Honourable Intent

Book I of The Hindolveston Septet

Jane Christie

Honourable Intent

ISBN: 9798366806107

© Gillian Stevenson writing as Jane Christie, December 2022

All rights reserved. No part of this publication may be reproduced,
distributed, or transmitted in any form or by any means,
including photocopying, recording, or other electronic or mechanical methods,
without the prior written permission of the publisher,
except in the case of brief quotations embodied in critical reviews and
certain other non-commercial uses permitted by copyright law.
For permission requests, email the publisher at the address below.

W: www.JaneChristie.com
E: JaneCristieAuthor@yahoo.com

Cover image: Gillian Stevenson
Cover design: Canva

Published independently by Robin Barratt:
www.RobinBarratt.co.uk

About the Author

Jane Christie was a Nursery Nurse and nanny before shifting rôles to that of a college lecturer. A confirmed scribbler since childhood, *Honourable Intent* is the first novel in her series of books entitled *The Hindolveston Septet*. Jane lives in Norfolk in the United Kingdom, and enjoys explosive cooking and walking, but not at the same time.

www.JaneChristie.com

Forthcoming Titles in The Hindolveston Septet

Book II: Bridal Wreath
Book III: Bookish Tendencies
Book IV: Inconvenient Truths
Book V: Hazardous Wagers
Book VI: Poetic Justice
Book VII: *Title to be announced*

For Kristen Bisten

March 2nd 1969 – June 7th 2015

"Mai kēia manawa ā mau loa aku"

Acknowledgements

I owe Kristen, Max, Joanne and Kim, a huge debt of gratitude for supporting, pushing, disagreeing and encouraging, and for not minding when dinner was late. To my mother for teaching me to read. And to my beloved Robin, for his love, patience and expertise, for making me laugh and believe in impossible things once again.

Spring, 1800.

Prologue

The start of the season, filled with high hopes and soaring dressmakers' bills, was invariably scattered with casualties; delicate flowers of maidenhood barely out of the schoolroom, forced to withstand the rigours of the ballroom might easily be crushed by the weight of parental expectation, or wither under the harsh gaze and caustic tongues of matrons, who with daughters of their own to be rid of, were scathing in their dismissal of perceived competition.

Beneath the veneer of formal gentility, routes and balls were fraught with danger, where the unwary might come to grief with no more than an unguarded word or imprudent gesture. Censure of a faux pas would be instantaneous and unremitting, and woe betide the foolish girl who put on airs and graces, or made an enemy of a fop whose dandified appearance concealed an icy heart and malicious tongue. Nor were the pitfalls limited to tonnish peacocks, popinjays, or vying mamas, for fraternising with rakes and fortune hunters could prove equally perilous, and judicious mothers took care to warn their daughters of such men, even if the former were alluded to in only the vaguest terms.

While onset of the season was greeted with trepidation by those whose duty was to ensnare a husband, if possible the most eligible, or at least a gentleman with a ready fortune, with their own come-outs consigned to history and their compassion in short-supply, the doyennes of the haute monde were free to disapprove, denunciate and enjoy themselves at the expense of the inexperienced.

However, it was not into one of these myriad pitfalls Maia Hindolveston willingly flung herself within the first hours of her first London season, but into something far more scandalous, salacious and, from the perspective of the gossiping witnesses, succulent.

Chapter One

The lamps flanking the St. James's Street establishment, flickered in the cool night air, while at the head of the stone steps the doors stood ajar, allowing the sound of jovial voices and occasional eruption of laughter from within to spill out into the dark street.

There was no need to observe the gallantries beyond those of accepted good manners within this most male of strongholds, for no woman ever set foot over the threshold, bar the cleaning women; not that they entered the premises by the front doors. Nor would the gentlemen who frequented the establishment have considered them in the same light as ladies of their esteemed acquaintance, indeed most would not have considered them at all.

Ignoring the sounds of revelry, the tall gentleman betook himself to a shadowed side-chamber, pausing to allow his eyes to adjust to the gloom, he frowned at the winged chair set close to the fireplace, until he was able to discern in the glow cast by the orange flames, the slight frame of a man seated within. The careless posture and closed expression supported what the brandy glass and lax grip upon it confirmed, that the chair's occupant was far from sober.

With increasing annoyance, the gentleman strode towards to the dishevelled figure of his cousin and loomed over the over the slouching figure in an a not entirely solicitous manner, indeed, his mien erred on the intimidating side of congenial. Upon first glance to a causal observer it might appear that the two were cast from a similar mould, however, closer inspection would reveal that one was but a pale echo of his dark elder. Those familiar with the pair would assert there was no comparison, indeed, when contrasted to his aristocratic cousin, it might be argued that the fellow slumped in the chair had be bestowed with favourable, even classical looks, while in his better-born relative the features contained a stark quality, giving the impression the gentlemen were the opposite sides of the same coin. The Duke of Bradenham's dark eyes were perhaps wider set than those of his cousin; his chin resolute and firmer; his cheekbones higher and his mouth a touch more generous. Impressive height and wide shoulders gave his Grace a distinguished air, which in vain his pale cousin had striven to imitate. Cosmo Bradenham might not make an effort to command respect, but nevertheless accepted it as his due without thought or question, in the same way he accepted the duties and responsibilities which were his by birthright. It was duty which accounted for his swift response to his cousin's barely legible request for assistance.

The inebriated gentleman squinted upwards in an attempt to focus upon the individual framed by the light of the flickering sconces from the hallway.

"Cosmo, s'at you? Sit down, you're givin' me a stiff neck, can't see you straight."

Reluctant to state the obvious Bradenham remained silent, waiting for some sort of explanation, with an effort, his intoxicated cousin attempted to haul himself upright in the chair, but finding himself exhausted by the exertion, slouched back once again.

"Damn it, what's to be done?" The gentleman waved his arm expansively, spilling brandy over himself, the chair and his boots.

The Duke continued to gaze upon the distasteful apparition, but remained silent, the indication of his mood plainly discernable in the glint in his dark eyes as they took in the state of his cousin. For a man with a reputation for fastidiousness, Percy Siddenham's jacket was unfashionably crumpled; his blond locks, usually so well-ordered, were tousled and greasy, his face sported more than a shadow of whiskers, and all-in-all he could have done with a wash.

Once again the brandy sloshed wildly over the dishevelled man's reeking boots, as well as those of this cousin, who stepped back to avoid further ignominy to his formally spotless footwear.

"It's a bloody mess and there's naught to be done about it," the inebriated gentleman complained morosely, then bringing the brandy glass to his lips he drained it, before shouting, "Wacton! Where are you man? I need more brandy."

Although the manservant appeared in the doorway, he made no attempt to do Mr Siddenham's bidding, for while drunkenness was not uncommon amongst the club members, no-one had ever seen a Siddenham anything other than in control and immaculate; others might sink deep into their cups on a regular basis, but Siddenhams were renown for their stamina. Even in a poor specimen like Percy Siddenham, such excesses were wholly unexpected.

The duke waved the man back, announcing in clipped accents, "Coffee I believe, Wacton."

"Damn ye' Bradenham, I said brandy and brandy's what'll have," Siddenham slurred. This in itself was enough to indicate just how much Percy had imbibed, for he would never have dared to address his cousin thusly had he been sober.

Unaccustomed to being spoken to in such a manner, the duke raised a haughty eyebrow, and intoned icily, "Percy, you are wasting my time. I do not propose to spend the evening watching you sink into oblivion, that you can do perfectly well without an audience, although if you take my advice, you will do it in less hallowed surroundings, but as you chose. Good evening," and turning on his heel Bradenham prepared to leave.

"Sorry," came the penitent reply from the chair. "But I'm in a devil of a fix, can't seem to see m'way clear."

"You astound me, however, I can do little while you are rather less than compos mentis. Call upon me tomorrow, I will not expect you early for I doubt you will arise with the lark."

There was movement from the chair as Percy made an effort to rouse himself. "Stay! I'll have the blasted coffee."

Seating himself, Bradenham waited, his steepled fingers against his lips, silently observing his cousin, but not until the coffee had been consumed did he permit the malefactor to begin his tale of woe.

With the draining of the last dregs Percy's shoulders slumped miserably. "I may as well tell you the whole, for you will hear it sooner or later, I have compromised a lady, Cosmo."

The duke's eyebrows threatened to disappear into his curling black mane in astonishment. "I believe I misheard you Percy."

"I know, damned funny ain't it?" Mr Siddenham laughed hollowly, his hands gripping the carved sides of the chair with such intensity that the knuckles began whiten.

"You will note I am not amused," drawled Bradenham's arctic accents. "Begin at the beginning, for I believe I have misunderstood you."

"Wish you had, but 'tis true and the deuced thing is she will not marry me."

"You leave me at a loss, cousin, but I dare say you will explain before one grows bored of this charade."

Unmoved by this frigid comment, Percy merely looked more morose. "I told you, I compromised a lady, but she will not have me."

"That at least is in her favour. Damnation Percy, have been fool enough to allow some scheming miss to make a mark of you?" The duke's disgust was evident, as he regarded Mr Siddenham through narrowed eyes.

Percy responded with a vehement shake of his head. "She'll not have me -"

"Forgive me, for unless I am missing some piece of vital

information, I fail to see the problem." Frustrated, Cosmo leaned towards Percy, then demanded with rather less finesse than he had hitherto employed, "What in hell's name is going on?"

"Ruined," Siddenham slurred, engulfed by another wave of self-pity.

Cosmo Bradenham's expression grew steely, he was beginning to doubt he would ever get to the bottom of what promised to be nothing more than tangle. Albeit a tangle of petticoats. "This time you exceed even my credulity, Percy."

Siddenham sighed and covering his eyes with his hand, tried to muster his wanting wits. "It was at the Wreningham route, three evenings ago," he paused, but receiving no encouragement from his austere cousin, Percy shook his head again, as if to dislodge his jumbled thoughts. "I had arranged to meet … well, it don't signify who I'd arranged to meet in the long gallery. Damn me, but Wreningham left his widow some deuced fine marble, and I wished to see 'em."

Having rallied briefly at the thought of the collection in Mrs Wreningham's long gallery. "We were in the gallery, such a place moves a man profoundly, and she -" he licked his lips at the stirring memory.

Bradenham raised his hand in order to prevent any further unwelcome intimate revelations. "Spare me the details Percy, let us move to the crux of the matter. I take it there is a crux, for thus far the tale is hardly edifying."

"We heard Lady Ormesby approaching," a glance in his austere cousin's direction confirmed that Cosmo indeed comprehended the severity of the situation, then added theatrically, "with that bloody Bellmont woman."

The duke's expression grew darker.

"You will appreciate that my predicament was dire." Mr Siddenham gave a sigh of indulgent self-pity. "When all of a sudden a lady arrives, takes one look at us and throws herself upon my neck."

Having not foreseen this turn of events, Bradenham was somewhat taken aback. "May one inquire as to the whereabouts of your amour during this affecting scene?"

"My amour?" It took the befuddled gentleman a moment to comprehend to whom his cousin referred. "Oh *her*, she was well-hidden behind the gel's skirts and the charming sculpture of Leda."

"Thus it looked as if the newcomer had been compromised?" intoned his Grace, coldly.

"Thoroughly, and I broke the button on my breeks. Damned nuisance."

"Which I imagine did little to prove your innocence."

Even more aggrieved, Mr Siddenham continued "Naturally, I was obliged to offer for her hand."

"It seems to me you were spoilt for choice," retorted the duke. "What of the lady with whom you planned the tryst, does she offer no objection, or am I to take it this was not a lasting union?"

Believing his obtuse cousin has missed the point, Percy raked his fingers through his greasy curls, demanding crossly, "What's to be done?"

"While your lack of judgement and discretion amaze me, I fail to understand why the lady has refused your offer, you are after all wealthy, with excellent connections. Why would she demure, what does she hope to gain?" His questions were purely rhetorical, although his next enquiry revealed a practical approach. "I assume you have spoken to the girl's father?"

Percy nodded. "The man claimed his daughter believed there was no reason to marry, and the incident was over. I don't want to marry the blasted girl but there is already gossip What's to be done?"

The duke rubbed nose thoughtfully, pondering the conundrum Percy had placed before him. To have been discovered in flagrante delictio whether it be with an experienced society matron, or an innocent, would undoubtedly sound the death-knell for Percy's social expectations. That the lady intended to remain un-wed would only compounded the scandal, for not only would she face ruination, but further ignominy would undoubtedly dog Percy's steps. For some the epithet of 'debaucher' was not a barrier to success, but it was unlikely Percy would be included amongst those libertines who not only got away with it, but whose exploits were positively celebrated. For reasons Bradenham could not fathom, doors to the ballrooms and withdrawing rooms of the upper echelon of society were held only hesitantly ajar for his cousin. This accounted for Percy's presence at the Wreningham route, along with such ladies Bellmont and Ormesby, although their condescension must have been something of a coup for the lowly Mrs Wreningham. To add debauchery to Percy's short list of questionable talents was hardly going to open doors for him beyond the infamous and disreputable. If Percy was correct and the tongues of society were already wagging, the possibility of permanent ostracism could not be underestimated. The Duke was not an emotional man, nor did he especially care for his cousin, who lacking the character, originality and charm to play the rôle of the rake with wit and style, would not fare well should he be shunned; the fact remained that Percy came under the chilly heading of familial duty.

"You are doubtless making a mountain from a mole hill,

however, even a molehill can fell the unwary, and I prefer this did not reach even hill-like proportions, it must be resolved. I will call upon the lady in question and inform her she will marry you as soon as a licence may be procured. I trust your estate is in order to receive your wife as soon as may be, for I do not believe it will do to install her in Warwick street."

The very notion of installing a bride in his town house was not only abhorrent but bordered on the preposterous, although Percy did not relish the idea of permitting the girl to stay unsupervised in his country house, nor had he any intention of allowing the inconvenience of marriage to discommode him unduly.

However, before he could protest, the duke held up his hand to silence any dissension. "You have sought my assistance, which naturally I will render, but it does not come freely, there are one or two strings attached." Observing Percy's expression, Bradenham could not help but feel that his cousin was about to be justly served. "You will take your wife to Hertford, and stay with her for at least what remains of the season, I will of course expect your wife to accompany you to Swanton Chatteris, at Christmas, if only to maintain appearances. Those are my only dictates, how you and your wife choose to live out the remainder of your wedded bliss is your own affair, an heir would be useful, but I will not place such a demand upon the girl."

Far from relieved at having the difficulty resolved, Percy looked even more miserable. "I know I should thank you Cosmo, and I do, but, damn me, it's abominable to be saddled with a wife in this manner."

"It would seem the lady is in agreement with you, so at least you have that in common, one can only hope it will be a lasting comfort to you both." Rising, the duke rested a booted foot upon the polished brass fender surrounding the fireplace. "It would behove you not make the girl's life a misery if you can possibly help it, who knows, you may find you are well-matched, if like you she has a penchant for long-galleries. Send her direction to me in the morning, I will call upon her after I have made a few enquiries."

His cousin looked startled. "Enquiries? Is there another way out of this?"

"I think not, for I believe the only solution is for you to don the manacles of marriage, but you cannot expect me to proceed without making enquiries regarding the lady in question."

As his cousin's face fell in dismay, Bradenham asked, not entirely kindly, indeed, had Percy been anything other than preoccupied by his own misery he might have noted the smugness of the duke's tone.

"Tell me, is she quite an antidote?"

Percy struggled to visualise the girl's face, before sighing deeply, sinking even deeper into despair. "Yes, quite an antidote," as he recalled his bride to be, the reluctant groom grimaced.

"One cannot help but be moved by your enthusiasm, but my dear Percy, you are going to have to learn to whisper sweet nothings in to your wife's ear."

Grinning broadly at his cousin's stricken face, his Grace strode towards the door.

Chapter Two

The Duke of Bradenham scowled at his secretary over the neatly ordered papers piled high upon the mahogany desk, and impatiently drumming his long fingers enquired, "You are quite sure she is whom she claims to be?"

Unmoved by the duke's expression, Harrington nodded solemnly. "Indeed your Grace, there can be no mistake, Maia Hindolveston is Viscount Nordelph's daughter."

Having set his secretary the task of discovering what he could about the girl, who in Bradenham's mind was either a seductress or a fool, Harrington had not disappointed, but then Harrington never let him down; he was one of the few individuals in Cosmo Bradenham's life who could be relied upon.

It had been an interesting morning, for in seeking out his acquaintances employed in high places, Harrington had been privy to several fascinating stories and anecdotes; salacious speculation, and as much hard information as it was possible to obtain without arousing the suspicions of those who were paid to be suspicious. Were it known his Grace was making enquiries about Miss Hindolveston, the tittle-tattle would soon spread, for duke's affairs of the heart was a subject of much speculation and, although even the most accomplished gossip-mongers were ignorant of the ladies who could be claim a place among the list of Bradenham's amours, it was not from a want of prying.

"Why am I not acquainted with Lord Nordelph or his self-promoting daughter?" his Grace demeaned. "I have endured the dubious honour of every tonnish, simpering miss being paraded before me for as long as I can recall, yet Miss Hindolveston appears to have neglected to make my acquaintance, an oversight which will shortly be corrected. What do we know of Nordelph, pockets to let?"

"The current viscount inherited the title two years ago when the previous Nordelph met an unexpected end, they were second-cousins."

"A-ha, that would account for it," drawled his Grace before adding with more interest, "how unexpected?"

Harrington was forced to hide a smile. "Unforeseen, your Grace, the viscount suffered an apoplexy, in delicate circumstances."

Eyes narrowing as he digested this information, his Grace nodded sagely. "Gerald Nordelph, I recall the scandal, until his death Miss Hindolveston would merely have been a poor relation, and even when promoted, would have been forced to bide her time in black gloves, but now she has thrown off her blacks she has launched herself upon the ton, quite literally."

Accustomed to his Grace's musings, Harrington continued, "Mrs Wreningham is the girl's aunt, Miss Hindolveston has been making her come out under the aunt's auspices."

"One assumes the mother is dead?"

Harrington shook his head. "Lady Nordelph is alive, but rarely leaves the family home in Richmond."

"A dying swan perhaps?" Bradenham frowned, but recalling Percy's description of the marble Leda and the emotions the effigy had aroused, hastily cleared his throat. "It accounts for her presence at the Wreningham route, but why was the damned girl brazenly wandering the long gallery, when she should have been safely chaperoned in the grand salon? Why she could she not make dull conversation like a normal chit?"

"Miss Hindolveston is hardly a chit your Grace, she has reached her majority, although I understand this is her first season."

"She is rather old to make her come-out, perhaps her parents hoped like a fine vintage, she would improve with age, sadly ladies of the ton rarely improve with age. Just look at my sisters ..." The duke shuddered melodramatically, his secretary said nothing; his employer might be right, but Harrington was too wise to audibly concur with such sentiments.

"Schoolroom misses seem to sour overnight, like milk, which is why they must be fired off before they can turn one's stomach or, in the case of my sister Regina, turn one bilious. Sensibly, Stanhoe had the foresight to keep his appointment with his maker before he had been married to my sister for twelve months."

The duke's sister had achieved widowhood before the first anniversary of her marriage, and it was speculated Lord Stanhoe had drunk himself into a early grave, for which Bradenham could not blame him. Happily, the death of her husband and the timely arrival of his heir had occurred within the same month, adroitly solving any difficulties regarding the late lord's estate.

"No doubt the arrangement suits them both admirably," Bradenham concluded, while Harrington remained judiciously quiet.

Examining the barely legible scrawl left by Percy containing, amid its spidery hieroglyphs, the direction of Lord Nordeph's residence,

Cosmo sighed. "One wonders why one should bother."

Upon receiving no reply from his impassive secretary, Bradenham tapped his fingers against the paper. "Harrington, your silence speaks volumes. Very well, I will persuade the chit to marry the damnable Percy; may it serve her right for playing the heroine, although it seems a harsh punishment. Perhaps I should call upon the questionable Mrs Wreningham before I meet Maia Hindolveston, what an odd name, why do you suppose one would call one's daughter after a Pleiades?"

"The Heavenly Sisters," mused the secretary.

"Indeed, although I doubt there is much heavenly about Miss Hindolveston if she has a penchant for accosting gentlemen in long galleries, one can only hope she will not make a habit of it once she becomes Mrs Siddenham. However, I feel bound to question why, if this was her first attempt, she chose Percy as her object? One would think she would display rather more discerning taste, not that it matters, she will certainly suffer the consequences of her foolishness, although being required to rescue the girl from ruination in this manner is distasteful in the extreme."

The duke looked up. "The subject distresses you, and as ever you are quite right, it is repugnant, we will not refer to it again, at least, not for the remainder of the day." He sighed as he watched rivulets of rain streaming down the window, keenly feeling the weight of family responsibility in this matter, yet he could not allow Percy's indiscretions to be Miss Hindolveston's downfall, even if the alternative might prove equally unpalatable to the girl.

***

It was perhaps an irony that having longed to be at home to callers of a more genteel variety than she was accustomed to receiving, the arrival of the Duke of Bradenham was by no means the social coup Mrs Wreningham had dreamt of. Indeed, his haughty presence in the good lady's withdrawing room was not entirely unexpected, although she wished heartily it could have been avoided.

Mrs Wreningham wished too that the ducal eye had not lingered upon the faded pink of the crewel worked damask covering her unfashionable Queen Anne chairs and sofas. However, she took comfort in the knowledge that she had possessed the forethought to replace the drawing room curtains with those from the morning room, when the rents and fraying edges in the sun-rotted cloth could no longer be concealed, for she never entertained visitors in the morning room, not being an early riser herself.

Mrs Wreningham was not alone in her trepidation, for her daughter Emmeline, a buxom girl with artfully constructed curls, lowered eyes and simpering smiles; whose come out was, by her own estimation, highly successful, bobbed a nervous curtsey, barely able to stutter. "Y - your Grace," when introduced to Bradenham.

John Wreningham, a male version of his gold and white sister, was older and more knowing than Emme in the ways society, yet he too found himself unequal to the occasion, and with little thought for his mother's peace of mind, hastily removed both himself and his sister from the duke's presence on the pretext of having a prior engagement. Mr Wreningham, like his sister, was not blessed with an abundance of empathy, and what sympathy he possessed was reserved almost entirely for himself. Maia should have known better, and John wanted no part in what promised to be a messy discussion; he felt no compunction in leaving his mother to deal with the aftermath, believing it was far better that he should distance himself from such matters.

Their departure suited Bradenham's purpose, for it would have been undeniably awkward to broach the delicate subject in the company of a debutante, even one as poor ton as Miss Wreningham. He hoped once Percy was married to Miss Hindolveston, that his cousin would have the good sense to distance himself from his bride's low connections.

It was not turning out to be a pleasant week for poor Mrs Wreningham, who had blithely anticipated that following her rout, her social status would be significantly improved. While it was true Lady Bellmont, together with Lady Ormesby, had paid her the compliment of an unexpected call, who could have foreseen with arrival of the tea would come palpitations of the worst variety? So unwelcome and shocking had been their news, poor Mrs Wreningham's aspirations had received the equivalent of an icy drenching. Nor had things improved when following her guests' departure, she had questioned her late husband's niece, who confirmed what the esteemed ladies had decorously and vindictively alluded to, with snide comments, lewd innuendo and delightedly shocked expressions.

Her peace of mind had received a further blow when despite her anguished hand-wringing, John's entreaties and Emmeline's copious weeping, Maia remained impervious to reason and propriety, calmly informing her aunt that "it would all blow over," before betaking herself back to Richmond with her strange little maid. In Mrs Wreningham's view, such storms rarely just blew over, but tended to linger, leaving catastrophic damage in their wake, for someone always seemed to recall the details of a scandal and was only too willing to remind others of the finer points, which might otherwise have been overlooked. Society did not care for young ladies who did not obey the strictures; the only exceptions to the rule were limited to those whose birth, wealth or connections provided more leeway than that given to others. With no title of her own to cling to, and no cachet of funds, Mrs Wreningham was well-aware of her tenuous social status, and being on the fringes of society meant she could not afford to set a foot wrong, or be tainted by familial association with a pariah, which was why Maia's departure from common decency was so galling.

So distraught was Mrs Wreningham upon Maia's departure, that she had snapped peevishly at her daughter. "Do stop frowning Emmeline! You will ruin your looks and your own betrothal is by no means certain, for pity's sake have a heart for my sensibilities."

However, her outburst had done little to improve the situation, for unaccustomed to being spoken to in this manner, Emmeline had merely looked more furious than ever, although she was glad to see the back of her cousin, having no wish to be likewise smeared by the gossip which must attach itself to Maia, and rather unwisely she voiced her sentiments. This prompted her mother, a woman with an eye to her own health, to declare her heart palpitations were a sign of something significant, perhaps even dangerous, and demanded the doctor be sent for. Finding nothing wrong, the sensible man made a show of shaking his head sorrowfully, before ponderously advising Mrs Wreningham to cancel her evening's engagement as a precaution against permanent damage to her wounded heart. As no chaperone could be arranged at such short notice, Emme was forced to remain at home with her mama, which did not please her in the least, although happily, their absence was noticed only by Emmeline's suitor and served to further inflame his decorous ardour, so all was not lost.

As His Grace the Duke of Bradenham was bowing over her hand, unable to hide her shattered nerves, Mrs Wreningham sat with a bump as her knees refused to hold her upright in such esteemed company.

The formalities thus observed, the duke dispensed with further niceties and got straight to the point: "I assume you know why I am here?"

With her heart showing every indication of resuming its palpitations, not trusting herself to speak beyond an incomprehensible squeak, Mrs Wreningham nodded dumbly, and waved her hand vaguely toward a chair, hoping that his looming Grace would sit.

He did.

"It would appear Mrs Wreningham, there is a problem. However, before I go about resolving it, I need to understand how such a thing came about. I understand Miss Hindolveston is your niece and a guest in your house."

Her esteemed visitor's disdain was abundantly clear, and poor Mrs Wreningham's eyes filled with indignant tears.

Being impervious to such feminine wiles as well-timed weeping and strategic hand wringing, her display of delicate sensibilities left the duke entirely unmoved. Miss Hindolveston might come from a reasonably good family, but at present her aunt was doing little to support the notion. If the girl was badly brought up, had been permitted a lamentably long-rein, or worse still, a free one, and had thrown herself at other men in her short career, it would be difficult to welcome her into the family. Although Cosmo felt duty bound to ensure the wretched girl joined its ranks before the scandal broke.

It was not a task he relished and irritated anew by Miss Hindolveston's ridiculous refusal of Percy's offer, he continued ruthlessly, "You permitted your niece to roam a long gallery unaccompanied, during a rout." He smiled condescendingly at Mrs Wreningham, as if awaiting a series of feeble excuses, not that he believed the woman possessed the ability to explain her apparently lax care of the headstrong Maia.

Forced by good manners and a natural dislike of silence to find something to say, Mrs Wreningham twittered, quite against her better judgement. "Indeed your Grace, my dear late husband's niece was passing through the long gallery returning to the drawing room from her chamber, where she had been mending a torn frill. Such a nuisance this fashion for frills, my Emmeline is forever tearing hers." But, finding his Grace unmoved by such frippery concerns, she made an effort to return to the point. "Maia assumed no chaperone was necessary as she merely going to and from her own chamber and there could be no harm -" her voice trailed away, the facts of the matter proof enough that the assumption was wholly erroneous.

"But that was not the case." His icy statement of the obvious would have frozen the most strident of discussions, and rendered Mrs Wreningham almost rigid with fear.

"Tell me," he intoned heartlessly. "Do you believe Miss Hindolveston guilty of the claims made by Lady Bellmont and Lady Ormesby?"

Mrs Wreningham's unwavering belief in Maia's guilt was not to her credit, despite having hitherto found the girl entirely truthful, but refusing be swayed by family loyalty, or Maia's steadfast declaration of innocence, she plumped irrevocably upon the side of what was bound to be society's sordid opinion. Confirming in a wavering voice, "I do, your Grace."

Her righteous indignation at the scandal hanging over Maia's dark head was fuelled by more than any passing concern she had for her niece's welfare, more importantly there was Emmeline's advantageous match to consider. Mrs Wreningham declared bitterly, "It was most unfortunate that Mr Siddenham ..." she paused, wondering if she dared to assign blame to the duke's cousin, "... was wandering the long gallery."

The duke ignored this momentary flash of resentment for in his estimation, while Percy was foolish, the wretched girl should have known better. He intoned coldly, "Your niece, despite being seen alone with my cousin in what can only be described as an indelicate position, is refusing Siddenham's offer. I am incredulous." But far from incredulous, he looked downright cross. "Have you spoken to the girl?"

"Indeed, your Grace." Mrs Wreningham recalled with a shudder how she had begged and implored Maia to accept Mr Siddenham's offer, trying without success to persuade the girl that she had no choice open to her but to accept his offer, no matter how unappealing it might be. But her anguished entreaties, and the suggestion that Maia's repugnance of the gentleman might have been better served in refusing his advances to begin with, rather than declining at this late stage, when he was the only means of social salvation, had been met by solid indifference.

"Does the girl comprehend the severity of the nature of her behaviour?"

"Your Grace, Maia informs me that nothing improper took place, she feels the -" Mrs Wreningham almost said 'affair', but managed to swallow the word before she choked upon it, "- incident will blow over, given time."

"Time? Miss Hindolveston may discover that time will drag on interminably while she is subjected to speculation and ridicule, for the ton will be paying close attention to the condition your niece may, or may not be in." Such indelicacy drew a gasp, but he continued mercilessly. "Although I doubt she will be permitted into even the basest of drawing rooms if she refuses my cousin's offer of marriage. This will not simply blow over, it must be resolved, the sooner the better, for the ton will believe nothing short of seduction took place. Indeed, judgement is already being passed on your niece, and will be passed upon my cousin if he is prevented from doing his duty by the girl; they must marry without delay."

Finding herself in agreement, Mrs Wreningham could only nod, the last thing she wanted was to be touched by a scandal which refused to be swept under the carpet, not when she had contrived and schemed to place her own daughter in the path of several eligible gentlemen; one of whom she believed was on the brink of making Emmeline an offer. The Wreningham purse was by no means bulging, and without a large dowry, or settlements with which to lure gentlemen of breeding and status, the fear that Maia's shocking behaviour would prove a stumbling block for Emmeline's suitor, was all to real.

As he observed the girl's wretched aunt with a gimlet eye, Cosmo was relieved to discover they were in accord, and he acknowledged her mute response with a satisfied. "Precisely. I will speak to Miss Hindolveston, the girl must be brought to heel."

Despite the seriousness of the accusation, Mrs Wreningham found the suggestion that Maia, or indeed any of the her late husband's strong-minded nieces, could be brought to heel, amusing. All the girls were shockingly wilful, with no comprehension of ladylike behaviour or decorum. Marriage to Percy Siddenham was the only course of action open to Maia, and if the wretched girl did not like it she only had herself to blame. She would not be the first young lady to find marriage unexpectedly thrust upon her, for society expected its debutante brides to possess an unblemished character, no matter how many seven-month babies were born following hastily read banns.

Cosmo noted Mrs Wreninghma's fleeting smile with growing disapproval, wondering what sort of family Percy was marrying into, if the woman found the intolerable situation even vaguely amusing.

Flustered anew by her visitor's obvious displeasure, Mrs Wreningham twittered nervously, "I did my utmost to persuade Maia, but she will not see reason and holds to the belief there is no need for her to marry Mr Siddenham." But finding herself unequal to the duke's growing ire, her voice trailed helplessly away.

"Will you inform the ton, and Lady Bellmont in particular, who is not know for her discretion, that your niece's reputation is in no way tarnished, and that she will not be marrying Mr Siddenham? Or would you prefer that I be the one to announce the tidings? I repeat, Mrs Wreningham, the girl needs to be brought to heel," referring to the damnable Miss Hindolveston, whom Cosmo already heartily detested, as if she were an errant dog, was perhaps not the best approach. But it was too late to consider such niceties. "If you would fetch your niece madam, I have a few things to say to her."

"Your Grace, I would gladly ask Maia join us, but I fear I am unable to do so, at present."

Any regret the duke may have felt regarding his insinuation that Miss Hindolveston was a dog in need of training, was forgotten, and his countenance grew grim.

"So, she won't see me, my reputation it would seem has preceded me."

"You misunderstand me, your Grace, Maia has already returned to her home, or I would willingly have her fetched."

With his face like thunder Cosmo declared, "In which case there is nothing more to be said. Good-day Mrs Wreningham."

Holding on to the threads of her composure, the lady managed to utter a tremulous "Good day," adding as an afterthought, "your Grace."

Her visitor, having inclined his head in curt dismissal of Mrs Wreningham's rustling curtsey, stalked from the room and, as his echoing foot steps receded, Mrs Wreningham sank back upon the sofa, fanning herself with one hand, the other clutching at her heart which was palpitating dreadfully, and tried to gather her scattered wits. She had heard tell the duke was a Tartar, but had certainly not expected to be spoken to in such a manner, it would serve him right if he did have the misfortune to interview Maia, who would not take kindly to his Grace's approach.

However, with the duke having left the with-drawing room, and Maia her house, Mrs Wreningham thought it best to wash her hands of the whole distasteful episode and concentrate upon getting her own daughter married off as soon as may be achieved, for her strained finances could not withstand a second season. Running a London house was an expensive business, despite Mrs Wreninham practising the most stringent of economies behind closed doors, and Emmeline, whose tastes were on the extravagant side of affluent, must be funded by someone with deeper pockets than those of her mother and brother. If Maia was foolish enough to refuse an offer from the cousin of a duke, then she did not deserve the slightest notice.

Really, it was too bad.

Chapter Three

Had the duke known how keenly his arrival at Delphic House was observed, he might have made an effort to look genial. As it was, the scowling gentleman who alighted from the carriage bearing the ducal coat of arms was a source of alarm, speculation and no small degree of amusement to the three pairs of violet eyes peeping from the damp shrubbery. Agog, they took in the tall crowned hat and fur collared redingote which gently brushed the tops of his spotless boots, as he strode across the gravel.

"Do you suppose he is will marry Maia?" Asked the owner of the youngest pair of eyes, anxiously twisting a tightly plaited skein of hair around her fingers.

"You are a goose," retorted her sister, with all the wisdom of an extra summer. "Of course Maia is not going to marry him, for he is dreadfully old. The other one was not so old, he was prettier too." She looked thoughtfully at the duke who, despite his apparently advanced age, was managing admirably to make his way from his carriage to the steps of Delphic House, entirely unassisted.

"It is not proper to say a man is pretty Cela, nor is this one ugly, he just looks cross, besides, how can you be certain Maia is not going to marry him?" wondered the owner of the third pair of eyes thoughtfully, and fretfully began sucking the end of an identical plait to that of her twin's.

"You are a goose too," Cela retorted indignantly. "If Maia were to be married, she would have told us." She looked down her nose at her younger sisters adding with an infuriating air of superiority. "She would have told me anyhow."

Unimpressed by their sister's delusions, the twins rolled their eyes at each other, then pinched their senior upon the arm, not unkindly but enough to remind Cela that she was talking nonsense. Maia might love them dearly, but even the twins knew she would not confide in them, not when there were other sisters closer to her own age with whom to share her secrets. Which was why the younger three counted concealment in the shrubbery amongst their talents, having long since discovered that girls with older sisters might find themselves omitted from the more interesting conversations, unless they occasionally took matters into their own hands; naturally this was just such an occasion.

The twins having meted out such justice as was quietly possible, held their collective breath, watching the man they believed to be Maia's prospective suitor, as he passed close to their hiding place. Once she was assured the gentleman was safely beyond earshot, Cela rose to her feet, catching her gown on a thorn as she did so; the damp, crushed and decidedly greened muslin tore, causing her siblings to hiss their enthusiastic disapproval.

Aster removed the end of her plait from her mouth and pointed out unnecessarily. "That is your third dress this week, what will mama say?"

Twirling her unravelling plait carelessly around her fingers, Mery warned gleefully, "Eley will say more." And she was right, the second of the Hindolveston sisters was not known for her reticence when it came to dealing with such wanton destruction.

However, anxious to reassert her seniority over her siblings, Cela ignored her torn dress and with her nose into the air and a hand over the rent muslin, announced conspiratorially, "If we hurry we can go through the conservatory and see him before he reaches the library."

It was as well Cosmo Bradenham did not observe the undergrowth undulating as if moved by an unseen hand, as the sisters stealthily made their way from the shrubbery to the side of the house. While mounting the steps, the duke was none the wiser of the damning pronouncements made regarding his age and person by such harsh critics as the three youngest Misses Hindolveston.

***

The sunny hall of Delphic House initially offered confusing insights regarding the nature of the family Percy would shortly be marrying into, adding to those always proclaimed by Miss Hindolveston's behaviour and the unfavourable impression given by Mrs Wreningham. But although the woman's pecuniary status had been obvious, his Grace did not judge solely upon such vulgarities, for her want of character had been far more apparent, and concerning. Being kept waiting for longer than he was accustomed only added to the disquiet which had been growing since Cosmo had read the scrawled missive from Percy.

Upon close inspection, the floral arrangement adorning the table proved to be no more than bedraggled greenery and wild flowers, vying for room in the overfilled vase with what looked remarkably like stalks of grass. Turning from the riot of questionable vegetation,

Bradenham perused the marble fireplace, which was not only adorned by statuesque carvings of semi-clothed figures from antiquity, but hanging above it was what could only be described as an uninhibited painting of the Muses, or were they the Graces, cavorting with a male deity? The artist had spared no detail, particularly when it came to the deity; not that the painter's skill could be called into question, only the location chosen to display the graphic portraiture. No wonder Miss Hindolveston had not been shocked by the statue of Leda and the Swan, which, by all accounts, was startling.

The duke's discomfiture increased as he became aware of the unabashed curiosity of two young ladies gazing down at him from the landing above; such scrutiny was wholly unexpected, accustomed as he was to misses who lowered their eyes at his glance and displayed respectful modesty when he deigned to speak. These audacious girls showed no such feminine sensibilities, but met his eye with unflinching interest, until Cosmo was forced to look loftily away in order to maintain some semblance of dignity. When he was sufficiently composed to raise his eyes once again, the girls had disappeared; it was only now, somewhat belatedly he reasoned, one of them must be Percy's bride, and wished he had thought to examine the pair more carefully. The notion did not improve his mood, nor did being kept waiting longer than was polite, or convenient.

It was perhaps as well, given his current frame of mind that Bradenham did not notice the wide violet eyes gaping at him from their relative concealment in the morning room. Nor was he aware of Cela's squeal as she shut her fingers in the door, to the mingled delight and horror of her younger sisters, who were enjoying the most thrilling of mornings.

***

For a man accustomed to deference, which occasionally bordered on obsequiousness, the wait in the hall of Delphic House seemed interminable, nor did Cosmo's subsequent ushering into the library dispel his mounting reservations. While it could not be disputed that the gentleman of mature years who greeted him was pleasant enough, and did not immediately give the impression of being a man who turned a blind eye to the debaucheries of his daughter, it was apparent that the duke's arrival had interrupted some sort of study. Seated at the library table was a boy, surrounded by a confusion of open volumes and papers covered with both childish scrawl and with a more precise script; while presiding over the disorder, a large globe stood proudly at the centre of the scholastic anarchy.

Other than the misrule of the table, the library was pleasant enough, its shelves rose to the ceiling, filling three of the walls. The volumes upon the uppermost shelves were reached by means of ladders affixed to a rail running the length of the book-lined walls, this was more than a mere show-piece library, for amid the hundreds, perhaps thousands of books, was housed a collector's soul. Had Bradenham been aware that the Hindolveston sisters were wont to amuse themselves by clinging to the ladders and pushed by their siblings would race along the rail, he would doubtless have disapproved; nor would the knowledge that the ladders would occasionally collide, tumbling the girls in different directions as they screamed with laugher, have improved his already dim view of the family. However, denied such insights, Cosmo was delighted to note the marble statues and busts, handsomely displayed around the room. Had he been burdened with less weighty matters, he would certainly have enjoyed a closer inspection, for not only did they appear to be remarkable, but were obviously of great antiquity.

With the formalities observed, the older gentleman spoke first, but not as his august visitor had expected, for instead of observing the usual pleasantries such as the state of the weather, the roads, or even his majesty, Lord Nordelph smiled benignly at his son and ruffled the child's dark curls affectionately,

"That will do for today Lysander, Plato can wait until the morning. Run along and see how those pups of yours are faring."

The duke who was not overly fond of children eyed Lysander Hindolveston warily, lest the boy should protest or otherwise make a nuisance of himself, but far from treating the visitor to a display of temper, Lysander grinned and ran off happily, allowing the library door to close behind him with a resounding bang. Cosmo winced.

However, Lord Nordelph's manners were by no means lacking, as having removed a pile of manuscripts, waved his guest to a chair and took the now vacant seat himself.

"I am delighted to make your acquaintance your Grace. I met your father only once, although of course that was many years ago."

While Bradenham was in no mood to waste time in making polite conversation, he was forced to delay broaching the unpleasant subject until the butler, who had silently entered the library in the wake of the boy's departure, had served the burgundy, and taking the proffered glass, Cosmo was surprised to note the vintage was as fine as anything found in his own cellars. This alone gave him hope that Nordelph might be a man with whom he could reason. Musing as he sipped, that in all likelihood the viscount would be delighted to have a daughter taken off his hands, especially if she were to marry a Siddenham, even if the Siddenham in question was Percy. After all, a man with seven daughters could not afford to be overly choosy when it came to marrying them off, for despite being endowed with a fortune, seven was an onerous number of females to be taxed with.

Finally, when his enjoyment of the burgundy could be stretched no further, Bradenham addressed the viscount, "I take it you have already spoken with my cousin, Percy Siddenham?"

Lord Nordelph looked quizzically at his illustrious guest. "Mr Siddenham did me the honour of calling upon me." Examining the gentleman seated before him, he concluded: "You are not alike and yet I had heard you shared a strong similarity, how odd."

The duke steeled his jaw, Nordelph was not making this easy, it was obviously a family trait, Siddenham would have to do something about it if he were to deal with his wife.

Draining his glass, he took the metaphorical bull by its horns. "You will appreciate the necessity of ensuring all is in order before the marriage, which is why I am here. I am not of the opinion that your daughter should bring with her a large dowry or property, beyond what you choose to settle upon her. Indeed, I propose what she brings should remain hers, Siddenham has no need to add to his fortune. Once all is signed we may proceed with the marriage, naturally Siddenham will procure a special license, that we may dispense with the reading of the banns; to delay will not improve matters."

Yet far from clarifying the matter, Cosmo's seemed to have bewildered Lord Nordelph. "There seems to be a misunderstanding your Grace, is Mr Siddenham expecting to marry one of my daughters?"

"My cousin will marry your elder daughter, naturally, it is the only path open to them."

"Is it?" The viscount's incredulity was not encouraging.

"Naturally," Bradenham reiterated slowly, as if addressing a man of particularly slow-wits, he was not a man blessed with infinite patience and this unpalatable duty was beginning to wear thin.

"My dear fellow, I believe we are at odds, for I fail to see why my daughter marrying Mr Siddenham should be natural, and pleasant though the gentleman may be, he does not seem to me to be the right sort of man for any of my daughters. I am at a loss to understand why he persists in the foolish notion that he will marry one of them."

With an effort Cosmo remained civil, for nothing would be gained by estranging the girl's father at this juncture. "My cousin, whom

I admit can be foolish, has compromised your daughter. Good lord, the act was witnessed and unless Siddenham marries the girl, she will be ruined in the eyes of society."

The ruined girl's father mused. "Foolish, yes, I believe there is something in your description of Mr Siddenham."

It was to be hoped that the viscount was hard of hearing, for Cosmo's sigh of incredulity was indeed audible, not that the duke was abashed by his lack of tact. Here he was, doing his utmost to save the man's wretched daughter from the ignominy of her own folly, and yet Nordelph had just questioned Percy's suitably, not to mention his acumen. Was the there no end to this madness?

His unspoken question was answered moments later when the library door was flung open and cause of his annoyance flew into the room.

Pausing only to draw breath, Miss Hindolveston dashed past Bradenham and, taking her father's hand, gasped, "Papa, you did not promise anything, did you?"

The girl's appearance, as well as her manner of arrival, was startling, with wide, violet eyes and a mass of dark corkscrewing curls spilling from beneath her hat; she was clearly out of breath as if she had been running, and Cosmo noted with a raking glance that she had mud upon her boots. Not the sort of lady who would excite any interest whatsoever from Percy, although that was hardly any concern of his.

Lord Nordelph's reply to his first-born was a gentle reproach. "My dear, how could I make such a promise on your behalf?"

The lady proceeded to drag her hat from her hair, causing the curls to cascade down her back, reminding the duke of Medusa, and hugging her father warmly, she planted a loving kiss upon his cheek.

"I should have known you would not allow yourself to be swayed, papa."

Her father patted her hand affectionately. "No matter who comes a-calling, you girls are not chattels to be bestowed upon a whim, you must decide for yourselves whom you will wed," and looking into Maia's eyes, which were a mirror of her mother's, he murmured pointedly, "or not." Lord Nordelph shook his grey head despairingly, to his enlightened mind the notion treating of his daughters as mere acquisitions, was unthinkable.

A man of lesser fortitude might have found the tableaux affecting, but Cosmo was entirely unmoved by the display of sentiment between the errant Miss Hindolveston and her unsatisfactory father. He had risen from his chair the instant the whirlwind of hair and muddy gown had made her unceremonious arrival proving, as if further proof were needed, that decorum was sadly wanting in Delphic House. He did his utmost to regain his equilibrium as he waited for the hoyden's father to make an introduction, for unlike his cousin, Bradenham preferred to adhere to the formalities. However, in this he was apparently alone, for when Lord Nordelph presented Maia to the duke, the wretched girl did not deign to curtsey in response to his curt bow of greeting, she merely inclined her head; her omission in acknowledging his station, both apparent and deliberate.

She was taller than Bradenham had expected, not that he had given this aspect of her being much thought, but in his experience schoolroom misses tended to be on the smallish side; more surprising than her height was the realisation that he had forgotten that she was no mere schoolroom miss, but a woman of twenty-one. How could this pertinent information have slipped his mind?

Miss Hindolveston was surprisingly elegant, and while her riding habit was severely cut and might almost have been masculine, but for the voluminous skirts and feminine figure which filled it, although he noted with disdain it was decidedly mud-spattered. More shockingly, with her hat clutched in one hand, and the hem of the besmirched habit in the other, Miss Hindolveston was oblivious that her carelessness revealed a good deal of her ankle and leg.

Drawing himself up his full and rather impressive height in preparation for the oration he expected to deliver, the duke was understandably put-out when Miss Hindolveston spoke-up before he could so much as utter a syllable.

"I am afraid you have wasted your time in coming here today, as I told Mr Siddenham when he called upon me at my aunt's house, and then again when he called here." Struggling to form her indignation into an acceptable declaration, Maia glared at the duke, who was taken aback by the intensity of her violet gaze. With an attempt to school her expression into something other than a snarl, she continued woodenly, "While I thank Mr Siddenham for his offer, I remain, unable to accept."

Bradenham wondered if it was his imagination, or whether she really was gritting her teeth.

"As there is nothing more to be said upon the matter, I bid you good morning ..." Maia added belatedly, in a half-hearted attempt at civility, "... your Grace."

The could be no doubting it, definitely gritted teeth.

Miss Hindolveston's summary dismissal was not met with immediate acquiescence by the duke, nor did it cause Lord Nordelph any disquiet as he beamed happily at his visitor. "I knew there had been a mistake, but all's well that ends well. Now, if you would excuse me, my wife is not in good health and I have already been away from her side for longer than I intended, I will leave you in Maia's capable hands."

A notion seemed to occur to the viscount, who said a trifle pointedly. "While there can be no impropriety in leaving you unchaperoned to finish the niceties, should you feel it necessary, I am sure of the elder girls would oblige. Good-day your Grace." With that Lord Nordelph absently bowed in Bradenham's direction and selecting a volume from the pile of books upon the table, hastened from the library, his mind already upon other matters.

Turning in disbelief to Miss Hindolveston, as she smugly peeled her gloves from her slender fingers, the duke announced ominously, "You are under a misapprehension if you believe the matter has reached its conclusion, for there is much to be said, and even more to be arranged; however, at this juncture you are required only to listen." Warming to his theme Cosmo continued, "You will marry my cousin within the week, you have sown into the wind my girl, and must now reap the whirlwind."

With no opposition from Miss Hindolveston, Bradenham embarked upon an entirely unplanned, although to his mind entirely necessary dressing-down. "Young ladies do not wander alone in darkened galleries, let alone cast themselves into the arms of gentlemen, nor do they wantonly kiss them before an audience; if they do, they must expect to pay the price."

Although the Maia had paled, she offered no objection and the duke began to feel he was making himself clear at last; once Miss Hindolveston understood the extent of her rôle in this pantomime, he could make the necessary arrangements and leave. It was possible she was innocent of society's ways, and that once she understood the ramifications of her actions she would meekly accept her marriage to Percy as a necessary evil.

"Marriage to Mr Siddenham is your only option, without his ring upon your finger you will be shunned at every turn, unwelcome by all, except of course by gentlemen eager to experience your reputation first hand."

Yet the duke was mistaken if he believed the girl would acquiesce to his plans, or even listen to a complete stranger elucidate the litany of favours she would be expected to bestow.

Maia exploded like a firecracker. "You horrible, odious man!" With her arms flailing wildly, she strode towards Cosmo, liberally distributing mud from her whirling skirts upon the floor, and to his dismay, upon his boots, as she levelled an accusing finger at his aristocratic nose. "How dare you think you can dictate to me? How dare you disparage me for a tarnished reputation which exists only in your own sordid mind." She prodded the duke in the chest, emphasising each word, "I will not marry your cousin, is that clear?"

While the duke had never seen an avenging Fury, he believed he would instantly recognise one should it cross his path, for it would look exactly like Miss Hindolveston; the revelation did not please him. However, unaccustomed to being spoken to in such a manner, the duke's reply was icy, "What is not clear is why you threw yourself at my cousin like a harlot; why you roamed un-chaperoned during a rout, when you should have been in the drawing room seeking a husband, but perhaps I am dull-witted; perhaps you will enlighten me."

In an effort to prevent herself from screaming at the sheer stupidity of this ridiculous, arrogant man, Maia gritted her teeth, her nails biting into the palms of her clenched hands, lest she do the unthinkable and strike the vile creature who stood before her. Was he deliberately trying to bait her?

Bradenham had been planning a long slow torture for his cousin, but from the look of the fury who, unless he was very much mistaken, was ready to draw blood, there was clearly no need; the harpy would exact a lifetime of remorse from Percy and he would be an eager spectator. Indeed, the duke was almost looking forward to Christmas, it was both appalling and entirely fascinating. However in the midst of her rage the girl seemed to recall something … his title no doubt.

Maia's quickly dispelled such pretensions. "Your Grace," again the gritted teeth, "I will not explain myself, nor do I seek your approval for my actions. If you chose to censure me there is little I can do to change your sordid and closed mind, even if I cared to."

Intending to respond, the duke was prevented from doing so by a slender hand held before his face; shocked to be on the receiving end of the arrogant gesture he was known to employ himself, he noted the small red half-moons where Miss Hindolveston's angry nails had scored her palm, and shamefully found himself hoping that the minor wound stung, just a little.

"I have not finished," the girl announced imperiously. "For I can hardly believe society can be so shallow as to shun me, when it is well-known that there are gentlemen who frequently spend a great deal of time in the company of ladies, or perhaps I mean women. Such a dual standard is laughable, particularly when my only crime was to seen with your cousin in a long gallery."

"Your crime, Miss Hindolveston, was not just to be seen with my cousin, but to be seen in his arms kissing him without restraint. Be assured, the ton does not take kindly to such bold seduction. While there have doubtless been Siddenhams with dented reputations however, their transgressions have for the most part been glossed over solely due to the shallowness of society. I say for the 'most part' because even the ton draws the line at young men who debauch innocent ladies and are foolish enough to be caught in the act. How you choose to ruin your questionable reputation is your own affair, however, it became my affair when you involved Percy in your scheme, and I will not permit Percy to be ostracised simply because you will not permit him to redeem himself."

"I see, so I am to be the sacrificial lamb," Maia stated matter-of-factly.

Her comment was greeted with a snort of derision. "There is no need for you to sacrifice yourself. Indeed, there is no reason why you should not be as content as the next married woman. Percy has an estate in Hertfordshire, following your wedding you will both remain there for the remainder of the season until the gossip has died down, when he will be free to return to London."

"And I?"

"You? You will make your home in Hertfordshire, unless Percy decides that you should reside with him in London; naturally as tradition dictates you will join your husband at my estate over Christmas.

Maia gave a murmur, as if having given the matter earnest consideration she were about to acquiesce, however, when she spoke her response was far from passive compliance. "I will not marry your cousin and that is my final word on the matter, if society shuns me then so be it, I care nothing for such nonsense, and am content to forgo the remainder of the season. The only opinions I care about are those of my family." At best this was a gross exaggeration, for none of the Hindolveston girls were reticent when it came to expressing their views, and the heated disagreements which invariably followed a discussion would certainly undermine Maia's claim of placing weight on collective family opinion.

The duke looked at her stonily, then with the ease of an accomplished card player laid his ace at her feet; his words cool and dangerous. "You have overlooked one small matter, but perhaps I overestimate its importance; perhaps after all it is of no significance." Assured that he held her attention, Bradenham said slowly and with great deliberation, "You have sisters I believe?"

Maia nodded, uncertain of the direction the discussion was taking. "I have six sisters."

"How tragic that your selfishness, your lack of propriety, must taint them also."

Her troubled violet eyes met the duke's mocking gaze, wary of where he was leading.

"My dear girl, you cannot believe with your reputation firmly established as a harlot, that your sisters will be able to make their come-outs in safety, surely you are not so naïve. The ton will be waiting for them, ready to pounce, to offer your sisters a warm welcome."

He watched the vile insinuation of his words hit home, he had found the chink in her armour; Miss Hindolveston might not care about her own reputation, but she would not risk harming her sisters. Yet as her spark of vibrancy faded and the girl appeared diminished and defeated, feeling as if he deliberately crushed something all the more remarkable for its rarity, Cosmo's victory seemed hollow.

He thrust the unwelcome notion aside and ruthlessly pressed his advantage. "At last you understand me. No matter how much you might protest your innocence, your conduct will not go unpunished. Neither of you will escape censure unless you abide by society's rules. Furthermore, if you insist in remaining unwed, first Percy and then your sisters will suffer for your transgressions."

His tone left Maia in no doubt that unless she complied and married Mr Siddenham, the duke would personally see to it that no mercy was shown to her sisters. With an effort she swallowed the rising panic threatening to overwhelm her.

"You will inform your father you have undergone a change of heart; that my cousin will suit you admirably and you welcome the alliance, leaving him in no doubt of your sincerity." Bradenham's dark eyes steeled. "Your father must believe that you are anxious to wed. After all, an eager bride is not uncommon. My man will draw up the settlement papers, once all is signed you will marry Percy by special licence, secure in the knowledge you have been a dutiful sister and daughter."

Waving a dismissive hand at her soiled habit, he stated disapprovingly. "I trust as a bride you will have less mud about your person than currently adorns you, for my cousin has exacting sartorial standards, no doubt you will bear that in mind when selecting your bride clothes."

With that he swept from the library without a second glance at the future Mrs Siddenham. As the door shut behind the departing figure, Maia's bravado finally deserted her and slumping to the floor she wept, messily and with abandon.

Chapter Four

While it is true that for some time after his carriage swept along the long drive from Delphic House, both the duke and Miss Hindolveston felt misery; perhaps only Bradenham experienced the cold clutch of guilt. Never before had he so ruthlessly annihilated a girl; inexperienced and ill equipped to spar with an expert like himself. He had not expected to feel remorse and was unable to fathom what it was about Maia Hindolveston that had irritated him so thoroughly he had been barely able to keep from shaking her.

Although the increasing distance between his carriage and Delphic House afforded Cosmo the opportunity to regain his equilibrium, he found himself wishing he could forget the entire incident, for despite achieving all he had intended, his method had not proved to be his finest moment.

Since assuming the title in his twentieth year, his Grace had done many things of which he was not proud, most in the name of youth and folly; he had even fought a duel, thus risking the slender thread of succession. However, his opponent's aim had gone wide of the mark and Bradenham himself had fired into the air as behoved a gentleman. Reminded of his past foolishness, the fragility of the unbroken line of ducal responsibility weighed heavily upon him anew, and he mused over the irony of securing a bride for the reluctant Percy, when it was he who needed to find a bride and set-up his nursery; having no wish to wait until he was in his dotage before he sired sons and risk leaving the title and estates to an heir who was still in the schoolroom when he inherited, or worse still; the nursery.

As Bradenham pondered the dynastic expectations he had yet to fulfil, an image of Miss Hindolveston sprang forcefully to mind; her hair tumbling down her back; violet eyes wide in consternation, and her face pale. Once again despair threatened to overwhelm him; he had crushed the ridiculous girl who had done nothing more than kiss Percy, although heaven only knew what had possessed her to do such a thing. He must indeed value family honour to serve Miss Hindolveston on a platter to Percy in this manner, for while the girl's reputation was undoubtedly at stake, so too was his wretched cousin's good standing.

He bent to flick some of the mud so generously imparted by

Miss Hindolveston from his well-polished boots, and wondered if Percy would appreciate his intervention any more than Miss Hindolveston, or even comprehend it was for their collective benefit.

Cosmo's efforts to restore his boots to their former glory were in vain, for he only succeeded in spreading the filth to his gloves and, leaning back against the squabs, the duke closed his eyes and rubbed his aching forehead in an effort to forestall what he suspected would prove to be a monumental headache; too late. He recalled the mud and, opening his eyes, examined with something akin to resignation his discoloured gloves, guessing that his brow likewise bore the marks of Miss Hindolveston's carelessness. Scowling, the duke's attention turned to the countryside beyond the carriage, for the sky was clear and the budding trees and hedgerows were filled with nesting birds, yet despite the obvious evidence of a world filled with hope, the drive back to St. James's square seemed both oppressive and interminable.

***

Maia remained slumped on library floor, sobbing until her nose was red and her eyes bloodshot, although her misery was more passionate and rage tinged than that of her nemesis. However, upon reaching the sniffing and hiccuping stage in her emotional outpouring, and with her resolve returning, she decided she had had enough of both the Duke of Bradenham and his loathsome cousin. Conducting an inventory of sorts of the duke's rudeness, Maia ruminated on the supercilious man's sneering dismissal of her grubby riding habit. Did he not know that staying clean was almost impossible when riding, particularly when one fell-off? She had a fleeting vision of being sent to her chamber to change, like an errant schoolroom miss, if her attire did not meet Mr Siddenham's exacting standards. Her snort of indignation forced Maia to wipe her nose upon the hem of her habit. She was amused to recall that Mr Siddenham had not been the epitome of sartorial perfection when she had first lain eyes on him in the long gallery, although to advise the duke of this would have severely undermined her claim of innocence.

The notion was sobering, as was the enormity of the situation. Lying in a shaft of sunlight, Maia sniffed. There had to be a solution, a way to protect her sisters and avoid marriage to Percy Siddenham. She did not doubt the sincerity of Bradenham's threat to ensure the ruination of her sisters if she did not comply, even if the task he had apparently set himself seemed to her to be Herculean, clearly he had not met her sisters. Yet she could not run the risk of jeopardising their futures. There must be alternatives open to her other than marrying Percy Siddenham.

She dismissed several possibilities as unpractical, and firmly rejected the idea of taking the veil. If she were to live a life of quiet contemplation and seclusion, she do that just as easily married to Mr Siddenham, where at least she would be afforded the opportunity of making the duke's life miserable, if only at Christmastide. However, comprehending a flaw, Maia was forced to abandon her prolonged punishment scheme; for doubtless the duke's wife was equally vile as her husband, and the prospect of being at the mercy of not only the odious duke, but also his equally odious duchess, was not in the least inviting, particularly when she could not be assured of successfully settling the score with his Grace.

With the prospect of marriage to Percy growing more unpalatable by the moment, Maia was further convinced that the drastic step must be avoided altogether. Of course remaining at Delphic House was out of the question; for she was in no doubt Bradenham would carry her kicking and screaming to a church, waving a special licence under her nose, whilst declaring that it was for her own good. Yet for her to stay at her home, defiantly unwed, could only seal her sisters' collective fate, therefore she must go, but where?

With no obvious solution presenting itself, Maia's violet gaze strayed to the shelves where yawning spaces bore witness to her father's scholarly notions of educating his children. For in his enthusiasm to illustrate a point, expound upon a theory, or seek the answer to a fiendish question, Lord Nordelph's fervour knew no bounds, resulting in plundered shelves and books piled high upon the table. Without troubling to look, Maia knew that the majority of the missing reading matter would be subjects closest to her father's studious heart; for she together with her sisters, had received many hours of instruction in all things classical.

For a man chiefly concerned with literary pursuits, the untimely death of his second cousin had brought Colkirk Hindolveston unlooked for and wholly unwelcome titles, estates and responsibilities; he would have preferred to be left in relative peace in his library, or caring for his beloved wife, for whom motherhood had come at a high price. While it could not be denied his inheritance of the viscountcy had made the arrival of a son after seven daughters all the more fortuitous, Colkirk's only regret was that it had cost his beloved wife her health.

The unexpected death of such a distant figure as Gerald Nordelph, had not been mourned by the girls, even if good manners and their mama had dictated they must be clad in black, and only as the prolonged period of mourning had progressed were they permitted to make the slow shift to purples and greys. Yet, sartorial restrictions aside, from the girls' perspective Cousin Gerald's demise and scandal surrounding it had been remarkably edifying, in addition to presenting the family with exciting possibilities. Attached to the viscountcy were riches beyond their youthful dreams; houses; carriages; estates and even, if the documents were to be believed, the remains of a castle. They had poured over the fusty velum documents which dourly pronounced the titles and entailments that were now their father's, together with their attached rights and responsibilities; the name of Frogshall Abbot had fascinated the sisters, even before they learned of its ruined walls and abandoned keep.

With her eyes gleaming, Maia stretched cat-like, feeling just a little smug, for Cousin Gerald had provided the perfect solution; she would go to Frogshall Abbot. That none of the family had yet visited the small estate was wholly unimportant.

The more she considered the notion, the more Maia was taken by the ingenuity of the scheme, and with her destination known only to her nearest and dearest, the ton would assume she had been banished; they could hardly ostracise Mr Siddenham if his bride vanished. Meanwhile her father would be seen to be exercising his parental authority in sending his errant daughter away, thereby vindicating himself; and with society's vengeful wrath duly satisfied, her sisters would be safe.

That Maia would not be able to return home until the older of her siblings had established themselves in society, did not worry her unduly, for Eley was but a year Maia's junior and might reasonably be expected to make her come-out next season. And given time, with the world ready to see Maia as the prodigal daughter, forgiven and restored to the bosom of her family, her presence would no longer be a danger to the younger girls.

Rising to her feet, Maia looped the muddy hem of her riding habit over her arm and swept from the library, her head held high. The Duke of Bradenham could go to the devil; it was just a pity that she would not be there to see it.

***

Convincing Lord Nordelph that his role in the unfolding drama was that of the outraged father, was harder than Maia had anticipated, for not only did Colkirk find the notion of banishing a wayward daughter to the furthest reaches of his estates distasteful, he refused to believe society would question Maia's innocence in the matter. It was his wife who finally reminded Lord Nordelph their daughters had been brought up to manage their lives as they saw fit, even if it meant that occasionally they might chose a path contrary to that of parental expectation.

An educated and well-read man, the viscount held enlightened views regarding his daughters, whom he had taken pains to instruct, placing before them the wisdom of the ancients. He had always treated them as equals, and valued their often voluble opinions. It had pained him to learn that the girls wished to take their places within the ton, the elite,who, to his erudite mind, were the least civilised quarter of society ruled by a barbaric and nonsensical set of rules and overseen by equally barbaric and nonsensical matrons; it was all most bewildering.

Colkirk did not understand how looks, dress and affectation could be prized above character and intelligence; it was true that witty individuals were revered, but the wit most appreciated by the ton was caustic, self-promoting and always at the expense of others. Wisely he kept his misgivings to himself and, if his heart sank when Maia first voiced plans for her come-out, only his wife was aware of the depths to which it plummeted.

The poor man was incredulous at Maia's suggested banishment, which not only flew in the face of reason, but undermined all the viscount hoped for his offspring. He saw no reason why the dual ogresses Bellmont and Ormesby should have their spurious beliefs confirmed, when all Maia had done was to shield her fellow-man, it was just a shame the man in question was un-likable as Percy Siddenham. But Maia was determined, a common trait amongst his daughters, who seemed to have inherited a stubborn streak.

It went against the grain for the poor viscount to be perceived - even mistakenly - as a tyrant who, gnashing his teeth, had commanded his errant daughter to never again darken his doors. How the girls laughed when Colkirk gnashed his teeth and pretended to be a monster; it was a game that had begun when Maia and Eley were barely knee high, and laughing had run from their beloved papa, terribly transformed. While the game always ended with the soothing of the monster's savage breast and reforming him. Society's monsters were not so easily recognisable, nor were they so effortlessly vanquished, but in the end Maia had won, although the viscount made the necessary arrangements with a heavy heart.

If their father was a reluctant participant, her sisters were enthusiastic supporters of the ruse; the three older girls in particular were adamant that Maia must avoid marriage to the unsuitable Mr Siddenham at all costs. They had listened to the tale with growing indigence and on Eley's part with mounting fury, for Maia believed it advisable to warn her sisters what was at stake should her plan fail, even if privately she felt the duke has miscalculated if he believed that Eley would be easily persecuted.

While the younger girls and Leander were left in relative ignorance, they knew Maia was going away and that her destination must be kept a secret. This did not prevent them from jumping into the fray with gusto as they attempted to assist with the packing, bringing useless and unhelpful items to be stowed in the trunk to the wails of consternation from their lady's maid-in-training, who was to accompany Maia. Lovelace Loveday helped dress and care for the seven sisters, and had agreed unreservedly to accompany Maia, but managed to undermined her commitment to the scheme by sobbing noisily at the prospect of leaving the other girls behind.

The farewell at the carriage door was a damp affair, with the three younger sisters and Lovelace Loveday weeping with abandon. Maia's goodbyes to her beloved mama had already taken place, quietly and privately.

Unable to leave her chamber to see her eldest daughter off, the quiet words of wisdom and encouragement Margaret Nordelph had privately imparted did much to lift Maia's flagging spirits. Lady Nordelph had good cause for her wholehearted support of the scheme, having seen her own sister bullied into an arranged marriage, with disastrous consequences, thus Maia was able to bid her mother adieu with a calm heart, although perhaps not entirely dry eyes.

At last, the escapee and her damp accomplice were installed in the coach which was to bear them to Norfolk. Although the final leave-taking was a protracted affair as the sisters each responded to the ordeal as befitted her nature. Taya mercilessly wrung her handkerchief until the delicate linen gave way under such rough treatment while, with a stump of charcoal in her hand, Alcy surreptitiously sketched caricatures of her weeping siblings, her own tears falling unheeded, as Eley, her expression murderous, glared at the younger girls who, making no attempt to disguise their emotions, were distraught and - Maia knew - enjoying themselves thoroughly. By contrast to his impassioned daughters, observing the scene with quiet dignity, Lord Nordelph shook his head in bewilderment, for his daughters not only seemed to be positively relishing the scene, but looked and sounded like a chorus in a Greek tragedy. The notion was rather unsettling.

It was left to Leander to add the final touch, as running from the stables, his black curls tousled and his knees grubby, he thrust a large basket though the open carriage door, panting breathlessly. "For you, so you will not be lonely."

In astonishment, Maia gazed into the soulful eyes of one her brother's beloved pups, while the benefactor stared at his feet in pleased embarrassment, and his sisters voiced their mutual approval. Having had her face licked soundly by the excited puppy, Maia scrambled out of the coach to give what seemed to Leander to be an overly affectionate hug; mayhem reigned as adieux were repeated, kisses exchanged and handkerchiefs sniffed into before the carriage was finally able to lurch its way along the sweeping drive.

To be certain of having the last view of her family, Maia leaned dangerously out of the window, waving wildly, while Lovelace scolded the puppy as it leapt excitedly from one seat to the other. Misjudging both the distance and the lurching of the carriage, it landed with a yelp onto Love's feet, causing the maid to squeal in surprise. Maia withdrew her head from the window and attempted to restore some order, firstly to the occupants of the carriage and then to her windblown hair observing, as the puppy settling down to chew the basket, that the journey to Frogshall Abbot promised to be a long one.

***

The sighs emanating from opposite corner of the carriage indicated that Lovelace Loveday was not enjoying the adventure; a journey which to Maia's mind was pleasurable enough, if one ignored the jolting. Even the puppy had at last settled, having chewed the basket and been thoroughly sick, it had fallen asleep, curled contentedly in the folds of a carriage-rug.

The disinclined bride speculated that it was perhaps easier to enjoy an escape if one were running away from the spectre of a disastrous marriage, offering encouragingly, "We should reach Frogshall Abbot by nightfall."

Far from cheered, Love gloomily responded, "I hope there ain't no frogs, nasty slimy things."

Whether there were frogs inhabiting the Frogshall estate was of little consequence to Maia, being understandably preoccupied with weightier matters, although she did her best to reassure Love regarding the likelihood of the creatures residency being restricted to Frogshall Abbot's ponds and waterways.

It was as well that for the time-being Lovelace's thoughts

were almost entirely taken up with frogs, which were by far the lesser of two evils, for the lady's-maid-in-training had heard rumours and speculation from below stairs regarding Miss Maia's sudden departure from Delphic House. Lovelace possessed a lurid imagination and was always willing to plumb the depths of a treasure trove of stories gleaned from older, but perhaps not wise, maidservants, who were happy to share their unbelievable, not to mention unenviable tales of ladies, at the hands of unscrupulous gentlemen.

Maia's own imaginings on that score were more than enough to contend with; she had woken flushed and breathless from dreams in which both a long gallery and the Duke of Bradenham featured, and although she was unable to see the face of the lady he pursued, from the darks curls she surmised it must be one of her sisters.

However, the journey was long, jolting and tedious, and Love was not one to permit her amphibious misgivings get in the way of offering her opinion on matters.

"I daresay the Frogs' Hall will be duller than London, mind you. That Mr Siddenham, well, he seems a shifty sort of gentleman and no mistake, if y'll pardon my saying so."

As Maia was in complete accord, no pardon was necessary, although she could not agree with Love's next pronouncement.

"Not like that nice duke."

Whether swayed by his station, or by the collective snobbery of the servants' hall, Lovelace held firmly to the belief that despite a touch of hauteur, the Duke of Bradenham was entirely satisfactory; naturally this afforded him more respect than his cousin. However, her censure of Mr Siddenham, and in particular the situation, alluded to rather than enunciated, into which poor Miss Maia had been thrust, was grist for her mill of wrongs.

"As if you'd do such a thing; his lordship might read them funny books to you, but there ain't no harm in that, 'tis only stories and foreigners after all, and I dare say they does things different in foreign parts."

Lovelace's loyalty might be unwavering, but it was as well Lord Nordelph could not hear her judgement upon his beloved texts. The lady's maid-in-training continued to mutter over Mr Siddenham's audacity in requesting Miss Maia's hand, as well as the failings of the viscount's library, until eventually subsiding into a mumbling sleep, she left Maia to stare out of the window in relative peace.

The cow parsley in the hedgerows was not yet open, but drifts of bluebells stretched enticingly under the trees, and dotted along the verges were clumps of primroses and daffodils. It was, she considered, a beautiful time of year. The bobbing yellow heads of the daffodils reminded Maia of the ball she had planned to attend this evening with her golden haired cousin, whose last communication had been a petulant missive, to which Maia had yet to reply. In one sentence Emmeline had mourned the loss of Maia's presence, if only to tell Emme how well she looked in her new gowns; while the next was a barely concealed lament regarding the tedium of being forced to stand while alterations were made by the seamstress. Emme went on to seek Maia's opinion regarding the gown best suited for the Aylmerton rout; how long she might expect to be kept waiting before Lord Stibbard made an offer and the likelihood of his providing her with an allowance before they were wed; she had even practised signing Lady Stibbard at the bottom of the letter that Maia might see how well it looked. It hardly an edifying epistle.

The carriage continued its lurching progresses through the burgeoning countryside, within Maia was lost to her daydreams; each roadside marker indicating that one more mile now distanced her from the hated Duke of Bradenham, together with the equally unworthy Mr Siddenham.

With its occupants secure, the Nordelph coach was for the moment, a haven.

Chapter Five

It was not often that the Duke of Bradenham had time on his hands, had he known his secretary would be absent from the house he might have delayed his return. It was bad enough that the appointment in Conduit street had been utterly tedious, but now he was forced to endure his own company, which he did with an air of resignation and not entirely good grace. While he did not eschew the notion of sartorial elegance, he had not relished the morning spent in Conduit street in the company of his tailor any more than he now wished to be alone with his mediations.

He perused the documents Harrington had left on the desk ready for his employer's attention, and pondered the wisdom of embarking upon the task before his secretary's arrival. Harrington might be a stickler when it came to ensuring that duke understood the complexity of the finer details, but it did not follow that Cosmo needed such things pointing out, rather that he preferred not to deprive the man of the satisfaction of imparting his legal wisdom.

"Wisdom," Bradenham snorted irritably; a thing sorely lacking when it came to his cousin, who had shown precious little over the Hindolveston debacle, beyond making the girl a half-hearted offer. If that were not sufficient, Percy's lack of prudence had been entirely eclipsed by the foolish stubbornness of his bride. Without Cosmo's intervention, Miss Hindolveston's future would be dubious indeed, not that he expected thanks from either the wretched girl, or his hapless cousin.

Yet the knowledge that by coercing Miss Hindolveston to begrudgingly accept the hapless Percy, he had circumvented the fate which would undoubtedly have befallen her, did little to allay the duke's pangs of guilt, knowing with certainty the years ahead would hold little happiness for Mrs Siddenham, for which she would doubtless hold him responsible.

Damn Harrington, where in hell's name was the man? He should be here, explaining each wherein-soever and forthwith, not blithely abandoning his employer to wrestle with remorse and the accompanying abyss of misery which had dogged Cosmo's waking hours since his painful encounter with the wretched Miss Hindolveston.

With more resolution than success, the duke turned his attention to the intricacies of estate accounting, Harrington would be well served to discover that bereft of his secretary's legal mind, his employer had managed to muddle his way through nonetheless.

***

When at last Harrington made an appearance, the Duke of Bradenham waved an expansive arm at the well-ordered documents before him upon the desk. "My dear fellow, I am in danger of questioning your worth, for I have waded through last quarter's accounts entirely unassisted, yet was in need of your expertise no more than a dozen times."

His secretary neither reacted to the jibe, nor more significantly did he offer an apology, but looking if not ruffled exactly, then certainly more than a little distracted, announced: "Your Grace, I have come from Richmond."

With the accounts paling into insignificance, the duke responded, "You have my full attention, pray continue."

"As you will recall your Grace, Forncett had an appointment yesterday with Lord Nordelph in order to finalise the marriage settlements."

Bradenham nodded, having himself directed his lawyer to call upon Nordelph. His steepled fingers touching lightly, he listened intently.

"Shortly after your departure for Conduit street, Forncett arrived here, greatly perturbed. His lordship informed him that the settlements were no longer required and dismissed him. In your absence, having received no direction for such an eventuality, Forncett sought my advice."

Although his expression grew grim, the duke refrained from interrupting.

"Knowing the importance of the marriage and the speed with which the union must be brought about, I went to Richmond to -" here Harrington hesitated, weighing his words with the care of a man accustomed to prickly legal complexities.

"Expedite the matter?" Bradenham grinned appreciatively. "Your worth remains entirely unquestioned Harrington. Please, continue."

While Mr Harrington was not given to excesses when displaying his emotions, his grim expression indicated that his tiding were not felicitous.

"His lordship informed me Miss Hindolveston has been sent from the house, thereby removing the necessity of marriage. He advised me that Mr Siddenham was no longer required to sacrifice himself in order to preserve the lady's honour."

"Dammed he is!" Leaping to his feet, the duke exploded wrathfully. As if to emphasise his ire, the chair toppled behind him, yet its resounding crash was ignored.

"Hell and damnation, you mark my words this is the work of that bloody girl. Ye gods but I shall get her to that damned altar if I have to drag her there myself. Nordelph would no more banish his daughter than I would become a saint."

Having erupted, Bradenham's fury gained momentum. "The vixen has done this to spite me, but this time the wretched girl has bitten off more than she can chew. I will make her sorry she ever set eyes on Siddenham."

Catching sight of his secretary's impassive expression, ruefully Cosmo ran his hand through his dark curls in a manner that was rather more boyish than ducal.

"Forgive me, Harrington, I am aware you do not share my sentiments regarding Miss Hindolveston, but surely you can see this is folly; running away will not still wagging tongues, nor will it nullify the damage done to the lady's reputation, but will serve only to inflame matters. The ridiculous girl has added unnecessary fuel to the fire, and is going to get burned. We must try to fathom out to where a young lady with an over-imaginative streak would banish herself, and how the feat was accomplished."

The duke became aware that Harrington looked just a little smug. "Again I beg your pardon, I allowed my irritation to get the better of me, there is obviously more to your account than I have heard, pray continue on with your tale."

Brushing aside his secretary's offer of assistance, Bradenham retrieved his chair, keen to hear the rest of what he suspected would prove to be a saga.

A man of quick wits, which was one of the reasons his employer held him in such high esteem, Harrington had wasted no time in ascertaining the proof of the banishment; sifting the facts from the web of fiction which had been spun around him from the moment he had set foot in Delphic House.

To this end he had wisely declared that he would retrieve his horse from the stables, rather than put the butler to the trouble of having the animal sent for, thus Harrington had contrived to cross the path of two of the Hindolveston sisters, although he had been forced to retrace his steps several times in order to bring the scheme to fruition.

A litter of boisterous puppies had contributed greatly to his success by distracting the girls, allowing rather more candid responses to his skilfully worded enquiries than the secretary had dared hope for, and had resulted in several pertinent facts above and beyond his subtle questioning.

As the conspiracy was unravelled, the duke began to feel marginally better. A real banishment left him little room to manoeuvre, short of abducting the reluctant bride, which even he was loath to do; but a feigned exile came with arguably few rules and certainly none Cosmo felt any obligation to abide by. Leaning back in his chair, the better to enjoy the fictitious tale, his eyes glinted.

"I assume Miss Hindolveston departed alone? No, let me guess- in the dead of night leaving behind her weeping mama and sobbing sisters?"

The secretary responded with a grin. "Your Grace has more genius for the dramatic than Miss Hindolveston, for she left in daylight hours."

"You disappoint me Harrington, I was convinced nothing less than a departure at midnight would suffice." He gave a long-suffering sigh. "Very well, if the girl was not thrown weeping from the house with no more than the clothes in which she stood, I was remiss to assume she left alone, perhaps after all there was a trusted retainer and at least one coachman to accompany her."

"Indeed, she was accompanied by two coachmen, two footmen and a maid," corroborated his secretary.

"It gets better by the moment, but one wonders if Miss Hindolveston has not heard of shutting the stable door after the horse has bolted. Too late she pays attention to the proprieties, but if she has learned her lesson it is woefully belated. What of the sisters, from your expression Harrington, one would guess they are from the same mould as their elder?"

"I have not met the lady in question, however, Miss Celaeno ..." Harrington was interrupted by a shout of laughter from his noble employer.

"Surely not? Nordelph cannot have named them for the Heavenly Sisters, no man in his right name would baptise his offspring after a constellation."

Struggling to suppress his own amusement, Harrington nodded. "It would seem so, your Grace."

Cosmo gave a sigh of despair. "It reminds me of my sister Julia. She would name her dog, Sweetling, and my father - against his better judgement - allowed her to do so, feeling sure the wretched animal like its predecessors, would not live longer than a few years. The animal out-lived my father, who never forgave himself for flouting his own rule of never allowing a child to name anything likely to live longer than a year or two. One wishes the same rule had been applied to Nordelph."

Believing it prudent not to comment upon matters pertaining to the duke's family, Harrington continued with his tale, "I was informed the Misses Asterope and Merope were distraught over the banishment of their sister."

"But Electra and Taygete are made of sterner stuff? Good lord, what was the man thinking?" The duke passed a hand over his eyes. "It's little wonder Miss Hindolveston made a lunge at the first gentleman she could get her claws into, having been brought up in a household with so little respect for the norms of society, even the names are at odds with what one would wish for one's daughters."

Harrington was somewhat taken aback, having never heard his employer refer to anyone's offspring in such parental terms.

"Remind me of the heavenly Maia's fate? The myth, the one for whom the star was named, seduced was she?"

His secretary nodded, just a little gleefully.

His Grace groaned. "Let us hope Miss Hindolveston does not share the same end, although I fear this ill-conceived banishment can only further endanger her. Does the foolish girl think tongues will not wag simply because she is unable to hear them?"

Cosmo's fingers rapped a tattoo upon the polished desk.

"I am tempted to put a notice in the Gazette announcing the betrothal of Percy to his Fury, just to keep the gossips at bay." His hand stilled as he mused. "One wonders if I did, whether the heavenly Maia would fly from her banishment to heap burning coals upon my brow."

"Would it not be wise to delay such an announcement until you have the lady in hand, so to speak, your Grace? After all, it may take some time to discover her whereabouts."

"I believe you are right to be cautious Harrington, you usually are. The heavenly Maia needs to be placed bound and most especially gagged upon the sacrificial altar before an official proclamation is made. However, first things first, we must advise my cousin of his temporary stay of execution. But his neck is not off the block, for the axe is sharp and will drop, eventually."

Much amused by this notion, the duke took a sheet of paper from the drawer and dipping the nib into the ink-pot, began to write firmly and with precision, his expression of amusement belying his true feelings.

Chapter Six

Hidden in the depths of Norfolk, Frogshall Abbott was certainly well-removed from society and its fascination with scandal. More importantly to Maia, she was safely beyond the reach of the odious Duke of Bradenham. Even without its lord and master present at the helm, Frogshall Abbot was a productive estate, and the unexpected arrival of a daughter of the house had caused much excitement and no small amount of speculation. Maia had been warmly welcomed by the servants and retainers; the former incumbent Lord Nordelph's second cousin, had rarely bothered with this remote outpost, despite insisting that a full compliment of staff awaited his whims and occasional unheralded visits.

Maia had expected some resistance to her untried hand upon the estate reins, but instead of being met with mere forbearance, the household were grateful for her appreciation of the decades of service, faithful care and painstaking attention they had lavished upon the ancient stones of this small, but delightful jewel in the Nordelph coronet.

The origins of Frogshall Abbot had long since been forgotten; how ever it had begun its career, it had without question ended it in ruins. Although there were clues amongst the detritus and rubble of a noble past, even if the hill which had once housed the keep and fortifications was overgrown, little remained of its former glory beyond scattered stones and the odd piece of intact wall. The house which stood alongside the vestiges of ancient history, was an impostor, built with the stones of its benefactor some centuries previously. The house might not be as romantic as living in a moated castle - with knights and an occasional dragon - but it was infinitely more comfortable.

Maia discovered that despite missing her exuberant brother and sisters, there was much to be said for being able to finish a thought without interruption; not to have to play endless games of Snakes and Ladders, or Cat and Mouse amid accusations and recriminations; not to have to mediate truces between warring sibling factions, for with so many strong-willed females under one roof such negotiations were often tricky and taking sides could prove a dangerous occupation. Instead she found pleasure in walking the tumbled walls, amid the wild flowers and long grasses; imagining knights of old seeking their lady's favour and riding bravely off to battle. Idly, Maia wondered about chastity belts, having read a book about such things in her father's library when she was fifteen while recovering from the glass-pox. Both the book and the glass-pox had left a lasting impression, although admittedly, the pox-marks had only been behind her ears and had long since faded.

As she chewed a blade of grass, Maia debated whether life had been easier with chastity belts, before reaching the conclusion that doubtless there had been haughty dukes who, upon questioning a claim of a faulty belt, would assume that the lady was both ruined and to blame; and after denouncing her from the walls would demand she marry his squint-eyed cousin. Not that Percy Siddenham had a squint.

Spitting out the chewed grass inelegantly, she scrambled a-top a piece of fallen masonry; it was so unfair, to be treated with suspicion. Papa always said that people despise their own vices and failings when witnessed in another. Could this account for Bradenham's harshness? Had he seen something within her which made him uncomfortable? Maia hoped so. Indeed, she hoped that whatever he saw gave him sleepless nights and made his life a misery.

***

Had Maia but known, she would undoubtedly have been satisfied, for the duke was indeed suffering. It astounded him how the girl who had the temerity to behave like a hoyden when confronted with her antics in the long gallery - the details of which he preferred not to dwell upon - had managed to give the appearance of abject devastation, leading him to believe she was ready to comply with his wishes, only to engineer a mysterious disappearance within a day. Had he not possessed a sceptical nature, Cosmo might have been taken in by the ruse, and believed Lord Nordelph had unceremoniously packed the girl off to avoid her tainting her sisters.

While the banishment of a defiant daughter was not common; several young ladies might be expected to be removed from London each season, hastily bundled off to family estates that they might rusticate in isolation until they had learned the value of dignity and propriety, or capitulated and agreed to marry gentlemen whom despite being held in esteem their parents, had not excited much enthusiasm within the romantic feminine breast. After a few weeks, or even months spent in lonely seclusion, the rejected suitor often seemed the lesser of the two evils, taking on the guise of some sort of knight errant, at least until after the wedding.

A daughter banished from home and hearth would be dismissed, wailing, with a hatchet-faced governess to act as gaoler, or perhaps dispatched to a particularly strict religious order, and while he struggled to imagine Miss Hindolveston in a wimple, the duke would have preferred she were safely locked behind the walls of a convent, contemplating her transgressions, rather than gadding about the countryside. Not that Bradenham believed for one moment Nordelph had thrown his daughter from the house, the whole affair smacked of a charade.

Despite his intention to treat the farce with the contempt it deserved, Cosmo found himself preoccupied with Miss Hindolveston's disappearance, and from a purely selfish perspective began to wonder if simply accepting this banishment at face value might prove the most prudent course of action. Percy could hardly be called upon to marry a girl who had vanished into thin air, and it would certainly make his own life easier if he did not have to track down an elusive, reluctant bride and return her to a less than eager bridegroom. And Bradenham doubted she would come quietly. This left abduction of the wretched creature as the only viable solution, but was he really prepared to add more drama to the travesty?

However, such meditations were meaningless, for not even he could abduct a lady who refused to be found, which was perhaps the most galling aspect of the debacle; not that Miss Hindolveston had defied him, but that she had done so with astonishing success. For not so much as a sniff of the girl had been found despite Harrington's painstaking enquiries.

Percy had been remarkably cheerful to learn he was not to be leg-shackled immediately, and was growing less concerned about society's wagging tongues with each passing day. While it was not entirely accurate to say that Mr Siddenham's stock had gone up considerably in the eyes of the ton, it was true that a newly perceived element of danger had enhanced his popularity with some of the young bucks who were eager to admit a would-be rake into their midst. Indeed, some tonnish doors which previously been held only tentatively ajar, were beginning to open a fraction wider in welcome to Percy, even if the gentleman himself generally preferred to socialise with his cronies and those who shared his particular tastes. He was certainly in no hurry for Cosmo to discover Maia's whereabouts and bring the girl back to be wed, although he was resigned to the fact that it would happen eventually, knowing Bradenham too well to doubt that his noble cousin would lay hands upon the runaway, sooner or later.

However, until such time as Percy was called upon to stand up before God and the clergy to plight his troth, he was happy to leave all the arrangements to Cosmo, who had already demanded that Percy go to the trouble of obtaining a special license in order to expedite matters when Miss Hindolveston was finally run to earth. Percy almost felt sorry for her; it would be no joke having Bradenham on one's tail, but recalling his own woes, not the least of which being that he was destined to wed the runaway, he stomped off to the house on Half Moon street, an establishment for select members, where within the perfumed walls Mr Siddenham might forget his unpalatable duty for the remainder of the evening. Percy might enjoy liaisons amongst artistically displayed statuary, but he was happy to pay for his ignoble pursuits; particularly when recompense meant one was allowed to indulge unchecked one's desires and proclivities, no matter how distasteful they might be.

***

The Duke of Bradenham paused in his pacing and stared down through the windows at the darkening street, his frustration evident, for very little in this scandalous episode made sense. For despite her hoydenish manners, Miss Hindolveston did not seem the sort to fling herself at a man's head, certainly not one whom she had clapped eyes upon only moments before, and putting aside familial loyalty, Cosmo found it hard to believe Percy was the answer to any débutante's dreams.

There was no denying the girl was difficult, decidedly so, but she was not wanting in wits, and to shock the ton simply because she could, would be foolish indeed. Besides, by all accounts it had been her idea to make her come out, so why would she deliberately jeopardise her success? Yet there could be no doubt, upon hearing the approach of Lady Bellmont and Lady Ormesby, although she had time to withdraw from the scene, Miss Hindolveston had chosen to stay.

The ambiguity regarding Miss Hindolveston's incomprehensible motives notwithstanding, the nature of the circumstance in which she had allowed herself to be discovered was by no means as perplexing, and the duke was not about to be swayed from his purpose. His resolve to bring about the marriage was perhaps spurred on by his growing irritation with Percy's behaviour; for having made a complete recovery from his short-lived bout of contrition, Mr Siddenham was giving every indication of thoroughly enjoying the season, while the girl who by Percy's own admission should be his bride, had simply vanished.

    Bradenham glared at the rain which was beginning to form puddles on the cobbles and growled to himself; cursing Percy for embroiling him in the affair. But despite his numerous misgivings, now the bit was between his ducal teeth, Cosmo could not let go. Dogged anew by the conundrum, he wondered again where a vague man like Nordelph would send his daughter, assuming that the man had been as complicit in the farce as Bradenham supposed; even Harrington with his quiet tenaciousness had been unable to discover the whereabouts of Percy's errant bride.

Chapter Seven

It was the frustrating lack of knowledge which drove the Duke of Bradenham to attend the rout given by his sister Aurelia, a household and event which under normal circumstances he would have done his utmost to avoid. Nor was his lack of family feeling by any means one-sided; for Lady Bawsey heartily disapproved of her brother whom she felt had shirked his duty for quite long enough. The merest mention of his name was enough to make the severe matron snort such censorious pronouncements as "Constantine should have set up his nursery years ago, does he want the line to fracture? I cannot understand all this shilly-shallying; he needs to do his duty."

However, Lady Bawsey was careful to keep her sentiments, if not entirely to herself, then certainly from reaching her brother's ears. Upon one occasion, she had gone so far as to forget herself and inform the duke that he should be busy filling the ducal cradle, not wasting his time in other directions, regarding his sister with abject disdain, Cosmo had remarked coldly, "My dear Aurelia, one is tempted to question your parentage, for you have the mind and soul of a farmer's wife. Am I a prize bull for stud?"

Mortified by such coarse sentiments, her ladyship satisfied her outraged pride by declaring privately to her husband that she hoped Constantine's future duchess would prove to be an antidote, who would worry him to the bone and produce ten daughters before the duke could sire an heir. From then on, feeling her arrogant brother was well-served, Lady Bawsey held her tongue - at least in his presence - although, her pronouncements were perhaps harsher on the future duchess, who as yet had done nothing to deserve such a fate. This evening however, it was with his brother-in-law, the object of Aurelia's vitriol wished to speak.

As his Grace made his way up the steps, Bawsey House was a beacon of light, the rain had finally cleared and sounds of laugher and chatter spilled from every window. The rout, for the benefit of the younger members of the ton, was not something Cosmo was looking forward to, but he needed information. What is more, he needed it quickly, and had no desire to be overhead by his sister; during the route she would be fully-occupied in her rôle as the gracious hostess, the timing could not have been more fortuitous.

On his way through the throng, Bradenham spoke at length with several of his particular acquaintances and made a point of glancing over the Bawsey girls, who were enjoying their first and second seasons respectively. The girls were surrounded by social moths drawn to their charms, and catching the eye of several of the fellows in question, the duke did not need to speak to inform the fluttering youths that the objects of their affections were under his protection. He was satisfied to note the moths stepping a few paces back from the dual flames of his nieces. It was, he reflected, time they were safely married off.

His avuncular duty done, Cosmo was arrested in his progress towards Lord Bawsey's study by the white-gloved hand of a lady upon his sleeve. He looked down in cold surprise.

"Your Grace," the lady who had waylaid him smiled coyly.

"Lady Stratton," acknowledging her presence with the cold incline of his head, Cosmo was surprised to find the movement reminded him of Miss Hindolveston.

The lady before him was of medium stature, daringly attired in gauzy yellow muslin, her gown clung so provocatively that it took Bradenham a moment to comprehend the lady must have dampened her chemise, encouraging her dress to mould to her figure, revealing much. It was something he had heard spoken of with relish within the confines of gentlemen's clubs, but had not actually believed that ladies of the ton would stoop to such desperate measures to attract attention.

Lady Statton lowered her eyes to her hand as it rested upon his sleeve and rubbed his arm provocatively, she then raised her eyes to his, a practised, enticing look.

"Well-met your Grace, I am surprised to see you here, for you once said such crushes were abominable, but perhaps I misheard, after all you were whispering in my ear and I find you such a distraction."

She dimpled seductively, her hand gliding to the back of his, tracing his gloved fingers. The duke withdrew his hand as if he had been stung.

The lady was commonly held to be beauty, but upon closer inspection Cosmo noted her brittle quality and theatrically provocative lure, with aversion.

"Lord Stratton, is he well?"

Blinking stupidly in response to his abrupt question, Lady Stratton stammered, "I ... would not know, your Grace."

Bradenham gazed stonily at the woman. "How remiss of me,

your husband resides upon his estate, in … ? You must forgive me Lady Stratton, I do not recall where you are from."

"Yorkshire, your Grace," she gazed reproachfully at him and, lowering her voice to a husky whisper, returned to her theme, "A long way from London." She sighed dramatically. "One gets lonely so far from home, I hoped you might bear me company, I believe we might both find amusement."

The carefully nuanced words dripped like honey, and the lady ran her tongue over her lips in a manner that made the duke frown. Brushing her hand sensuously across the deep décolletage of her clinging gown, she gazed at him from beneath calculatingly lowered lashes, unaware that far from entrancing him, the duke was revolted by her overt lasciviousness. He recalled how the wretched woman had hounded poor unsophisticated Stratton from their first meeting. Stratton was an acquaintance, a genial, good-natured man, not gifted with an abundance of intelligence, who had been dazzled, flattered and finally seduced by the lady's considerable expertise. However, having triumphantly married the object of her devious affection, Lady Stratton felt no compunction to remain by his bedside when her husband had broken his back in a fall from his horse, and leaving him to his misery, had returned to the ton, in her own mind already a widow.

Unbidden, an image of Miss Hindolveston arose in Bradenham's mind, Lady Stratton did not compare favourably to Percy's raven-haired fury.

"You must hold me excused Lady Stratton, I have matters to attend to. Give my regards to your lord, when next you see him."

His nod of farewell was dismissive to the point of rudeness, and left the lady no option but to curtsey, biting her lip as she reflected upon the lost opportunity, and curse inwardly at her mismanagement of this notoriously prickly duke, while Cosmo stalked away without so much as a backward glance.

Lord Bawsey was where the duke anticipated he would be; in his study chair beside the fireplace where, having done the bare minimum in order to placate the demands of society and perhaps more importantly the dictates of his wife, his lordship had retired, feeling remarkably fatigued.

"Allow me to join you Bawsey, one can, after all, have enough of polite conversation," observed Cosmo.

Bawsey nodded, his face even more flushed than usual, doubtless due to the excess of brandy as much as an excess of warmth.

"The ladies love all that talk, but dam' me I'd rather sit here." He took a fortifying draught from his glass. "Still, one must not complain, not when there are still Ursula and Lavinia to be rid of." Lord Bawsey's voice grew peevish. "Aurelia assured me Ursula would take during her first season, but here she is, still eating me out of house and home, and costing a fortune in faradiddles and whatnots." He gave a shake of his grey head, his jowls wobbling ferociously as if to add weight to his words. "When the time comes Bradenham, have sons - for daughters are too costly." Shifting uncomfortably, his lordship heaved a sigh of dissatisfaction.

"I will bear it in mind." Cosmo assured Bawsey, and recalling the social moths fluttering about the Bawsey girls, enquired, "Has either girl received an offer?"

His brother-in-law nodded, his eyes closed as if striving to block out a painful memory. "Naturally they have had offers, three for Lavinia and one for Ursula, but none of 'em acceptable and I turned 'em down, damned impudence."

"What do the girls say?"

Bawsey, who had taken on a morose aspect, looked stunned at the notion. "Say? Why nothing, what has that to do with the matter? The day I ask either girl for an opinion is that day I sign m'own death warrant. Good lord Bradenham, 'tis clear ye don't have daughters."

"Not that I am aware of ..." the duke conceded dryly.

"Yes, well," harrumphed his lordship. "You take my advice, when the time comes say naught until all is settled, once you have signed the settlements their tears and carrying on will count for nothing. Not that Aurelia will countenance such nonsense; she'll see to it the girls marry where they are told." He chuckled and waved a plump hand dismissively. "Once they get caught up in bride clothes and whatnots, they soon dry their eyes. T'was the same with my sisters; lord but they cried for days, until the first appointment with the mantua maker, then t'was nothing but gowns, bonnets and gloves."

Bradenham recalled with a shudder the hysteria attached to his own sisters' betrothals. However, both this experience and his brother-in-law's attitude contrasted sharply with the more temperate philosophy towards matrimony he had encountered in Delphic House, a point he noted with irritation.

"There are some who say it is better to marry for love."

Lord Bawsey harrumphed once again. "What nonsense! Cannot think why you of all people would say such thing, good lord man, whatever next?" Getting into his stride, the elder gentleman continued, "Your cousin married for love and look where it got her. I will admit, they make a fine-looking pair, but damn it, she could have wed a dozen others better born and with deeper pockets too."

"You speak of Constance."

"Siddenham should never have given his consent, nor you for that matter. You could have prevented the marriage. If y'ask me, the pair of you made a damned mull of the whole wretched business. Aurelia says, and I do believe she's right, that Constance should have married well-above Lyth-Hudson, you should have sent the bounder about his business."

Bradenham said nothing.

"Tis too late now of course, even if the reckless fool died, Constance has those boys of his to manage and no other man would take her on, not with those ill-mannered brats snapping at his heels and pulling on his purse- p'raps when they are older."

Remaining silent, Cosmo drew himself up fractionally in hauteur.

"I dare say you are right," Bawsey nodded sagely, mistaking Bradenham's icy annoyance for mute agreement. "Better to say nothing, but such an alliance would not do for my girls, not that Aurelia would countenance such poorly planned scheme."

"Should Constance require a second husband, I have no doubt that even with her ill-mannered brats in full voice, she would not want for suitors, she never did before."

"She still don't, from what I hear. Damned funny way carry on, but Lyth-Hudson don't seem to mind. Although I tell ye plain, I should not like Aurelia to make such a spectacle of herself."

Cosmo ignored the unlikely event of his stolid sister inflaming the ardour of another suitor. His charming cousin Constance, like her brother Percy, was blonde; a beauty who had married the dashing Rowland Lyth-Hudson during her first season. There was no question theirs was a love-match and, at the time, there had been little objection raised by members of the family, other than Aurelia.

Bawsey's complaint about the union alluded to the indisputable fact that during their marriage Rowland had won and lost several fortunes at cards, including his own. Twice. Constance had shown no undue emotion when confronted with a litany of her husband's reckless gaming habits and loss of income by the unsympathetic Lady Bawsey. Tossing her golden head, Connie had merely laughed. "My dear, he will simply have to win it all back, for I have ordered the dearest hat from Locks, and Rowland must buy me a new landau to go with it, although I dare say a barouche would be more the thing." This had caused a rift between the Bawseys and Lyth-Hudsons, at least on the part of the Bawseys.

In addition to their disapproval of Rowland's excessive

gambling, the staid Bawseys were shocked that Constance was the object of rumours, suggesting intrigues, liaisons and even a scandalous affair. Yet far from ostracising the beautiful Mrs Lyth-Hudson and her dashing husband, in a rare and surprising display of indulgence, the usually censorious matrons of society treated the pair as if they were but children, incapable of adhering to the accepted norms of behaviour and decorum. Yet despite Rowland Lyth-Hudson's gaming and his wife's apparent profligacy, they were a golden couple who were adored by the ton. Perhaps because they were so delightedly shocking. The doyennes of the haut monde found it impossible to condemn someone who was just as likely to win a king's ransom at cards as he was to lose it, and accepted whichever hand he was dealt with equal equanimity and, providing Constance did not take a string of lovers and flaunt them in the face of society in the guise of a performing troupe, she would remain a-top her pedestal. It was an anomaly indeed, for most were not afforded such benevolence.

Reminded of the reason for his visit, Cosmo inquired, "What do you know of Nordelph?"

"Nordelph?" Bawsey frowned, his mouth gaping with the effort of recollecting his numerous acquaintances. "Nordelph you say?" he repeated as if the name might jolt his memory. "Can't say I cared for the previous earl. Damned strange and kept low company, not the sort one would invite to house. The new fellow is some sort of distant relative, damned fortunate too, for there are some tidy estates I believe, besides the one in Norfolk. I am surprised you have forgotten, for Nettleton abuts it on the coast side, although I'm deuced glad I sold it. What need did I have for an estate in Norfolk, when yours is so handy? Why d'ye ask? Got daughters has he?" The last question was accompanied by a baffled glance in the duke's direction.

"Seven," Bradenham confirmed, bitterly.

"Good lord!" Gasped Bawsey, with the utmost sympathy, adding hopefully, "antidotes?" With two daughters still in the schoolroom he might be forgiven for hoping the Hindolveston girls too had been blessed with plain features, for neither the Bawsey girls would need competition when the time came for her to enter to fray of the ballroom, but perhaps their looks would improve between now and then, their sceptical papa fervently hoped so.

Cosmo's response offered Bawsey little comfort. "I have seen only three of the girls, although they were most definitely not antidotes, in fact quite the reverse."

His brother-in-law enquired suspiciously, "What? Are you to wed a Hindolveston when Aurelia has been throwing well-connected chits at your head for years? She will never forgive you." He took another sip of brandy and added censoriously, "The Hindolvestons are not good ton."

Cosmo's dark eyes glittered in the firelight giving him a sinister air. "I intend Percy to marry the elder Hindolveston girl."

"Percy?" His lordship choked. "Good lord! Percy you say? To wed an Hindolveston?" Bawsey harrumphed, attempting to digest this wholly unforeseen snippet of rather startling information. "Never saw Percy as a marrying man, but far be it from me to interfere. Does Aurelia know?"

Bradenham suppressed a shudder at the prospect of his sister's predictable reaction to the news that a mere Hindolveston was to wed their cousin. "She does not, nor do I intend to inform her of the fact until it is accomplished, rendering her objections obsolete."

Lord Bawsey nodded sagely. "Very wise. When it comes to marriage it is best to inform the womenfolk when all is done with. Still, I dare say marriage will be the making of Percy, and not before time."

The duke rose from his chair, somehow he doubted that even Miss Hindolveston could achieve such a feat, but not one to dwell upon the things of this world which were beyond even his control, he merely inclined his head at his brother-in-law and turned to go.

"One can but hope. Good evening, Bawsey."

***

The calm of the evening was shattered, as striding into the hallway, the duke shouted to his secretary: "The witch is in Norfolk. Now we have her!"

The pronouncement caused his butler to express his consternation by a sharp intake of breath, and blinking rapidly, as he waited to relieve his Grace of his curled brimmed beaver hat, gloves and silver topped walking cane. The startling declaration also brought Harrington to the library doorway, a large ledger under his arm, although his reaction was perhaps more measured than the relatively emotional outburst of the usually expressionless butler.

Cosmo's triumph belied the frustration he felt, how could he have been so blind? Maia Hindolveston's hiding place should have been obvious. But he had entirely forgotten that Frogshall Abbot, the estate owned by Nordelph, abutted the ugly manor house of Nettleton, close to his own Norfolk estate. His father had settled Nettleton on Aurelia upon her marriage to Lord Bawsey who, with his bride's blessing, had sold it almost as soon as the ink was dry upon the deed. In the unlikely event that Lady Bawsey might feel the need to rusticate in the depths of Norfolk, she would never be content to reside in a mere manor house, not when the magnificence of her brother's ducal estate Swanton Chatteris, was at her disposal.

"She has gone to Frogshall Abbot."

Harrington looked perplexed. "Frogshall Abbot?"

"The estate beyond Nettleton. I had completely forgotten it - or indeed that it belongs to Nordelph. I fear I am losing my touch Harrington."

His secretary scratched his head in amazement. "I had no idea it was one of Lord Nordelph's properties."

"Bawsey has his uses, though heaven knows they are few and far between. Yet while my brother-in-law plays the fool, you may be sure he knew to the groat the sum of my sister's settlements before he made an offer for her, settlements which included Nettleton, a rather unattractive manor and if my sadly lacking memory is correct, Frogshall Abbot lies to the north of Nettleton."

Understanding dawned at last upon Harrington. "And Nettleton lies beyond your estate. She has run straight into the lion's jaws - so to speak - your Grace."

The lion's lips twitched. "Precisely, and at this moment she is within an hour of Swanton Chatteris. The witch was right under my nose all the time."

Ever to the point, Harrington enquired sombrely, "How to you intend to proceed?"

Bradenham had been so focused upon discovering the whereabouts of Maia Hindolveston, that beyond locating her he has not formulated a plan. However, there could be but one course of action.

"I shall leave for Norfolk immediately, I intend to bring Percy's bride back with me, if I have to throw her across the saddle. You may advise my cousin he will be wed by the end of the week."

All things considered Cosmo decided, of the two of them Harrington had the less enviable task, Percy was not going to be pleased, the thought buoyed him greatly.

Chapter Eight

The approach to Frogshall Abbot was lined with trees, and in the meadowland beyond, cattle grazed contentedly, lifting their heads to stare in bovine curiosity at the unusual figure, they lowed softly at the intrusion before turning their attention back to the rich pasture.

The duke's interest in the estate was not solely that of a fellow landowner, for he was characteristically moved by the ancient scattered stones which littered the meadow, the tumbling flowers and lush pastureland which imbued Frogshall Abbot with a soporific sense of tranquillity. In an effort to retain his wits, Cosmo gave himself a shake - both metaphorically and physically. This was no way to approach matters, had he not known better he might have been tempted to believe a web had been spun over the estate by the witch. Or did he mean spider? Witch or not, it would take more than the likes of Miss Hindolveston to get the better of him. He had planned his visit with the utmost care; this time things would go as he intended, this time he had the measure of his opponent. He also had the upper-hand, for Maia Hindolveston had no inkling that her hiding place had been discovered.

Marshalling his thoughts and suppressing any lingering doubts he may have nurtured regarding the suitability of Miss Hindolveston as Percy's bride, the duke continued towards the house; the wretched pair had made their bed and he intended that they should lie in it. Although once the knot was tied he would wash his hands of the whole sordid business.

The stable lad, with whom he left his horse, was delighted to have charge of such a noble beast. But it was not the care of his thoroughbred which caused the duke misgivings; he reminded himself that Maia's young brother would one day be Lord Nordelph, and it would be as well to manage things adroitly to avoid any lingering enmity between the two families. Although once Maia was a Siddenham, her allegiance naturally belonged with Percy's family first and foremost. Indeed, the current Lord Nordelph should be grateful to him for taking the trouble to prevent the Hindolveston name from being dragged through the mire.

The scruffy footman who had admitted the visitor eyed him

with interest, showing him into a large hallway, with twin staircases ascending regally upon either side. Thankfully there was no repetition of the drooping flower arrangement which had been such a feature of the hallway at Delphic House. An elderly butler approached with unhurried, creaking steps, but had to be informed twice of the duke's name, before the scruffy footman took it upon himself to bellow, "The dook of Bradmum," which did little to impress the duke, but certainly resolved the dilemma.

Cosmo anticipated being shown into the library or salon to await Miss Hindolveston's arrival. Instead however, a small woman of middle years bustled forward. The butler stepped aside to speak to the woman, in the same leisurely manner he had approached the duke. She gazed at Cosmo in fascination, absently drying her hands on her apron as she listened to the information the butler imparted in a loud whisper.

It was to be hoped the woman would not feel it necessary to chaperon Miss Hindolveston, for Bradenham intended to speak plainly to the future Mrs Siddenham, and preferred not to have an audience, no matter what propriety dictated; they were after all in the country and country ways were more relaxed than those of the capital.

"Your Grace." The woman stepped forward and dropped a low curtsy, evidently her manners were better than those of her mistress. "I understand you wish to speak to Miss Hindolveston."

The duke inclined his head, but saw no reason to speak.

"Miss Maia is gone from the house. Riding. I do not expect her to return for some time, but will inform her of your visit, your Grace." With that she bobbed another curtsey. "Good-day, your Grace."

Cosmo wanted to ask if Maia had taken an attendant with her, but he could hardly question the woman, then it dawned on him, he was being summarily dismissed from the Nordelph household … again.

***

As she approached the lonely beach, Maia felt a mounting excitement; she had never before seen such a vast expanse of water. As she reached the end of the tall pine tress heralding the wide arc of the bay, her heart began to beat faster. The trees gave way to a strip of peat marsh, flanked by grass-topped dunes, and beyond white-capped waves rushed to meet the ridged sands.

Even the fresh breeze which blew her hair from beneath her hat could not dim the joy of that first breathtaking glimpse of azure sea, and from her vantage point a-top one of the estate horses, Maia tried to fix the memory of the sights and the sounds into her soul forever. The surging water reminded her of a lapis lazuli necklace belonging to her mother, and with an aching heart Maia wished her once vibrant mama could share the beauty of this moment. Struggling to swallow the lump in her throat which threatened to overtake her, she took a deep breath.

The beach was deserted, which was perhaps as well for Maia had no intention of obeying the dictates of decorum, not when she could ride along the water's edge with the wind in her hair. Kicking the horse on, they splashed through the shallow water of the peat marsh towards the dunes, the Hackney picking up speed as they reached the firm, damp sand beyond. Free of the rigid confines of her station and sex, Maia threw back her head and laughed. Throwing her hat from her head, she pushed her hand through the tangled profusion of curls tumbling around her face, and raising her face to the sun she allowed herself to dare to feel truly happy, it was an intoxicating feeling.

***

Beneath the pine trees, hidden from view in the shade cast by the lower branches, the thoroughbred flicked his tail in irritation at the gathering flies. His rider had not expected to find himself on a beach and mused wryly that his valet might never forgive him if he ruined his top-boots, although it would be a worthwhile sacrifice if he achieved his aim.

Any sense of tranquillity the duke may have experienced upon his approach to Frogshall Abbot had abandoned him during his return along the tree-lined avenue; leaving in its wake an irritation Cosmo was beginning to associate with Miss Hindolveston. Returning by a circuitous route to Swanton Chatteris in an attempt to regain his equilibrium, he had spotted the unmistakable figure of Percy's unwilling bride atop a horse far too large for her, disappearing down a narrow track. Despite being engulfed by misgivings, his Grace had followed at a respectful, if ominous, distance. What was the wretched girl doing gallivanting about alone; what the devil was she thinking?

Ruefully, Cosmo considered that he should have anticipated his visit to Frogshall Abbot would not go to plan; although he could hardly accuse the Miss Hindolveston of trying to avoid him when she did not know he was in the county, which could only mean that she had a talent for making things difficult without even trying. Yet if he expected Maia to behave in a ladylike manner, Bradenham was sorely disappointed as, with growing incredulity, he observed the girl carelessly toss her hat upon the sand and laughing, urged the ridiculously large

Hackney into a windswept canter, the sound of the horse's hoof bets deadened by the sand.

Sitting tall in the saddle, the duke craned to watch until Maia was almost out of sight then, wheeling her mount around, she returned, thundering along the beach, her hair streaming out behind her and skirts flapping. Bradenham was transfixed. He had intended to escort Miss Hindolveston back to Frogshall Abbot, but with his plans evaporating, all he could do was gaze.

As the horse slowed, Maia kicked her leg from about the pommel of the side-saddle and sliding, landed in the sand with rather more skill than grace upon the sand. She bent to retrieve her abandoned hat and, as the breeze ruffled her hopelessly tangled curls, a thought seemed to occur to her. Tossing aside her hat once again, Miss Hindolveston sat without ceremony upon the damp sad and, after removing her boots, lifted her riding habit and proceeded to roll down her stockings, neatly sliding each one from her elegant, pointed toes. Bradenham groaned, his mouth suddenly dry.

After making a careless pile of the discarded items, taking the skirts of her habit in one had and the horse's bridal in the other, Maia walked towards the surging water. The sea was bitingly cold as it swirled around her ankles and legs, but unperturbed she threw back her head and laughed.

While the sensual caress of the water was soothing, it produced a heightened awareness and Maia could not ever recall feeling so completely alive, making her long to leave her cumbersome gown in the untidy heap and dance in the waves. However, Maia was wise enough to know that the remote beach could not guarantee total seclusion, and she had no desire to risk being spotted by a fisherman; being disgraced in both the town and the country would be the outside of enough.

So, resigned but determined not to allow the day to be spoilt by proprieties even she could not ignore, Maia splashed along happily beside her horse, kicking the water before her and covering her habit in the fine salt spray, together with a liberal shower of wet sand.

Cosmo was enthralled despite himself, and watched her bend down to pick shining shells from the water. She placed one or two in the pocket of her riding habit, the rest she returned to the sea by throwing them beyond the cresting waves.

She padded lightly along the shoreline leaving barely a trace of a footprint in her wake, the horse training behind her.

Bradenham almost gave himself away when Maia's long legs became ensnared in the skirts of her habit, which by now were heavy, wet and cumbersome, causing her to tumble, she landed heavily upon the wet sand, barely out of reach of the surging water. Restraining himself with effort, the duke was rewarded for his fortitude by the sight of Percy's bride scramble to her feet and vigorously attempt to brush her rear free of sand; in vain the girl twisted herself around only to again become entangled in the unwieldy skirts and unable to maintain her balance she fell for a second time, her bare legs hopelessly entwined in the yards of heavy, sopping cloth. As the sea frothed about her, rushing along her legs and thighs, Maia threw back her head and laughed.

Bradenham was hypnotised.

Wiping tears of mirth mingled with salt spray from her eyes, Maia held the Hackney's reins between her teeth as she wriggled clear of the teasing water, hitching her skirts above her knees until she was free of the clinging cloth and could stand once again. With a final wiggle Maia shook the sand from her backside, the droplets of water on her legs glinting in the sunshine.

For the first time since the days of his youth Bradenham found himself in the unusual predicament of not being entirely sure how to proceed. He had planned to be firm with the girl, not allowing her to gain the upper hand. Now, painfully aware Miss Hindolveston had no notion she had been observed, Cosmo had no desire to draw attention to his presence, and having watched the joyful expression so intently, his desire that she should return immediately to Frogshall Abbott had diminished significantly. Indeed, he could think of nowhere he would rather be at that moment that on the beach.

The reminder of his errand sobered the duke's soaring elation, as did his awareness of not trusting himself at this juncture to be capable of coherent conversation with the Fury. When Miss Hindolveston shook out her sodden skirts and allowed them to drape uncomfortably about her, it occurred to Cosmo that the clinging material hid legs which were still damp with salt water, and would be cool to the touch. This knowledge, as fascinating as it might be, was not going to improve matters, so it was that with a mixture of reluctance and resolution the duke gathered the slack reins and turning the thoroughbred towards the pasture, wished he had not witnessed the past minutes, for the lasting imagine of his cousin's wife's bare legs was going to make Christmas a damnably awkward affair.

With her attention fixed upon the removal of sand from between her toes, Maia did not notice the flash of sunlight as it caught the horse's gleaming bit, nor was she aware of the duke's brooding glance over his shoulder as she began brushing the damp sand from her underskirts.

**

It was a sober man who rode through the gates of Swanton Chatteris. The miles between the beach and his estate had provided ample time for contemplation, leaving the duke with the notion that Maia Hindolveston was not the only one wanting sense. He had been given the opportunity to address the girl in the seclusion of the beach, where she might have argued and protested to her heart's content. However, with no witnesses, he would have been spared any embarrassment. Then, having dealt his final crushing blow, the matter would have been settled. He should be riding back to London with Percy's bride-to-be firmly contained within his carriage, instead all he had to show for his afternoon was the unpleasantly guilty notion that he had spied upon the wretched girl, and damned uncomfortable ride home.

A fortifying brandy strengthened any temporary lack of resolve. Cosmo was confident that tomorrow he would take Miss Maia in hand, meanwhile, her housekeeper would doubtless inform the girl of his arrival so that at least she would be expecting him, although he hoped that being forewarned was in this case, not forearmed.

Chapter Nine

If the Duke of Bradenham expected to be received in a civil manner the following day, he was sorely mistaken. Having not slept well, he was not in the best of humour as he handed his hat and gloves to the scruffy manservant who had answered his imperious summons; curtly biding the man to inform Miss Hindolveston that the Duke of Bradenham wished to speak with her.

The young man might perhaps be forgiven for taking quiet delight in informing the haughty duke that Miss Hindolveston was not at home, nor was she expected to return for some hours.

Incredulously, Bradenham inquired as to her whereabouts, but while the servant's appearance might be lacking, his demeanour was certainly up to snuff. Stiffening, the man replied with reticence that he was unaware of Miss Maia's particular movements.

The duke was forced to bite back the retort that he has seen more than enough of the lady's particular movements upon the previous day to last him a lifetime. Duly shown to the library, Bradenham was abandoned to bide his time.

The library was an antiquated but nonetheless splendid affair, with books too numerous to count confined behind the wire mesh screens of the bookcases. The hearth was cold, and although the fire had been laid ready, it was not needed on such a beautiful spring day. An ancient refectory table of black oak, benches flanking its well-polished sides stood to one side of the chamber, while to the duke's chagrin a decidedly haphazard arrangement of wild flowers stood upon the table, their earthy fragrance scenting the air. The buzzing of early bees in the flower borders below the open sash windows could be heard.

With a sigh Cosmo sat in one on the high-backed, deeply winged chairs set before the hearth to await the arrival of Miss Hindolveston. He supposed he must have dozed, his poor night's sleep demanding recompense, for he was not aware of the passing of time until he was startled by the noise of a window being opened to its fullest extent and the sound of boots scraping over the sill.

At first the duke assumed Frogshall Abbot was the object of a burglary, but hearing a curse whispered from feminine lips, he smiled and settled further back in the chair, like a lion in his den, waiting.

***

When she had been informed upon her return the previous afternoon of the unexpected visit by his Grace the Duke of Bradenham, Maia had been silently furious; although she had done her best to keep her wrath to herself. She had tried her utmost to prevent the wretched man from casting more than a shadow upon her day, albeit a long one.

Her patience had been further tested by the housekeeper's assumption that the duke was an ardent suitor who had gone above and beyond to demonstrate intentions of a lasting nature by making the arduous journey all the way from London to call upon her. The kindly Mrs Dalling obviously expected Miss Maia to be thrilled and flattered to have inspired such attention from a man of the duke's standing.

Maia had been forced to bite her tongue, until at last she could relieve her frustrations upon the hapless pillows in her bedchamber, sending them thudding against the bedposts in dull protest at the injustice of the world. He may have found her, but that meant nothing; the man was only a duke, even he could not force her to marry Percy.

Could he?

Dismissing such thoughts as nonsense, Maia had passed a reasonably calm night, despite once again dreaming of a long gallery in which a young woman with a profusion of corkscrew curls threw herself with abandon into the duke's open arms. She had woken to find her bedclothes upon the floor and the sheets horribly tangled, but worse than this was she she had not been able to see which of her sisters was being so capably seduced in her dreams.

After breakfasting rather earlier than she might otherwise have done, Maia decided the day was too beautiful to waste waiting for an unwelcome guest to glare down his nose at her and issue decrees she had no intention of following. Not that her lack of compliance or enthusiasm would deter him, however she was not about to sit and twiddle her thumbs until the duke deigned to appear with a face like thunder. It was by far a better plan to avoid the man altogether than to await and unnecessary scene, which is why Maia took herself from the house, taking the puppy with her.

Setting off to through the woodland and across the meadows, she soon forgot about the duke's presence as she picked wild flowers, lay in the grass watching the industrious insects, and dozed in the sunshine. It was only when pangs of hunger reminded her of the passing of time, that with her arms full of flowers and a tired puppy trailing behind her, Maia made her way back to the house.

A group of stable boys were crowded in the stable-yard, admiring a thoroughbred with a mixture of respect and caution, indicted that the odious man was in the vicinity. Duly warned, Maia was confident she could evade him until eventually the duke grew bored and betook himself back to London; after all such a man must have better things to do than lie in wait forever.

Anxious to conceal her return from the servants, as well as her unwelcome guest, and assuming that the wretched man would have been shown into the grand salon or even the morning room, Maia made her way along the shrubbery. With a defiant gleam in her violet eyes she recalled with satisfaction how she had opened the library windows that very morning, having noticed that the room had a musty air. Squeezing past plants and shrubs, she pushed up the open sash window until it was sufficiently wide to allow her to pass through, Maia seated herself upon the ledge and swung one leg over the low still. Juggling the flowers from one arm to the other, she leaned over the ledge to retrieve the panting puppy from the trampled herbaceous border; the animal wriggled unhelpfully and licked Maia's face with enthusiasm.

"You wretch! Stop or I shall drop you."

There was a scuffling as she deposited the puppy on the library floor.

"Now, behave yourself you horror, or we shall both be in for a scolding."

The corners of the duke's mouth began to twitch in amusement, from his vantage point of deeply winged-chair, the large looking-glass above the fireplace was clearly visible, and although he was concealed by the shadows, Maia's reflection was perfectly illuminated. He had been stunned to observe Miss Hindolveston clamber through the window, and equally startled to hear her refer to him both as a 'wretch' and a 'horror', until he realised that she was speaking to something bedraggled, with four legs.

"Sit there and do your best to look as if you had not just eaten the lavender, which might not be poisonous, but cannot possibly be good for you. Be a good-boy while I arrange these."

Noting that 'these' were the flowers which Miss Hindolveston seemed intent on dropping upon the floor, Bradenham wondered what Percy would say if the girl brought wild flowers into his library, not that the future Mrs Siddenham would need to, for Percy's estate had a perfectly good hothouse filled with flowers no matter what the season, as well as a perfectly good housekeeper whose job it was to arrange them. If the duke's smile was replaced by a resolute grimness, it was hidden from view.

Unaware of his presence, Maia began to thrust the wood anemones, cuckooflowers, heartsease and bluebells into the already overflowing arrangement, leading Cosmo to question whether arranged was indeed an apt description for what was happening upon the library table, deranged seemed a more appropriate explanation. While darting between her feet, the puppy caused Maia to scatter even more flowers over the floor, the table and, to its great delight, the puppy itself.

The excitable animal attempted to bite at the wild blooms, then settled down to worry some of the longer stems, growling happily as their pungent aroma filled the room, sending Maia into peels of laughter.

"Really Monk, have you no soul? That is no way to treat flowers. If the duke could see you he would think you were a disgrace! Never mind my darling, we are well-matched you and I!"

With this she bent down, kissed the puppy on the nose and rose to look straight into the eyes of the Duke of Bradenham, standing tall and impassive before her.

"Indeed Miss Hindolveston, and I would be right."

Cosmo suppressed the urge to smile at Maia's wholly unladylike reaction, while other ladies of his acquaintance might have feigned a swoon, or clutched a trembling hand to still their troubled breast, not so Miss Hindolveston, who had definitely indulged in a full-blown squeal followed by an unexpected oath, exclaiming her surprise loudly and proficiently. She also managed to drop the remaining flowers, while the puppy delighted by the commotion, jumped up in excitement at Maia's skirt, adding paw prints to the profusion of grass stains already decorating the soft muslin, before turning his attentions and muddy paws to the duke.

"Down sirrah!" Commanded Bradenham.

The puppy promptly sat on Cosmo's feet, its tail thumping rhythmically on the floor. The duke raised an eyebrow at the animal in mute disapproval, for the puppy was now drooling on his glossy top boots.

"Well," exclaimed Maia in disbelief. "He never does that for me. Monk, you are a horror, just look at my poor flowers."

The duke's incredulity intensified. Flowers? Had the witless girl not noticed his boots?

"Why on earth did you make me jump like that?"

Frowning at the small dog as he removed his trapped feet

from beneath the adoring animal, Cosmo ignored Miss Hindolveston's second question, responding to her first with more than a touch of cynicism.

"I dare say the animal knows when he is mastered, which at least bodes well for one of you." Rounding on the lady, his tone grew steely. "Miss Hindolveston, I do not appreciate being led on goose chase by your foolishness. We must waste no more time, we leave for London as soon as your maid is able to gather your belongings."

With her eyes blazing, Maia responded, "I do not think -"

But what Maia thought Bradenham could only guess, for at that the moment the puppy was copiously and comprehensively sick, covering the tops of his well-polished boots.

The duke's scowling dismay as he stared in horror of the errant dog, forced Maia to compress her lips in an effort not to further disgrace herself. But despite her best intentions, the man's compete disdain, coupled with the ridiculousness of the situation, was too much for the irrepressible Maia. With a barely suppressed snort of laughter, she clasped her arms around herself and collapsing helplessly onto the edge of the table, laughed until she cried.

While Cosmo could be amusing and was frequently witty, he did not recall anyone laughing at him, certainly not within his hearing, therefore this was a new and not entirely pleasant experience for the beleaguered duke. Indeed, to have a small, scruffy animal relieving the contents of its breakfast, together with a disgusting mass of half-eaten flowers over his beautiful top-boots, while its hoyden owner exhibited an undignified display of mirth, making no attempt to control either herself or her flea-bitten mongrel, was the outside of enough.

Yet it could not be denied that Miss Hindolveston presented an arresting sight, with her hair tumbling about her face, her eyes unnaturally violet, tears of mirth flowing freely, and her head thrown back in complete abandon to the emotion. This was not behaviour to which Bradenham was accustomed, and was a far cry from the missish giggles and delicate simpering of the affected ladies of the ton, who would not dare to indulge in such an outrageous display at his expense.

It is possible they might have remained for sometime, Bradenham glaring first at the dog and then Maia, who rocked with laughter, whilst tears of merriment rolled unchecked down her cheeks. However, the sound of Maia's mirth was overheard by Mrs Dalling, who despite her dismay, took control of both the puppy and the duke's boots. Monk was swiftly dispatched to the stables in the arms of the footman, with Maia calling instructions after them, requesting that Monk be given plenty of water to drink and allowed to sleep-off the after-effects of over-indulging in flower arranging.

Alas, the duke's boots were not so easily dealt with. While the housekeeper hesitantly suggested his Grace should remove the offending items, that they might be cleaned as best as could be achieved; Bradenham was reluctant to relinquish his prized boots into any hands other that those of his valet, who treated them with a pleasing, if slavish attention to detail. However, it was clear the offending boots could not remain in their current condition, although the duke could not possibly remove them in front of Miss Hindolveston, one of them at least had to observe the proprieties.

Gleefully grasping the situation, Maia had no compunction in making the most of it, and addressed her unwanted guest scornfully, "I apologise for Monk's unfortunate welcome, your Grace, and leave you in Dalling's capable hands. Good day."

Scarcely able to believe the audacity of the wretched girl, dismissing him as if he was a mere youth, the duke could only watch as Maia inclined her dark head in an approximation of condescending leave-taking, but being severely hampered by his soiled boots there was little he could do, and with the housekeeper present he could hardly attempt to restrain Miss Hindolveston. However, he had not ridden all the way to Norfolk to be dismissed so easily and his response was terse, "I will call upon you in the morning."

This was no request, it was an ultimatum, and Maia recognised it as such. But equally hampered by Mrs Dalling's presence, as the housekeeper benignly awaited the removal of the offending boots, Maia could do no more than grit her teeth. Yet she was not about to be cowed and pausing in her progress to the door, raised an unmistakably mocking eyebrow at him.

As she resumed her retreat, her smirk left the duke in no doubt as to the victor of this second skirmish, but if he had underestimated his opponent upon previous occasions, he would not do so again.

***

The duke's steely resolve might have been further strengthened had he known the amusement his current predicament caused Miss Hindolveston, as she retold the story of Monk and the Duke of Bradenham to her maid. That Love, shocked to the core, did not enjoy the tale as much as Maia had anticipated was disappointing, for the lady's maid-in-training was shocked to the core, and admonished Miss Maia so keenly that had his Grace been party to the scolding, it might have provided a little balm for his wounded pride - although it would have done little to help his boots.

Chapter Ten

The duke was understandably infuriated upon his arrival at Frogshall Abbot shortly after nine the next morning - having given what he believed to be clear instructions regarding his expectations to Miss Hindolveston - to be informed by the butler that Miss Maia was not at home. However, saving his withering response for the lady in question, Bradenham awaited what he anticipated would be a poor excuse for her absence; this was obviously a ruse on Miss Hindolveston's part to avoid a confrontation she had no hope of wining.

The elderly butler was relieved to be prevented from offering the haughty gentleman the explanation with which he had been furnished regarding the absent Miss Maia and, as the housekeeper bustled forward, he was content to defer to her superior knowledge in the awkward matter, being unaccustomed to discussing such things.

Cosmo was momentarily distracted by Mrs Dalling's scurrying curtsy, which made him wonder how the woman managed to curtsy as she walked, and he reigned in the caustic comment which, despite his good intentions, he had been dangerously close to making. He was grateful to the housekeeper for her ministrations of the previous day, for although his valet had been horrified by the state of the duke's boots, the woman had done her best to rectify the damage done by the errant hound.

"Your Grace," Mrs Dalling bobbed another curtsey. "Miss Maia is not at home, she was called away ... to assist -"

The housekeeper faltered, hesitant to explain to the lofty Duke of Bradenham that Miss Maia had gone to assist at the confinement of the one of the estate workers, an unwed one at that. It was certainly not a situation in which most young ladies of Maia's ilk would expect to find themselves, although Maia had not so much found herself in it, as dashed towards it with abandon.

Taking a deep breath, Mrs Dalling rallied; she was after all a country girl and if she was not mistaken, the duke knew what was what. "Your Grace, Miss Maia has gone to see to a girl in her first confinement."

Bradenham somewhat taken aback, banished with regret any notion he may have held of hunting down Miss Hindolveston and giving her a good talking-to.

The housekeeper continued, anxious the duke should not think ill of her mistress. "The poor girl is naught by a young thing and Miss Maia would go, although she ought not, for the poor girl got caught out and by all accounts is making a rough do of it."

Lowering her voice Mrs Dalling spoke conspiratorially, "I hope as how Miss Maia will not be frightened by seeing such things before time and be put off, you'll pardon me speaking so freely, your Grace."

With horrified comprehension it dawned upon Bradenham to what the woman was alluding, and the rôle she mistakenly envisioned him playing in the scheme.

He was further dismayed when brightening visibly, the housekeeper added, "Miss Maia might listen to you, your Grace, if you were to put your foot down and have her come away."

Having formed the distinct impression that Miss Hindolveston had been entreated not to attend the confinement, but had refused to listen to reason, Cosmo did not believe for one moment the ridiculous girl would give credence to any argument put forth by himself. Far from it, she was entirely likely to stubbornly remain should he add his weight to the argument. Miss Hindolveston would be well-served if the experience frightened her witless, not that it would matter to him, nor he suspected, to Percy. The conceiving of offspring and their arrival into the world was part of a wife's duty - to be coped with or not - it was certainly none of his concern whether Maia went to her bridal bed terrified of the outcome. He has no intention of involving himself in the birthing of an estate brat who, by the sound of things, was a bastard to boot. Babies were none of his affair, not yet anyway.

These ridiculous delays were not helping matters; the duke had planned to allow Maia time to arrange her bride clothes, but no longer - the wretched girl would be wed to Percy within the hour of their arrival in the capital, in her riding habit if needs be. Recalling the sand upon the backside of Maia's riding habit, Cosmo cleared his throat, finding his neck cloth unaccountably restrictive.

"Inform Miss Hindolveston that I shall call upon her in the morning and I expect her to be here to receive me." With a curt leave taking of the housekeeper, and his face like thunder, Bradenham betook himself to retrieve his horse.

Gathered around the pump in he stable-yard a group of men wagered with laughter and coarse speculation upon the outcome of the birth Maia had hastened to attend. Cosmo supposed that regardless of their station men were much the same, such wagers were regularly placed in the London clubs, although with considerably higher stakes than those being risked over the pump. The greatest speculation was usually concerned with the paternity of scions of the ton, but without irrefutable proof to support a hypothesis, money seldom changed hands, the only thing lost were the reputations of the ladies involved.

As he turned the thoroughbred from the stable-yard, he began his return to Swanton Chatteris, by way of the boundary between Frogshall Abbot, and the Nettleton estate, curious to see how the land previously held by his father had fared since it had been sold by the grasping Bawsey.

Cosmo was a fair man, who usually acted with clear reason and sound judgement, although forbearance had not hitherto featured highly when it came to a catalogue of his virtues; however, unable to rail against the cause of his woes, there was little to be done but accept with grim resignation that once again Maia Hindolveston had sent his plans awry.

***

The cottages nestled beyond the plantation of ancient trees, not far from the boundary with Nettleton, did not require a landowners eye to distinguish them as estate cottages. Nor could there be any doubt that within the farthest dwelling a woman laboured, for it was a warm morning and with the windows thrown open, the girl's cries could be heard by all who passed by.

In the shade of a tall Whitebeam, a young man sat whittling, a drift of pale wood shavings testimony to the long hours of waiting. From time to time his gaze would seek the upper window, hopeful that it would reveal something of the events unfolding behind the open lattice. At the duke's arrival he rose to his feet, brushing away the clinging flakes of wood from his from his shabby breeches and touched his forehead respectfully.

Bradenham was not given to facile pleasantries, nor had he any wish to linger - particularly in his current frame of mind - but the which assailed their ears could not be ignored, nor could the man's reaction to it, as with the colour draining from his face he gaped fearfully at the window. Cosmo dismounted the thoroughbred, his eyes following those of the expectant father; it was likely Maia was not the only pair of hands helping with the troublesome business of helping a child into the world. At that moment Maia's flushed face appeared, framed in the small window, not unlike a particularly vibrant miniature by a grand master.

A second ear splitting screech from the cottage caused the young man to drop his knife and, sinking to his knees, held his head despairingly in his calloused hands.

The duke was accustomed to seeing his fellows drinking themselves noisily under the table in any number of the clubs he frequented, not to mention stern gentlemen, well-fortified by brandy, resolutely awaiting the arrival of a long-awaited son and heir, but he had never seen a man in such abject misery. Then again he had never before been in the vicinity of an actual birth. Like most men of the ton, he knew where his duty lay in the begetting of an heir, and was content that should be the extent of his participation, with the onset of his wife's confinement his rôle in the proceedings would have been adequately accomplished. It had never occurred to him that he might find himself anxious for the outcome of so perilous an undertaking, therefore the young man's anguish lay entirely outside his experience.

For once, any attempt to adhere to the comfortable formalities was cast aside, and Bradenham stroke briskly over to the hunched figure, muttering encouragingly, if a little woodenly. "All will be well, babies are born everyday, the world over." Although even he was unconvinced by the trite words of cold comfort which blithely ignored the perils attached to the undertaking.

The expectant father nodded towards the window,. "Tis good Miss Maia's come, for the old 'un did say how my Rosin was -" he gulped, but unable to voice his fears, repeated, "tis good Miss Maia's come -"

Noting the young man's red rimmed eyes, Cosmo wondered how his sisters had managed during their not infrequent confinements, particularly in the absence of their mother, who had not lived to see her first grandchild. He doubted the presence of Regina, his eldest sister, had proved a satisfactory replacement and for the first time he pitied both Aurelia and Julia.

"Has your ...", he had been about to say 'wife', but recalling the absence of the legalities, rephrased his enquiry, "... are there no others who might assist?"

The response was a dour shake of the young man's shaggy head. "No." Having no notion of whom he addressed, or the gentleman's elevated position in society, the young father bridged the abyss between them with more ease than he might otherwise have done, had he been aware of the coronet which hung over the gentleman's dark head.

"No ma, no sisters neither."

The duke fervently hoped the expectant father was not going to list all the female relatives the mother of his child was apparently lacking, as the cries of the labouring woman startled them anew, although he suspected his companion's groans were more in self-pity than sympathy for his de facto wife. Resigned that his fate was temporarily entwined with that of the unborn child, Cosmo tethered his precious horse to the weathered wooden railing bordering the burgeoning cottage garden, and joined the young man to await for news from within.

***

The arrival of Mr Siddenham's despised cousin did not please Maia in the least, and while she was taken aback to observe the lofty duke in company with the lowly estate-hand, she felt heartily sorry for the young man, being forced to endure such odious companionship during the nerve-wracking wait was adding insult to injury. The poor fellow had been forcefully thrust through the cottage door the previous evening by the old woman who served as a midwife, admonishing him to "keep out of the way", with such vehemence that the prospective father had not dared to cross the threshold, but had spend the night huddled miserably under the great tree, as afraid of the unearthly noises emanating from the upper room of the cottage as he was of Old Sally.

It had been he who had run across the parkland in the first streaks of the misty dawn, with the message that Miss Maia's name was being cried out by the suffering girl, who had seen the lady in the great park and perhaps viewed her as some sort of benefactor. or else, in her terror, believed Miss Maia might save her from the careless attentions of the ancient midwife.

Mrs Dalling had objected as far as she had dared at the impropriety of an unmarried young lady of breeding assisting at the birth of an estate baby. She had not liked to mention the word 'bastard' but, after alluding to the young mother's lack of good Christian morals, had subsided into a reproachful silence while Maia packed a basket of items she considered necessary for such an event, obstinately refusing to be influenced by Mrs Dalling. She knew what her mother would wish and therefore where her duty lay. She had willingly hurried through the dew-laden grass to the cottage - whether she went to be of assistance from a sense of sisterhood, or *noblesse oblige*, Maia did not stop to wonder.

Rosin had been overjoyed to see the lady whom she considered her new mistress, as if Miss Maia's presence would somehow turn the tide of her suffering. That the lady's arrival coincided with the first rays of sunlight touching the small window, did much to encourage the labouring girl. The supply of clean bed linen and cloths, purloined from the indignant Mrs Dalling's linen press, together with Maia's own bottle of scented water, certainly improved the squalid bedchamber in which Rosin's child was to be born.

In days of old the grubby midwife might have been condemned to the rigours of the ducking stool which, from Maia's point of view, would have done wonders for her cleanliness. As it was she insisted that Sally wash her hands and arms, despite the old woman's evident annoyance. However, holding the lady in too much awe to argue, Sally had only grumbled under her breath as she stumped to the well, where she made a great show of splashing herself from the bucket hanging from the windlass. That she returned damp but not much cleaner was not lost upon Maia.

The long hours passed slowly, and there was little to occupy her other than to air the thin wraps and swaddling clothes which Rosin had come by in readiness for the baby; they were a threadbare collection and had clearly seen better days. The labouring girl's cries were distressing and Maia could do no more than try to comfort poor Rosin, who wanted only to be free of the terrible pains. Beyond the window the morning was warming and birds sang joyfully in the branches, Maia idly wondered what the duke would say when he discovered she was not awaiting his arrival as he had commanded. However, he was banished from her thoughts by the sounds of distress from the girl upon the bed.

There was no denying that the girl was suffering; she appeared to Maia - who was the ripe old age of twenty-one - to be terribly young, yet there was nothing unusual in that, and Rosin would not have gone to her lover's bed either unwillingly, or in ignorance. Unlike the young ladies of the ton who frequently went to their bridal beds both reluctantly and innocently, Rosin would have been well-aware of the possible outcome of a summer's evening spent amid the ripening corn.

Maia shuddered at the notion of own bridal bed should she be forced to wed Percy Siddenham, and wondered again at the fate of her aunt, who at barely seventeen had been married against her wishes to a man nearly forty years her senior. The morning after the wedding the young bride had taken her life. Not for the first time Maia puzzled over what could possible have taken place during that nuptial night which had caused poor Aunt Maria to throw herself down the stairs. The myriad possibilities further strengthened Maia's resolve to never marry Mr Siddenham.

As the sun rose higher, the little room under the thatch grew oppressive; all three women suffered from the heat, while clad only in a patched shift the labouring Rosin was sweat-soaked, her hair plastered to her forehead and neck.

The chamber with its low, sloping roof was sparsely furnished. A battered old bedstead held the stained, sagging straw filled pallet upon which numerous arrivals to and departures from this world had been made; in one corner a wooden chest stood drunkenly, containing the young couple's meagre possessions, a wedge shoring up the chest's roughly hewn inadequacies; in a pool of grease upon a chipped saucer lay the remains of a tallow candle long since burned down to a stub, and on a battered milking stool lay Rosin's stained and patched gown, discarded where she had thrown it.

Despite these meagre trappings of poverty the pathetic chamber boasted a view from its tiny window which was unrivalled in any of the cottages upon the estate, even if the great park stretching majestically into the distance was partially obscured by the low thatched roof. Under the eaves starlings nested, the hatchlings scrabbling in the rough reeds of thatch, as their elders flew to and fro, busily feeding their young and quarrelling noisily.

Throughout that interminable day the midwife made Rosin pace the room, for there was no birthing stool to hasten the child's delivery or to ease it's arrival, but when the girl could no longer put one foot before the other, the old lady reluctantly allowed her to slump exhausted upon the lumpy bed. Worn out by the long hours of suffering, Rosin was making the most of the brief moments of respite afforded her between the pains which were increasing in intensity as well as rapidity.

The shadows were lengthening when bending to examine the girl who, ceasing to care about such indignities, barely noticed the old woman.

Sally muttered darkly, "Tis not far off now."

The midwife's tone concerned Maia. "Is all well?" she whispered, having no desire to further alarm Rosin.

Sally shrugged her shoulders and held out her hands in a gesture of helplessness, murmuring her doom-laden response, as if it were a prophecy, "Her own ma died birthing."

Aghast at this pertinent information which gave Maia belated insight into the girl's terrors, she knelt beside the bed and, taking Rosin's work roughened hand, smoothed back the girl's straggling hair that she might offer some comfort.

"It will soon be over."

Rosin looked up fearfully, but was unable to speak; her voice hoarse from the long hours of screaming and crying.

"You must work for just a little longer," Maia encouraged, although the notion must have made the exhausted girl's heart quail.

There was no need for further explanation as the pains Rosin felt were evidenced in her grimace and the grip of her hand upon Maia's, as a nod from Sally indicated that it was time for Rosin begin pushing. Helping the girl to her feet, they led her to stand in the narrow doorway, where gripping the worn wood until her knuckles turned white, Rosin braced herself against the jamb, straining, her guttural sounds loud and desperate.

Maia felt as if she too were spun into the arrival of this child and forgot all else; nothing existed beyond that which was unfolding in time honoured fashion and, irrespective of Rosin's fears, would reach its inevitable conclusion in it's own good time.

***

As awkward situations went, waiting with an expectant young father with whom he had little in common, ranked highly. But worse was in store as Rosin's grunts and cries resonated from the open window. That each man avoided looking at the other came as a relief to both, for there was nothing left to be said, but Cosmo did not think he was mistaken in believing he could hear Maia's firm voice faintly above the moans, encouraging and praising Rosin.

The abrupt cessation of Rosin's misery was as startling as the sounds of her struggles had been, and although just moments before both men would have given much for the unearthly noises to stop, the sudden silence was equally unnerving. Bradenham drew a silver hip flask from the pocket of his jacket and, unscrewing the lid, handed it wordlessly to the young man, who drank deeply before returning the exquisitely worked item to its owner with a nod of gratitude. All-in all, Cosmo considered as he lifted the flask to his lips, birth - like death - was a great leveller.

***

The old midwife had seen more births than she could recall and more deaths than most; it had been her gnarled hands which, sixteen years before, had helped Rosin into the world, and had but an hour later closed the eyes of her mother as she departed from it. The weather-beaten face gave away very little, yet what Maia read was sufficient to cause a lump in her throat and tears to sting her eyes; for the baby Rosin had worked so hard to bring forth had not lived long enough to draw breath. The tiny limp figure was lifeless, while slumped across the lumpy pallet Rosin began to wail, a pitiful, dull cry.

The child lay impossibly still amid the cloths, her minute fingers curled lifelessly against hands which would never be held, her ruddy curls an echo of her mother's, and although Maia choked back a sob, she could not prevent her tears from falling.

Yet, as Sally roughly moved her hand across Rosin's heaving belly, her faded eyes filled with hope and she whispered, "Another?"

Maia's dawning elation as the comprehension of the midwife's meaning became clear was mingled with fear for the exhausted girl, and it seemed impossible that the broken and weeping Rosin could endure more labouring. But endure it she must, for like its sibling, this child's arrival could not be delayed.

Drawing Rosin's shaking hand into her own, which was none to steady, Maia asked her gently, "Did you know there were two babies? Twins."

The girl lifted her tear-stained face, her weeping momentarily arrested. "Two?"

Robbed of almost all comprehension by grief and exhaustion, Rosin struggled to piece together what Maia was saying. But as she was again gripped by the unmistakable pains, Sally grinned a toothless smile and commanded: "Stand up, now push girl- PUSH!"

Chapter Eleven

The sun was setting when Maia stepped from the cottage. Weary and aching she paused upon the threshold to breathe the clean, cool air. At the first sign of movement the young man jumped to his feet and hastened along the path, leaving his noble companion to rise stiffly. The duke could not have explained why he had chosen to spend the day as he had, yet despite being both uncomfortable and undeniably hungry, he had been unable to leave the man alone in his misery, even if they had passed the majority of the day in fraught silence, broken only by moments of stilted conversation, which had dwindled with the passing of the hours until it had ceased completely.

At the man's approach, Maia spoke softly. "Thomas, you have a fine son."

But despite having waited for such tidings, the man seemed incapable of comprehending what Maia was saying and gazed dazedly at her.

"I am sorry, your daughter was still-born."

This too was beyond his understanding; for like Rosin, the possibility of there being more than one child had not occurred to him. But there was a question weighing heavily upon him and, dreading the answer, he spoke but a single word. "Rosin?"

"Rosin is well, as is your son," reassured Maia.

"My son," Thomas repeated.

"Go up and see them, Rosin is asking for you."

Gathering his scattered wits, the young man asked, "The little gel miss, what of her?"

"She -" faltering as the image of the pale, still child arose before her, Maia answered softly, "I told Rosin I would take her to the ice house and would speak to the curate, myself."

The ice house provided cool a resting place for those awaiting burial during the warmer months, and the young man gratefully nodded. As for the resolution of the other difficulty, Thomas did not believe himself equal facing the curate, let alone encouraging the man who had a reputation for a legalistic point-of-view to bury the child within the churchyard precincts.

While it was common for the clergy to refuse burial in

consecrated land to a child born out of wedlock, Maia was determined not to permit such a travesty to pass unchallenged, hoping the Hindolveston seal of approval upon the stillborn baby would mean that the curate might turn, if not a blind-eye, then certainly a forgiving one, to the irregularities surrounding her conception.

"Thank you miss. I dursn't know how to thank you ..."

"Then I beg you not to. Go up to Rosin, she is anxious to see you."

Maia followed the fleet footed Thomas as he bounded through the door, but while he sped eagerly up the narrow stair, Maia returned only to place her shawl about her shoulders and take the small, carefully wrapped bundle into her arms. She squared her shoulders, closed the door behind her, and made her way towards the rickety gate.

It was there Cosmo met her, his dark gaze noting her pale face and the bundle she carried. Holding the gate open for her, Maia absently passed through. Neither of them spoke as they made their way through the ancient woodland of the great park, even the duke's stately horse was subdued, and in the quiet of the twilight the world seemed unusually peaceful.

Cradling the precious bundle, Maia tried to reconcile the past hours and, with the calm which surrounded her, wondering if the difficulties of the day had any bearing upon the remarkable lack of animosity the duke was currently displaying.

"It was good of you to remain, it would have been a lonelier wait for the poor man had you not," she reflected. Then asked, puzzled,"Why did you?"

Cosmo took in Maia's appearance, the unruly ringlets hanging down her back, which had escaped from the sombre braid she had so hastily fashioned that morning; her gown crumpled and marked, the sleeves still pushed back from her arms; her tear-stained cheeks and strained face.

"Let me take the child -"

"No!"

Maia's reaction took him by surprise, but no more so than her immediate contrition. "Forgive me, that was discourteous and I did not mean to be. She is so very tiny and ..." Cosmo heard her voice tremble, "I am taking her to the ice house."

"I guessed as much."

Undaunted, Maia put out her chin defiantly. "And then I shall speak to the curate."

Silence fell between them as they walked, until at last the duke enquired, "Would it be preferable if I spoke with the curate? I expect he would be more amenable if I were to deal with him."

"And less likely to argue with a duke about where this poor soul should lie?" Maia retorted, adding a moment later, "Forgive me, that was ungracious and uncalled for."

It was undeniably frustrating, but Maia could not allow her annoyance to stand in the way. Mr Thorpe, the curate, would be overawed by the duke and more likely to allow the frail little body she held so tightly to lie within the churchyard. For once Maia conceded, having no desire to allow her foolish pride to be a stumbling block in swaying the curate.

"Thank you. Doubtless Mr Thorpe will be more reasonable should the suggestion come from you."

As they walked through the shadows, each engrossed in their own thoughts, a companionable peace settled between them. Stumbling against a tree root which had forced its way though the winding path, rather than drop the bundle which had been entrusted to her care, Maia made no effort to prevent herself from tumbling. Instead she closed her eyes, shielding the still body against further injustice. Her fall was broken by a pair of strong hands, which caught her and held her fast until she could catch her breath, before setting her upon her feet once again. Frowning at the fragility he had not previously been aware of, the duke said reproachfully, "You are exhausted, I should have sent for your carriage. Allow me to carry the child."

Maia shook her head."Thank you, but I prefer to walk than to sit in the carriage." She paused, puzzling over her turbulent emotions. "And I am not so weary, just sad." A lone tear trickled down her cheek, but turning her head so that the duke would not notice it, Maia brushed it aside. "She is not a burden," Maia's voice wobbled and, not daring to speak further lest she betray her emotion, she hugged the bundle even closer than before. However, Bradenham had observed both the falling tear and Maia's surreptitious wiping of her cheek.

There was no denying it, Miss Hindolveston was unlike any other tonnish maiden - indeed, unlike any women Cosmo had ever met; women who indulged in outrageous displays of tears, tantrums and torrid varieties of emotional manipulation, seeking to display what passed as feminine sensitivities to their best advantage, or to simply get their own way - for whom crocodile tears and insincere emotions were de rigour. Objecting to manipulation by flights of female fancy, the duke had been known to offer ladies of his intimate acquaintance exhibiting such behaviour, his handkerchief and a cold departing shoulder. Yet the single tear, and Maia's attempt to hide it, had succeeded where numerous ladies of the ton had failed with their exaggerated displays of nerves; feigned fainting, copious weeping and promises of decline. Bradenham was moved by the girl whose grief for the child was real, no matter how she might try to conceal it, and not merely a sham intended to elicit sympathy. Her dignity and determination, which he had hitherto dismissed as nothing more than infuriating stubbornness, was something of a revelation.

Cosmo placed a firm hand under Maia's arm, ready to steady her should the need arise, yet he was not foolish enough to delude himself that Miss Hindolveston's silent acquiescence was a victory in her submission, for she barely seemed to notice his presence, let alone his guiding hand.

The stable yard was deserted but for two of the stable boys who gazed curiously at the new arrivals. However, the startling news that Miss Hindolveston had undertaken the rôle of midwife was now common knowledge, and recognising not only the daughter of the house but equally pertinently the nature of the wrapped bundle in her arms, the boys removed their caps respectfully, leaving Maia to pass by in hushed silence.

***

Even by daylight the ice house was a gloomy affair, nestled in the wood beyond the stables. The domed subterranean outbuilding was seldom entered, and in the half-light it seemed a forbidding place; the only sound the echoing of the dripping ice. Cut from the lake during the winter months and packed into layers of fragrant sawdust and straw, the blocks of ice were protected by the thick walls of the ice house until such time as they were needed, making the isolated chamber an ideal temporary resting place for those who had embarked upon their final journey, until a more permanent arrangement could be made.

Shivering, Maia placed Rosin's child into the chill darkness and having placed a silent benediction upon the baby, closed the heavy door behind her. Nothing more could be done for little girl until an understanding had been reached with the curate.

The stirring wind caused the leaves above their head to rustle, it caught Maia's shawl as she clutched it about her and blew coiling strands of hair across her pale face. Perhaps too it revived her, for when she addressed the duke, her voice was steady, although her eyes were suspiciously moist. "It was kind of you to remain with Thomas."

There was no mistaking the authenticity of her gratitude, although it was obvious to Cosmo that the girl was much shaken by the events of the day.

"Thomas," he mused, "is that his name?"

Maia stared at him incredulously. "Do you mean to tell me that you spent an entire day with the man and did not discover his name?"

The duke responded primly. "There was no one to introduce us, besides, the subject did not arise."

"What did you talk about, if introductions were not made."

Frowning in an effort to recall, Cosmo supplied with mock hauteur, "We discussed the weather, very seasonable, for the time of year."

At this Maia's mouth dropped open, both at the ridiculousness of men, and the revelation that the odious duke had make a joke.

Reaching up Bradenham placed two fingers under her chin and gently closed Maia's mouth. "The expression does not become you my dear," he added with a grin, "besides, you might catch a fly."

Chapter Twelve

The ducal bedchamber was not a place normally associated with solitary contemplation, nevertheless as he stared out of the window into the night, the duke was lost in thought and very nearly at the mercy of conflicting emotions.

As the gathering wind blowing through the trees reached a crescendo, a splatter of rain ricocheted off the glass and trickled its way down the pane. Involuntarily Cosmo reached to trace its progress, frowning at the conundrum before him. Things which had seemed reasonable in London, now appeared to be clouded. The missive from Harrington awaiting him upon his return to Swanton Chatteris, had been consigned to the flames in what Cosmo's sisters would have termed 'a nasty fit of temper'. Poor Harrington, his employer mused, must have had the devil's own time composing the tactful communication, which contained within its neatly written pages what the duke guessed was a heavily edited report of the gossip and scandal already permeating the refined air of the upper echelons of society. The salacious version doing the rounds in Mayfair's drawing rooms would be even less edifying.

Tasked with the unenviable commission of informing his Grace, that Mr Siddenham's name was being bandied about in intimate and distasteful connection with Maia Hindolveston's, Harrington's diplomatic epistle, despite its delicacy, had nevertheless caused Bradenham to brutally crush the pages, before being forced to smooth out the creases in order to continue reading.

While the secretary had applied his customary thoroughness to verifying the identity of the chief rumourmonger, Cosmo had guessed the distasteful descriptions circulating the ball rooms in the guise of common-knowledge were the work of Lady Bellmont, Harrington simply confirmed his employer's suspicions. It was further to Harrington's credit that far from gloating over Percy's misfortunes, the details of the tonnish gossip were imparted in the most diplomatic of terms - his intention only to prevent Mr Siddenham, and by association the duke himself, from further speculation and dishonour; knowing that the duke would wish to be apprised of the status quo, he remained his Grace's obedient servant.

Unable to reconcile the salacious behaviour of which Maia was not only accused, but had been confirmed by none other than Percy himself, with a girl he knew to be principled, if unexpected, Bradenham closed his eyes. Unbidden, her image filled his mind; the tousled curls and violet eyes. Did she know she was as transparent as glass, every emotion revealed in her expression?

With a groan the duke wondered what the devil was wrong with him, what was he doing thinking about Percy's bride? Leaning his dark head against the cool window pane he groaned again; his cousin's bride, he had almost forgotten the very reason he was here. To be so distracted from his purpose Maia Hindolveston must truly be the witch he had considered her to be. But witch or not, she would marry Percy.

The prospect of Maia's fate were she not safely under his ducal protection was not a pleasant one and there could be no more delays. With his resolve thus bolstered, the duke betook himself to bed.

Chapter Thirteen

As she stood at the library table, picking idly at the drooping flowers in their vase, Maia debated whether she might be able to slip away unseen in order to avoid what she anticipated was likely to be a trying conversation. She had been pleasantly surprised the duke had not forced a discussion the previous evening, it would after all have been the ideal opportunity. However, he had simply taken his leave of her, adding almost as an afterthought that he would call upon her in the morning. It had not even sounded like much of a threat, although Maia was reasonably sure it was.

Wrinkling her nose at the fouled water in which the wild flowers wilted, she decided with resignation, that in light of his willingness to speak to the curate, she owed the wretched man the courtesy of an interview. If only he did not nettle her so; she rarely argued with anyone other than her sisters, yet the duke seemed to bring out the worst in her.

Still pondering the conundrum, Maia picked up the heavy vase in order to take it to the scullery, for the pungency of the water was far from pleasant, and stepping back knocked against something as unexpected as it was unyielding. Twisting in surprise, she bumped against the table, splashing a few drops of the slimy water from the vase onto the obstruction's boots and down the front of her gown, causing the fabric to pucker.

"Oh!" She squealed, but perceiving whom it was, frowned. "You seem to have a nasty habit of sneaking up on people ..." adding belatedly, "... Your Grace."

However his Grace did not reply, he was busy looking down at his boots, forcing Maia to bite her lip in an effort to prevent herself from laughing at his expression of undisguised horror.

With a last rueful glance at his boots, the duke turned his attention to the cause of the mishap, "What is so amusing?"

Trying to contain her glee, Maia responded not entirely convincingly, "Nothing your Grace, nothing at all."

The sound of scrabbling preceded the exuberant arrival of Monk, who bounding into the library, make straight for Cosmo, and jumped up, his tail wagging in delight. Most pertinently, his muddy paws illustrated that the hound had been digging in the herbaceous border.

"Down sirrah!" Bradenham ordered.

The dog's instant obedience upon hearing the command produced an irritation in Maia.

"You need not think you have taught him to sit, for I have been training him for days, it was just a matter of time."

"Do not disregard incentive, Miss Hindolveston," Cosmo retorted crushingly. "Doubtless you tried to teach this poor animal to obey, but what he needed to discover was whom commands his respect."

With her temper rising at the man's audacity, Maia was about to launch into a tirade against the duke's arrogant, high-handed ways, when she visibly checked herself and, returning the dripping vase to the table oblivious to the watermark it was bound to leave, absently wiped her wet hands upon her skirt and took a deep breath.

"I am not going to quarrel with you, no matter how provoking you might be. I will listen to what you have to say, for we both know you are here to lecture me on the many and varied reasons I should marry your cousin. Once you have done so, and I have told you again that I am not going to marry Mr Siddenham, we may say our farewells and you can return to London. Your absence must have noted, perhaps even lamented, whereas my humble presence, or lack thereof, can hardly have been noticed at all, so none of the things you feared will come about."

Bradenham's gaze grew steely. "Can you be so sure? Would you risk your reputation on such conjecture?" Before she could speak he held up his hand to prevent any interruption. "Would you risk the reputation of my cousin?" Dropping his hand he awaited her response.

"Your Grace, you will forgive me if I speak plainly -"

"Are you telling me you have not done so thus far? I must have remarkably thin skin to have been wounded so."

Maia ignored the jibe. "You have spoken of Mr Siddenham's reputation, but surely there is nothing in this absurd situation which can harm him in anyway." She snorted in disgust. "If anything it will only serve to enhance his reputation in keeping with other members of his- of your -", her voice trailed off as she recalled to and of whom she was speaking.

Cosmo finished her sentence coldly. "- other members of my ilk?"

Maia nodded.

"Like others of my ilk, my cousin might be a paragon of

virtue, but never before has he been accused of deflowering virgins in long galleries. You will no doubt forgive my plain speaking, Miss Hindolveston."

"But he did not deflower me," spluttered the horrified Maia.

"I am delighted to hear it, but irrespective of the facts, rumours of a most sordid nature are being whispered. Doubtless wagers have already been placed in the betting book at Whites, regarding the gender of Siddenham's bastard."

Remembering too late the events of the previous day, the duke had the grace to silently curse his clumsiness. "I should not have said -I did not mean -"

Maia was in no mood to listen to trite apologies and countered triumphantly, "When there is no child then the rumours will stop and no one will win their bets."

"Just because there is no obvious outcome does not mean an event has not taken place. The ton will simply deduce that you are barren, or that a child did not take, this time."

While Maia gasped at his candour, Cosmo continued, "As far as the ton are concerned you have been seduced by my cousin. That you did not cry out or scream for assistance implies that you were a willing participant."

"Which is why I came here, to avoid distasteful speculation."

"For how long do you plan to stay? Long enough for society to assume that you have borne Percy's child and farmed it out on the estate?"

Maia's face turned white in horror. "How could they possibly think so? Not that I am going to bear a child," she added, weakly.

"That is precisely what the ton will think, that you have been banished from the unsullied sight of your sisters while you bear Percy's bastard."

Wearily Maia closed her eyes. "I did not think of that, I did not realise the ton believed that -"

"That is exactly what they think, and such speculation will forever hang over your head unless action is taken, and taken swiftly. This madness must end, you must marry Percy. Once you are wed and no eight month child is born, the ton will forget the events leading up to your nuptials. More importantly you will be protected by the association with my name, and Percy will not be suspected of the seduction of an innocent, or worse."

"Is that what they are saying?"

"It has been voiced by those with nothing better to do with their time than cause evil."

"I do not understand, Lady Bellmont and Lady Ormesby, were the only witnesses and even they could not see clearly for it was rather dark, their claims are based on conjecture alone, nothing more."

"It would seem Lady Bellmont has a vivid imagination, for her description leaves little upon which to speculate, stating that you were clearly being intimate with Percy. I might add that Leda and the Swan feature in her description, perhaps you were led astray by their an example."

Maia laughed despite herself. "Mr Siddenham is very swanlike. But how can she say such things? Why does she say them?"

"It might be argued that the blame can be laid almost entirely at my door, I refused to fall into her trap three seasons ago when she attempted to ensnare me for her daughter. Perhaps unable to strike at me, Lady Bellmont's wrath has fallen upon Percy."

"Can nothing be done to silence her?"

"The woman is a toad!" Cosmo declared with feeling. "Nothing short of lead-shot between the eyes will stop her."

"Surely she cannot hate you so much that she would ruin the lives of two people simply to inconvenience you." Such cruelty was impossible for Maia to comprehend, particularly when she was barely acquainted with the woman. A thought arrested her: "Wait, either I was a willing participant in the debauchery, or I was not, Lady Bellmont cannot claim both. How does she explain it?"

Despite himself, Bradenham was amused by Miss Hindolveston's clarity, as well as her forthright approach. "From what I understand, the lady asserts that you were lured to the long gallery, where Percy forced his attentions upon you. Encouraged by Leda's example you discovered Percy's advances were not so unwelcome after all."

"Making us both villains of the piece," Maia declared in disgust. "Mr Siddenham is painted as a violent, lustful man and I, as woman entirely without morals. Either way I am ruined." While the words were spoken quietly enough, there was not mistaking Maia's revulsion, at both the notion, as well as the lady behind the twisted version of events.

"I'm afraid so, for although the grande dames may turn a blind eye to their own indiscretions, they will not tolerate the same behaviour in others, and a blatant disregard for the proprieties will always attract more than its fair share of censure. Seduction in the long gallery is not for young ladies, and you may be sure Lady Bellmont will not permit the incident to drop, but will continue to whisper words of poison until Percy is painted as a debaucher of the most vile hue and you are not safe anywhere in London."

Maia narrowed her eyes, thoughtfully. "What you said to me in Richmond, about my sisters, is that true?"

"Indeed, the ton will be waiting for them like wolves."

"I don't see how my marrying your cousin will make a difference."

Aware that Miss Hindolveston was at last treating the situation with the gravity it demanded, nevertheless, it gave Cosmo remarkably little pleasure to deliver what he knew would be the final blow.

"Percy has made no mistakes, until now; being discovered with you was his first rather dramatic plunge into scandal. However, if he marries you, the talk will come to nothing. Meanwhile, your indiscretions will be put down to pre-wedding passion, all will be wrapped in clean linen and the suspicion of rape and debauchery forgotten."

Unconvinced, Maia questioned bitterly. "That is the difference?"

The duke tried again. "The difference your marriage to Percy will make, is that you and your sisters will be protected by the name of Siddenham. Percy is after all my heir until such time as I make the necessary arrangements to beget my own; as Percy's wife, at least until I marry, you will be viewed as the next Duchess of Bradenham, the potential of a title will protect you. It does not do it underestimate the power such a title holds."

Maia was horrified. "Percy is your heir?"

The current duke nodded. "Unless I marry and have a son, Percy will inherit, as the son of my father's younger brother."

"Have you no brothers?" Her enquiry was perhaps a touch desperate.

"Only sisters.".

"I had no idea." The resolute lift of the girl's chin should have warned Bradenham, as she announced with finality, "I cannot possibly marry Mr Siddenham."

Having believed he was at last making headway in persuading Miss Hindolveston, her declaration was all the more galling.

"Hell's teeth woman, what now?"

Maia's eyes flashed angrily as she rounded on the duke. "I am not the sort of woman who lures the heir of a dukedom into marriage, nor will I be seen as one, it would be ..." her irritation almost getting the better of her, Maia was forced to pause momentarily, "... like selling myself."

Cosmo snorted unsympathetically. "There are ladies who have been kicking themselves since your escapade, wishing they had possessed the foresight to cultivate your passion for art; I doubt they consider such a stratagem as selling themselves."

Furious, Maia stamped her foot, actually stamped her elegant, silk slippered foot. "Let him marry one of them, I am not such a woman and I will not be painted as one."

"You have already been painted as far worse my girl. While it is not the outcome either you or Percy might wish for, marriage to my cousin is the only option." He raked his hand through his dark hair. "You are not dull-witted, why can you not see this cannot be avoided?"

Glaring at Bradenham incredulously, Maia intoned, "You are too kind your Grace, not dull-witted? How unutterably generous of you to say so."

Cosmo's hands itched to take Maia by the shoulders in order to shake some sense into her, at least he assumed that was what they were itching to do.

***

In the corridor beyond the library doors, catching sight of the under-footman and a young housemaid crouching by the partially open door, Mrs Dalling hissed her disapproval, for the pair were listening intently.

Unabashed, the housemaid giggled, her apron held to her mouth in delight. "You should hear 'em Mrs Dalling, fightin' like cat and dog."

Far from sharing the amusement of the eavesdropping pair, the housekeeper responded by swiping at the housemaid's rear end with a firm hand.

"You wicked girl, off with you before I box your ears."

Mrs Dalling rounded on the under-footman whom she held to be the guiltier of the pair due to his superior position to that of the lowly housemaid. Folding her arms across her chest, she eyed him sternly.

"And you should know better than to spy on folk."

As he turned to return to the kitchens and sculleries, the man had the grace to look abashed, even if his remorse was only fleeting, for leering over his shoulder he whispered, "She's giving 'im what for, a regular vixen she is, an' him top lofty an' all."

This was too much for the housekeeper, but before she could deal the under-footman a sound blow to the ear, he dodged out of reach, leaving her to retort to his departing back. "I want no gossiping mind, you keep your thoughts to yourselves."

As she paused to listen momentarily to the furious voices within the library, Mrs Dalling smiled to herself and, smoothing down her skirts with a deft hand, murmured thoughtfully, "A regular vixen and him top-lofty? We shall see." She was after all a country woman and knew that a spark was required if the flame were to burn brightly.

Within the library a stalemate had been reached; with too much to lose by admitting defeat, neither was willing to concede. Mrs Dalling's muffled scolding had forced the pair to sink into undignified hisses and whispers, each convinced the other was entirely unreasonable. With the interview in danger of declining even further, Cosmo had been forced to take a step back, his hands firmly by his sides in an effort to prevent himself from shaking Maia Hindolveston until her pearly teeth rattled in her curly head. He stood at the fireplace with his back to the damnable girl, one booted foot resting upon the polished fender. With a matching expression of fury etched upon her face, Maia obstinately crushed the remains of the wilted flowers and with her hands fully-occupied, was thus prevented from wringing his ducal neck.

It was Bradenham who broke the silence. "You cannot allow Percy to pay the price for seduction when he is innocent of the crime, you must marry him."

Behind him, Maia glared at the wide shoulders and made a snarling face, baring her teeth at his back.

"You would do well to remember that I can see you, Miss Hindolveston."

Having forgotten the looking-glass hanging over the fireplace, Maia had the good manners to blush. Nevertheless she made the face again to ensure the duke knew she meant it.

He sighed a long-suffering sigh. "Why I should be so anxious to welcome such a hoyden into my family is entirely beyond me, doubtless I shall live to regret this day."

"Be advised if I marry Percy, you will both regret this day," retorted Maia with spirit.

"Miss Hindolveston, when was the last time your father put you over his knee?" Inquired the duke innocently.

Maia hefted the large, wet vase from the table into her hand and lifted it level with her shoulder. "Just you try it," she warned.

His eyes sparkled wickedly as he took a step closer. "Is that a request, or a threat?"

"If you dare raise a hand to me, I promise you will rue the day you heard my name."

"Too late," intoned Cosmo cuttingly. "For I have been ruing that day for quite some time."

The unwieldy vase began to slip from Maia's grasp, with a gasp she attempted to catch it with her other hand, but missing it, it fell to the oak-boarded floor, sending a tidal wave of slimy water over both Maia and the duke, before shattering with awful finality.

Bradenham gazed incredulously at his sodden boots, while Maia tried not to laugh; her lips compressed so hard they turned white, her violet eyes betraying the mirth which seemed bound to explode forth sooner or later.

With a joyful bark Monk bounded forward, having hidden at the sound of shattering porcelain, his tail wagging as he approached, eager to investigate the source of the commotion.

"No Monk!" Maia cried in consternation and reaching down grasped at the broken china in an attempt to keep Monk's twitching nose from the jagged edges. However, the duke took a more authoritative and arguably more effective approach to the impending catastrophe by commanding the dog to "SIT!"

Monk sat, his tail thumping upon the floor as it wagged.

"Ohhhhh."

Aware that her hand was stinging Maia dropped the cause of her discomfort, which broke into infinitesimal pieces, for the shard she had so hastily snatched up had left behind it a gash across the palm of her left hand.

Cosmo pushed the sniffing Monk away with a dripping foot. "Let me see."

Reluctantly Maia relinquished her injured hand into the duke's outstretched one, wincing as he firstly inspected the laceration, then pressed gently against the sides of the wound, which was now bleeding profusely. However, feeling just a little overwhelmed at having her hand held so closely she said nothing.

"It appears to be a clean cut, but we must staunch the bleeding before you stain the woodwork," the duke pronounced cheerfully.

With that, still holding Maia's hand in his, leaving her no option but to follow in his wake, he strode across the room to the bell-pull to summon assistance. The pair were shadowed by Monk, intrigued by the trail of bloody droplets crossing the library floor.

Chapter Fourteen

Never in all his years of service had Watton known anything like it. Under normal circumstances, the duke was the most considerate employer a valet could wish for, not given to excess wear and tear upon his clothing, he always dressed in the first style and never expected Watton to scrimp on quality when it came to purchasing small clothes. Nor did his Grace require a stern eye with regard to his taste in attire; all-in-all he was a most pleasing employer, a bit top-lofty perhaps, but Watton liked that in a gentleman.

Life had been pleasingly harmonious until this unexpected jaunt to Norfolk. As a rule, Watton enjoyed his visits to Swanton Chatteris, for his position as the duke's valet placed him in a rank of rare standing within the household. In addition, he could always be relied upon the bring the choicest morsels of gossip, as well as the latest news from London, thus assuring his welcome at the Bradenham country seat.

Yet there was discord within Watton's well-ordered breast, not once, or even twice, had his employer returned with his top boots in less than perfect condition, but thrice.

Observing his valet eye the offending boots with disdain, Cosmo intoned, "I echo your sentiments Watton, and offer my most abject and humble apologies. Would it help if I were to tell you, despite the evidence to the contrary, that I did not wade across a stream, I was merely in the line of fire, so to speak."

Watton's silence declared an eloquent disbelief.

"As unlikely as it sounds, nevertheless it true. However, the implement, or perhaps I should call it a weapon, for that was its intent, slipped before more permanent damage could be inflicted upon my person. So, while I sympathise with the Herculean task I have placed before you, I am glad it is only my boots which require attention and not my skull, as was undoubtedly the plan."

Watton was aghast. "Your Grace? Someone threw something at you?"

"Indeed, but instead of a baptism she merely washed my feet. I wonder if she detected the subtle reference, I think perhaps not, for she failed to offer her hair as recompense with which to dry them." The duke appeared amused by the recollection. "But perhaps the Ark is a more apt analogy."

Despite being thoroughly confused, Watton was accustomed to his employer's musings - which he frequently found baffling - and removing the thoroughly anointed boots, went to work that peculiar form of magic upon them which in the duke's eyes, made him worth his weight in gold; marching off with the offending items held at arm's length, lest they foul his pristine sleeves.

***

Prodding at the wrapping upon her hand, Maia considered it fortuitous that she had injured her left hand and not the right, for it would have taken even longer to accomplish the task of writing letters to her family, and necessitated an explanation for the injury and subsequent deterioration of her hand-writing. As it was, she could simply fail to mention this most recent of episodes in the library, just as she had failed to mention that his Grace the Duke of Bradenham had followed her to Norfolk. Some things were better left unsaid; such knowledge would only serve to upset her family and her mother needed no additional concerns to undermine her already failing health. As for her sisters; were they aware the wretched duke had followed her to Norfolk, Maia knew only too well how swiftly their imaginations could take a Gothic turn, or worse still a classical one. She shuddered at the thought of Eley's reaction, her sister was not known for restraint.

With a sigh Maia perused the letters requiring a reply, hoping to find something amid the closely written pages to which she might respond, for writing about the happenings in her own life was out of the question. Amid her aunt's missive, filled with her hopes for a lavish wedding for Emmeline, were severe misgivings regarding Maia's shocking pronouncement not to marry Mr Siddenham, lest Emme's esteemed fiancé baulk at the notion of being associated with a family whose ranks contained a woman of questionable morals.

"I believe it would be best for all concerned -" wrote Mrs Wreningham, *"- for you to consider carefully your disastrous resolution to refuse the generous offer of marriage made by such an eligible and well-connected gentleman as Mr Siddenham, before making a foolish and hasty judgement, repentance will come too late to salvage your reputation. Remember always where your duty lies. How I feel for your dear parents, most particularly your poor dear mama. You must return home knowing that it falls to you to set a shining example of filial duty, one to which your sisters will aspire."*

Seated at her escritoire, her bandaged hand resting on the

side of the desk, appealing to what she hoped was her aunt's better nature, Maia tried to temper her reply, but had no intention of misleading Mrs Wreningham.

"I am sure dear aunt, you will do all within your power to ensure this unfortunate incident does not linger as a scandal, but is quietly forgotten in the hubbub of the season."

Feeling enough had been said upon a subject which held no fascination, Maia then wrote at length, and in what she hoped would pass as heartfelt rhapsodies, in reply to the descriptions of Emme's betrothal gown and plans for her trousseau, knowing the subject would delight her aunt and distract her from lingering over an incident Maia considered closed.

By contrast, Emmeline's letter to her cousin was filled with chatter regarding the whirl of parties and soirées she had attended. Emme was thoroughly enjoying her first season, and described vividly her new dresses and slippers, hats and pelisses, as well as the less tasteful, or even downright hideous creations worn by other young ladies, also making their come-outs. Maia could not help feeling that it made uninspiring reading.

Emme wrote too of her fiancé, Lord Stibbard, and of the gifts he had showered upon her; jewels, trinkets and tokens of his considerable regard. She wondered if Maia would return to London before the wedding in late August, for it would be a shame if Maia missed viewing the bridal gifts, which Emmeline anticipated would shortly begin to arrive. Complaining that if Maia did not come back soon, Emme would be Lady Stibbard and, having made the long journey to Scotland, would be presiding over her new husband's manor for the shooting season.

It all seemed dreadfully dull, indeed Maia shuddered at the prospect of spending one's honeymoon stuck in a chilly manor with a hunting party and little to do but wait for a man like Stibbard to return, eager to regale his bride with tales of trekking across soggy highlands, hunting grouse. It was as well Emmeline did not seem to mind; indeed she was looking forward to playing lady of the manor, content to be affianced to a man more than twice her age. Lord Stibbard had conveniently buried two wives, neither of whom had produced a single offspring, and it had been rumoured he was on the hunt for a third wife. In the first hours of the season his rheumy eye had alighted upon the buxom, simpering Emmeline, who despite her considerable charms had very little of value in her golden head. However, Stibbard was not interested in Emme's head, and was well-pleased with the doe-eyed beauty, in much the same way a horse-breeder might view a brood mare.

Having successfully secured two wives, his lordship did not doubt his success in obtaining a third, and wasted no time in turning Emme's empty head. When her brother informed Emmeline that Lord Stibbard had offered for and been given permission to wed her, both she and their mama were delighted. After all, Emmeline would become a lady upon her marriage, John Wreningham therefore had no qualms in agreeing to a match which would see his sister wed to a man older than their own mother.

It puzzled Maia how someone as vivacious as her cousin could consider marriage to Lord Stibbard, with whom Emme had little in common, what on earth would they talk about? Grouse?

With her left hand causing some discomfort, Maia winced as she began the letter to her family, carefully making no mention of the duke. Instead she related several of Monk's adventures, knowing the tales would delight her siblings, although the most amusing of the exploits she was forced to leave untold.

***

Maia's slumbers were destined to be fitful; for disturbed by the throbbing of her hand, sleep eluded her. Her mind was a-whirl with things which by the light of day she would dismiss as fanciful; she found herself speculating whether a kiss could reveal a gentleman's character, if so what did Percy Siddenham's kiss disclose? Strictly speaking, she had been the one who had pressed her lips to his, which was hardly a kiss. It was certainly not worthy of all the fuss, or the duke prowling round like a wolf on the hunt. Not caring for the imagery such an analogy provoked, she rolled over and burying her head in her pillow, attempted to banish all thoughts of the duke from her mind.

When she finally slept, she dreamed of a long gallery, a lone swan flying overhead, and the Duke of Bradenham, a girl encircled his arms. It was obviously one of the Hindolvestons, for no other girl of Maia's acquaintance had dark, spiralling curls, which fell with such abandon. The duke seemed fairly abandoned too, and Maia awoke, warm and flustered, cursing the wretched man for another disturbed night.

Chapter Fifteen

Mrs Dalling eyed Maia dubiously as the girl stood before the gilt looking-glass in the morning room. Maia frowned at her own reflection as she clumsily attempted to tied her bonnet strings. For although she would not admit it her hand was hurting, her fingers were swollen and the mother-of-pearl buttons at the wrists of her coat-dress had only been fastened with great difficulty. The announcement that she intended to go for a walk had not meet with the housekeeper's approval.

While she knew the reason for Mrs Dalling's stern gaze, Maia choose to ignore it, blithely retying the ribbons with fingers that would not comply with her wishes, until at last Mrs Dalling reached up to the slippery ribbons, tying them firmly and just a little too tightly under Maia's chin, pursed lips signifying her censure of Miss Maia's actions.

Maia stretched her neck experimentally to ensure she could still swallow and, discovering she could, beamed at Mrs Dalling, "I will not be long, the walk will do me good and it will get Monk out from under your feet."

The housekeeper sniffed disapprovingly "He'd not be under my feet if he were in the stables, where he belongs."

Unaware of the pronouncement, Monk gambolled happily around Maia's legs.

"Poor Monk, did you hear that? Banishment, what a cruel world it is."

With a snort of indignation at such nonsense, Mrs Dalling enquired pointedly, "His Grace will be here asking after you and what must I tell him this time?" She shook her head at the memory of the previous day. "The poor man was as white as a sheet when he called for water and bandages. Perhaps he can't stomach blood, being a duke."

Unable to agree with the housekeeper, Maia considered the varied and frequently bloodied dukes to be found in the history books she and her sisters had poured over, convinced that had the need arisen Bradenham would be the sort to take up arms rather happily, certainly with enthusiasm. But pushing aside the stirring image of the wretched man wielding a broadsword, she picked up a posy of flowers from an octagonal table standing by the long windows.

"I doubt the duke will make the ride over this morning, but even if he does, I will be back long before the he arrives." She sniffed the posy sadly. "Rosin's little girl was buried yesterday, I wish to see where she lies and put these flowers on the grave, I suggested by the hawthorn hedge would be the prettiest place, for it is covered with May blossom and might bring Rosin a little comfort."

Despite her disapproval of the girl's gadding about the estate, Mrs Dalling was unable to argue, Miss Maia was a grown woman and the housekeeper was not in a position to voice her objections, other than to let her displeasure be known in her own inimitable way.

As Maia disappeared from view along the sweeping avenue, Monk running in enthusiastic circles after his mistress, sniffing distractedly, making her way back to the kitchens, Mrs Dalling muttered gloomily, "And it looks like rain."

***

The dew-laden cobwebs sparkled in the patchy sunshine, while in the woodland beyond the meadow, the hammering of a woodpecker hunting insects amid the oaks and elms could be heard. While distracted by new scents, and the sniffing out of field-mice and voles, Monk scampered here and there, his tail wagging furiously.

Maia held onto her hat against the gusts of wind which tugged at her curls. "As persistent as the duke", she thought. Yet she could not evade him forever, nor could they continue to bicker at every turn. The matter must be settled and the duke made to understand that she was not going to capitulate. Perhaps then he would return to London and leave her in peace.

Her meditations were interrupted by Monk who, having trapped a vole under a paw, seemed uncertain what to do with it and barked, first at the vole, then at Maia, inordinately proud of his achievement. The vole, making the most of the opportunity slipped from beneath the puppy's paw and scurried away into the long grass.

"You wretch, you scared the poor little thing."

Bending down Maia fondled the dog's ears lovingly, obligingly the puppy rolled over for her to rub his underside, wriggling with delight.

Thus distracted, the walk to the churchyard took longer than Maia had intended, and by the time the pair approached the church the sky had grown darker and the air was chilling rapidly. Undeterred, Maia lifted the latch on the lych-gate and went in search of the baby's resting place.

The tiny grave was covered with recently cut turf, a rough-hewn cross marked the baby's resting place, tucked away against the hawthorn hedge, well away from the tombs of the more prosperous members of the community, separated in death as she would have been in life, by her birth and station.

Maia placed the posy upon the mound, glad the hawthorn hedge was already dotted with white buds of May blossom. She was grateful to Bradenham for arranging to have this unimportant, still-born child buried beneath such a beautiful bloom of commemoration. The memorial was more fitting than any cold, stone monument afforded to the affluent lying in eternal rest not far away.

She was preparing to retrace her steps to the lynch-gate, when Maia noticed Monk sitting patiently behind her, the still form of a mouse in his jaws.

"Oh Monk!" Her exclamation was more one of surprise than a scold, she patted his fluffy neck tenderly.

"Good boy, but please don't bring me any more."

Wondering what to do with the limp carcass Monk had obligingly dropped it at her feet, Maia felt the first heavy spots of rain.

"How vexing, I expect someone will say the rain is a good thing and that the fields or gardens need it, they always do, but I would prefer to stay dry."

There was no need to look down at her red-kid half-boots to know they were already dew soaked, the rain was certainly not going to improve them, so picking up her skirts, Maia made a dash for the church door, calling to Monk as she ran.

The church was dimly lit and chill, but it was better than getting wet, and Maia had no wish to return to the house soaked to the skin and thoroughly bedraggled. Although, she mused, arriving in such a state might convince the duke once and for all of her unsuitability as a bride for Percy Siddenham.

Seating herself in a back pew close to the open door, Maia heard Monk snuffling about the wooden kneelers, investigating the distinct possibility of mice. She untied the damp bonnet and placing it in her lap, began to smooth the puckering ribbons, wondering what the curate would say should he discover a puppy in his church.

"Never mind Monk, we shall think of Mr Coleridge, *'He prayeth best, who loveth best; All things great and small; For the dear God who loveth us; He made and loveth all.'* I am sure that means you too."

Reassured by this notion, Maia waited for the downpour to end, listening to the heavy drumming of the raindrops, she absently smoothed the hat ribbons between chilled fingers, as Monk continued in his quest for mice.

Neither of them heard the church door quietly creak on its ancient hinges, nor did they hear the soft step of well-made boots upon the tiled flooring, for the beating of the rain had intensified and was now accompanied by the rattle of hail, drowning out all other sounds.

Indeed, Maia heard nothing at all, and only momentarily felt the blow to her temple which felled her, after that she heard, felt and saw nothing for sometime. She was certainly oblivious to being slung unceremoniously over the shoulder of her attacker, her inert form enclosed within the voluminous folds of a man's cloak. With no knowledge of being tossed into the black Berlin coach, Maia was unaware that the doors bore no crest, the driver wore no livery, or that the blinds were carefully drawn over the windows.

Perhaps it was best for all concerned she was not able to see the man who had rendered her unconscious, as the carriage moved off along the lane, towards the country town of Fakenham. For while being abducted must always be a shock to the sensibilities, even those possessed by an Hindolveston, it is more perhaps shocking to be abducted by a complete stranger.

Chapter Sixteen

The oaths uttered by the duke as he paced the Turkey carpet in the charming morning room of Frogshall Abbot, were fluent and varied. To his credit he had managed to curb a similar response when he was informed by the ancient butler - in what was fast becoming a monotonous habit - that Miss Maia was absent.

His temper had not improved, when having been kept waiting for the best part of an hour, Mrs Dalling entered the chamber and, expecting to see the lady in question, was evidently surprised to discover the duke was alone.

"I beg your pardon your Grace, I was wishing to speak with Miss Maia."

"That makes two of us," muttered Cosmo, sotto voce.

"Has she not returned?" The housekeeper sounded anxious, and peered through the long windows at the rain which was falling heavily, intermingled with an occasional flurry of hail.

"Perhaps you would be so good as to inform me of Miss Hindolveston's whereabouts, for I am tiring of the game she insists upon playing."

Thoroughly concerned for her young mistress's whereabouts, Mrs Dalling grew even more perturbed.

"Miss Maia went to the church to lay flowers on the child's grave, but that was hours ago, she will be soaked to her skin, and your Grace will beg my pardon, but she didn't ought to have gone out this morning. She looked... " Mrs Dalling paused, "downright poorly, if you'll pardon me for saying so."

At this pronouncement Bradenham's fury abated. "Was the injury bothering her? Did she complain of pain?"

The housekeeper snorted with mixed pride and derision. "Complain? Miss Maia? I should think not your Grace, she never said a word, but I particularly noticed she was having trouble a-tying her bonnet."

"Did you not think to stop her from walking?"

Mrs Dalling drew herself up, primly, "I should think I did your Grace, but Miss Maia was that set on going, there was no arguing with her."

Cosmo could imagine only too well.

"But miss said she would be back."

The woman's emphasis indicated to Bradenham that Miss Maia's word was apparently her bond.

The rattle of hailstones against the window pane caught their attention and, noting that the rose garden beyond now lay beneath a fine white covering, resigned, Bradenham turned to the door.

"If you would be so good as to have my horse brought round, I will go in search of the errant Miss Hindolveston."

Bobbing her usual curtsey whilst on the move, Mrs Dalling hurried to find the under-footman.

***

As a man brought up upon a country estate, the duke was aware of the vagaries of spring; one moment warm and sun-filled, the next hailing and nipping at the buds on the trees, as well as at one's nose and fingers. But this knowledge did little to improve his frame of mind as he pulled up the high collar of his greatcoat and peered out from under his sodden beaver hat. A rivulet of icy water trickling down his neck caused Cosmo to muse that leaving Miss Hindolveston to punish Percy for what remained of their natural lives was not going to be sufficient recompense for all he was currently enduring.

He looped the thoroughbred's reins through the hitching-ring, strode through the lynch gate towards the church porch and open door beyond. Halting in the doorway he strained to see into the gloom, but could distinguish very little. As he stepped over the threshold he felt something other than the tiled floor of the nave beneath his feet; although it took him a few moments to discern that he was standing on a small pile of dead mice. He groaned, Watton was going to give notice if presented with boots in any condition other than perfect. However, all thoughts of upholding his valet's exacting expectations were banished as Cosmo's attention was caught by a scuffling, heralding Monk's arrival.

The hound gambolled along the aisle, wagging his tail delightedly as he dropped the bloodied corpse of a rat upon the ill-fated boots. The duke closed his eyes in mute protest, and giving the macabre offering a flick with one defiled foot, added it to the pile of small corpses.

He had expected to look up into the laughing eyes of Miss Hindolveston, and felt a stirring of disappointment to discover she was not enjoying his displeasure. Nor was she anywhere to be seen.

Wondering if Maia had entered the church at all, he glanced methodically into each pew to ensure she had not collapsed and was lying, half hidden by the high pew backs. She was not. Nor did he believe she would have abandoned the dog.

There were signs that someone had been in the cold nave; not only had the church door been left open, but the wooden kneeler in the last pew was lying at a rakish angle, and the unpolished floorboards bore faint patches of moisture. The duke's dark eyes narrowed as he discerned the outline of a footprint, partially obscured by the shadow of the bench-seat, strangely the footprint was facing the seat, not away from it as it should have been had Maia rested there. He placed his own booted foot over the damp print, as he thought, this was not the mark of a woman's shoe, but of a man's.

Despite the dog's presence, Cosmo was tempted to dismiss the notion that Miss Hindolveston had taken shelter in the church, until he caught sight of a length of red ribbon peeping out from beneath the pew. He bent to retrieve the incongruous object, only to discover it was attached to a damp straw bonnet. His attention was arrested by what appeared to be red circles upon the faded floorboards of the pew-stall, and on the dark polish pew-seat itself. Closer inspection confirmed that they were droplets of drying blood.

As a child, Cosmo had intensely disliked the wooden dissected map his tutor had insisted he use; the droplets, hat and footprints forcefully reminded of the damnable puzzle, jumbled pieces which made no sense until one had placed them all correctly and revealed the picture. Why did this puzzle make no sense? Perhaps like a half-completed puzzle, there were pieces missing.

Calling to Maia's dog, Bradenham hurried out to his dripping horse waiting disconsolately by the horse trough. It was with chagrin he realised the puppy was not going to be able to keep pace with him, even if it managed to avoid the thoroughbred's hooves. With a shake of his damp head at his folly, Cosmo placed the wriggling, muddied Monk within the folds of his great coat. He was rewarded for his efforts with a vigorous and thorough face licking all the way to Frogshall Abbot, where Maia's housekeeper anxiously awaited tidings of her mistress.

***

The duke's return did nothing to relieve Mrs Dalling's disquiet; she had expected his arrival to correspond with Miss Maia's and viewed the gentleman's solitary arrival with misgivings, eyeing the rainwater as it ran from him in rivulets with further dismay. But his only companion was the bedraggled dog, whom the duke placed unceremoniously upon the floor.

"No sign of her Dalling?"

Cosmo winced inwardly as he heard himself address the woman with what sounded suspiciously like an endearment. However, noticing nothing untoward, Mrs Dalling shook her head, watching in mystified silence as the duke deposited Miss Maia's bonnet upon the hall table.

"I found this, with Monk in the church, but Miss Hindolveston seems to have performed a vanishing act. I take it the bonnet belongs to her?"

He declined to mention the blood he had found in the church, believing that at this juncture it would only to frighten the housekeeper, adding a sense of panic to an already perplexing conundrum.

Mrs Dalling nodded in mute response to the question.

"I must speak with your stableman and anyone else who was in the vicinity of the meadow or church this morning. I need to know if anyone saw Miss Hindolveston, or anything untoward."

Mrs Dalling picked up Maia's damp bonnet and held it anxiously, "Untoward, your Grace?"

"Miss Hindolveston has gone to some trouble to avoid me over the past few days, but I am concerned something is amiss, particularly if she is - as you mentioned earlier - not quite herself. In which case, time is perhaps of the essence?"

Taking the hint that immediate action was required, the woman betook herself to the scullery.

While he waited there was ample time for Cosmo to arrange the pieces of the mystery, although nothing in this dissected puzzle gave any indication of the overall picture. He would not put it past the girl to elude him once again, yet he did not believe she was the histrionic sort who enjoyed playing an elaborate game of hide-and-seek, laughing gleefully up her sleeve as she watched people anxiously searching for her. He smiled ruefully; Maia was not one for such childish indulgences. She was more likely to stand nose to nose with him, damning him to the very devil, her eyes blazing, or else hurl something at his head, telling him exactly what she thought.

His reflections were interrupted by the approach of a man of middle-years, his weather-beaten hat clutched nervously to his chest, his discomfort at setting foot over the threshold of the house - out of familiar territory - was apparent. Being prodded none-to-gently by Mrs Dalling, did not help matters.

"Your Grace, this is Repps," she announced grandly, adding in an undertone,"Go on man, his Grace will not bite you."

The groom gave a stiff bow, not daring to look Bradenham in the eye.

"Yer Grace," he mumbled, only to receive another wince-inducing prod for his efforts.

Mrs Dalling hissed, "Speak up man, tell his Grace what you told me."

Despite the need for haste, Cosmo restrained a smile, it was clear who ruled this roost and he would not care to be on the receiving end of one of Mrs Dalling's bony-fingered jabs.

Goaded into speech, Repps glared crossly at the housekeeper.

"Yer Grace, the woman did say," here he sniffed disparagingly, "how you wus askin' about the miss. Now, I in't sayin' I se'n 'er, but one o'the lads wus takin' a mare up the farrier, bles't critter cast a shoe 'us mornin'-" he paused to recollect his thoughts. The duke knew better than to interrupt, the man would get to the heart of the matter more swiftly if left alone, and he cast a warning glance at the housekeeper, who quickly retracted her finger from the vicinity of Repps's back.

"The lad did say 'e saw a bloomin' gert coach comin' along the spinney, 'e had ter jump up the hedge, or ut'd've knocked 'im in-ter next week." Another sniff indicated the dangers of such recklessness. "The mare wus that upset she wus a-kickin' 'un shyin', the lad come in a-cursing, says 'ow the driver or'ter be strung up."

"Could the boy describe this coach?"

The man shrugged his shoulders. "Black, but I in't never sin 'un as weren't black. No crest, the lad did say that, as the only 'un what'd 'ave a big Berlin like that u'd be you, yer Grace." He added thoughtfully, "But t'wen't you were ut?"

Bradenham's countenance was like granite. "No, it was not."

Chapter Seventeen

The return of Maia's senses did not bring clarity, but the painful realisation that her head pounding dreadfully, and she seemed to have a throbbing in her right temple. She tried to recall the events which had preceded this painful moment and, opening her eyes, peered into the gloom, wondering if she were dreaming. Although it seemed unlikely that even the most vivid of nightmares would be accompanied by such discomfort.

But if she were not dreaming, where was she? And why did she feel as if she were in motion? And why could she hear the sound of rain, so close by?

"You awaken, Miss Hindolveston." A languid voice she did not recognise broke into her muddled thoughts.

Trying unsuccessfully to push herself into an upright position upon what appeared to be a carriage seat, Maia discovered her wrists were bound, and was forced to slide helplessly down once again.

"I suggest you remain where you are, you will undoubtedly be more comfortable." The voice sounded amused in a detached sort of way, as if her welfare was of no concern.

"My head hurts, did I fall?"

The response was both immediate and succinct, "No."

"Who are you?"

"Interesting that you should enquire about my person, rather than wonder where you are," the voice mused sardonically.

"Yes," agreed Maia, closing her eyes, as the pain inside her head increased. "That too." There was little she could do but remain slumped upon the seat, as she tried to make sense of the situation and regain her befuddled wits.

The carriage, for there was no mistaking the rattle and lurch of the coach despite the drawn blinds, was dimmed but was not in complete darkness, and although Maia's face was half-buried in the seat, by squinting she could discern the outline of man in a high hat, whom she presumed was the owner of the languid voice. His profile was distinctive; boasting a high forehead and long, straight nose, yet try as she might should could not recall having previously made his acquaintance.

A particularly sharp jolt as the carriage lurched into a rut, sent her sprawling to the floor at the voice's feet, and when Maia tried to right herself, with the continuous movement of the coach and being hampered by her bound wrists, it proved a pointless exercise. Begrudgingly the man leaned forward and placing none too gentle hands beneath her arms, hoisted Maia onto the seat once again, but now she was upright. Perhaps more surprisingly, he grabbed her ankles and placed her still damp kid-boots upon the squabs next to him.

"Brace you feet here," he instructed, adding shortly, "'if you fall again you will stay on the floor, for I will not pick you up a second time."

Although confused, in pain and feeling nauseous, Maia had sufficient wits to hold her tongue, and resting her head upon the bouncing carriage seat, tried to focus on the outline of the gentleman.

"Do I know you?" She asked after a few moments.

His response was a curt "No."

The brevity of his conversation offered little reassurance, nevertheless as she assimilated the snippet of information and struggled to align her scattered understanding into something akin to a coherent train of thought, Maia was encouraged to learn that although her memory might be patchy when it came to recalling the events of the morning, her mind remained reasonably sound, for she had not thought she recognised the man.

Looking around the carriage she enquired, "Where is Monk?"

Irritated, the man snapped, "There was no monk, your wits are clearly disordered. Sit back and be silent, that the journey might be infinitely more pleasurable for both of us."

Maia, uncharacteristically, did as she was bidden, for she was feeling decidedly unwell.

As the carriage lurched along the rough, narrow roads, occasionally swerving to avoid deep ruts, despite the sense of revulsion she felt at sitting with her ankles and the tops of her half-boots exposed, Maia did not remove her feet from the opposite seat, for it was an excellent way to brace herself. And by anchoring her back against the hard cushions behind her, she was able to ride out even the worst jolts.

In the gloom the gentleman remained motionless. Unperturbed by the motion of the coach, he sat bolt upright, his eyes occasionally straying to his travelling companion, before closing once again, as if bored by her presence.

The drumming of rain upon the roof began to subside and with it the gloom and, as light began to creep around the blinds covering the windows, the interior of the coach grew noticeably brighter. Yet despite trying to piece together that morning's events, Maia could remember nothing except tying her bonnet ribbons. She frowned, no, she had not tied them, Mrs Dalling had done so. She looked down at her hands and bound wrists, recalling how she came to injure her hand, and wondered if the duke would be even more furious than he had been previously, when he discovered she was not waiting for him at Frogshall Abbot as he had instructed. Doubtless he would assume she was avoiding him again, would eventually get bored and return to Swanton Chatteris in a foul mood.

A sickening thought gripped her; could it be possible that, having grown weary of her arguments and prevaricating, the duke had arranged for her to be abducted? Would she find herself being forcibly wedded to Percy Siddenham, in some Gothic candlelit ceremony? She stuck out her jaw defiantly; Bradenham was very much mistaken if he thought she would be coerced into marriage, for not only was the bride required to speak her assent during the plighting of her troth, but she would rather sacrifice her reputation than make her vow were the damnable duke dictated.

The stranger glared at her. "Stop grinding your teeth."

Unaware that she had been indulging in this childhood habit, Maia was surprised. But as the gentleman turned his disdainful gaze from her and resumed his somnambulant pose, Maia reconsidered; her hypothesis was obviously flawed. She had no doubt that the Duke of Bradenham would not hesitate to accuse, bully or goad her; nor would he have any qualms in attempting to manipulate or even blackmail her, but an abduction seemed entirely out of character, unless he were the one doing the abducting. He might, she reasoned, throw her over his shoulder in a fit of temper, but she could not see him employing someone to do the job on his behalf. But despite such disturbing thoughts, and the disastrous predicament in which she found herself, shaken by the pitch and roll of the carriage, and fatigued by her sleepless night, Maia was unable to prevent her eyes from closing, and as if in imitation of her companion, she drifted into an uneasy slumber.

More than once the gentleman leaned forward to reassure himself she was still breathing. He had not thought the blow to her head had been so great, but then again he had never before rendered a girl unconscious by such a method. Sucking his fair moustache meditatively, he reflected that the experience had been remarkably satisfying. He was incredulous and grateful the girl slept through the change of horses at the busy coaching-inn to the south of Fakenham. The route was a crossroads on the main highway between the market town of King's Lynn, to the west, and the port of Great Yarmouth, on the North Sea. There were better horses to be obtained at other inns, but at this overrun establishment there was little likelihood that the Berlin's presence would be noticed amid the hustle and bustle; at a less frequented inn the Berlin might have occasioned comment, but 'The Bull' was awash with people and horses, and coach's arrival and hasty departure went unnoticed.

It was in many respects the trickiest aspect of the whole escapade, but having planned to gag his captive before the Berlin drew-up at the coaching-inn, he had decided against disturbing the sleeping girl and trusting that his notoriously good luck would hold, he allowed Maia to remain un-muzzled and undisturbed.

As the Berlin lurched on its way, new horses between the shafts, the stranger smiled sardonically, perhaps abducting young ladies for modest fee would become his stock in trade. He drew a thin finger across his lips, perhaps not so modest after all.

***

It had taken what seemed an inordinate amount of time to set the wheels of pursuit in motion, for there was much to be arranged before the duke was able to relinquish the responsibility of overseeing the finer details into Mrs Dalling's capable hands at Frogshall Abbot, and his valet's more hesitant ones at Swanton Chatteris.

A message had been dispatched to Watton, instructing him to pack such items as his Grace might require for a stay of unknown duration, and together with Yaxley, the coachman, grooms and a stable lad, to betake themselves without delay to Frogshall Abbot.

Watton received the instructions with misgivings, for his employer had not couched his orders in neatly tied phrases, although it was perhaps not the wording of the missive which caused the valet unease.

Gallivanting about in this manner was not how his Grace conducted his affairs; either those of business or the other variety. Nor was he given to bolting across the countryside on a whim, dragging his prized Cleveland Bays after him. However, Watton knew better than to question the duke's orders therefore, as swiftly as could be achieved, the stately coach was made ready and with the duke's coachman, grooms and valet a-top, and excited stable lad behind, clutching his cap and occasionally picking at his nose, they hastened on their way.

As the heavy carriage rattled along the narrow lanes, its owner was already some distance away, urging the thoroughbred on with increasing resolve.

***

While the duke's progress was marked by an urgency and steely determination, preparations at Frogshall Abbot had a more feverish air, and in the end it was Mrs Dalling who supervised the packing of Maia's trunks, as she attempted to calm Lovelace Loveday's untimely indulgence in a touch of histrionics. On the duke's orders, the lady's maid was to accompany the coach, and had been warned to prepare for a protracted journey. But despite giving every appearance of being an unwilling participant in the hastily contrived pursuit of her mistress, Love was enjoying herself immensely.

"Where am I a-going Mrs Dalling?" wailed the girl, draping herself artistically over one end of the trunk.

The housekeeper, who was attempting to fasten the trunk's unyielding straps, brusquely pushed the lamenting Lovelace out of her way, before resuming her struggle with the stiff leather.

"If the duke knew the answer to that there would be no need to hurry. Get out of my way girl, if you keep the coach waiting you'll answer to his Grace." Mrs Dalling was pleased to note Lovelace looking suitably overawed

"You are to follow along with Mr Watton, his Grace's valet. You'll be in safe hands I dare say, but for goodness sake don't start a-crying again, I've heard tell Mr Watton is as top-lofty as the duke, so mind your manners and do as you're told."

Trying to overcome her imaginings concerning all that might befall her upon such an adventure, Love gulped and sniffed alternately, her eyes wide in trepidation, a heavy cloak drawn about her too long travelling dress. Upon being informed by Mrs Dalling of the active rôle the duke expected her to play in the unfolding mystery of Miss Maia's unseemly disappearance, Love had fled shrieking to gather her possessions and change into her highly prized travelling-dress, handed-on to her by the missing Maia. She wished ruefully she had bothered to take the dress up, but having not expected to make a journey quite so soon, the bothersome task had not seemed significant but, like her sisters, Maia was tall and the gown was far too long for the diminutive maid.

After tripping twice over her skirts, Lovelace quickly learned to hold the heavy twill well above the ground, in what she hoped was a regal fashion. However, Mrs Dalling soon abjured her of this notion by telling her that she looked like a child play-acting, which did nothing to help Lovelace's wails. But before the harried housekeeper could demand that Love rectify the situation, shouts were heard from the watching under-footman, announcing that the duke's carriage was in sight. Moments later they heard the sounds of hooves and wheels scattering the gravel along the avenue, as it sped towards the house.

To Watton's annoyance, precious minutes were wasted as Maia's hastily packed trunk and boxes were corded and secured behind the coach. Their departure was further delayed by the crowd of admirers from the house and stables, who pushed forward to gaze at the horses and coachwork. To make matters worse, Lovelace, who was enjoying being the centre of attention, clung to Mrs Dalling, snivelling messily, until taking note of the valet's irritation, the housekeeper pushed the wailing girl up the step and into the grand coach.

She handed lamenting Love a packet of paper wrapped cheese, a half loaf of bread and two small apples, together with the warning, "Not to get crumbs on his Grace's upholstery." Adding, "and mind you be good and take care of Miss Maia, when you find her."

The necessity of blowing her nose upon the corner of her voluminous apron prevented Mrs Dalling from issuing further instructions to the overwrought girl.

Seizing his opportunity, the valet elbowed Yaxley the coachman in the ribs, hissing, "You'd best be quick, lest we be here all day."

The carriage lurched on its way, Love waving in mute farewell, before her sensibilities overcame all rational thought and sinking back against the squabs, dampened them thoroughly with her tears, as well as her running nose. Yet by the time the carriage reached Fakenham, Love was enjoying the sensation of the landscape racing by her eyes at a remarkable rate, although his Grace's upholstery would forever bear the marks of the journey.

***

The second change of horses made just beyond the town of Swaffham, passed without mishap, but although inside the warm coach Maia slept on, the Berlin did not go completely unnoticed.

The coaching yard of The Red Lion was a bustling, noisy place, and Mellis, the innkeeper, boasted that his lads could unhitch a team of spent horses and hitch a fresh pair, or in the case of the mail-coach and larger carriages, four or even six horses, in less time than at any other inn in the county. The mighty Mellis, a noted local pugilist, had blacked the eye of more than one argumentative rival by way of proving his point. However, upon the morning of the Berlin's arrival, there was even more commotion than usual surrounding the London mail-coach, causing customers and lads alike to delay in order to watch the spectacle. The mail-guard, taking exception to the way in which the lad hitching the fresh horses to the mail-coach had looked at him, had with some asperity called the lad's antecedents into question.

Much affronted by the enquiry, the lad suggested that the guard might "Come have a taste o'me fist." The acolyte of the mighty Mellis, having learned well how best to make a statement.

The guard, feeling secure a-top the coach clutching his trusty blunderbuss, with a brace of pistols in his pockets and the power and majesty of the King's patronage behind him, declined none too politely. Whereupon it was deemed by the lad and several young men to whom the lad's parentage was no mystery, that the guard was "the milk pissin' by-blow of a waspish trull." To say nothing of his own unknown sire, whom it was speculated had long since discovered that "'is nutmegs were a-missin'" while "a-pissin' pins and needles."

This was met with howls of laughter from the onlookers who had nothing better to do with their time than encourage the lad. Indeed, several of the gentlemen were preparing to add interest to the fracas by sweetening it with a wager. The guard might be armed to the teeth, but the onlookers would require the lad's assistance when it came time to harness fresh cattle to their own chaises and carriages, so knew with absolute certainty which of the two horses to back, even if the decision was perhaps a tad tactical.

The argument came to a natural, if as far as the spectators were concerned, all too swift end when Mellis of the iron fist emerged from the inn's doorway, his sleeves rolled to his elbows, ready to strike the first blow upon whomever was responsible for delaying the mail-coach. With the law duly laid down, Mr Mellis hastened back to the tap room, eager to assuage the thirst of his customers who could apply themselves to the task now the other distractions had been removed.

The lad contented himself by barring his buttocks at the departing coach, to the feigned indifference of the guard, indifferent to the catcalls and jeers from the lad's cohorts which accompanied the display.

It was into this parting shot of the melee that the Berlin made its entrance, and having re-buttoned his breeks, greatly buoyed by the vanquishing of such a foe as the mail-guard, and feeling particularly cocky, the lad dared to ask the coachman seated high upon the Berlin. "What is the shades a-doin' of being closed on such a day?"

The coachman, a naturally surly individual, at first snarled that the lad should, "Attend to the horses, afore the master asks what the hold-up is about." But upon reflection, wishing to leave no mystery in the Berlin's wake, jerked his head towards the closed coach door and leering down at the lad whispered in a conspiratorial manner, "happen the master is finding a way to pass the journey."

The lad grinned in acknowledgement and winked gleefully at the coachman, then whistling, set about un-harnessing the blown horses, well-pleased with the day.

***

For all of his efforts to follow in the Berlin's wake, Cosmo remained in ignorance as to its final destination, concluding that it would help matters considerably if he understood the purpose of the apparent abduction, for Maia's disappearance could be nothing less. While he was no expert on the subject, he was under the impression that most young women when abducted, were removed from London, to be taken into the wilds of the country, for the culmination of their abductors' nefarious deeds, and were not as a rule, snatched from rural ecclesiastical sanctuary.

From what Repps had related, the duke guessed the Berlin must be headed for Fakenham, but beyond there he had no notion in which direction Maia would be taken. Although he was anxious to make up the distance between himself and the coach, Cosmo was forced to stop in order to speak those he passed on the rough roads, and with deeps pockets with which to reward the possessors of pertinent information, he was able to follow the Berlin with some degree of accuracy.

With the slim thread at which he had clutched becoming something more substantial, Bradenham could only hope that his confidence that Watton would follow his instructions to the letter, were not misplaced, Any deviation would cause the strand to become hopelessly entangled, and should it break all would be lost for both Percy and Maia. Miss Hindolveston's rescue could not be from one compromising situation to another; the proprieties had to be observed, and to accomplish this a suitable compliment of servants was necessary.

He was hot and thirsty by the time he reached The George Inn, in Fakenham, and expecting the Berlin to have changed horses at the coaching-inn, Cosmo was dismayed to learn that no such coach travelling southwards had stopped that day, although the lad busily shovelling the filthy yard recalled having seen a Berlin pass-by sometime earlier and suggested it has stopped at The Bull. Cursing fluently, to the great delight of the lad, the duke went to the tap room to leave a message for Watton.

The innkeeper did not trouble himself to halt in supping from his half-filled tankard, and was somewhat surly at the notion of relaying a message when there appeared to be no immediate monetary incentive for the service. Sagely the duke reassured the man that he would be paid once the message had been faithfully imparted. The nature of the gentleman's person was not totally lost upon the tipsy innkeeper, who bit back the retort he would have unleashed upon a lesser mortal, and gruffly assented to the arrangement.

Staying only to swallow a mellow mug of ale, Cosmo swung into the saddle once again, following the settled dust of the Berlin's wheels, wondering whether its final destination was sufficiently close to warrant forgoing the change of horses. Had the abductor made a bolt for the border, the chase would certainly have been longer, but at least the journey's end would be obvious, for Bradenham was no wiser with regard to the abductor, his intent, or where this chase would end.

Upon one thing he was resolved, that he would wring Percy's neck, once he had found, rescued and wrung Maia's.

***

Lovelace Loveday was enjoying herself greatly, although she had panicked upon dropping the bread Mrs Dalling had adjured her to take extra care with, but slipping from her hands before even a single bite was taken, it landed upon the seat, showering the carriage's interior with a fine covering of crumbs. If this were not enough to contend with, having gathered most of the crumbs into her clammy hand, the coach lurched to a standstill, causing Love, the crumbs and the partially wrapped cheese, which had been lying in her lap, to fall, liberally redistributing the crumbs once again. Sadly the cheese and found its way beneath her foot, leaving a greasy mark upon the polished floor.

She had done her best to rectify the problem, kicking the scattered breadcrumbs into a corner of the carriage and deciding to sit next to the cheese stain, that her long skirts might hide the mark. With such domestic arrangements resolved, Love sat back to enjoy the experience of travelling like a lady.

Her only other concerns came when the carriage drew up at various coaching inns in order to change horses, or to discover whether his Grace had left a message for Mr Watton. Peeping out of the window nervously, Love was taken aback by the curiosity of passers-by gawping at the lone figure in the magnificent travelling-carriage. Feeling as if she were trespassing, she shrank back against the squabs to avoid the stares.

However, Mr Watton, who had initially been somewhat supercilious, was kind enough to notice the maid's nervousness when he looked in upon her. "Chin up my girl, don't be afraid you ain't done nothing wrong."

"But Mr. Watton, sir, they was all lookin' at me." Love wailed.

Watton nodded sagely. "They'll gawp at anythin' most of 'em, think how miss must feel with all eyes upon her. Set yer back straight my girl, and give 'em something to stare at."

Giving her a wink, he closed the carriage door with a bowing flourish, intoning sycophantically, 'Yes m'lady, as you wish m'lady', much to Love's delight. Despite his natural inclination towards a well-ordered household, Watton was rather enjoying the escapade. Thus far at least.

***

While the Berlin had a good head start, and Bradenham had made frequent stops in order to verify that the coach had passed by, to ensure that despite all appearances he was not on a wild goose chase. He was an excellent horseman in command of a thoroughbred; the Berlin meanwhile, was cumbersome; its coachman was far from skilled and it was not making good speed.

While there was much in his favour, Cosmo's disquiet could not be entirely assuaged. Indeed, the lad at the Red Lion, with whom he had spoken, had added to the duke's concerns. The lad recalled the coach, identifying it as a Berlin and responded with enthusiasm to Cosmo's enquiries surrounding the direction the coach had taken. Sniffing richly and wiping his nose upon the back of his hand, the lad had elaborated with graphic speculation on the entertainments enjoyed by the Berlin's occupants.

"Blinds wus drawn, t'was my guess the dragon was a-ridin' St. George."

His lewd actions mimicked his description and overcoming an inclination to break the youth's jaw, Bradenham was careful respond in kind; now was not the time to stand on ceremony or to take out his frustrations upon the hapless youth. It would, he reasoned, be advisable not to draw further attention to the situation by acting as if he were an outraged lover in pursuit of the Berlin. Instead, playing the rôle of a friend following the coach at a respectful distance, would avoid difficult questions.

The duke agreed that it sounded very much like his comrade, who had a hearty appetite for experiencing the view while making arduous journeys, and the youth guffawed appreciatively.

After leaving a message for Watton with the mighty Mellis - who recognising a gentleman of quality when he saw one, was only too willing to oblige, and throwing the lad in the coaching-yard a crown for his troubles, Bradenham swung himself into the saddle once again.

While he was concerned for Maia's welfare, he did not believe she was being successfully debauched as the lad seemed to think; she would hardly have been a willing participant, and he would have wagered that any stranger attempting to lay hands upon her person would have his head knocked off, the long gallery and Leda, notwithstanding. However, preying on his mind the prospect of Maia being debauched, even unsuccessfully, did not amuse him, although he reminded himself that this obsession with Maia Hindolveston's state of virgo intacta would have to stop. Once she was irrevocably shackled to Percy, Maia's welfare would be out of his hands and he would be able to put all thoughts of her out of his head, once and for all.

***

The unremarkable hired horses had covered many miles before Maia awoke to find the carriage warm and stuffy; the dark shades obscuring the windows radiated warmth and the air was stale. She licked her lips, trying to push the sensation of thirst from her thoughts.

"I have refreshment, if you would care for some."

The stranger's offer surprised Maia, although his tone was not one of concern and she shook her head; suspicious that anything he gave her to drink was sure to be drugged.

His disparaging snort indicated that he comprehended the reason for her reluctance. "Am I to be wounded by your lack of faith?"

Maia tried to weigh up her companion, wary of angering the man, who for now held the balance of power.

"What makes you think I would trust you?"

Her abductor shrugged dismissively. "It matters not, you may drink or remain parched, the choice is yours."

Withdrawing a bottle from a pocket concealed in the upholstery, and neatly uncorking the stopper with his teeth, he drank a long draught before offering the drink to Maia, who tentatively took the bottle and sniffed at it suspiciously, trying to discern its contents.

"Lemonade, I believe," came the bored reply to her unasked

question. "Too bitter for my taste, not that lemonade is too my taste, but perhaps it will be to your liking, but then again, beggars can hardly be choosers, can they?"

Reasoning that her abductor was unlikely to drug himself, Maia took a hesitant sip and was relieved to discover it was indeed lemonade, although he was right, it was horribly bitter. However, grateful to have her thirst assuaged, Maia drank deeply and passed the bottle back to the man, who languidly waved it aside.

"Keep it, you may require more before we reach our destination," he handed her the cork.

Maia took another long draught, before attempting to re-cork the bottle, her efforts hampered by the bindings securing her wrists. After watching her fumblings with increasing irritation, her abductor produced a small penknife and, prising the blade from its handle with his thumbnail, leaned forward.

"Hold up your wrists," the command was terse.

Maia did as she was bidden, holding her breath as the blade tugged at the strips of cloth binding her wrists, which gave easily under the lethal edge and dropped limply into her lap. The bounds had not been unduly tight, nevertheless Maia was glad to be able to move more easily and to regain some degree of independence.

Refreshed by the lemonade she felt sufficiently buoyed to enquire conversationally, "Where is our destination?"

The gentleman snorted, "My dear Miss Hindolveston, I have no intention of discussing where we are going, or indeed of discussing anything with you. Do you suppose me to be some sort of fool, or perhaps a villain from a tale who carelessly reveals his strategy to the hapless heroine, in order that she may plan her escape?" His voice grew cruel. "You are very much mistaken if you believe you will escape."

Finding her throat to be exceedingly dry, Maia reached for the lemonade, glad to avoid the necessity of responding to the ominous warning.

The remainder of the journey were spent in bouts of prolonged sleep and brief wakeful thirst, and by the time Berlin drew up in the coaching yard of the Wagon and Horses in Newmarket, the bottle was empty and Maia was drunk.

Chapter Eighteen

The last hours of Cosmo's journey were perhaps the most arduous, for not only was he saddle weary, but having finally caught sight of the elusive Berlin, with its mismatched, ill-kempt coaching-inn horses running clumsily in harness, he grew anxious for his own Clevelands, despite the precautions he had taken for their care. Runton, the duke's most trusted groom was to be left with the prized horses when Yaxley, the coachman, considered the pair were winded, although it was to be hoped Runton, would have the foresight to check the condition of the stables before permitting the bays to reside there, even for one night.

As the Berlin made its way through the heath-land, passing flowerless broom and forlorn sheep, the duke discovered that remaining out of sight upon the empty highway was more taxing by far than chasing after the carriage in a frenzied pursuit, along country lanes well-shielded by high hedgerows. However, by careful reining-in, together with judicious pausing along the truly exposed stretches of highway, Bradenham managed to maintain his distance admirably and avoid being seen by the coachman, or the carriage's occupants.

While it would have been easier to call the Berlin to a halt and, having hauled Maia from within, return to Frogshall Abbot with her in the saddle before him. Not that the mode of transportation would please her; it simply would not do, although she would be a captive audience and perhaps by the time they reached Norfolk she would have acquiesced to becoming Mrs Siddenham. At least with the drawn shades, the wretched girl was hidden from prying eyes; a-top his horse she would effectively be paraded for all the world to see. Imaging her response at being ordered to ride before him in the saddle, Cosmo laughed aloud.

He was not laughing however, when he realised the Berlin's final destination; comprehending with horror that Maia's abductor was taking her to Newmarket. Didn't the damn-fool know this was the day before the Second Spring Meeting The entire place would be heaving with the massed ranks of the racing fraternity and assorted hangers-on, like a bloated corpse riddled with maggots. Maia was reasonably safe within the confines of the Berlin, but the same could not be said once she reached Newmarket. It seemed an odd location to seduce someone like Maia Hindolveston, although the duke would have been hard-pressed to come up with an appropriate alternative, but then again seduction was not foremost on his mind.

As unsatisfactory as Newmarket undoubtedly was, The Waggon and Horses Inn, on the busy Newmarket High Street, seemed an even more unlikely location in which to entice Miss Hindolveston; particularly when the White Hart, a coaching in just down the High Street, was both larger and more popular, and boasted a more genteel clientele.

Halting at the crossroads, Bradenham watched the carriage's occupants disembark into the cool evening air and make their way across cobbles into the inn. From this distance he could only see Maia's abductor in profile, and was unable ascertain his identity. As the man placed a proprietary hand upon Maia's waist Cosmo stiffened, causing the thoroughbred to sidle uneasily in response.

It seemed strange that Maia did not appear reluctant to enter the inn, nor did she seem to notice the fellow's hand at her waist, and the duke wondered with a sinking heart whether the lad at the Red Lion was right. When it came to it, what did he really know of Maia Hindolveston, other than she had thrown herself at his cousin?

Finding no answer, the duke watched the empty Berlin being taken to the rear of the coaching inn, that the horses might be unharnessed and stabled, making it clear that Maia and her captor were going nowhere in the immediate future.

***

Watching the world pass by was thirsty work, and hunching even further over his ale pot, the old man shifted on the rickety bench in his spot under the inn's window. It was a prime position for a man who had nothing better to do than observe the comings and goings of the inn's patrons.

Raising the half-empty tankard to his lips, he idly watched the carriage lurch to a standstill on the uneven cobbles; the mangy horses blowing, their sides heaving with exertion. The driver made no attempt to jump down to assist his master, but merely touched his hat in curt greeting as the gentleman opened the carriage door from within.

A fair-haired gentleman alighted with care, and leaning back into the Berlin, reached to assist a dark-haired young lady, who appeared to be struggling to finding her feet now that the continual movement of the carriage had ceased. She stumbled, firstly upon the step, and then upon the uneven cobbles, but was steadied by her travelling companion who placed his hand upon her waist. Yet the expression upon the gentleman's face was not one of kindly concern; indeed it seemed to the old man that he looked downright nasty, gazing at the lass as if she were dirt.

The old man had seen it all before, he had witnessed the arrival of scores of young men and their doxies; mistresses; paramours, or in some cases reluctant misses, who needed encouragement and subtle coercion to take the last irrevocable step over the threshold. This one looked a little worse for wear, but she was not reluctant, and he wondered if the comely wench knew what was in store for her. Taking another sup from his ale pot he watched the couple from beneath hooded eyes, pitying the poor lass, not that he entirely blamed the fellow, for she was a rare piece. But not liking the look of the gentleman, the old man kept his observations to himself.

***

Tucked away down Drapery Row, surrounded by narrow streets and crowded tenements, the Bushel Inn, was one of the older establishments in Newmarket, boasting a cock-pit in its cellars. Its proprietor, the grasping Trunch, knew that despite not offering the finest ales, or most salubrious of surroundings, the gentlemen who descended upon Newmarket, hopeful of improving their fortunes with calculated wagers upon fine horseflesh, might be persuaded to part with a portion of their winnings in reckless gaming upon the bloody outcome of skirmishes between the feathered prize fighters, belligerently engaged in a battle to the death.

The Bushel was certainly no place for a lady, and as he dodged the lines of tattered washing slung across the narrow backstreet, the duke doubted Watton would be impressed to discover his employer had engaged a parlour in this unprepossessing of places. However, it could not be helped, for the Bushel was within strolling distance of the Waggon and Horses, albeit careful strolling if the filth strewn cobbles were anything to go by.

From his spot behind the tap, where he might observe his patrons as they passed through the shabby portal, calculating to the groat what each man was worth and more importantly what each would spend, Trunch would direct the fastidious Watton to a side-parlour, his glee palpable as he rubbed his grubby hands together. While with horror it would dawn on the valet, as he read the missive from his employer, that he was to await further instruction, possibly even staying the night. Bradenham almost wished he could watch the scene unfold, however, he had more pressing matters to attend to.

***

Long before the Berlin reached a jolting halt on the cobblestones, Maia discovered she was feeling decidedly unwell, and putting the indisposition down to a bout of carriage-sickness, wondered in a muddled way if the journey disagreed with her. By the time the coach reached its destination, Maia was beyond rational thought. With the opening of the door, allowing light and fresh air to penetrate the coach's stuffy interior, she noted fuzzily, that her abductor was a blonde gentleman and, disliking his thin lipped sneer and malignant air, decided he was not in the least handsome. Although it is doubtful she would have been able to articulate such sentiments had a formal enquiry been made. Perhaps, more pertinently, she did not notice anything untoward in being hurried across the cobbles and into the inn.

As they crossed the threshold, the gentleman informed Maia "You need rest, I will see you to your chamber."

She nodded dully and did not even protest when she was shown into what was obviously a bedchamber for more than one person.

Yawning and stretching, Maia recalled that she hadn't eaten for some hours, announcing loudly: "Gruel."

"I beg your pardon?"

"Gruel. It is given to invalids and I believe I would care for some." Maia spoke as if she were giving the man orders, then hiccuped gently to herself.

Her abductor's response was brusque, for he was unaccustomed to being addressed in this manner. "I have business to attend to and will lock the door on my way out, for I would not want you to be disturbed, however, I will leave you some lemonade."

With this he closed the door, and allowing the wooden latch to fall into place, turned the key in the lock.

Once alone, Maia discovered she was not hungry after all, merely thirsty, and catching sight of the bottle the gentleman had placed next to the smoking tallow candle on the deal table. She smiled; at least she wouldn't die of thirst in his absence.

***

Pocketing the key to the room, Maia's abductor allowed himself a moment to gloat. It was, he mused, so very easy to ruin a young lady -

delightfully so - and betaking himself down the narrow staircase, he went to the tap room for a fortifying drink. While kidnapping was not an arduous pastime, it was somewhat tiring, not to mention being unutterably dull, and Miss Hindolveston's company was far from fascinating. Her conversation in particular had been tedious, but perhaps that was hardly surprising when one took into account the blow to her head and the potent mixture contained in the lemonade bottle. Doubtless she would regain her wits once she had eaten, but the girl was more malleable while under the influence, and he had no intention of directing that food be taken to the bedchamber. Besides, hunger would soon be the least of her concerns.

The tap room was filling with newcomers arriving ahead of the race meeting; anxious to secure lodgings, discuss form and place wagers, nosily enjoying the novelty of being away from their regular haunts.

The gentleman was well-satisfied, assured that in addition to his judicious foresight in securing a bedchamber in advance, luck was with him. For in getting Miss Hindolveston to the chamber unseen, no one would be able to accuse him of coercion, or claim the girl had been an unwilling participant in a seduction concluded under duress. Not that such allegations would matter once his aim was achieved.

He looked appreciatively at the crowd of eager faces, knowing that tomorrow morning when he led the debauched figure of Maia Hindolveston down the stairs, the tap room and hallway would be seething with men, and all eyes would be upon her. Beneath the dirty-blonde moustache his thin lips curved into a malicious smile; when she descended upon the morrow the obvious and natural conclusion would be reached.

Delighting in his ingenuity, Maia's abductor did not notice the hunched figure of His Grace the Duke of Bradenham, his hat low over his brow, as he nursed a mug of ale. Not that he would have recognised the duke, even if he had espied him, having not had the privilege of making the noble gentleman's acquaintance.

***

Gently swaying to and fro, Maia clasped the edge of the bed and wondered why the room persisted in spinning so alarmingly, concluding after a few dizzying minutes that she must still be suffering from carriage-sickness. Her younger sister Mery, was prone to the affliction, which was at best inconvenient and at worst unpleasant for all in the immediate vicinity. But while Mery made a swift recovery once the carriage had ceased to move, Maia found herself growing increasingly bilious.

From her swaying vantage point on the bed, she could see through the window overlooking the rear of the inn. In the courtyard below horses were being unharnessed from carriages, and thoroughbreds led away to be groomed and fed. Maia puzzled over the number of gentlemen who seemed to be arriving, for there did not appear to be any ladies.

She fuzzily wondered if the gentlemen were going to a ball, or perhaps a rout, but concluded with a hiccup. "They are not dressed for a ball." Yet despite the dearth of knee-breeches and dancing shoes, there were sufficient top-boots, Hessians and artfully arranged neckcloths amongst the assorted race-goers, to please even her cousin Emmeline. "Definitely not dancing."

Maia's pronouncement was followed by another unladylike hiccup. Mercifully the bottle of lemonade provided by the gentleman was substantial, and certain that a tumbler-full would alleviate the aggravating hiccups, Maia rose unsteadily from the bed and poured herself a generous glassful of the clouded liquid. She returned with a thud to the lumpy, compacted horsehair mattress, in order to savour it, finding it strange she had previously not much cared for lemonade, perhaps it was an acquired taste.

***

The duke's method of communicating with his valet while travelling proved an admirable one, although it was with a sinking heart that Watton read the missive from his employer instructing him to proceed to Newmarket, where further direction would await him at the Bushel Inn. The valet was not personally acquainted with the cock-pit, not being a gambling man, nevertheless its reputation preceded it.

He was somewhat disconcerted to find himself tangled in yards of grimy washing hanging across the street, as he sat a-top the coach, while the stable lad clinging to the back of the crested carriage shouted cheerful obscenities at the group of filthy urchins running in its wake, much to the amusement of Yaxley, the coachman and Pigot, the groom - men, who in the valet's opinion, were sadly lacking in consequence.

Grimly cuffing the grinning lad as he hopped from his perch, Watton passed through the Bushel's weathered columns and with a disdainful sniff, went to make enquiries about his employer. It was too dark to continue their wild goose chase; to do so would only invite the likelihood of mishap. But still Watton clung to the hope that the message Trunch delivered into his carefully manicured hands would instruct him to proceed to a more refined establishment.

Alas his hopes were in vain, even before he had finished reading the direction, Watton was aware of the calculating gleam in the proprietor's eye. The valet grew frosty, Bradenham may be a duke, but it was he, Watton, who currently held the purse strings and woe betide any man who attempted to cull more than his due from his Grace's deep pockets.

***

The tap room of the Waggon and Horses was hot and noisy, and Cosmo was growing increasingly restless. Maia's abductor had not moved from his seat for sometime, and Bradenham, too tall to be comfortable in the narrow alcove for long, needed to stretch his legs. It seemed to the cramped duke, that the man had no clear plan of action, and he wondered if seduction were indeed the abductor's object. If so, what the devil was he doing kicking his heels, drinking ale and sharing pleasantries with his fellow drinkers, with whom he appeared to have no more than a passing acquaintance?

The inn became steadily more crowded, until the smell of spilled ale and warm bodies was overpowering. But despite being undeniably tedious, the time spent in the tap room provided the duke with ample opportunity to ponder how he might effect Maia's release. Chasing after the Berlin was all well and good, but it would be for nothing if he failed to liberate Maia, unscathed.

Should her abductor go upstairs, all the duke could do was burst in upon them before irreparable damage was done. However, that did not solve to problem of how to get Maia out of the coaching inn unseen - for short of making her vanish into thin air, Cosmo could not see how it might be achieved, and the Waggon and Horses was no place for a well bred, unmarried lady to be seen in the company of a gentleman. Indeed, every wench, serving maid and woman under the age of sixty was on her guard, for anything in skirts was considered to be fair-game by the majority of the prowling males. It was a foregone conclusion that any woman who made her way through the male sanctuary of the inn would be a willing participant of whatever followed, and the less particular gentlemen did not object to sharing.

He watched a slovenly young woman collecting used ale pots from the grimy tables, clearly relishing the attention of being the token female in the tap room. When roughly molested by a florid man missing his front teeth, she threw back her head, laughing delightedly, stale ale spilling from the pewter pots as she wriggled at the man's groping, much to the enjoyment of the gathered race goers.

The duke shuddered; even without her antics in the long gallery, to bring Maia Hindolveston through such skirt-sniffing predators would be social suicide for the girl, but to leave her upstairs in her abductor's grasp was unthinkable.

At last the abductor began to push his way through the throng. Finishing his ale Cosmo glanced cautiously about before rising, ensuring there was no one present who might recognise or hail him. He took pains to hunch his shoulders in order to disguise his noteworthy height, and with his hat well-down, prepared to follow the stranger, but instead of making his way to the stairs as the duke had anticipated, the abductor headed towards the door leading to the cobbled street.

When the man paused on the threshold, Bradenham was forced to halt abruptly, feigning an interest in a tattered bill posted upon a low beam, and although he could not hear what was spoken, or to whom the words were addressed, it was clear an altercation was taking place, and from the manner in which he brushed and dabbed at his sleeve, it seemed someone had spilt something upon Maia's abductor. Waiting in the doorway as the man picked his way across the filthy cobbles, there was no question of Cosmo following in pursuit and leaving Maia alone at the inn, which was now a heaving mass of men. He did not care to consider what would happen in this melee should Miss Hindolveston's presence be discovered.

Forced to sidestep a drunken man who barged unheeding through the door, Bradenham narrowly missed bumping into an old man seated upon a bench; the fresh porter stain upon his filthy breeches and the pool of dark liquid splashed over the cobbles at this feet, bearing testimony to the altercation the duke had in part witnessed.

The old man spat extravagantly and stared stonily at Bradenham, who nodded by way of a greeting.

"Allow me refill tankard, yours appears to have met with an accident."

The old man looked doubtfully at his would-be benefactor, then sniffed his assent, nodding in the direction of the abductor's disappearing back. "Yon devil, damn'd mutton-monger."

"He was perhaps in a hurry," speculated the duke.

This was met with an indignant harrumph.

"For what? To go to Queen Anne's with yon wench awaiting 'is pleasure upstairs, poor gel." The old man leaned forward conspiratorially, "Got a nasrty look about 'im, woun't wish 'im on no gel and her a-wobbling' on 'er pins." He shook his grizzled head sadly. "T'won't stop 'im, I seen 'is sort afore, an 'er a proper lady."

He continued to shake his head in contemplation of Maia's fate, then gave a chuckle. "Were I thirty years younger I'd not be leaving a wench like 'er a-waiting." He wheezed in appreciation at the memory of his youth, wiped his nose on the back of his hand and sniffed richly.

His interest piqued, Bradenham clarified, "Queen Anne's you say?"

The old man sniffed again. "May the pox take 'im."

His gaze following the direction the blonde haired abductor had taken, Cosmo agreed. "You are likely to be right."

Attracting the attention of the slatternly serving girl was not difficult, and she sidled up to the duke in anticipation of his attentions, brushing against him provocatively. She was disappointed when the gentleman requested only more porter for his friend. However, when he enquired about rooms, the girl with every expectation of a profitable encounter, advised him there were no lodgings to be had for the night.

She added speculatively, "I knows of a chamber what can be 'ired by the hour, or if the gentlem'n ain't partic'lar, the stable ain't but a step away."

Repulsed, Bradenham declined.

***

Although it was long after dark, the streets were still thronged with people, as Maia's abductor threaded his way along Moulton Road, for race meetings attracted business of more than just an equine nature to Newmarket.

Savouring the prospect of an evening spent in Queen Anne's Coffee House, he was in no rush to reach his destination, nor did he desire to immediately return to the male companionship of the tap room, or to spend more time with Miss Hindolveston than was absolutely necessary. She was not the sort of woman with whom he cared to share an evening's pleasure. She was, he considered, more of a business venture.

With a thin, supercilious smile, he pushed open the door of what had once been a bustling hub of intellectual domination, where business and conversation were as important as the coffee consumed by its patrons, now however, the consummation of an entirely different business was practised within its walls.

As he stepped over the threshold and was greeted by the queen of Anne's herself, the abductor's contemptuous expression was replaced by one of predatory malevolence.

Chapter Nineteen

As the evening progressed, the noise from the public rooms below grew steadily louder, raucous and with a sinister edge to it that Maia was unable to explain, but as she was struggling to put words together in a coherent fashion, it was perhaps hardly surprising. Despite a lack of verbal agility, her senses seemed to be heightened; sounds were clearer, and Maia felt as if she were experiencing the world for the very first time, in a way that was so overwhelming she thought she might burst.

She had lost track of time since the gentleman had departed from the chamber,; he may have been gone for hours, or perhaps only a few minutes, and she tried to remember if he had mentioned something about food. But finding she was unable to recall not only this, but also a great number of things, she removed herself in rather a wobbly fashion to the only chair in the chamber, for even in her confused and somewhat euphoric state, its rush seat was preferable to the lumpy mattress.

The wooden door-latch clicked up and down in its bracket, making Maia start. But the door had been carefully locked by her abductor and did not open, even when pressure was applied from the other side. A pale, wavering light shone under the gap between the door and the threshold; shadows of movement rising and falling, and fixated upon interplay between the light and darkness, she was utterly rapt.

The latch moved peevishly, as the door was briefly but ferociously rattled.

"Maia?" A deep voice hissed through the keyhole.

Unmoving, Maia responded with a hesitant "Y-yes?"

The voice came again. "Thank heaven, I do not suppose you have the key to this damned door, do you?"

Maia shook her head absently, wondering why the voice was so familiar.

"Maia, can you hear me?"

"Yes, I can hear you. Can you hear me?"

On the other side of the bedchamber door the duke was somewhat taken aback, had the woman lost her wits? He had heard what he had always believed to be vastly exaggerated tales of untutored young ladies left witless following an unexpected, or particularly robust first liaison, but he hadn't expected Maia to be the fainting type.

Cosmo's expression grew grim and his hand shook, causing him to spill the stinking, melted tallow from the candle onto his boots.

He hissed through the keyhole. "Stand aside from the door." Upon receiving no response, he asked shortly, "Did you hear me?"

"I can hear you." Maia wondered why could she hear a voice yet was unable to see anyone.

Pausing to gauge the level of the din rising from the revellers below, the duke braced himself. A drunken individual had just made a particularly rousing speech against the upstart Bonaparte who, if the news from the continent was to be believed, was intent on taking on the might of the Habsburgs. His words were greeted with shouts and enthusiastic jeers, the upstart not being a favourite among the race-goers. With the noise reaching a crescendo, Cosmo applied a ducal shoulder to the wooden door and lifting the latch free of the keep, gave an almighty shove.

The lock held fast but the ancient cross-boarded door gave a crack - its dried timbers snapping beneath the considerable force before it gave way completely. Easily pushing aside the door, which was now in two halves, Bradenham held his candle aloft and peered into the chamber. While remaining seated, Maia gazed in rapt fascination at the fractured door.

Although Miss Hindolveston gave the distinct impression of being decidedly tumbled, with her hair cascading about her shoulders, Cosmo was encouraged that she was not weeping and that despite being grubby and creased, her gown appeared to be intact. He was relieved to note that the bed was unused, not, he considered grimly, that an unused bed meant much.

Even by the light from the poor candles the girl looked ashen-faced, the bandage on her hand was worn and loose, and there seemed to be a dark patch at her temple. This was not the Maia Hindolveston with whom he had stood nose-to-nose; the Fury was missing. A placid shadow of her former self in her stead, she made no movement as he entered the chamber.

Placing his candle upon the table, Cosmo knelt at Maia's side, and looking intently into her eyes tried to ascertain if all was well, but receiving only a vacant response, he took her hands and began to chafe her cool fingers.

"Maia, do you recognise me?"

She focused upon his face with difficulty, and to the duke's great relief she nodded.

"Are you unharmed?" Such a question must surely cover a multitude of sins without the need to be specific.

Maia pondered for a moment, then withdrawing her hand from Bradenham's, she pointed to her temple.

"It hurts, here -" wincing as she touched the shadowed bruise, she held up her wrapped hand, "- and here."

A closer examination of the wound to her head revealed it was not bleeding, but in the dim light it was impossible to discern the severity of the injury. It was likely Maia was suffering the effects of a blow, it would certainly account for her unnatural and unnerving docility, making Cosmo all the more anxious to remove the girl to safety, without delay. The noise from below indicated things were getting out-of-hand and he did not want any drunken pleasure-seekers to stumble their way into the chamber now the door was no longer intact.

"Can you stand?"

It had not previously occurred to Cosmo that Maia might not be in a fit state to be rescued. Nevertheless he offered her his hand, encouraging her to rise to her feet. Wobbling, Maia stood briefly, then lurching forward, leaned heavily against him, forcing Bradenham to take her by the waist. He was puzzled she had made no attempt to prevent herself from falling, but waited, hopeful that she might show some spirit and object to his familiarity, or at the very least regain her balance. But she remained slumped against his chest.

This was getting them nowhere, and the sound of voices beyond the door added to Cosmo's growing unease.

"Maia, STAND!"

Greatly irritated, the precipitously unbalanced girl frowned at him, struggling to focus, and announced, "Shhhh, I have a headache and you are not improving it."

Bradenham heaved an audible sigh of relief, at least she was coherent.

"Did you bring me gruel?" Sounding peeved, Maia inspected the duke, as if expecting him to bear a tray. "No, it was not you who was to bring me dinner, it was … Oh, I do not know." She waved her hands dismissively at her own confusion, the bandage unravelling as she did so, and prodded the duke's chest with a slender finger. "Who is to bring my gruel, if not you?"

Had the situation not been so dire, Cosmo would have laughed at its ridiculousness, but there was no time for frivolity. He manoeuvred Maia until she was leaning against the deal table, where she wiggled, trying to get comfortable.

He did what he could to reassemble the fractured door and by wedging the ladder-backed chair against the two halves, was able to foster the impression that the door was indeed intact, at least to a casual passer by. Even if the latch were lifted the lock would hold fast, the damage would only become apparent if someone attempted to push the door open.

Content that the door was as secure as was possible given the damage, Cosmo turned to see Maia returning a bottle to the table and delicately wipe her mouth upon her fingers. Taking the bottle he sniffed warily at what remained of its contents, but unable to identify the concoction was forced to take a small sip, only to spit the liquid onto the chamber floor in disgust.

Maia responded cuttingly, with a flash of her former spirit. "Has his Grace never before tasted lemonade?"

Cosmo glared at her. "Of course I have, but this is not lemonade, this is 'La Fée Verte'."

It was clear from Maia's dismissive snort that she considered the duke to be a fool.

"I have no idea what you are talking about, green faeries indeed. I am forced to question his Grace's ... your Grace's ... your judgement if you believe such creatures exist. I can assure you it is lemonade." Then confided as if she were a connoisseur, "Although it is a touch on the bitter side."

"Hmm ... " Bradenham regarded the girl shrewdly. The presence of 'La Fée Verte' in the lemonade accounted for much, although there was certainly more than just a mere presence of it. Wormwood was bitter even when mixed with anise and fennel; more than bitter, it was potent, and while she was not completely intoxicated, Maia was clearly not herself. 'La Fée Verte' had truly cast her spell, even if it had been diluted with lemonade.

The girl would not have heard of the noxious drink, and would not have recognised what she had surreptitiously been given; even in the gentlemen's clubs there were few who were familiar with the potent brew. Maia was unlikely to have drunk anything stronger than orgeat, so it was a miracle she had not fallen into a stupor - or worse still - cast up her accounts completely. The duke was grateful for small mercies.

He had made his way along the landing in search of Maia with no specific plan in mind, but had seized the opportunity provided by her abductor. It was said the queen of Anne's did not offer up her girls for a tup'peny tup; gentlemen frequenting her establishment were expected to pay handsomely for the privilege, but in return the range of delights on offer was limited only by the participant's imagination, or purse. Repugnant as the notion might be, Cosmo hoped Queen Anne's would buy him some time.

Maia's abductor was not alone in his pursuit of carnal pleasure, as the shouts and laughter from beyond the chamber door attested. The bedchamber latch rattled furiously, as one of the drunken men stumbled to his own room.

A slurred voice wheedled. "Wench, open the door, there's a good gel- d'ye hear, open the door -" It was not Maia's abductor, for the voice was of a much older man.

"This room is occupied, seek your pleasure elsewhere and leave me to mine," growled the duke, in fine imitation of the inebriated interloper, who with a sense of hopeful anticipation, had happened upon the locked chamber by chance.

As the man's footsteps trailed disconsolately away, the duke wasted no more time and raising the sash window overlooking the rear of the premises, thrust his head and shoulders over the low sill, looking into the cobbled yard below.

Beyond the yard came the familiar whinnying of the horses from the stables, however, the crowds of new arrivals had dispersed, seeking lodging, ale, or companionship of one sort or another, leaving an assortment of gigs resting forlornly upon their shafts.

The yard was lit by lanterns providing murky pools of light in their immediate vicinity, but they could not penetrate the into night beyond their reach, forcing Cosmo to strain to see anything in the darkness. His relief at hearing the approach of horses, their hooves echoing upon the cobbles, was palpable, as his travelling-chaise drew up in the deserted yard, his horse securely tied behind. Seated primly a-top, beside the sturdy Yaxley, Watton searched for some clue as to his employer's whereabouts, for the letter delivered into his hands at the Bushel Inn, by a disreputable old man, had not been particularly informative, or clean.

Although the duke was silhouetted against the flickering candlelight in the window, it took strenuous waving and hissing before he was able to attract Watton's attention. It took the mystified valet what seemed like an age to clamber cautiously onto the cobbles and fastidiously picked his way across the muck laden yard, until he stood directly beneath the chamber window. Cosmo was forced to learn perilously out of the window in order to whisper impromptu instructions to the incredulous man, who swallowed hard at the directions, not daring to argue with his noble employer.

All-in-all, Watton considered, blanching at what was expected of him, staying put at The Bushel would have been the lesser of the two evils, even if the prospect of a noisy evening filled with the sounds of revellers enjoying a cockfight was not entirely palatable. But it was too late for that now.

Withdrawing into the chamber, the duke helped the unsteady Maia to her feet, fixated with the shadows flickering upon the ceiling cast by the smoky, guttering candles. She had been oblivious to his hissed conversation with his valet.

"Look," she murmured, touching his face with her hand, she directed his gaze upwards. "See them dance- do you dance?"

"Not, if I can avoid it," came the crushing reply. But to no purpose, as continuing to be mesmerised by the leaping rivalries of darkness and light, Maia gave audience to visions Bradenham could only imagine, further intensifying his urge to choke the life from her abductor.

While manoeuvring the befuddled girl to the open window was not difficult when her attention remained transfixed upon the fluttering shadows, but for all her dreaminess, getting her to clamber under the raised sash through the open window was quite another matter. He straddled the sill, one booted foot firmly planted upon the chamber floor and took Maia's hand.

"It is important you to do all I ask."

Maia blinked, but said nothing.

"Can you do that?"

Miss Hindolveston nodded, her dark curls bouncing.

"Come, I am going to help you to climb down."

Taking her by the hand, Cosmo drew Maia towards the open window, but despite his matter-of-fact approach, she pulled her fingers from his grasp and began to back away from him towards the bed, her bewilderment apparent. The duke climbed back into the bedchamber and, with his hands outstretched, took a step towards the bed, urging Maia to come to him, wondering how he was to get the girl to safety if she refused to comply.

Almost too late, he realised, that in her witless condition Maia misunderstood his intent, and he hastily took a step back, allowing more space between them.

He pointed down to the yard below, explaining gently, "Look, there is my carriage, do you see?"

Warily curious, Maia stood on tiptoe, that she might see the carriage without stepping closer to him, and straining to see, caught sight of movement in one of the chaise's windows, palely illuminated by a lantern hanging from the inn wall.

She was puzzled by this and enquired, "Is someone there?"

The duke, relieved that a new claim had been made upon Maia's wandering attention, affirmed. "Your maid has come to join you, you must climb down to her."

As if the preposterous suggestion were the most normal thing in the world, Maia nodded obligingly; her chief concern lay in how the lemonade bottle might be carried during her descent. But as she removed the bottle from the table and considered whether the small pocket in the seam of her gown might suffice, Cosmo relieved her of the noxious solution.

"Should you require a drink, I dare say we will find something to your taste once you are down, and it would be a pity to drop it in our haste."

She wrinkled her nose, looking regretfully at the bottle in his hand. "Too bitter, by far."

As he straddled the low sill, the duke was pleased to observe the dependable Yaxley had the carriage in place; in the gloom he could just discern Pigot, at the horses' heads, keeping them steady while the lad attempted to calm the thoroughbred.

With his back against the window frame, Cosmo gauged the position of the carriage; it was lower than he had anticipated, but it would have to do, he had no intention of climbing down to the curved carriage roof and attempting to catch Maia, knowing she would refuse to jump down to him. The only solution was to lower Maia into Watton's waiting arms. Even under these trying circumstances Bradenham found this amusing, although he was glad that due to their need for concealment, Watton would be reduced to mute protestations.

By leaning far over the sill, in a grave whisper the duke was able to impart to his valet the hastily improvised scheme, and despite the semi-darkness, he was sure Watton flinched at the idea of laying hands upon the person of Miss Hindolveston. However, any arguments the horrified man may have been about to utter were nipped in the bud when his employer's beaver hat unceremoniously descended from the upper window into Watton's shaking fingers.

Barker & Co., makers of fine carriages, had not anticipated the roof of their particularly magnificent travelling-chaise might one day be required to effect an escape, consequently had neglected to add such refinements as ease of access and generous footholds, a flaw which caused Watton to struggle even more than his employer had foreseen.

More at home in the duke's well-appointed dressing room than undertaking the rôle of performing acrobat, the fastidious valet slithered as he attempted to stand upright, but unable to balance he wobbled alarmingly, reluctant to unbend his knocking knees.

"Hell's teeth man, stand up!" Exhorted his employer, watching Watton's antics with misgivings. "You will never reach her hunched over like that."

To the valet's credit he did not respond as he might have wished, but holding his tongue, swayed unsteadily as he stood a fraction taller, his knees locked in a half-standing, half-crouching position; whether at this moment he was reconsidering his future in the duke's employ was not apparent.

Satisfied that Watton was as close to being in place as was likely, Cosmo turned his attention to Maia, and, having secured the loose wrapping upon her hand hoping the wound would not be put under too much duress, he drew her to sit beside him upon the sill. Maia seemed to be unaware of either her change in position - from standing to sitting - or the duke's skills as a nursemaid; she had been trying to catch a glimpse of her maid in the carriage below, although in her current rather muddled state she was under the impression that Love had come to see the miraculous dancing shadows upon the ceiling. How the lady's maid-in-training was to gain access to the chamber, Maia knew not, for there was a chair blocking access to the doorway. Overwhelmed by the conundrum she sighed.

It was clear Maia was not going to play an active rôle in her rescue, and having no desire to risk an argument by trying to get her to comply, the duke took the girl by the waist. He had not expected to find his face buried in her curly hair, nor could he have predicted that when surrounded by the trailing tendrils he would breathe deeply; but as the silken corkscrews attached themselves to his unshaven face, Cosmo knew he would live to regret the indulgence.

Before she could object, he gathered her legs and skirts and lifted them over the sill, so that Maia was seated with her back to the chamber, her legs through the open window, the duke's arms firmly around her slender waist.

"I am going to lower you down to your maid. Do you understand?"

"Yes, that she may see the shadows too?"

While Bradenham had no idea to what Maia was referring, of one thing he was certain; that seated upon their precarious perch was neither the time nor the place to discover where her muddled mind had wandered.

"I shall take your arms and lower you down, we must be very quiet so that you may surprise her. My valet will catch you, so there is no need to be afraid."

Maia snorted scornfully, offering a tantalisingly brief glimpse of the real Maia Hindolveston: "I am never afraid." But, being scrupulously honest, even when held in the clinging arms of 'La Fée Verte', she added, "except for spiders, I do not care for spiders." Reminded of her dislike she shuddered violently in Cosmo's encircling embrace, threatening their collective equilibrium one way or another. It was he decided; more than enough.

With a firm hold of the girl's waist, the duke knelt beside the open window. Swiftly and without warning, giving Maia no time to react or resist, he took her weight in his arms, allowing her to slowly slide through his hands until he was holding the girl firmly by her wrists, her legs dangling above Watton's bobbing head.

A-top the slippery carriage roof the valet was trying to maintain his balance while averting his eyes from the shocking sight of Miss Hindolveston's underskirts and waving, stocking-clad legs.

"Watton ..." hissed the duke urgently. "Look what you are about - bloody catch her man."

Despite being slender, not only was Maia tall, but at that moment she was also a dead-weight as Bradenham dangled her through the open window, so it was with relief that he saw Watton reach up and hesitantly grasp hold of Maia's swinging legs, for with his muscles locked and leaning as far out of the window as he dared, the duke had been terrified lest he drop the girl.

Secure in the knowledge that his man had her, Cosmo allowed Maia to slip slowly through his fingers until she landed with a muffled thud, a flurry of skirts, a ripple of dark tresses and a muffled exclamation, upon the shocked valet.

With no time to ease his aching arms, the duke clambered over the sill, careful to ensure that the sash-window slid closed behind him; he had no desire to make Maia's way of escape obvious. Grasping the edge of the sill was both tricky and painful, but as he was about to drop onto roof of the travelling-chaise, to his dismay, it began to move.

The hired horses had not taken kindly to the late-night sojourn and as Watton had clambered onto the roof of the carriage, had grown increasingly skittish. The arrival of a passenger falling from the skies had unnerved them so thoroughly that Pigot, who had been holding their heads, had a job to steady them. He too had been somewhat distracted by Miss Hindolveston's startling and wholly undignified arrival, and it took him some moments to gain possession of his wits and bring the horses and carriage under control. Meanwhile, from the box upon the travelling-chaise, Yaxley murmured soothing sounds at the duke's thoroughbred as it sidled nervously, neglected by the wide-eyed and open-mouthed stable-lad, who was agog to see a lady descending in such an unexpected manner.

With the carriage steadied, Watton belatedly comprehended the pressing need to clear the way for his employer's imminent arrival, and closing his eyes as if to disassociate himself with the distasteful business, heaved the lady aside, as Cosmo dropped, landing neatly beside the wriggling turmoil of legs, hair and underskirts that was Maia Hindolveston.

Greatly relieved to relinquish the care of Miss Hindolveston into the duke's capable hands, Watton slid recklessly from the sloping carriage roof and scuttled back to his seat beside Yaxley, who would never view the valet in quite the same way again. Thus it was left to Comso to disentangle Maia from the yards of muslin which threatened to engulf her. Indeed, he had almost succeeded when the sound of approaching footsteps upon the cobbles caused him to halt, knowing that the slightest movement would attract unwelcome attention, and Maia was in no position to be discovered at this juncture. Come to that, neither was he.

He placed a hand over her mouth to ensure she made no noise, and did his best to hide Maia's disarrayed white underskirts beneath his dark coat and breeches, although this meant that he was all but lying upon the girl. Miss Hindolvston's outrage at this indignity was palpable.

The owner of the heavy footfalls echoing around the stable yard walked with deliberation across the cobbles and proceeded to relieve himself against the against the wall. While perched upon the coachman's box, Watton sat bolt upright, as if his demeanour alone could detract from the farce being played out a-top the carriage.

With the ostensible purpose his visit to the stable-yard completed, the man paused and peered up at the roof of the travelling-chaise, allowing Bradenham to distinguish the wrinkled features of the old man for whom he had procured the porter, the same old man who had delivered the duke's hastily scrawled missive to Watton at the Bushel Inn, instructing the valet to bring the carriage to the yard of the Waggon and Horses.

"I can see yer busy," the disreputable fellow announced blithely, "but the gel's gent is on 'is way back, 'e's a-talkin' with another gent down the street." With that he doffed his battered hat respectfully in the duke's direction, as if gentlemen indecorously arranged with young ladies upon the roofs of travelling-chaises were a common sight, then stumped his way back to the front of the inn.

The lady, having had enough of the large, stifling hand, bit it with remarkable thoroughness.

"Oww …!" the duke exclaimed, hastily withdrawing his smarting hand.

Maia lifted her chin defiantly, asserting, "I could not breathe."

"Your continued ability to converse rather undermines your argument," retorted Cosmo dryly, his face but a hand's breadth from the belligerent Miss Hindolveston's. A furious wriggle from the girl reminded him that not only was she still pinned beneath him, but that from his perspective the situation was far more dangerous than he had first comprehended, prompting him to hastily remove himself from the hazard.

The duke's hand was still smarting as he settled himself in a corner of his carriage, the oval bite mark across his palm with each tooth perfectly imprinted - his reward for the day's hardships. However, while appreciation for his considerable efforts might to be in short supply, Maia was delighted to be reunited with her maid, even if the bewildered Lovelace could not make head-nor-tail of anything Maia related, but listened wide-eyed, making the appropriate noises of interest and wonder when she deemed it necessary. Therefore, despite the distinct lack of promised lemonade, Maia was well-pleased, although still rather inebriated.

With its occupants hidden from view behind the closed blinds, Yaxley drove slowly from the stable yard, under orders not to draw further attention to the already unusual sight of a magnificent travelling-chaise, emblazoned with a ducal coat of arms, departing from a less than salubrious inn, during the middle of the night, with a thoroughbred high-stepping behind.

***

Well-satisfied with his evening, Maia's abductor strolled towards the Waggon and Horses, with no purpose in mind other than the manner in which he would bring the task he had undertaken to its conclusion. His progress was arrested upon the inn's cobbles when he was hailed by a gentleman whom he recognised as an acquaintance. It was he considered a happy coincidence, as ever luck favoured him.

They spoke of horses, of the runners in the Second Spring Race, the state of the appalling roads from London to Newmarket, and of mutual acquaintances, before the gentleman bemoaned the lack of congenial female company to be found before such race meetings.

"Naturally, all the tastiest morsels are tied up in London,

being paraded before eligible parti and kept well away from gentlemen of our ilk," he sighed.

Maia's abductor smirked knowingly, "Not all."

Incredulously his acquaintance enquired, "Have you a bit o'muslin tucked away somewhere?"

Not foolish enough to believe good fortune was sufficient to secure the ultimate victory in this particular quest, but assured of his own cunning, the abductor did not waste the opportunity to establish and confirm Miss Hindolveston's downfall, and to promote his own distinctly dubious reputation.

He chuckled. "Not just a bit o'muslin as you so delightfully put it, for the lady is no Cyprian, but you must hold me excused, she awaits my company and I … " he licked his lips as if savouring the prospect, "… am anticipating hers."

Much impressed, his acquaintance declared. "A lady! Well done old boy!" As an afterthought placed an eager hand upon the abductor's sleeve, "I do not suppose- I mean to say- when you have finished?"

Maia's abductor smiled unpleasantly, his thin lips contracting tightly over his teeth. "My dear fellow, I intend to keep the lady occupied all night." With a nod to his acquaintance he elbowed his way through the men thronging about the inn's doorway and disappeared from view.

With no reason to question the condition of the bedchamber door, which from the outside certainly looked intact, Maia's abductor was unaware the door had been tampered with, and the chair Bradenham had wedged to keep the two halves together served its purpose. So well had the duke secured the two halves, that even when the man turned the key in the lock and lifted the latch, he failed to notice the splintered boards. It was only when the door did not yield to his touch that he encountered the obstructing chair.

An unsteady reveller staggering along the landing paused to watch in amusement as Maia's abductor struggled to push open the bedchamber door. He enquired sympathetically "Reluctant filly is she?"

Maia's abductor ignored him, calling out as encouragingly as he could manage, through gritted teeth, "My love, you are wise to take precautions in such a place as this, but 'tis only I, let me in my dear."

Not taken in for one moment, the drunken reveller laughed and called out to the unseen woman he believed had locked the door upon her amour. "Be a good gel m'dear and let him in, it don't do to keep a man standin' on ceremony!" He roared appreciatively at his own wit, clapped the abductor on the back, and resumed his swaying progress towards his own chamber, saying encouragingly, "I hope the filly sees you across the finish line before the night is done."

The gentleman was forced to wait until the stumbling footsteps had receded before he could resume his attempt to access the chamber, and as the chair slid away under his forceful shoves and the two halves of the door came apart in his hands, horrified he stepped around the fractured sides of the split wood and into the chamber. It was empty but for two tallow candles on the deal table, both burning low in their dull brass holders, each surrounded by a pool of stinking, melted fat.

Wheeling round the gentleman began to search for Maia, not that the room afforded many hiding places and, having lifted the stained cover and looked beneath the wooden bed frame, it was clear that the girl had gone. He struggled to comprehend what had happened; for the door had been locked and no one knew where Miss Hindolveston was concealed. Nor was she in any state to summon assistance, of that he was sure.

He attempted to reassemble the splintered door, that he might understand the events leading to the girl's flight, but lacking the duke's height and strength, the abductor struggled to manage the unwieldy halves. Confused he realised that the chair had to have been placed against the door from the inside, thus the damned girl had been in the chamber in order to do so, but the knowledge brought no clarity and he sucked his narrow moustache meditatively.

A glance down into the empty stable yard offered no insights, for the creature could not have jumped, not without breaking a leg, or perhaps even her neck; besides the window was closed with not so much as gap left open to allow the stench of the tallow candles to escape. Sitting upon the bed the gentleman tried to make sense of it. However, for the present at least, his luck - as well as his insights - had run out. As unlikely as it might seem, the damnable Miss Hindolveston had indeed vanished.

Chapter Twenty

The lurching coach ground to a halt, one wheel lodged in a pothole, forcing it to lean precariously to one side. The shrouding darkness was almost as impenetrable outside as it was within the carriage.

While relieved at the respite from the chaise's jolting, with more concern for his guest's well-being beyond their immediate comfort and, fearing the possibility of robbery, the duke removed the pistol from the pocket concealed against the squabs. However, far from a band of murderous cut-throats, the perfunctory knock upon the carriage door revealed his own valet, who had not expected his employer to be thus armed and was naturally rather taken aback to find himself staring into the barrel of a travelling-pistol, even one so finely decorated.

The survival of the party's only means of illumination was by no means certain, as the quivering lantern in Watton's hand shook, and it seemed the guttering flame was in grave danger of being extinguished. However, being a man who believed in maintaining his composure, no matter how trying the circumstances, instead of following his impulse to throw the lantern into the air and, shrieking, run to safety, the valet stood his ground.

Despite being muffled in a great coat and scarf, Watton was chilled to the bone and thoroughly miserable; the fact that he did not wait for his employer to speak first to enquire why they had stopped, testimony to the depth of the valet's distress.

"Your Grace, Yaxley asks if you might reconsider and allow us to turn back to Newmarket."

Although Watton had been overjoyed not to spend the night at the Bushel Inn, he considered this foray through the darkness to be decidedly ill advised, not to mention slow-going. Every muddy puddle and rut in the road were cause for concern, lest one of the hired horses should miss its footing, or the coach lose a wheel. While for all their gleaming brass, the carriage-lamps cast barely enough light to justify their upkeep. Indeed, the valet would gladly have delivered his employers deep purse upon a salver into Trunch's grasping hands, than have to endure one more terrifying mile, anticipating certain death at the hands of footpads, or a broken neck from tumbling into a ditch.

Roused from her waking dreams, Maia sat up and blinked in the unaccustomed lamplight, wondering why the sun seemed to be bobbing upon he end of a staff. While thoroughly bored with their flight from Newmarket, her maid was curled in a ball, wedged securely in a corner of the carriage. With her cloak wrapped about her, Love snored gently, her mouth open, unaware of the carriage's lurching halt, or the unnerved thoroughbred's whinnies of consternation, causing the valet to feel disproportionately annoyed that she could sleep in relative comfort, whilst he was being jolted to the bone and cold to boot.

"Where are we, exactly?" Cosmo had tried to keep track of their progress, but the carriage's lowered shutters and the all-encompassing dark meant that once beyond Newmarket he could not have said with any degree of certainty where they were.

The valet relayed the enquiry to Yaxley, seated high upon the box. The reply was terse and audible only to Watton and the duke, for somewhat preoccupied, Maia was staring at Watton trying to recall where she had met him. However, with the incident upon the carriage roof uncomfortably fresh in his mind, the valet preferred to busy himself with the lamp, rather than meet the lady's eye.

The tidings were not auspicious, for despite the fact that Miss Hindolveston was safe, with her maid in attendance - for propriety's demanding sake -, they could hardly spend the remainder of the night by the wayside in the middle of Cambridgeshire. They must reach somewhere by sun-up where due ceremony could be restored to the party without too many questions being asked.

The cause of the day's upheaval yawned. "Where did the driver say we are?"

"Bottisham -" Bradenham repeated brusquely.

"Oh." Maia considered his response, then echoed vaguely, "Bottisham." Frowning, she repeated, 'Bottisham' again, as if the word had significance beyond being their current location, then announced, "my god-mother lives in Stow-cum-Quy."

Upon receiving no reaction to this statement, she clarified in a long-suffering tone, as if pained by the duke's apparent obtuseness. "Stow-cum-Quy, near Bottisham."

This was the straw Cosmo had been hoping for and he clutched at it gratefully. "Your god-mama?"

Maia appeared to be bored with the conversation, but explained as best she could, given her spinning head. "She is mama's dearest friend, and is god-mama to us all."

To be god-mama to all seven sisters seemed to be taking devotion to friendship to extremes; it was bad enough dealing with but one Hindolveston. It was to be hoped that Maia's mama had possessed the good sense to pick a docile woman to stand as god-mother to her numerous daughters.

"Is she the sort of women who would be shocked should you arrive unannounced upon her doorstep in the middle of the night?"

Maia looked scornful, "Of course I would be announced, her butler is most particular."

Cosmo rejoined icily. "That was not what I meant."

Maia leant against the squabs, closed her eyes and rested her head upon the shoulder of her sleeping maid.

"Maia, are you listening to me?"

"Mmm ..." came the dreamy response.

"Wake up Maia, this is important. Can your god-mother be trusted to hold her tongue, or is she liable to cause a scandal?"

Without opening her eyes and apparently oblivious to the gravity of the situation, Maia murmured disapprovingly. "You have an unhealthy preoccupation with scandal."

Believing the likelihood of further coherent communication with Miss Hindolveston was highly improbable, the duke turned to Watton, who had observed the exchange with some degree of awe, having never before been party to such casual treatment of his esteemed employer.

"You heard Miss Hindolveston, we hasten to Stow-cum-Quy."

The valet hesitated. "Your Grace, may I enquire how Yaxley will know the house?"

As if to undermine the duke's summation of her current mental capacity, Maia responded laconically, "On the Lode Road. Big black gates with a gatehouse. Fenmere Park ... " before subsiding into a fitful sleep.

"Big black gates," reiterated Cosmo, rather more gleefully than he felt.

"Thank you your Grace, miss," Watton gave a deferential bow, which was slightly marred by the gust of wind which caught the carriage door, closing it more firmly than might be considered to be courteous; at least it was to be hoped it was due to the night breeze, rather than a rather than a manifestation of the valet's pique.

As the carriage lurched on its way, the duke settled as best he could. He had not envisaged the possibility of turning to Maia's relatives for assistance, and the notion was not a comfortable one. With no indication of what sort of woman this god-mother might be, Cosmo could only hope she would not prove to be a blue-stocking, who eschewed male-company, or worse, asked impossibly pertinent questions of the variety he preferred not to answer.

Yet another rut jolted carriage's occupants, banging the duke's head forcefully against the window-frame, and as he rubbed his aching forehead he hoped Percy was utterly miserable.

Chapter Twenty-One

The Dowager Duchess of Alconbury was unable to sleep, not that such an inconvenience perturbed her unduly, having discovered upon the untimely death of her beloved duke, ten years previously, that sleep could be an elusive bedfellow.

However, being a woman who disliked boredom, rather than await the slow passing of wakeful hours filled with melancholy, Caroline preferred to read; write letters to her numerous god-children; play the spinet; draw, or - when the whim took her - to entertain. Her liaisons were so discreet that no-one other than the participant ever knew with any degree of certainty with whom she had conducted an affair. Whether her conquests included within their envied ranks men possessing position and wealth, or merely wit and intellect, only Caro was aware, for the elite group remained ignorant of each others' identity. Perhaps, more importantly, upon the conclusion of the liaison her lovers always remained on amicable terms with the dowager, who never alluded to former paramours and never made comparisons.

Having returned late that afternoon from a gruelling stay with her daughter, whom a month previously had been brought to bed of a large, bawling son, the dowager was enjoying the blissful solitude of her own company. It had been a difficult time, and Caroline had almost lost her beloved only-child; had she done so not even her red-faced, screaming grandson would have proved sufficient consolation. Happily Charlotte had recovered from the ordeal, while having been duly admired, the child, still screaming, had been entrusted into the care of his nurse. It was as well his sire's country seat was a sprawling one, with nurseries sensibly situated some distance from the parental apartments.

Perhaps her own experience had coloured the dowager duchess's views of childbirth, she had not had an easy time during the long trial of Charlotte's birth, and her beloved husband had paced, ashen faced, watching the sun rise and set twice, before being regretfully advised by the physician that the duchess had produced only a daughter.

The duke however, was overjoyed that both his wife and child had survived not only the hazardous ordeal, but the equally perilous ministrations of the doctor. For the regret it transpired, was that of the physician, whose clumsy care had greatly contributed to Caroline's suffering, and ensured that the duchess would produce no more offspring, certainly not the son the good doctor assumed the duke was honour bound to sire. His Grace was not a man to bargain with God in vain, and having prayed ceaselessly for the safety of his adored wife, had no wish be rid of her, not even for a son.

The ton had watched agog, as the duke made provision to place all of his un-entailed property, incomes and investments in his wife's name; advice was sought and taken and the ensuing document was drawn up with all due ceremony; his Grace making sure the witnessed deed was indisputable. This done, the duke continued to invest, speculate and accumulate with renewed enthusiasm, so that upon his sudden death, when their daughter was but ten years old, the new dowager duchess discovered what her husband had gleefully informed her of on several occasions, that she was probably the wealthiest woman in England. While the news did nothing to bring back her beloved duke, Caroline was wise enough to appreciate the gift he had given her and sensible enough to enjoy it.

***

The yawning footman who sleepily unbolted the great doors of Fenmere Park, was grateful to hand the imposing figure of the Duke of Bradenham into the capable hands of the dowager duchess's equally imposing butler, who unlike the footman, had taken the time to don his breeks before leaving his chamber.

That no shadow of disapproval, or indeed any emotion flickered across the man's face, as if receiving unexpected guests in the middle of the night was a normal occurrence, should have indicated to Cosmo that Fenmere Park, was the residence of a singular woman. However preoccupied as he undoubtedly was, perhaps the oversight was understandable, although like the butler, Bradenham's demeanour gave no indication there was anything out of the ordinary about his arrival.

As if he were paying a courtesy call within the bounds of accepted society hours, he advised the butler, "Miss Hindolveston has arrived." Adding for good measure and with a touch of hauteur, "I am Bradenham."

The name was not unknown to the man, who bowed in acknowledgement of the duke's rank, "Your Grace," and departed to enquire whether the dowager was at home to the duke, accepting without question that she would be at home to Miss Hindolveston, no matter what the hour.

Left to kick his heels, Cosmo appraised the lavish surroundings, noting the fan vaulted ceiling and stained glass windows with interest and appreciation, although the obvious splendour was concerning, for he could not help thinking that impoverished gentry might have proved easier to manage. Yet Maia had anticipated no problem with their arriving in this unseemly manner. But then again, Bradenham recalled grimly, it was Maia's unseemly manners which had launched her into this disaster in the first place.

A tactful cough brought him back to earth. "Her Grace will be delighted to receive you, your Grace."

Her Grace? Unaccustomed to being at such a social disadvantage, the duke frowned; the wretched girl had failed to mention that her god-mother was a duchess. However, there was no time to dwell upon the possible ramifications of this oversight, for the butler was looking enquiringly towards the great doors, as if questioning Miss Hindolveston's presence. The duke steeled himself for the next painful chapter in this tale of woe, knowing it was not going to be easy getting Maia out of the carriage.

"Miss Hindolveston is … a little unwell," he offered vaguely. "She may need assistance."

"Indeed your Grace."

Showing no disapproval or undue judgement, the butler beckoned to the young footman yawning at the end of the vast hall, and together they hastened down the steps to the carriage. The open door revealed a wide-eyed, pale-faced Maia. Hatless, her hair resembled that of Medusa's and her walking dress was reduced to a mass of rumpled fabric; she certainly did not paint a picture of propriety, but then again Cosmo mused, propriety was hardly Maia's stock-in-trade.

Upon seeing the butler, whom she evidently recognised, she smiled beatifically, while Heydon greeted her as if there were nothing in her arrival to arouse suspicion.

"Miss Hindolveston, welcome back to Fenmere Park."

Somewhat unsteadily, Maia allowed herself to be handed down from the carriage and stumbled her way up the steps to her god-mother's house, clutching Bradenham's arm on one side, and the footman's upon the other, while the man silently vowed never again to answer the door in the middle of the night without first donning his britches. However, he had no need to be concerned, for Maia did not even notice.

***

The dowager duchess kissed her god-daughter upon the cheek, bidding her to sit down, adding, intrigued, "Before you fall down, dear."

It was all Cosmo could do not to groan aloud, for having no desire to advertise his ignorance by inquiring of her butler, he had not known the identity of 'her Grace' until he has entered the withdrawing room, and even then could scare believe his ill-luck. Caroline Alconbury was not unknown to the duke, although he had never spent time in her company, or even spoken to the woman, beyond the social niceties dictated by good manners. An oversight he regretted, for the dowager's reputation preceded her.

At forty, Caro was still an alluring woman. But it was not her looks alone which attracted the interest of the gentlemen of the ton, for all those whom the duke had heard speak of her did so with the utmost respect. Self-assured, she possessed an eloquence which was as appealing as the intelligence and humour which made her eyes sparkle, it was little wonder that men, weary of brittle beauty and empty charm, spoke highly of her. It would, Cosmo reminded himself, have been far easier to deal with the wife of a country squire than Caroline Alconbury.

With Maia safely ensconced upon the chaise-longue, the dowager regarded the duke searchingly, a glint of amusement in her eyes.

"While I am always delighted to see my god-children, am I to assume this is not merely a social visit?"

Cosmo hesitated, inhibited by the butler's continued presence, he had no desire to provide fodder for below-stairs gossip, but Caroline casually waved her guest's concern aside.

"Heydon is a trusted friend and has been in my service for more years that I care to count. You will discover my household are discreet to the point of obsession, for if one cannot be free within one's own home there is little point in residing there. You may be candid Bradenham, for I expect we shall need Heydon's invaluable assistance if we are to prevent a scandal." She paused and gazed serenely at the duke. "I take it that is why you are here."

An astute woman, she was aware this was not a comfortable position for the haughty Bradenham to find himself in; seeking assistance, shelter and guidance from someone he barely knew. It was, the dowager considered, very good for his soul.

The tale took some telling, even with the judicious omitting of some of the pertinent facts pertaining to his hounding of Maia, and the glossing over of others, for Cosmo was of the belief that he needed to make an ally of her god-mother, not an enemy. Maia herself, remained mute, half-sagging, half-reclining upon the silk covered chaise-longue, whilst the duke recounted his expurgated version of the past weeks, days and subsequent hours.

Without interrupting, or giving any indication of her thoughts as he spoke, other than to other than to give her god-daughter an occasional thoughtful glance, the dowager gave Bradenham's narrative her utmost attention, until having reached his conclusion, she announced: "It is a tale worthy of Mr Lathom himself."

Before the duke, somewhat nonplussed could respond, Caroline continued, "I take it you have not read the 'Castle of Olloda'? What a pity, I find so many gentlemen have not. Utter nonsense of course, but extremely diverting, perhaps Mr. Lewis's 'The Monk' would be more to your taste?" Her speculation in his literary interests exhausted, the dowager turned her attention upon Maia. "My love, when did you last eat?"

Cosmo was staggered; what the devil was wrong with the woman? Here he was doing his damnedest to avert a catastrophe, and all she could do was to enquire about inconsequential nonsense.

"At breakfast, but it does seem a dreadfully long time ago," Maia responded wistfully, her voice shaky with exhaustion.

Eyeing the duke critically as he leant against the marble fireplace, the dowager stated censoriously, "Hindolveston girls are made of sterner stuff than this, but no doubt her spirits will revive once she had eaten. I am amazed you did not consider it."

Feeling thoroughly reproved, Bradenham held his tongue; while he had enjoyed mugs of ale and such delicacies as might be hastily snatched along the way, Maia had not been so fortunate. Indeed her only fortification had been intended to be the means to her undoing.

"It is high time you went to your bedchamber my love, please do not bother to ague, for it is entirely pointless. I expect Miss Maia's belongings have been taken to the usual chamber, Heydon?" So saying Caro took her god-daughter by the hands and raised the drooping girl to her feet, adding as an afterthought, "I assume Maia does have belongings with her?"

The duke nodded, wondering how the wretched woman had so quickly managed to gain the upper hand, clearly the dowager's reputation - sterling though it may be - had not done her justice.

However, blithely unaware her character was undergoing such scrutiny, Caroline continued, "In that case my dear, Knapton will bathe your poor sore head and help you to bed, your hand may require some attention too. Heydon, please see that a tray is taken up to my god-daughter's chamber, something warm I think." Wrinkling her nose as she thought, she added, "and easy to eat. Maia, I will be up to say goodnight to you shortly, but despite the hour, may I remind you that you must be ready to leave for church in good time tomorrow?" And kissing the girl upon the cheek, the dowager dismissed her into Heydon's capable hands.

As the door closed behind the departing figures, the dowager duchess sat upon her chair beside the fireplace and gazed quizzically at the duke, who was clearly irritated by what he considered to be a frivolous response to the dire situation.

"I hardly think Maia's attendance at church is a high priority, madam."

Caroline was not intimidated by the man, no matter how he might seethe with righteous indignation. Well-used to the attempted manipulations and undermining by men of power she waited, knowing there would be more ire to come, before the duke was ready to listen to reason and wise council.

"It is nonsensical to pack Maia off to her bedchamber, when we have yet to decide upon a plan of action. I have too much at stake to allow all my efforts to have been for naught." Cosmo paused, waiting for an apology.

"Indeed?" The dowager's response was frigidly polite. "Yet you have overlooked one small detail, if Maia is seen by my side tomorrow morning at St. Mary's, it will be assumed she returned with me from sojourning at the home of my daughter, thus with no effort we will have established an alibi. Indeed, with her whereabouts duly vouched for by the priest, there will be no need for further explanation, and the only other authority interested parties will be able to question will be the Almighty himself."

Caro's green eyes flashed at Bradenham, irritated by his lack of foresight. "You will get no sense out of Maia this night, she is clearly exhausted. Good heavens man, you say she has been hit over the head and stolen from her home; drugged by some hellish wormwood concoction. She has been certainly been half-starved, and was to be raped, before you dropped her out of a window. And if that were not enough, she has been driven through the night. Yet you wonder at my sending the girl to bed? Your cousin will not thank you if his bride-to-be is witless before she has a chance to repeat her vows." If anything, the duke's countenance grew grimmer than before, but ignoring his thunderous expression, Caroline Alconbury continued. "After we have made our Sunday come-out before the clergy, will be time enough to make arrangements. Maia will not be able to travel before the morning." Sighing, she exclaimed crossly, "Such is the inequality which exists between man and woman, for while we must awaken early and appear in our church finery, you may lie-abed as you will and partake of a peaceful breakfast unencumbered by such niceties."

Rising, the dowager eyed Cosmo thoughtfully, then murmured almost to herself, "But perhaps Bradenham, when all is taken into account your position is not to be envied, after all."

With this she inclined her head, and the duke found himself being shepherded from the salon by the impassive Heydon, who saw to it that his Grace had all he required to ensure his stay at Fenmere Park, was as comfortable as possible. Inexplicably, Cosmo had never felt more uncomfortable in his life.

Chapter Twenty-Two

Awaking in the familiar splendour of a chamber she had known since childhood, Maia could not imagine what had disturbed her, until she caught sight of Love peering at her from behind the bed-curtains.

"Love! What on earth are you doing?" She spoke more sharply than she intended, but it had been a trying night, after a trying day.

The maid jumped and gave a squeal. "Sorry miss, but I was tryin' to get a look-see at that bump on yer 'ead."

Lifting her hand from beneath the warmth of the bedclothes, Maia touched the tender wound on her temple, wincing slightly she sat up. "Does it look shocking?"

Love shook her head vehemently, doing her best to reassure her mistress. "Not so bad as what it were last night, last night yer looked fair milled, like a side o'mutton."

While her description might have embellished the truth and was certainly far from flattering, it could not be denied that the ministrations of Caroline's housekeeper had proven beneficial. Mrs Knapton had insisted on bathing Maia's head, cleaning her hair and the wound, before she would permit the exhausted girl to retire for the night. Too weary to object, Maia had submitted with a docility the Duke of Bradenham would have found astounding.

Scrambling from the bed to stand before the looking-glass, Maia surveyed the damage. Yet despite the wound to her head being minor, the swelling remained noticeable which, together with the bruise and abrasion, did nothing to improve either Maia's frame of mind or, as far as she was concerned, her looks. It was bad enough to have endured the indignities of the previous day; how she was ever going to be able to look Mr. Watton in the eye, she did not know. But to be forced to rise from one's bed after a legion of ordeals, and to have to attend church as if nothing had happened, was the outside of enough. Now there was the added obstacle of explaining the injury to her head.

Love peeped around Maia's arm as she glared grimly at her reflection.

"You know miss, if we was to shape yer hair a bit different and yer was to wear that straw bonnet, the one what matches the blue pelisse, no one 'ud notice it."

Maia mulled the suggestion over, as Lovelace continued, "An' the gloves is loose enough to slip over that bandage, if we trims it a bit."

Having forgotten her hand, which she became aware was still sore, doubtless being dangled through the window of the inn had not contributed to its healing, Maia poked experimentally at the loose wrapping covering the wound.

While encouraged at not being met with resistance, which was unusual when dealing with the Hindolveston sisters, Love continued, "An' that new pelisse looks a treat miss."

Thusly attired, Maia awaited her god-mother in the hall, as was the custom at Fenmere Park on Sunday mornings; the dowager preferring to breakfast quietly alone with a book and coffee, to bright conversation over ham - or worse still - sweet chocolate served in bed.

The redoubtable Mrs Knapton, the dowager's housekeeper, had dispatched to Maia's chamber a tray of breakfast fare she considered suitable for a young lady who had suffered a severe ordeal, although it had been met with a disparaging sniff by the lady who deemed it food fit only for an invalid. However, despite long held reservations regarding coddled eggs and thinly sliced bread, Maia had enjoyed the light repast far more than if had she been forced to face a hearty meal in the sole company of the duke, which she believed would be sufficient to ruin even the most determined appetite.

Stepping from the last stair, the dowager beamed approvingly at her god-daughter. "You look much better my dear. Did you sleep well?"

Maia confirmed that, given the circumstances, she had passed a far better night than she might have expected.

"I expect you were exhausted, but let us not dawdle for it would not do to be late. Where I wonder, have I put my ...?" Caro looked about vaguely. "Winch, you think of everything," she addressed her lady's maid, who with an expert eye had located the dowager's missing prayer book even before her noble employer discovered it was missing.

Handing the well-worn volume to the dowager, Winch primly tweaked the collar of Caroline's pelisse before possessively removed an infinitesimal speck of dust from her bonnet, while Caro waited meekly for the indomitable Winch to finish her ministrations - like a child being made ready by her nursemaid. Maia could only hope that Love would not get any ideas, for she could see the maid hovering at the head of the stairs avidly taking in every detail.

***

The duke had been surprised to discover he was to breakfast alone; for having expected to see either or both ladies, he had planned his arguments accordingly. Despite his disappointment he managed to do justice to the dishes on offer, returning to the sideboard several times to refill his plate, much to the gratification of her Grace's cook, who enjoying a culinary challenge had set to work to entice the unexpected male appetite, with a will.

He was tempted to lurk in the hall in an attempt to waylay Maia before she left for the church, but having no desire to instigate what was bound to degenerate into a heated discussion, Cosmo betook himself to the library where he passed a quiet hour gazing out of windows at the garden and great park beyond, although the pastoral scene did nothing to improve his temper.

***

Despite the undeniable luxury of the Alconbury chaise, Maia was ill at ease. For although Love's careful arrangement of her hair covered the deepening bruise and angry abrasion on her forehead, it was not a natural style nor, as far as Maia was concerned, was it attractive; requiring numerous hair pins which poked relentlessly. To make matters worse the deep brim of her silk and straw bonnet, intended to shield the wound, was horribly restrictive and Maia longed to tear it off and have a really good scratch.

Surreptitiously reaching a tentative finger under the brim of her bonnet, Maia moved her hair aside the better to feel her temple, observed by her god-mother who was seated upon the deep squabs on the opposite side of the chaise.

"My dear, I feel sure you do not need me to remind you that it would be preferable not to draw attention to your head, pretty though it may be." Adding sotto voce, "Nagging is so dull for both parties."

Maia withdrew her hand and sighed, waiting for the inquisition she knew must surely follow. She had been apprehensive about the drive to the church, for the dowager duchess had excellent timing and rarely made the mistake of rushing things. In Caroline's case biding her time invariably yielded results, and Maia had known that once they were alone in the chaise there would be no wriggling out of answering difficult questions. Yet for all her concerns, the ride was more than half over and still the subject of the long-gallery had not been broached, although Caro must surely have heard the gossip which the duke claimed was already the talk of the ton. Nor had the dowager enquired of her involvement with the wretched Bradenham.

Such suspense was not adding to her comfort, and Maia had almost convinced herself that it would be less painful to introduce the difficult subject herself, when her god-mother spoke.

"Once we arrive, leave the talking to me my love, you are a shocking dissimulator, although I dare say you have improved since last I saw you. Nevertheless, I believe it would be preferable for you to play the rôle of demure maiden, no matter how difficult you may find it." Her green eyes twinkled with amusement. "We can always put your reticence down to an affliction of the heart."

Maia ignored this remark, enquiring, "What story are you going to tell them?"

Her god-mother looked smug. "Story? No story is necessary my love. I shall simply permit them to draw their own conclusions and having done so, shall leave them in ignorance of the real facts, so much tidier than an outright lie."

"Where will they conclude I have been?"

"Do not be witless my dear, naturally people will assume you have been with me, visiting your god-sister and your god-nephew."

"Is there such a relationship as that of god-nephew?"

"My love, you are being difficult," Caro pointed out mildly.

"If I am asked for my opinion of the new viscount how should I reply?"

The dowager looked thoughtful. "Perhaps in this case honesty is not the best policy, for the poor child is decidedly ugly; rather red and makes far more noise than one would expect from one so young, and I confess to having grave misgivings about his ears. However, it would be fair to describe him as taking after his sire's side of the family, and that is how I shall describe him. At least until he is out of leading strings, by which time he will doubtless have progressed to being a fully-fledged hell-born babe. One can only hope his parents will contrive to provide him with several siblings, although that might prove risky, for they might all turn out like little Ingham. But perhaps he will outgrow it. Now, quickly my love, give your cheeks a pinch for we are here and you are still dreadfully pale."

Pressing her lips together to suppress her giggles. As the five bells rang a joyful peal from the bell tower, Maia obediently pinched the roses back into her cheeks, and followed her god-mother down the chaise steps.

The nave of the parish church was thronged with an eclectic

mix of inhabitants from Stow-cum-Quy, and its outlying farms and hamlets who, although parting for the dowager to pass, nevertheless slowed her progress to the Alconbury pew, as she paused to make polite enquiries into such matters as ailments, crops and the condition of a prize pig. Following in her wake Maia did her best to look as if she had not been kidnapped, drugged, rescued and was, unless she was very much mistaken, about to be married against her wishes to man for whom she felt nothing. All things considered, it was an admirable performance.

With its beautifully intoned liturgy, the Eucharist was the service Maia most enjoyed when visiting St. Mary's, particularly when the parish priest kept the sermon mercifully brief. Today was such an occasion, for Mr Chedgrave was a man who liked to get to the point; having more elevated matters upon his theological mind than the sound of his own voice. Yet what the sermon lacked in loquaciousness, it made up for in convolution, and Maia's was not the only mind to wander.

The uncomfortable suspicion that the duke might be right, had grown steadily from an insidious whisper to a roar Maia could no longer ignore. If she were to be the target of every rake, cad or roué, her life would hardly be worth a straw. She could not expect Bradenham to dash to her aid every time she was hit over the head and carried off, particularly when his only interest in her was to ensure she was leg-shackled to his cousin. Once the duke accepted that she had no intention of marrying Mr Siddenham, he would have no reason to protect her virtue. Maia gave a shudder, not wishing to think what might have occurred had Bradenham, not unceremoniously dropped her from the window of the Waggon and Horses.

Her meditations were interrupted by a sharp elbow from the dowager, who had been trying to catch her god-daughter's attention, and jolted back to the present Maia quickly deposited the coins she had been clutching into the offertory plate held before her by the shaking hand of the verger.

During what was left of the service, Maia attempted to focus upon Mr Chedgrave. But dropping her hymn book twice and her book of Common Prayer once, she was forced to wonder if the blow to her head had caused more damage than just discomfiture. The notion that she might be rendered as clumsy as her sister Cela, whom it was said could not keep hold of anything for more than a few moments without dripping, spilling or breaking it, was worrisome.

Knowing the arrival of her grandson had garnered much interest, Caro did not hurry to leave the church following the dismissal, but sat as if in silent contemplation, allowing the parishioners to congregate around the church door; wisely delaying her exit that she might answer questions only once, yet be heard by many, while Maia went to inspect the brass beneath the cancel arch, depicting Sir John Anstey and his 16 offspring.

It was to Maia's great sorrow that Sir John's poor wife Johanna, was almost completely obliterated from the brass, believing that the lady must have died from exhaustion at the effort of producing 12 sons and four daughters. Their numerous offspring however, were pictured kneeling at their sire's feet, gazing at him in mute adoration for all eternity. It was, Maia thought, typical and decidedly unfair. She had been fascinated by the brass since her first visit to see her god-mother, as a small child, presumably during one of her own mother's many confinements, although the injustice of the brass had only become apparent to her in recent years. Now as she stood before the memorial, she imagined Bradenham would have a similar epitaph and doubtless his own wife would be similarly obliterated, should any woman be foolish enough to marry the wretched man.

A touch upon her arm indicated that the dowager was ready to leave, and together they made their way into the leafy, spring sunlight, where the throng awaiting them was hushed, anxious to hear first-hand the news of the safe delivery of her Grace's grandson.

At the head of the crowd stood, the parish priest who despite being unsure if the rumours which surrounded the dowager were true, nevertheless was delighted to welcome his most illustrious parishioner back to the fold. Mr Chedgrave was painfully aware that should the speculation be correct, it fell to him to save her soul. Not that the scholarly man gave much credence to gossip, particularly when the dowager gave the impression of living a blameless existence. Although he was forced to concede that occasionally she was a tad too forthright for comfort.

"You return to us with glad tidings and the blessing of your god-daughter's presence." Mr Chedgrave announced ponderously and having made a protracted blow to Maia, he continued, "Welcome once more to St.; Mary's, Miss Hindolveston. Tell me, my dear, is the blessed child so recently arrived much like his mama? How we miss the dear countess."

Unable to respond Maia hesitated, allowing Caroline to intervene. "You must excuse my god-daughter's reticence, she is too tactful to say within a new grand-mama's hearing, that the viscount is already rather a handful."

The priest beamed, both at the news and Maia's delicacy of

feeling. Clutching his hands together in an effort to contain his fervour. "Such a joy to welcome new life, but your Grace must have been distraught to leave your daughter to return home, even with Miss Hindolveston to bear you company."

This was obviously a barefaced lie, for Caro did not look in the least bit distraught. Indeed, she had been greatly relieved to leave the squalling child - finding it far easier to feel affection for her grandson from afar.

However, she sighed gallantly, and with a quiver in her voice which almost fooled Maia, said, "It is why I am determined to take my god-daughter to London, it would be wicked if she were to miss the entire season just to keep me from moping."

Caroline smiled bravely at Maia, who was well-aware that it was a smile of triumph and not, as the crowd of eager spectators believed, one of noble duty and maternal courage. Really, Maia mused, her god-mother had missed her vocation.

Mr Chedgrave was delighted at such a show of devotion and crowed, "If only other god-parents would take their vows to guide and nurture their god-children as seriously as your Grace."

The dowager nodded sagely at the reverend gentleman. She did not trust herself to continue in this vein, nor by the look of things, could Maia be counted on to say anything remotely sensible.

With a deftness borne of practise, the dowager turned back to Mr Chedgrave. "May I hope to see you in town during the remainder of the season, or you will you be occupied with matters ecclesiastical?"

The scholarly man, who despite his preoccupation with his calling, was on excellent terms with his cousin Lord Babingley, pondered the question while trying to recall something rather worldly, although important nonetheless.

"My dear wife and I will be attending the come-out of my cousin's elder daughter, such a dear child." Overcome with emotion the man was unable to continue.

Caroline laid a calming hand upon his arm. "How delightful, I intend to honour my god-daughter with a ball and hope you, your cousin and your dear wife will attend."

Mrs Chedgrave, who was standing behind her husband hanging on to every word uttered, looked as if she might swoon with joy. However, realising this would cause her to miss important snippets of conversation, sensibly rallied and managed a wobbly curtsy in Caroline's direction. She was not disappointed with the dowager's response.

"I look forward to seeing you both and renewing my

acquaintance with your cousin."

Maia's expression of incredulity at the news that a ball was to be given in her honour threatened to undo the silken thread of Caroline's careful spinning, and taking her god-daughter by the arm, the dowager nodded her farewells.

As Maia was handed into the chaise by a liveried footman, Caro hissed, "That was easy, was it not? One wonders why men feel the need to complicate matters so."

Chapter Twenty-Three

By the time the scheming communicants returned to Fenmere Park, the complicated duke was pacing the library in frustration. With barely concealed irritation, he made a perfunctory bow of greeting as the dowager duchess entered, but only nodded curtly at Maia, who responded by affording him the same degree of respect.

Caro sighed; abandoning any hope she may have nurtured that this was going to be an easy morning. Nevertheless, as an arch manipulator, she had no intention of allowing her plans to be ruined by a petulant duke and, taking a seat upon the long sofa facing the columned fireplace, the dowager smiled pleasantly at the irascible gentleman.

"Whilst you have passed what I trust was a pleasant morning, Maia and I have been working ourselves to mere shadows, but the job is done, Maia's alibi is firmly established."

Cosmo gritted his teeth at her bright smile; the blasted woman may have had her way in pulling the wool over the priest's eyes, but he fully intended to lead the next skirmish to a victorious conclusion.

"Just so, as soon as Maia ..." he hastily corrected his familiarity, "Miss Hindolveston is ready, we will proceed to London with all due haste. If we make good time Maia- Miss Hindolveston and Percy may be married tomorrow."

He detected a sharp intake of breath from Maia, who wandered distractedly before the long windows. She had not uttered a word since entering the room, but if Bradenham was waiting for her to react, he was not to be disappointed for the outburst was both swift and cutting.

"Do you mean to tell me the chase yesterday was in order to hand me over to Percy? One wonders why you troubled yourself; it would have been far simpler to leave me where I was, for it seems I am reduced to being nothing more than a mere object, to be snatched here, or married off there, while my own wishes are overridden by all and sundry."

Before Bradenham could respond to what seemed to him to be a tirade of accusation and deeply distasteful observation, the dowager duchess spoke up. "My love, while I am loathe to interrupt, I must request that you run and fetch my shawl, the plum coloured Norwich silk. I believe I left in my chamber, or perhaps the withdrawing room, for I collect that I was there last evening."

Observing her god-daughter's hesitation, stemming from a reluctance to abandon her argument so early in the proceedings, Caroline gave a shiver for good measure. "I found the chaise rather chilly, but this time of year can be quite frigid."

Despite her suspicion that she was being sent upon a fool's errand, Maia could hardly argue with such an entreaty, although Caroline's beaming smile and instruction of 'I feel sure it is in the blue salon, or possibly the morning room' as Maia closed the library door, did little to dispel her mistrust.

Entirely unmoved by the dowager's ruse, Cosmo enquired coldly, "Madam?"

Caroline regarded him with amused green eyes. "I needed to speak with you privately. Maia will, I think, not find the shawl which I took the liberty of hiding before we departed this morning. Norwich silk is so useful and so very warm, it is the worsted they add to the silk, you know."

The duke was not about to be distracted, not even by Norwich silk, and returning to his theme was determined to leave the dowager duchess under no illusion as to his purpose.

"I shall take Maia to London today, I intend her to marry Percy. You knew that last night." His last remark carried a marked degree of petulance.

"I heard what you said last evening and neither my memory nor my understanding are faulty," retorted his hostess acidly. "However, I note my god-daughter did not receive this news with the unmitigated joy one might expect a bride to exhibit."

Exasperated, Bradenham regarded Caro in disbelief; he had gone round and round upon this very subject with Maia, must now do the same with the dowager?

"With all due respect, the events of yesterday can only add weight to my argument. Maia has become a talking point within the ton and must marry Percy, if she is to ever have any degree of safety. Until they are man and wife she will be the object of vile speculation and the target of every rake who hears her name. Do you not see the danger in which this ridiculous prevarication has placed her? The abduction only puts the final seal to the disaster."

Caroline said nothing.

"If Maia had married Percy, within a few days of the incident in the long gallery, the gossip and danger would have died a natural death, but now ..." Cosmo swept his arm expansively, emphasising the endless danger to which Maia had needlessly subjected herself.

"You are certain Maia was abducted by such a man, by a rake?"

Her question was unexpected and Bradenham's eyes narrowed. "Whom else?"

The dowager fixed the infuriated man before her with a penetrating green gaze. "Why was Maia abducted?"

Taken aback by such a simple question, Cosmo protested. "Is this really necessary?"

A slender hand stayed his argument. "If you insist upon pursuing this line of reasoning, I believe it is absolutely necessary. Let us for argument's sake say that the object of Maia's abduction was ravishment. Very well, if that was her captor's intent, he was singularly inept; for the man had ample time in which to avail himself of my god-daughter's charms and yet made no effort to do so."

"As I explained to you last night, I precipitated his return to the inn before the violence could be perpetrated."

Caro's eyes gleamed. "Consider if you were in his shoes Bradenham, if you had gone to the considerable trouble of kidnapping Maia; of incapacitating her, drugging her; taking her all the way to Newmarket and installing her in an inn, would you delay the task in hand? Would you put off her ravishment?"

The duke was startled.

The dowager continued smugly, "As I thought. I see you comprehend my point."

Bradenham was nonplussed. "For whatever reason he delayed the- his- the-"

Caroline supplied unnecessarily, "Ravishment?"

"Conclusion to his plan - it is hardly important."

"Ravishment -" repeated the dowager cheerfully. "But why take Maia all the way to Newmarket to ravish her; there must be a host of equally suitable locations where the ravishment could have taken place. Good heavens man, they were in an enclosed carriage, were they not?"

"Has anyone ever accused you of having a devious mind?" Growled his Grace, wishing the dowager would not keep saying 'ravishment'.

Caro nodded. "Upon several occasions, it is considered an asset." Delighted by his discomfiture, she welcomed Maia's return, as her god-daughter swept into the library, leaving neither of its occupants in any doubt of her frame of mind.

"My love, were you not able to find the shawl?" Caro enquired guilelessly. "No matter, I will simply sit just a little closer to the fire, and now here is Heydon." Caroline beamed delightedly at her butler.

"Heydon, how splendid, you have brought tea, how warming, the carriage was just a little chilly, was it not Maia?"

Sipping her tea a few moments latter, the dowager considered how remarkable it was that neither Maia, nor Bradenham, were capable of conversing. While she doubted the relative calm would continue, it was pleasant to enjoy one's tea without the facile chatter and attendant anxieties which always seemed to surround young lovers.

Although the request to find her god-mother's shawl had seemed benign enough, it was a wild goose chase and Maia knew it, as certainly as she knew that the withdrawing room, morning room, blue salon and Caro's bedchamber would not yield results. She disliked being manipulated, even with a touch as deft as the dowager's, and as she marched off in search of the elusive shawl, Maia felt like a fool. Worse was yet to come; for in her current state of irritation, searching for the evasive shawl provided ample time to realise that despite successfully avoiding the noose of matrimony to the odious Percy, she had been deluded in believing that the dratted duke would abandon his plan.

Closing the withdrawing room door behind her more forcefully than was necessary, she concluded that the events of the previous day had not been so very terrible. It was true, the blow to her head had left an unsightly mark, but nothing lasting. Nor had any permanent damage been inflicted upon her person. A thought arrested her progress; was her success in eluding debauchery due only to Bradenham's timely rescue? Would the outcome have been different had the wretched man not dropped her from the window? Did this mean she was indeed regarded as a fallen woman, viewed as an object of lust and nothing more? It could not be denied that to have been educated and expected to use her intelligence, only to discover that men were only interested in her for quite a different purpose, was lowering indeed. What of her sisters? Her flight to Norfolk had been to protect them, but there could be no protection for the sisters of a wanton who was found embracing Percy Siddenham, and was then almost debauched in a coaching inn. It really was too unfair.

Accompanied by these uncomfortable thoughts, Maia marched crossly from the withdrawing-room to her god-mother's bedchamber and even glanced around the blue salon, but finding no sign of the elusive shawl she returned empty-handed to the library.

That the ruse had been intended to prevent her from saying something unfortunate, meant that a petulant Maia expected to find an uncomfortable silence awaiting her. What she found was that her arrival had coincided with Heydon's, together with tea tray, for Caro was an avid tea drinker despite the exorbitant price of the revered leaves. The civilised ceremony did much to soothe Maia's nerves, although interestingly it did not seem to have the same effect upon the duke, who barely touched his fragrant cup, and she wondered if he would have preferred something a little stronger.

Placing her cup in its saucer, the dowager looked expectantly at Bradenham. "Your plan was to return to London today." This was not a question, simply a statement and Caro continued smoothly. Maia and I will be departing for my house in Berkeley square, tomorrow." Before the duke could argue she breezed on, "I am going to beg your indulgence and ask you to delay your return to coincide with ours, it would be delightful to have some accompaniment on our tedious journey."

Despite her carefully worded request, Caroline did not sound as if she were begging, nor did she wait for the duke to respond. Even as a crushing reply was forming upon his lips, the dowager stated calmly, "I will be taking Maia under my wing - so to speak. Indeed, the timing could not be more auspicious."

Cosmo glared at her, but before he could give voice to his displeasure, Maia interjected bitterly, "I am tired of being treated as if I were not here, as if my opinion did not matter, or as if I were too frail, or too foolish to make my own choices."

Her violet gaze turned upon Bradenham. "I understand your desire to protect your cousin, but your Grace, can you understand how wretched it is to be informed you have no choice in the matter, but must marry someone to whom you have spoken no more than two words. To be advised that you must conform to his expectations and that you are deserving of such a fate?" She raised her hand to prevent the duke from interrupting. "I have heard all of your arguments and do not need to be told again what I am, or what the ton consider me to be; you have said it more times that I care to count."

Caroline looked bemused, her green eyes alight with glee. "My love, you are upsetting the his Grace."

Almost light-headed now she had said what was on her mind, Maia declared with feeling, "Good, for he really is the most odious creature."

"Dear," chided the dowager, "the duke is a guest and I must object to you calling him odious, at least within his hearing. After all my love, he did go to some trouble to prevent your ravishment."

Cosmo winced and wondered why the blasted dowager insisted in repeating the word with such relish.

Maia sighed. "Do not remind me, how I wish he had not." Cosmo was perhaps justifiably shocked by such an admission, and her clarification did not improve matters. "Because now I shall have to marry his dreadful cousin, one cannot help feeling ravishment might have been preferable."

While the duke was not the only one to be taken aback by Maia's sentiments, Caroline concealed her consternation more successfully. "My dear, that's rather drastic - marrying Mr Siddenham I mean."

"You must see that I have to marry Mr Siddenham," Maia wailed despairingly. "Unless I do so Eley, Taya and the rest will suffer the same fate as I."

"My love do be sensible, you cannot all marry Mr Siddenham," Caro snorted in amusement.

"Not that," Maia explained. "I meant they will be debauched- can you imagine?"

"Vividly," the ever-practical dowager retorted pragmatically. "Eley would shoot any would-be abductor with his own pistol, and no man in his right mind would kidnap Taya, she would prose him to death, the girl could argue the hind leg from a donkey."

Maia wrinkled her nose. "I do not recall that the abductor had a pistol."

"Such facts would not deter Eley," was Caro's dry response, before turning her attention upon Bradenham. "It seems felicitations are in order, for I collect this has been your aim. Is it not gratifying when we realise our aims and ambitions? You must be overjoyed." She eyed the duke thoughtfully for he did not look overjoyed, in addition, it was fascinating to note that he was utterly bereft of speech.

Maia on the other hand was positively wretched, and having made the pronouncement, her bravado drained away; leaving her resigned one moment, and furious the next.

Looking from one to the other, the dowager concluded that nuncheon would not be a joyful affair, deciding that she would be forced to take to her bed with a diplomatic headache, perhaps even for the remainder of the day. Should there fail to be a marked improvement then a mysterious feminine ailment would be called for, Caro believed such things were very useful during tedious domestic trials of this nature.

Chapter Twenty-Four

Leaving strict instruction that she was not to be disturbed - at least not by either of her guests - the dowager duchess betook herself to her chamber. Naturally such directives did not apply to Heydon, that most trusted of men, who did not need to be told that a tray bearing the light noon-time nuncheon which her Grace enjoyed as part of the ritual of observing country hours at Fenmere Park, would be most welcome. Having risen early to attend church, Caro had no intention of starving just because Maia and Bradenham were at loggerheads, and there was no doubt about it, the pair were still at odds, despite the duke having got his own way.

Miss Hindolveston's capitulation had taken Cosmo by surprise, for he had begun to think the wretched girl would never acquiesce to his demands, and although he should have been delighted by this unexpected turn of events, he was unaccountably troubled. Not that anything had been discussed, arranged or agreed upon, for Maia's startling surrender had halted all discussion and sent both women in search of solitude; the dowager to her apartments claiming a headache brought on by fatigue, and Maia to wander aimlessly beneath the row of elm trees some way from the house, leaving Cosmo to watch her distractedly from the anonymity of the library.

So it was that when she paused in her meandering to brush surreptitiously at her cheek, Maia was observed. It was a gesture Bradenham had witnessed before, and it cut him more deeply than any barb Miss Hindolveston had flung at his head. As she brushed at the other cheek, Cosmo found himself torn between an overwhelming sense of self-loathing, and hatred of his cousin. Not being a man given to brooding introspection, he opened the doors to the terrace and stepping outside, grimly made his way down the stone steps to the gardens beyond.

With her mind elsewhere, and the wind rustling the branches of the elm trees, Maia did not hear Bradenham's approach across the soft lawns. Like her god-mother, Maia's head ached, causing her to seek refuge away from the house, but even amid the beauty of the spring day she could not escape the vile notion that she would soon be Mrs Percy Siddenham, tomorrow if the duke had his way in the matter.

Her mediations were interrupted by a firm touch on her arm, and jumping violently, she wheeled round, her hair breaking lose from its complicated new arrangement as she did so. Maia reached to grasp the writhing mass before it tumbled around her shoulders, feeling disadvantaged and horribly gauche, why could she not behave like the well-brought up lady she was supposed to be?

"You do not need to tell me that once I am wed to your cousin, I will need to bring my hair under control," Maia announced with some asperity. "For I already know it; I will have it cut short like my god-mother's, doubtless it will be easier to manage."

Trying to imagine the girl with short hair, Cosmo found he could not. While there was no denying that the duchess's auburn hair worn cropped in halo of curls about her head was most becoming, the suggestion that Maia's ridiculously unruly ringlets be shorn, was shocking.

A thought seemed to occur to the girl, "Does Mr Siddenham like the fashion for short hair?"

"I have never discussed hair fashions with my cousin," the duke retorted irritably, as much disturbed by the image her words had conjured, as by the vision which stood before him, her hair spilling through her slender fingers.

She could not remain rooted to the spot for the remainder of the day, clutching in vain at her tumbling tresses, and so Maia gave up the fight and allowed the weight of her hair to fall. The dark tangle blew across her face like a veil, before she could toss her head and threw the locks over her shoulder. Cosmo looked on in mute fascination; having never before met a woman whose hair seemed to have a life of its own, he found himself wondering if cutting it would be akin to murder.

Unable to fathom the frown on the duke's face, Maia eyed him warily.

"What should I know about Mr Siddenham? If I am to be his wife it would be helpful to know more about him other than the fact he has a penchant for the classical, at least where statuary is concerned." Maia's voice had a brittle edge to it.

"What would you have me tell you?" Still distracted by Miss Hindolveston's hair, Cosmo was at a loss to know how to respond. "Would you know about his worth? His estate? His family?"

Maia stared at him coldly. "No your Grace, I would know about the man to whom I must plight my troth. I must promise to obey my husband and would like to have some inkling of what I might expect, and what will be expected of me."

The duke snorted. "Obey? I believe I would like to see such a thing, while you may vow obedience Miss Hindolveston, I doubt you are capable of keeping the oath."

Rallying at this dig, Maia glared at him. "No matter what you may think of me, I do not take my promises lightly, as you will see. For you said yourself we are to spend Christmas under the same roof therefore you will be a witness to my 'obedience'".

This stark reality was a sobering prospect and Cosmo did not need to be reminded of the ties that would forever bind them.

Maia continued bitterly, "For we are destined to belong to the same happy family, are we not?"

"Maia ..." the duke pleaded. "Can we not be friends?"

"Friends?" Greatly taken aback by the audacity of the request, which was entirely at odds with the man's treatment of her, Maia gazed incredulously at him. "No your Grace, I do not believe we can."

Cosmo opened his mouth to speak but her raised hand halted his words. "You see, I cannot forgive your part in this catastrophe."

"Forgive me?" He spluttered. "I was not the one seen with you in the long gallery ... I was not the one in your arms ... I was not ..."

But finding his own explanation insufficient, Cosmo took Maia by the shoulders, perhaps in order to shake her some sense into her, or perhaps simply because he could no longer contain himself. Whatever the reason, the duke found himself inexplicably and thoroughly kissing his cousin's bride.

Chapter Twenty-Five

The Dowager Duchess of Alconbury had always taken a keen interest in her estates and gardens, holding that spring was by far the most satisfying time of year, even if one was so often required to miss the profusion of bluebells in the ancient woodland which bordered Fenmere Park. The London season could not be halted, even for the most beautiful of spring-times, and this year Caro had a reason to take her place in the hubbub of society. Indeed it would be good to be back in London once again, particularly when she had such a diverting purpose with which to amuse herself.

Wasting no time, she had written and dispatched the directive to the housekeeper of her Berkeley square residence, instructing the good woman to remove the Holland covers from the furniture; unswathe the chandeliers, and employ such additional staff as was necessary to ensure the smooth running of a house, which once again would host balls and parties. Meanwhile, Heydon was selecting which of Fenmere Park's servants would depart for London the following morning.

The wheels of the dowager's exodus were already in motion.

A movement amid the great elms caught Caro's eye, and standing that she might better peruse the attractive Forget-Me-Nots which grew in profusion about the stately trees, she was perfectly placed to observe the lithe figure of her god-daughter as she ran towards the house, her hair billowing behind her. With her green eyes narrowing thoughtfully, the dowager's attention focused upon the tall gentleman who stood alone beneath the gently swaying branches of an ancient elm, his gaze fixed upon the fleeing figure.

Finding the view from her bedchamber window to be even more satisfactory than usual, Caroline smiled to herself, softly singing a somewhat bawdy ditty her beloved husband had been known to enjoy. She was more than ready for the tray Heydon brought in to her shortly thereafter, for although a diplomatic headache might be advantageous, the notion of forgoing asparagus soup was unthinkable.

***

It was an awkward couple who sat down to nuncheon in the splendour of the dowager's vaulted dining room; the gilded looking-glass behind the sideboard reflecting and multiplying the pair as they sat in mute silence at the immense oaken dining table. It was a chamber in which to entertain a throng, and was not intended to host an intimate gathering … or a warring couple.

Convinced that her god-mama would have recovered from what could only be a tactical-headache, having never known Caro to suffer from such a malady, Maia was surprised to discover the table was laid for only two.

The duke too was dismayed, having assumed their hostess would be there to mediate what he suspected would prove to be a difficult repast. While he would have preferred excuse himself, turn on his heel and leave cause of his distress to her nuncheon, Cosmo could not consign her to a lonely meal in this cathedral of a room. He allowed the footman to push his chair under him, another liveried footman having performed the same office for Maia. Resigned, he sat expressionless as Heydon decanted the wine, and a footman served asparagus soup; wondering how long it would be before he could, with any degree of decency, beat a hasty retreat.

With polite conversation next to impossible, and real conversation out of the question, the pair sat in uncomfortable silence, broken only by the occasional sound of a heavy silver spoon against the fine Sèvres porcelain. The meal seemed to take an eternity and even when the soup had finally been consumed, a footman brought in co,ld meats and fruit. Having struggled to manage the soup, Maia did not feel equal to facing either the delicately carved beef or chicken, yet to run away from Bradenham at this juncture would be weak-spirited - and Maia was no coward. That she had fled the garden was a source of embarrassment; he was bound to assume she had run from him. The truth of the matter was that as unexpected as the duke's embrace had been, her response had been even more startling. She had not expected that upon receiving her first real kiss, she would kiss back, although Maia doubted she had mastered the art, which was hardly surprising; for she had not anticipated being kissed so very thoroughly, or to enjoy it as much she had done.

Naturally her exchange with Percy Siddenham in the long gallery was discounted as no more than a desperate measure, for not only had she not enjoyed the encounter, but strictly speaking he had not chosen to kiss her, and certainly not with the enthusiasm Bradenham had shown.

Maia's eyes were drawn to the duke but, finding herself

looking at his lips, she gazed hurriedly away. What was to become of her if she could not look the man in the face? How would she to get through Christmas?

Now that she had agreed to marry his dreadful cousin, was he testing her? Would he be convinced she was nothing but an adventurer - even if it were not her fault, for he had kissed her first? Had he set a trap into which she had fallen? Would he assume she was the sort of girl to throw herself at every man who crossed her path? Jabbing vehemently at an unfortunate hothouse peach with her fruit knife, Maia felt crosser than ever with the wretched Duke of Bradenham.

Meanwhile, at a loss to know what to say which might begin to excuse his behaviour in the garden, Cosmo barely tasted the excellent asparagus soup, despite not leaving so much as a drop. Not that he wanted to dismiss what had happened, and although it was doubtless wrong to kiss the affianced bride of his cousin so passionately, he could not bring himself to regret it. Perhaps if he had considered the ramifications of such an act, Cosmo would not have kissed the girl, but he had not thought of anything other than the dratted Maia Hindolveston.

The duke frowned, he was known for being a man who considered wisely and acted prudently, yet he had just made the biggest mistake of his career for which he would no doubt pay, in spades; forced to endure family occasions in the company of his cousin's wife. The girl would be so close and yet entirely beyond his reach.

Looking up from his plate, about which he had been pushing the same piece of game pie for some time, Cosmo looked straight into Maia's violet eyes. She looked instantly away. Possibly, he considered, it was time to abandon family tradition and travel to the Continent at Christmas instead, particularly now they were no longer guillotining the nobility in Paris. Perhaps they might make an exception in Percy's case, not that it mattered much, for at that moment Bradenham could quite cheerfully have throttled his cousin himself.

***

Caroline looked up from the book she had not really been reading, for her mind was engaged elsewhere, and enquired, "How goes it downstairs?"

Pausing in his removal of the nuncheon tray, Heydon frowned minutely, a gesture his employer considered spoke volumes.

"Oh dear, as bad as that?"

"Your Grace, nuncheon was a somewhat silent meal."

"And where are they now?"

"Miss Maia is taking a turn about the orangery, while his Grace, I believe, is instructing his valet regarding their arrangements for London."

"Indeed." Caroline was thoughtful.

Having been in the dowager's employ long before the ninth Duke of Alconbury, exchanged his rôle and become one of the formidable ancestors of the unworthy tenth duke, Heydon voiced his concerns quietly, as was his custom. "Might I suggest that his Grace's valet is a most efficient man and will doubtless effect his Grace's departure without delay."

Understanding his meaning, Caro leapt to her feet. "You are quite right, I need to put a spoke in Bradenham's wheel before Maia is leg-shackled to that fool Percy Siddenham. If the duke will not see reason, we must prepare to do our worst to poor Watton, for I feel sure Bradenham will not leave without his valet. Naturally I would prefer to avoid such drastic methods, I always feel it is less than sporting to render a servant insensible, particularly one as worthy as Watton."

The dowager smoothed her gown as she disclosed, "Did you know it was Watton who caught Maia when Bradenham dropped her from the inn window?" Noting the indomitable Heydon's expression of mingled awe, horror and amusement, Caro nodded. "Rather magnanimous of him was it not? Perhaps we will leave nobbling Watton as a last resort. In any case, I would rather Bradenham make the right decision for himself." Smiling serenely at the wry look which passed across her butler's face, she conceded: "The right decision for my god-daughter that is, for which he will need encouragement."

As she swept through the door, the dowager duchess did not see Heydon's smile of appreciation dawning in her wake.

***

Maia was enjoying the warmth of the orangery, finding it soothing to stroll amongst the trees growing in the humid air, the spring chill kept at bay by a number of stoves located at strategic intervals throughout the long, sunlit building. That the orangery was situated some distance from the house had been a contributing factor in Maia's decision to walk there, rather than in the conservatory adjoining the house. The duke was less likely to find her here, and even if he did come searching for her, she would be well-hidden by the sweeping foliage and fragrant orange blossom. Yet having taken the trouble to saunter undisturbed, she was not sure why she should feel a sense of disappointment when the orangery doors opened to reveal the dowager duchess.

"My love? Ah, there you are."

Thwarted in her half-hearted attempt to conceal herself behind a large wooden tub containing a lemon tree, Maia was forced to step sheepishly forward and submit her cheek to be kissed affectionately by her scheming god-mother.

"We must make plans for our removal to London," Caro announced briskly. Observing Maia's confusion, the dowager breezed on, "we must make amends for having missed so much of the season, I mean to take you with me to Berkeley square."

Maia's face clouded. "But I have agreed to marry Percy Siddenham, I imagine his Grace is expecting me to accompany him to London, you see he is in rather a hurry to bring about my marriage to his cousin."

The dowager dismissed these frippery concerns with a wave of her hand. "What nonsense. Of course it is entirely your own affair if you choose to marry Percy Siddenham, I shall not interfere, but there is nothing to prevent you from staying with me and continuing to make your come-out before you wed. Indeed, if Charlotte had not chosen to present her husband with an heir with such abominably bad timing, I would naturally have overseen your first season. Surely you would not be so cruel as to deny me the pleasure?"

Sighing as the fleeting prospect of routs and balls under her god-mother's glittering auspicious were snatched away, even before they had begun, Maia's disappointment was bitter. Her come-out had been far from splendid, limited to a tedious curtsey before the Queen, and a dull rout with far-reaching consequences.

"I think the duke has other ideas." She intoned dully.

"The duke be hanged!" Retorted Caro with feeling. "Really Maia, I am surprised at you. This is not some tragedy fit only for that wretch Shakespeare's quill, and you are not, nor have you ever been a Desdemona. Neither are you a ghastly Ophelia ... really, that man has much to answer for. My love, it does not do to simply go along with a gentleman's plans, unless they are in keeping with your own. We shall make our plans and the duke may fall in with them, or not. As he wishes."

The gleam in her god-mother's green eyes gave Maia hope for the first time since she had arrived at Fenmere Park, of what she could not say, perhaps only of a stay of execution, but it was sufficient.

"I suppose I must marry Mr Siddenham eventually, but it will be good to dance before I am dragged up the aisle."

A languid voice from beyond the sweetly scented trees

reached her ears. "What a singularly unattractive portrait of a bride you paint, Miss Hindolveston."

Turning sharply at the sound of the duke's voice, Maia was taken aback, having kept a wary eye upon the doors to the orangery, she had not expected to see him emerging from behind a blossom laden tree.

She remarked coldly, "One might be tempted to suspect you of eavesdropping, although such an accusation would be unseemly." As the eldest of eight siblings, Maia particularly disliked being spied upon.

Unaccustomed to being addressed in this manner, Cosmo's eyes blazed at the denunciation, although he remained wisely mute; having no wish to further jeopardise the wretched girl's already low opinion of him.

The dowager stepped into the breach, placing a restraining hand upon Maia's arm. "You have discovered us plotting against you Bradenham, and you are outmanned, or do I mean out-womaned?"

The duke's expression was stern, but still he said nothing, while at Caro's side Maia bristled with indignation.

With a disarming smile, the dowager continued, giving no indication that she anticipated the duke to cavil. "Maia and I will be departing for London in the morning. I will not ask you to join us in my carriage, for doubtless you would find it dull to be shut in, I think instead you had better ride-attendance, it is always so much more convenient to have a gentleman in one's company."

Bradenham spoke through gritted teeth. "Maia will indeed be going to London, but she will be leaving with me."

This proved too much for Maia, who exploded wrathfully, "I have agreed to marry your cousin, but I will not be treated as if I have no voice. Worse than that, you treat me as if I am merely an inconvenience, to be wedded, bedded and no doubt got with child at your whim."

Incredulous, Cosmo's face was a picture of horror at her voicing the unspeakable, the unthinkable, but not the unimaginable.

However, Percy's bride had not yet finished. "Make no mistake, I will go to London, as and when I please and with whom I please, and I will marry Mr Siddenham at my convenience, not yours."

Holding up a hand to prevent him from interrupting her flow of vitriol, as she paused to draw breath, Maia continued. "Tomorrow I will depart for London with my god-mama, who has kindly invited me to join her in Berkeley square, an invitation I have accepted. Mr Siddenham may wait upon me there. I have said that I will marry him and I will keep my word, but I do not intend to be bullied by you, nor will I speak again on this odious subject."

With that Maia swept majestically past the duke, through the tiled orangey and having given further vent to her feelings by slamming the door so that the glass rattled, made her return to the house.

Longing to follow the wretched girl, although to what end he hardly knew, Cosmo found his arm being taken by the dowager, who proceeded to take a turn about the tree-lined pathway. It would have been churlish to snatch his arm away in a fit of pique, which left him no option but to stroll with the scheming Caroline. It long before the dowager broached the delicate matter.

"Why the unseemly haste for Maia to marry your cousin? To rush her to the altar can only inflame the speculation you are so anxious to avoid."

Cosmo's response was terse. "You know what occurred in the long gallery, you know what the gossips are already saying."

The dowager snorted disparagingly. "I know that you are the Duke of Bradenham, and I, the Dowager Duchess of Alconbury. Good lord man, if we cannot steer our way through this mull then we do not deserve all that has been bestowed upon us. Neither one of us has ever allowed the ton to ride roughshod over us, and Maia will be under my protection."

"She was previously under her aunt's and look where that got her."

"Her aunt is a fool, with rather less wit than my infant grandson. Maia's papa, while a loving and wise man, is not always practical, and entrusting Maia into her empty-headed aunt's fluttering hands was neither well-considered, nor sensible, but it is too late shut that stable door."

Aware that she had Bradenham's attention, Caro prepared to capitalise upon it. "Your heart's desire to see Maia firmly wedded to your cousin need not be thwarted by her taking up residence with me for the duration of the season. It will simply mean that instead of a shamefully small wedding; a clandestine affair, we will between us contrive to send the happy couple off in a more regal manner, as befits a member of your family. The gossips may whisper amongst themselves, but under our shared protection there can be no need for haste. Why should Maia not experience a little of the season before she is, as she so eloquently said, 'wedded and bedded' by your cousin. The more experience she has of the ton, the better she will fare in it."

Caroline was forced to bite the inside of her cheeks to prevent herself from smiling, for she had not been mistaken in believing the duke had blanched when she had repeated Maia's words.

He swallowed hard, then taking hold of himself, regarded the dowager, his gritted jaw the only indication something was amiss.

Yet as much as disliked having his plans interfered with by Maia's meddlesome god-mother, it was true that Caro could provide social protection for Maia in a way he could not, allowing for a formal betrothal to take place, swiftly followed by a large wedding, which would place Percy and his bride beyond the reach of scandal, particularly if it were well-attended by his family, as well as hers.

"Very well. But there must be a formal betrothal within the week, any longer will leave them both open to ridicule, the most vile speculation and in Maia's case, danger."

Halting in her progress, the dowager turned her green gaze upon Cosmo. "There is one more thing I would like you to consider, you said Maia had been seen in Percy's arms."

The duke appeared to be momentarily unable to articulate, but upon clearing his throat, he spoke stiffly, "The account is not entirely accurate ... Maia had her arms about him ... she was kissing him."

The revelation was met not with a shocked response, but an indulgent smile. "Just so. Yet you have spent some time with Maia and must by now have gained some insight into her nature. Did you never think to enquire why she was kissing your cousin, whom both you and she claim until that evening, Maia had not met?"

Cosmo looked abashed, recalling only too clearly the slurred intelligence his cousin had shared that night in Whites.

Observing the effect of her words with no small degree of satisfaction, the dowager duchess opened the orangey door and suggested benevolently, "You would do well to weigh what you know, against what you think you know. They are perhaps not the same thing at all."

Chapter Twenty-Six

All in all, Mr Watton was not having an easy week. But having spent the better part of the morning unpacking and repacking his Grace's belongings he had so hastily assembled before their departure from Swanton Chatteris; smoothing the crushed neck cloths and shirts, and refolding the small clothes, his equilibrium had in part been restored. The valet's greatly shaken soul had been further soothed by polishing the duke's top-boots, although some scuffs and marks remained which no amount of spit and polish would remove. Just as poor Watton would bear some memories like scars; having never before in his long and stolid career been called upon to lay hands upon the person of a young lady.

However, just when order had been restored to his Grace's clothing - as well as to the valet's tattered dignity - believing they were to return to that male bastion Bradenham House, the duke had dealt Watton another blow; they were to stay another night at Fenmere Park, and far from an exclusively male ensemble returning to London on the morrow, they were to accompany the dowager duchess and Miss Hindolveston.

From the set of his Grace's jaw, Watton could see his employer was far from delighted with this turn of events, not that the valet himself relished the prospect of setting eyes upon Miss Hindolveston once again. Although it was marginally better than having to catch her while balancing a-top a carriage. Shuddering at the memory, Watton shook his head in disbelief; it was not like his Grace to be dictated to by a pack of women, not like his Grace at all.

Such was the valet's disquiet that he sought solace in giving the duke's boots another rub, in the hope that if it accomplished nothing else, it might give vent to his frustrations. Certainly a little more elbow grease might shift the more persistent scuff marks and ominous smears of what appeared to be tallow fat, and stains reminiscent of dried blood. He had been forced to resort to the old stand-by of Bayly's blacking until such time when he could mix his own lethal concoction; the potent mix did not travel well and Watton was loathe to mix it within view of other servants - for his receipt was a closely guarded secret.

Hoping to improve the inferior blacking by systematically spitting upon his employer's boots, the valet stoically took his cloth and began to rub, wondering, as he did so, where this would all end.

***

Giddy with excitement at the prospect of residing at dowager's London house for the remainder of the season, and dressing Miss Maia for parties, routs and balls, Lovelace Loveday was a-quiver; for the maid had felt the misery of being forced to remove to the wilds for Norfolk far more than Maia.

Since arriving at Fenmere Park, Love had been overawed by Miss Winch, the dowager's lady's maid, who was not only stern, but was a stickler for such things as clean gloves and the removal of mud from the hems of gowns. Upon seeing how nicely turned-out Miss Hindolveston had been for Holy Communion, Winch's dour face had been wreathed in smiles. She had even gone so far as to praise Love for her ability to render the crumpled gown wearable again. Winch had gone on to unbend sufficiently to make some helpful suggestions with regard to the care of velvet bonnets, and mentioned a receipt for the cleaning of silk, which she promised her acolyte, worked a treat.

Lovelace gratefully memorised all Miss Winch had imparted with a reverence bordering on awe, and the notion that she would spend more time with this veritable treasure trove of wisdom was enough to send the girl into raptures. She was, however, careful to contain her enthusiasm while folding and re-packing her mistress's possessions; having no wish for the intimidating Winch to cast her eagle eye over Miss Maia's trunks and band boxes, and find any cause for reproof.

***

Pacing restlessly upon the terrace, Cosmo was oblivious to the birdsong; as the blackbirds called their last arias of the day. Deep in thought he considered the words of the dowager - for the woman was right, he had been so intent upon the fact that Maia had kissed Percy, he had failed to wonder why. What would make a girl throw caution to the wind and needlessly ruin her reputation?

Of late, this preoccupation with Maia in his cousin's arms was an image which had haunted Cosmo, causing him sleepless nights and a restlessness previously unknown to the duke.

Recalling the evening when Percy had confided to him the

events in the long gallery, although Cosmo had questioned Maia's involvement in the clandestine imbroglio, Percy had failed in supply a satisfactory response. Much in the same way that Maia had failed to supply a satisfactory motive for her reluctance to see the thing to a tidy conclusion, or her willingness to see her own name dragged through the mud.

He raked his hand through his dark hair in frustration; what the devil had the dowager been talking about?

A blackbird, belligerently defending his territory against a newcomer, flapped in consternation as the duke stalked down the terrace steps and across the lawn; his foot prints visible in the already damp grass. Unwittingly, his pacing took him to the line of ancient elms where he had so briefly held and so unexpectedly kissed Maia. He leaned against a ridged elm-trunk and looked across at the great house. His gaze naturally seeking the windows, from which light blazed forth into the deepening twilight. A movement in an upper window drew his attention, revealing Maia in what was obviously her bedchamber. He watched her turn to speak to someone, probably her maid, then settle herself upon the window-seat.

In the concealing gloom beneath the tree, Cosmo was invisible to the girl; she was illuminated by a candelabrum. And although he should turn away, he stood, mesmerised, as Maia drew her knees before her, and rested her chin upon them.

When Maia draw the clasps and pins from her hair, freeing it from its temporary bondage, the duke was transfixed, hardly daring to breathe. Shaking the dark mass about her face, she ran her fingers through the tangled tresses, staring unseeing into the darkness beyond the window. Cosmo had always believed he led a charmed existence; he had never envied anyone and certainly never wished to be anyone other than himself. Until this moment. Yet, as he stood beneath the sheltering elm watching Maia trailing her fingers through her spiralling curls, the duke would have changed places with his cousin without a second thought.

***

While Maia was oblivious to the duke's presence, from her own darkened chamber, Caroline had observed Bradenham crossing the lawn. Waiting, she watched him return shortly thereafter. As he approached the house, she leaned forward, hopeful that the light from the open library doors might provide sufficient radiance for her to catch a glimpse of the duke's face. Although Cosmo did not hesitate, but quickly crossed over the threshold and disappeared from view, the dowager smiled to herself nevertheless. It was a smile of satisfaction.

Chapter Twenty-Seven

In the crisp air of the hour before dawn, Percy nodded his thanks to the doorman and handsomely slipped that gentleman a token of his gratitude, reflecting as he did so that it paid to keep on the right side of such men; employed for their brawn as much as for their demeanour.

Saluting his thanks, the doorman closed the door behind the departing figure as Mr Siddenham buttoned his thick collar against the chill. Striding confidently down the high steps of the town-house, he made his way along the empty, echoing street.

He was not a frequent customer of this particular house, preferring not to be associated with any one business, instead Percy chose to distribute his patronage among several such establishments offering a similar selection of fine wares. It was a necessary evil - although undeniably useful to have easy access to such houses, particularly in light of the events of the preceding weeks. Since then he had been more wary of the well-bred ladies of the ton, for the escapade at the Wreningham rout had very nearly been his undoing. As it was, he had come dangerously close to being leg-shackled to Maia Hindolveston. Shuddering not only from the cold, but at the idea of being wed to such an unappetising long-meg, he walked on. With no figure to speak of, the girl was not by any means his idea of a comfortable female; if one was forced to have a wife at home then it made sense to have one it would not be a chore to put to use. Damn Bradenham! Percy ruefully considered that he should have known better than to take his woes to his meddlesome cousin; but that was what an excess of brandy did for a fellow, befuddled the wits. He had been in shock and had not known how to proceed, having never experienced such a thing before. Moreover, he had been terrified the escapade would ruin him. All the same, he should have been more wary than to involve his cousin.

Still, it had turned out for the best; the girl had refused to marry him and it was common knowledge that he had formally offered for her, he had made certain of it. Indeed, the unmitigated disaster he had anticipated had not come to pass, and would have blown over entirely but for Cosmo's high-handed ways. Percy chuckled to himself; the girl had been too clever for his noble cousin, unexpectedly haring off to Norfolk like that, forcing Cosmo to follow snapping at her heels like a hound baying for blood. In due course his cousin would see that in addition to the improprieties and the fact that she had been adamant in refusing his proposal, the Hindolveston wench was not a suitable bride for a Siddenham, and the matter would be allowed to rest, Cosmo was after all a stickler about such things.

In the meantime, while it rankled for a man of Percy's classical looks and excellent breeding to have to pay for his pleasures, he was not about to risk another close-call with matrimony and, as he approached the steps of his house in Warwick street, Mr Siddenham had every reason to feel well-pleased with himself.

***

Percy might not have felt so self-satisfied had he known - as he threw off his boots and left his linen upon the floor for his long suffering valet to discover - that, as he did so, the Dowager Duchess of Alconbury's travelling-chaise and coach were being made ready, and that the stables at Fenmere Park were alive with activity.

There was little to be done to improve the look or gait of the hired horses from the Bushel, and they had duly been returned to Newmarket; the groom who had been dispatched with them returned to Fenmere Park, declaring that the beasts would have been better served had they been put out of their misery altogether.

The dowager's handsome offer to loan the duke a well-matched pair from her own stables to harness to the coach, which was to convey his Grace's valet and baggage, had been met with enthusiasm by Yaxley. Nor did the fine black Hackneys led out by the dowager's stableman disappoint. They certainly made amends for the deficiencies of the hired horses; causing Yaxley to declare that it would be no shame to be seen driving the high-steppers, which was more than could be said for the disreputable nags from the Bushel. Watton had been right in his pronouncement of Trunch, as a conniving, thieving, son of a whore.

Greatly impressed by the quality of the dowager's stable, leaving Pigot to currycomb the duke's thoroughbred, Yaxley made it his business to inspect the rest of her Grace's horseflesh; supposing there was no point living cheek-by-jowl to Newmarket if you did not take advantage of the breeding stock to hand. However, upon voicing this opinion to the dowager's coachman, who was supervising the preparation of the carriage bearing the Alconbury ducal crest, the man laughed and, breathing heavily upon the brasswork he was busy polishing, grinned, "'Er Grace don't just buy prime cattle, she breeds 'em too." Then with a sage nod, as if imparting a closely guarded secret, he added, "'Er Grace alluy's backs a winner."

Permanently on the lookout for insider information, Yaxley was elated, and betaking himself to the duke's carriage, flicked away a few dust motes which had dared to stray onto the polished leather, whistling as he did so.

It was as well Mr Siddenham slept on in blissful ignorance, for despite having worked hard with the assistance of a well-paid tailor to create the illusion of being a discerning gentleman of fashion, if truth be known, he was not noted for having a good eye or excellent taste in so many things, horses being but one of them.

Chapter Twenty-Eight

As she stepped stiffly down from the carriage into the twilight, Maia stifled the urge to yawn; it would have been rude, and while she felt no obligation to show Bradenham the least courtesy, neither did she feel inclined to go out of her way to be discourteous.

The duke made no comment as he handed her down. It had been a long day, although accompanying the dowager's travelling-chaise and attendant carriages on horseback had been preferable to sitting in the carriage, facing Maia all the way to London, their knees almost touching, his senses aware of her presence for the entire excruciating journey. He had expected to feel a sense of relief upon reaching Berkeley square, which heralded the end of an episode he would prefer to forget, but instead he felt deep misgivings about leaving Maia in her god-mother's care.

Caroline Alconbury meanwhile, was already halfway up the steps; her skirts billowing behind her as she ran girlishly to where Heydon awaited her arrival, anxious to be beyond the threat of rain from the looming clouds. Caro was thrilled to be in London once again, with the prospect of an unexpected season ahead of her, although more immediately she was looking forward to of a cup of tea.

Retracting her hand sharply from the duke's, Maia spoke. "I assume you will send Percy to wait upon me." This was not a question, merely a terse observation.

"Indeed, he must make you another formal offer, which you will formally accept." Rather unnecessarily Cosmo added, "I shall witness both the offer and your consent."

She paused in the act of arching her back to stretch her cramped muscles and began rubbing her rump and thighs, in a way the duke wished whole heartedly she would not.

"I would expect nothing less, your Grace."

Cosmo held out his hands as if appealing to her sense of fair play. "I can hardly be blamed, after the dance on which you have led me."

Although she sighed bitterly, Maia was nevertheless resigned to her fate. "Is it too much to hope that you will not be accompanying us upon our bridal night? Because I feel obliged to advise you that it would be too much to bear."

Finding himself floored by the image her words conjured, Cosmo's response was harsh, "Too much to bear indeed, Miss Hindolveston."

Without waiting for her to reply, or bidding her good-evening, he strode to where a lad waited holding his horse and, mounting swiftly, the duke betook himself in the direction of St. James's square, leaving Maia to wonder what on earth was wrong with the man. He had nearly achieved his purpose, why was he now so distant, so stiff?

Not finding any answers in the first drops of rain which began to fall upon her bonnet, Maia dashed up the steps just in time to avoid the downpour, as the heavens opened.

***

If the duke's secretary was taken aback to see his employer infuriated and dripping upon the hall floor, he did not show it - knowing that when it came to the duke; to expect the unexpected. Harrington was therefore rarely flustered. What he noted with interest was that despite his employer's pronouncement that Miss Hindolveston was to marry Percy Siddenham, the duke appeared to draw little satisfaction from the knowledge.

Discarding his soaking greatcoat into the waiting arms of a footman, Bradenham stalked into the library, awaiting directions Harrington followed.

"We shall have to get the damnable Percy to make a formal offer of marriage to the wretched girl. Once that is done then there will be no wriggling out of it and lord knows Harrington, she's clever enough."

It was his secretary's opinion that Mr Siddenham was more than cunning enough to wriggle out of most things. But as ever, Harrington kept his thoughts to himself.

"I believe I should be the one to inform Percy that he will shortly be betrothed, I presume he will be at Whites, this evening?"

His secretary looked doubtful; Mr Siddenham had not been frequenting Whites as often as he had in the past, and although Harrington had kept a discreet eye on the gentleman, thus far he had not been able to discover where Mr Siddenham spent the majority of his evenings.

"A betrothal, your Grace? May I take it there is to be no marriage by special licence?"

Bradenham sighed ruefully. "Harrington, before I answer that may I enquire, have you ever met the Dowager Duchess of Alconbury?"

"I do not recall having done so, your Grace."

"If you had, all that I am about to relate would make sense, but before I begin let me clarify; Caroline Alconbury is Miss Hindolveston's god-mama, which seems to me to be something of a misnomer."

Standing dripping upon the library rug, Cosmo proceeded to tell his secretary all that had happened since he had departed for Norfolk. The duke's damp clothes steamed gently, giving Harrington the impression that his employer had been to the gates of hell and back, but had perhaps only been slightly singed.

Chapter Twenty-Nine

Of the two letters presented to Lord Nordelph whilst he oversaw his son and heir's translation of a Greek text, the viscount eagerly read the first; a missive from his eldest daughter. Having known nothing of Maia's adventures in Newmarket, or her subsequent stay at Fenmere Park with her god-mama, Lord Nordelph was pleasantly surprised, if a little mystified to discover his daughter was staying with the dowager duchess in Berkeley Square. However, as his lordship was frequently mystified by his daughters, the sensation was nothing out of the ordinary.

While Maia's letter indicated that she was happy enough, it contained little of interest for a man whose passion was the study of all things classical, and excusing himself from Leander, who appeared to be wrestling successfully with the archaic manuscript, Lord Nordelph took both Maia's letter and the second unopened communication to his wife who was resting in her morning room.

"My dear, there is a letter from Maia, and if I understand matters correctly, she is no longer in Norfolk but is with Caroline, in London. Although I do not understand how the event came about. Caro has written also, perhaps it will explain matters fully. I do wonder at Maia's lack of clarity; I had hoped the girls would manage to avoid this nonsensical fashion for vagueness."

Waving his hand vaguely at the letters, Lord Nordelph handed them to his wife who, for all of her apparent invalidity, had a sharp eye for detail.

While her scholarly husband sat by her side reading a book he had discovered in his pocket, Margaret Nordelph perused the sketchy outline from her eldest daughter, wondering greatly about the events which had taken Maia to Fenmere Park, and from thence to London.

Breaking the seal upon the second missive, Margaret mused that it was as well Colkirk had not read the letter from her dearest friend; it would only have served to further disturb his peace of mind. For Caro's communications were invariably characterised by blottings, jottings and frequent underscoring - the dowager duchess invariably wrote as she spoke and seldom censored herself.

Lady Nordelph, who had known Caroline, since the cradle,

read the letter twice and smiled as much at what Caro had neglected to mention, as at all she had alluded to. Satisfied that Maia was indeed in safe hands. Her mama carefully folded the epistle and tucked it under her pillows for safe keeping, well-away from the curious eyes of her numerous offspring.

There was a reason she had chosen Caroline Alconbury to stand as godmother to her daughters, and resting her head upon her pillows, reassured that all would be well, Margaret slept the sleep of the just. While her husband engrossed in his book, read on, oblivious to all else.

***

The news that her niece had returned to London, was met with grave misgivings by Mrs Wreningham.

"I hope this means Maia has finally seen sense and is to marry Mr Siddenham," she remarked peevishly to Emmeline, handing her daughter the letter Maia had so thoughtfully written.

Emme said nothing, but read the communication with interest.

Her mama continued more cheerfully, "She does not mention him, but perhaps the betrothal is not yet formal. Never mind, until such an announcement is forthcoming we shall contrive to ignore Maia." Noting that her daughter was startled by this pronouncement, Mrs Wreningham added, "We must ensure the scandal does not touch you, or it could ruin your marriage plans, my love. And to think Maia had the audacity to behave in such a manner under my own roof, after I had taken the dratted girl under my wing, out of the goodness of my heart, to ensure she made a decent come-out. She thinks of no-one but herself, and has certainly not considered how such conduct might reflect upon me. It does not bear thinking about. However, I shall contrive to put it from my mind." She gave a sniff of self-pity, then rallying looked approvingly at her daughter. "It is too diverting is it not, to consider that shortly you will be Lady Stibbard?"

Wrinkling her pert nose, Emmeline puzzled. "Mama, how can we ignore Maia, if she is staying with the Dowager Duchess of Alconbury? Mama, she is a duchess."

Mrs Wreningham waved a dismissive hand. "Nonsense, Caroline Alconbury is nothing but a dowager, what is more, I have it on good authority that the current duke barely speaks to her. She is merely Maia's god-mama, and I expect she has taken foolish pity on the reckless girl. Caroline has not been in London since her own daughter's come-out, some two or three seasons ago, caring for Maia will give her something with which to occupy herself. Doubtless they will remain very quietly in that ridiculous house of hers in Berkeley square, for not even Caroline will wish to draw attention to Maia's shocking situation by entertaining. We shall not notice them, I am sure it is by far the kindest approach, as well as being the most expedient."

Having reached this conclusion, Mrs Wreningham turned her attentions to more important matters. "Emme, my dear, I think it wise if you refrain from indulging in more cake, I know that Lord Stibbard greatly admires your figure, but if the modiste has to let out your gowns once more I fear she will grow distracted, nor does such treatment improve the look of the gown and they were exceedingly costly."

Hastily Emmeline withdrew her hand from the cake plate, looking suitably chastened.

***

"Just look at 'em Mister Burnum, ruinated and to think, Mister Hobbes made 'em special for his Grace, not a month since. I barely got 'em broke in, but he goes chasing about the place, and lord only knows what else, 'tis enough to break a man's heart."

Watton gazed sadly upon what had once been his employers exquisite Hessian boots, which were now beyond even his redemptive talents and, shaking his head sorrowfully at the duke's butler, the valet waved a contemptuous hand over the expensive footwear.

Pausing in his egress, Burnum deigned to look at the stained boots, shaking his head in consternation, anxious to impart his own tale of sartorial woe. "I knew of a lord when I was first in service, what was terrible hard on his boots. It fair made my heart bleed for his valet, the man could never hold his head up. Can you credit it Mr Watton?"

As it happened Mr Watton could credit it only too well. "I shall have to take his Grace in hand. Mister Hobbes will not be well-pleased, him being such a particular man and that high-handed. I tell ye Mr Burnum, I am a-thinking we shall give Mister Peel a try, 'tis to be hoped he will not give a man so much lip when the boots is ruinated."

Nodding in stout agreement, the butler continued upon his way, leaving the valet to ponder how he was to persuade the duke to take his custom to a new and as yet untried boot-maker. Finding no immediate solution, Watton attempted once again to remove the stubborn residue of tallow grease from his Grace's top-boots, although even his own receipt for blacking had thus far proved unequal to the task.

Chapter Thirty

Faced with the thorny task of persuading Maia that a visit to the modiste was not only desirable but necessary, with more forbearance than she felt, Caro shouldered the responsibility for the outing, explaining, "It has been more than two years since I have spent the season in London, it would not do to be seen looking like a ragbag, what would people say?"

Maia eyed her god-mother warily, for not only was Caroline rarely concerned with the opinions of others, but more pertinently, she was always expensively and tastefully dressed in the latest style; her silk finery never screamed of one dressing to impress, although impress she invariably did. Comparing her god-mother's flawless sensibility with her aunt Wreningham's disastrous forays into the world of fashion, Maia was well-aware of the gulf which existed between the ladies; for despite claiming to be impoverished, Mrs Wreningham spent a shocking sum on finery but rarely looked well dressed. A king's ransom would be spent upon Emme's trousseau and bridal clothes, forcing Mrs Wreningham to penny pinch in other ways.

Seeing Maia's frown, Caroline enquired brightly "Did you receive a letter from your cousin? May we expect a visit from her? What does she say of your betrothal?" She had guessed the letter Heydon had brought into the morning-room was from Emmeline Wreningham, for the girlish scrawl addressing the missive had been plain to see.

"The letter was from Emme, but I do not expect her dance attendance upon me, for she is busy with her own betrothal and bridal plans, trousseau and wedding clothes. Can there really be so much to prepare before one marries?"

Tactfully Caro did not respond, having no doubt that Miss Wreningham was avoiding her cousin and the taint of association with one who had caused such a scandal. She noted that her god-daughter seemed to have neglected to tell Emmeline her own news; that of her impending betrothal to Mr Siddeham.

The dowager deftly distracted Maia from dwelling upon the subject of matrimony, announcing, "My dear, it is far too soon to expect callers, after all we have hardly had time to draw breath. Besides it is such an unfashionable hour. But before Bradenham and his cousin arrive to pay their respects to you, let us seek the advice of Madam Aiguille. Greek street is not where one might expect to find a modiste of her skill, but she is undoubtedly worth the effort, so we shall turn a blind eye to her address. You must tell me what you think, for I am convinced her French accent has a touch of brogue, but perhaps I misjudge her."

The merest mention of the possibility of Duke of Bradenham and Mr Siddenham calling upon her, unfashionable hour or not, was enough to send Maia rushing for her bonnet and reticule.

So it was that Caroline Alconbury and her god-daughter were safely ensconced in the Greek Street modiste's, with the excitable Madam Aiguille, when the duke strode up the steps of the Berkeley square house and knocked solemnly upon the recently replaced door knocker.

***

Madam Aiguille was a diminutive, lumpy, vivacious woman of middle years, with what could only be described as borrowed, impossibly golden ringlets, pinned to the edge of her lace trimmed cap. The irascible French woman moved with a speed Maia found quite breathtaking; talking and imperiously waving her hands, while her golden ringlets bobbed in furious accompaniment. She had fallen upon the dowager with alacrity as soon as Caroline set foot over the threshold of the workroom which also served as the modiste's consulting room.

She scolded the dowager for staying away from London for so long. "I zink, zat per'aps you 'ad died, but non, no one ees telling me zat you are no more, so I zink, ach, she ees upzet wiz moi."

The woman's accent was puzzling, and Maia could not place it. There were occasional lapses into what might have been brogue, but Madame Aiguille spoke so swiftly that it was difficult to be sure.

Proceeding to measure her esteemed client, by the simple expedient of demanding that she turn around, the modiste assessed the dowager's curves with an approving eye.

"As I zought, you 'ave not changed, your size she is perfect- Zo, I will make you ball gowns? Ow many? Ten, twelve? You will need ze day dresses, walking dresses and carriage dresses, non?"

While the dowager and the modiste sorted through bolts of silks, gauzes and cotton voiles, the Frenchwoman's hands accentuating her words, Maia watched, fascinated. She had always enjoyed visits to the seamstress and her first brief foray into the ton had naturally meant she had required ball gowns and day dresses. Observing her god-mother taking such an active rôle in discussing and arguing, not merely putting herself into the hands of her modiste, was a revelation, having firmly been told what to wear by her aunt Wreningham's staid modiste, while her aunt nodding in agreement at all the dour pronouncements. At the time Maia felt she had selected her gowns reasonably well, as far as she have been permitted, but realising that she was now in the presence of genius, she was agog.

At last with the negotiations and selection completed, the dowager and Madam Aiguille turned as one, each eyeing Maia's figure with a considering and - in the modiste's case - calculating eye.

Leaning behind her, Madam Aiguille rummaged through ells of rustling silk upon a work table, until with a cry of triumph she found what she had been seeking. "Now, we shall zee." Muttering to herself, she leafed through the pages of the modiste's bible, until she reached the page she had been searching for.

The fashion plate depicted a woman clad in what appeared to be a diaphanous gown, designed in the classical style. To Maia's mind the bust-line was shockingly low, revealing far more of the well-drawn young lady's ample charms than was strictly necessary.

Addressing the dowager while appearing to ignore Maia, the Frenchwoman explained, "En Paree et es wore zo," by way of demonstration she placed her hand against Maia's breast, whilst holding up the fashion plate beside her.

Maia blushed as she looked down where the modiste was indicating; as if a young woman in decent society would allow herself to be so shockingly displayed, then noticed with horror her god-mother's considering look.

The modiste continued, still ignoring Maia. "But 'ere in Londres, it must be worn zo." She raised her hand a little higher than it had previously been, but as far as Maia was concerned, still far too low to be decent.

Meanwhile Caroline, who was nodding in agreement, took the book of fashion plates from Madam Aiguille, and studied the drawing carefully.

"With I think, white roses embroidered at the hem, not red. It is Maia's first season after all, and red roses have rather drastic connotations, don't they?"

The modiste beamed her concurrence. However, before the unholy alliance were completely carried away, Maia spoke up, "I have no need of more gowns, my aunt Wreningham saw to it that I have enough to be decently dressed for the remainder of the season, and it is not as if I have many engagements to attend. I am sure I have sufficient."

While Maia sounded as if she believed this nonsense, the modiste threw he hands up uttering theatrically "Quelle horreur." Stating that Maia must be a lady of "supreme sang-froid" to believe "zat you could ever 'ave enough gowns." This was followed by a stream of indistinguishable French, which Maia suspected no self-respecting governess would demand her charges be able to translate.

The dowager duchess suppressed her amusement as she waited for the torrent of Gallic to stop. And when momentarily exhausted by the outpouring of dismay Madam at last paused for breath, Caro made the most of the opportunity by fixing Maia with a firm lift of her eyebrows and a gentle reproof.

"It was very kind of your aunt to oversee your wardrobe, but do consider my love, your circumstances have altered since then, you have different expectations now, especially in light of your new family. All eyes will be upon you, so let us give them something -" considering her words carefully, the dowager hesitated.

Maia eyed the fashioned plate and muttered "Something dramatic to look at?"

Her god-mother smiled. "I am not sure that was the word I was searching for, but I see you comprehend my meaning."

"God-mama if I were to make an appearance dressed in such a gown, I have no doubt his Grace would either throw his coat over me, or insist I marry his cousin instantly, before any more of me was revealed!"

"Indeed?" Maia did not notice the dowager's wry smile.

Caro continued, "I will be purchasing your come-out gowns, in addition to your trousseau, as my bridal gift to you. Let us begin. My dear I will not be argued with, so please do not waste time by attempting to do so."

The modiste, accustomed to ignoring the gossip and discussions of her more affluent clients, appeared to pay no attention to either the dowager duchess or her attractive god-child, until Caroline indicated she should to begin to cut the parchment in order to measure Maia for the numerous garments she would require, and returning to the fashion plate, the woman continued as if there had been no interruption. Removing the girl's bonnet and unfastening her hair, the modiste moved the loosely gathered mass and held it high at the back of Maia's head.

"Your 'air, must be warn a la Grecian, zo." Standing at arm's length to study the effect, she nodded solemnly, adding, "Not a la Roma," and pushed the dark tangle to the front of Maia's head in order to illustrate the difference between the two hairstyles.

"I 'vill make you a princesse, you 'vill zee."

Maia was torn between refusing the generous gift and wanting to throw her arms about her god-mother's neck and kiss her. In the end she did neither, but smiled gratefully at the dowager, her violet eyes shining.

Caroline kissed her cheek affectionately. "Just so my love, you are wise not to argue with me, there really is no point, besides, you are too beautiful for me forgo the opportunity to dress you. One has so little joy these days, and now that Charlotte has had a boy, who knows how long it will be before I have such joy again."

Her dramatic sighs fooled no-one, least of all her god-daughter, but aware of the hand of Madam Aiguille at her breast, Maia frowned. "Very well, but I refuse to wear a gown so shockingly low." The modiste sighed in frustration and raised her hand fractionally.

Maia took the woman's hand and raised it again. "There, that will be perfect."

Behind her, unseen by Maia, the dowager caught Madam's beady eye and, without saying a word, Caro held her hand against her own breast and making sure the modiste was attending, lowered her hand significantly, saying, "And I think perhaps a more fitted sleeve than the one in the plate, after all Maia is beautifully slender; it would be a shame to make her look as if she were puffed up."

The modiste beamed her appreciation, rejoicing as a woman of business, as well as an artist, for here was a young lady whom it would be not only lucrative, but also a thrill to dress.

"Mademoiselle will be ze belle of ze ball," she sighed happily. And for once the shrewd Madam Aiguille, meant every word.

***

It was some hours later when Maia returned to Berkeley square, elated and exhausted; she had poured over dozens of fashion plates, discussed endlessly the minutiae of trimmings, buttons and embroidery, as well as the properties and benefits of crepe de chine over gauze, until her head had spun. It had been a revelation to discover that her god-mother was an authority in such matters, for she had taken for granted that Caro's exquisite attire was due solely to the skill of her modiste.

They were greeted by Heydon, bearing the dowager's silver tea tray. He informed them that the Duke of Bradenham had called upon Miss Maia, shortly after their departure. However, after waiting for sometime, he had left his card, promising to call again upon the morrow. With supreme dignity Heydon omitted to mention that his Grace had appeared to be rather peevish, or that his vow to return had been somewhat terse.

Greatly annoyed, Maia picked up the calling card bearing the duke's name, one corner folded upwards to indicate that it had been left by Bradenham himself rather than a servant, and flicked it unconsciously with her fingers.

She announced pointedly, "God-mama I fear I shall miss the duke's visit tomorrow, for I cannot delay in visiting a milliner. Such pity his Grace did not seek to enquire whether or not I had a previous engagement."

The dowager smiled appreciatively, as she deftly unbuttoned her gloves at the wrists, before peeling them from her slender arms. "Indeed, I am glad you have taken matters into your own hands, for I feared it would fall to me." Seeing Maia's questioning look, she added gently, "I was referring to the milliner, my dear."

Chapter Thirty-One

The notion that he would be indulging Maia in another game of cat and mouse had not crossed Cosmo's mind as he made his way to Berkeley square, therefore he was justifiably taken aback upon handing his hat, gloves, walking cane and calling card to the impassive Heydon, to be informed that the dowager duchess and Miss Hindolveston were not at home.

Determining that the pair were indeed gone from the house and not merely disinclined to receive visitors, the duke waited; expecting an explanation for Miss Hindolveston's failure to keep what he had assumed was a fixed engagement.

The explanation however, was not forthcoming, and he was forced to announce, "I will await their return." Which, given the circumstances, seemed the lesser of two evils; having no desire to spend the entire day lurking in the vicinity of Berkeley square or, worse still, returning later only to be advised that the ladies were again not at home.

As ever, Heydon showed no undue emotion, but merely inclined his greying head in acknowledgement of his Grace's request, and showed the noble gentleman into library; for the dowager duchess had been clear in her instruction that his Grace was to be allowed to "cool his heels for as long as he likes." That her green eyes had twinkled with wicked delight as she imparted the direction, Heydon did not see fit to mention. Nor with wisdom bourne of experience, did he advise the duke that her Grace was unlikely to return for some hours; for enjoying trips to the milliner, the dowager usually required several footmen to convey her purchases from her carriage.

Meanwhile, the faithful butler was under orders to serve his Grace a fine claret, for Caroline was of the opinion that while Bradenham deserved to be left to his own devices, there was no point in infuriating the man beyond endurance. At least, not until she was there to enjoy the spectacle of the Duke of Bradenham, being so effectively thwarted.

The dowager's Berkeley square residence boasted a library known for exerting a sense of calm over most of the gentlemen who - upon occasion - were deposited into its rich mahogany interior. Sadly, it did little to soothe Cosmo's irritation. He paced, sat, stood and stared out of the window at the waving branches of the plane trees in the square beyond, with varying degrees of distraction. He even read for a while; Heydon having thoughtfully placed copies of the London newspapers upon the reading table. Yet even this usually restful venture was doomed to failure upon the discovery halfway through a fascinating account of the attempted assassination of the king, that one page within *The Morning Post* was missing. Presuming either Maia or the dowager had committed this act of vandalism, Cosmo crossly folded the newssheet, abandoning it upon the polished table, as the French mantle clock struck with a delicate and precise chime.

He had been kept waiting for two long hours.

Unaccustomed to such casual treatment, the duke was not in the best of tempers as he received his beaver hat, gloves and cane from Heydon's capable hands, and with due care, attention and ceremony was shown out of the house.

His ire mounting with each step, Cosmo made his way along Bruton street, and was not altogether delighted to espy his cousin in conversation with one of his cronies. He had not yet requested the pleasure of Percy's company since his return to London, telling himself it would be prudent to wait until his interview with Maia to arrange the time and location where Percy would be delivered to make the girl a formal declaration.

From his vantage point the duke was surprised to notice what a dandy his cousin had become. Like the duke, Percy had always favoured spotless linen and enjoyed the benefits of expensive tailoring, but Cosmo could scarcely believe his cousin's newly achieved, overly confident and entirely tasteless rendering of sartorial elegance.

Such was the confusion in the manner in which his neck cloth was tied, that it took Cosmo some time to discern that far from being a haphazard and overly complicated arrangement of Percy's own design, it was merely a poor attempt at the Mail Coach. Furthermore, there was something distasteful about Percy's boots, although whether the heel was quite as it should be, or the tassels were longer than one could wish, Bradenham could not determine. The overall impression was far from inspiring, and left Cosmo wondering whom his cousin was aping, and when this change had begun to manifest. Assuming of course that Percy was blindly mimicking someone, and this distressing display was not simply due to an appalling lack of taste.

Engrossed in conversation, Percy did not notice his cousin, and was greatly taken aback upon parting company with his companion to find Cosmo at his elbow, having not been aware of his return to

London.

Mr Siddenham covered his confusion by greeting the duke with unnecessary bonhomie. "Cosmo, my dear fellow, how delightful to see you, I take it you are empty-handed for I see no weeping bride in your wake." He gave an affected laugh. "No doubt you have seen sense and realised we made a mountain out of a petticoat molehill." Amused by his own wit, Percy flicked a speck of dust from the sleeve of his rather tight, well-padded jacket. How the ladies of the establishments he frequented had swooned over the jacket, which privately he admitted magnificently enhanced his somewhat lacking physique.

Percy's comments left the distinct and distasteful impression that he considered his involvement with Maia on a par with a discreet dalliance with an experienced matron, with no-one any the wiser; it was certainly a far cry from the brandy sodden plea for help he had made that evening in Whites.

Casting a raking glance from the top of his cousin's well-oiled locks, to the tops of has tasselled boots, the duke allowed his disapproval to show. Not being a man to mince his words, he pronounced coldly, "You resemble an upstart cit, not a gentleman of the ton. One can only hope your wife will contrive to make you see sense."

Percy paled, his bravado fading. "M-my w-wife?" he stammered.

"Surely you did not think I went jaunting all the way to Norfolk, at the beginning of the season, with the sole object of returning with your bride, only to neglect to see the thing through?"

When Percy did not comment, noting his cousin's distinct lack of gratitude, Cosmo smiled sardonically. "Your appreciation overwhelms me."

Spluttering in a most un-gentlemanly way, Mr Siddenham's head reeled as he tried to comprehend the ramifications of what he had just been told. While assuming an air of bored disinterest, Bradenham waited, not particularly patiently.

"But- but- I- I assumed you would decide- that is to say -" gathering his scattered wits, Percy appealed to his cousin's family pride. "The girl is hardly a suitable choice for a Siddenham."

The duke glared at the dandy. "My dear Percy, as you so succinctly, if ineloquently informed me in Whites, you compromised the lady, therefore you must marry her." His dark eyes were hard. "Miss Hindolveston is a lady; she was compromised; you will marry her. Do I make myself clear? I have not spent the past week rusticating in Norfolk, in order for you to decide the incident in the Wreninghams' long gallery is of no consequence." Warming to his subject Cosmo continued, "If you think to wriggle out of your obligation, allow me add a little more weight to the argument by advising you that Miss Hindolveston is in London."

Although incredulous at this startling piece of information, Mr Siddenham said nothing.

"She is in the care of her god-mama, of whom you may have heard, the Dowager Duchess of Alconbury."

At the mention of the dowager duchess, Percy's already pale face took on a grey hue. In her ignorance, Mrs Wreningham may have underestimated the dowager duchess's far reaching hand, but Mr Siddenham was aware that Caroline Alconbury was a force to be reckoned with.

Percy swallowed hard and murmured faintly, "I had no notion."

"Miss Hindolveston has finally agreed it would be expedient for you to marry, although there may be a delay of sorts; for while I had anticipated the wedding would be carried out swiftly and privately, the dowager duchess has other ideas."

Visibly brightening at this encouraging development, Percy's hopes were soon dashed when Cosmo continued ruthlessly, "As Miss Hindolveston's god-mama, the dowager believes it behoves her to bring the girl out in a manner befitting the Siddenham name, and the coronet which might indeed be hers, for as my heir is it entirely possible that your wife will be the future duchess. In the dowager's care your bride-to-be will be protected for a while at least from possible scandal, and we may effect to present this marriage in more palatable light to both families."

Percy looked even more horrified. "Not a big wedding?"

His cousin nodded, adding viciously, "With all the attendant hullabaloo, just think how my sisters will enjoy themselves, and Constance will be overjoyed to see you leg-shackled at last, although it is too bad her boys are not old enough to attend, for there will be a sad shortage of males within the bridal party. You know of course, that your bride has dozens of sisters?"

"Dozens?" Mr Siddenham yelped, looking as if he were about to cast up his accounts.

Recalling the numerous times he had wished to throttle his cousin over the past days, Bradenham nodded gleefully. "Dozens." He was about to add that Percy's children would never want for doting aunts, but upon recalling whom the mother of Percy's children was to be, discovered that the desire to throttle Percy had not been assuaged, indeed, it seemed to have intensified.

"I intend to introduce you to Miss Hindolveston, that is to say to introduce you to her formally, and after you have offered for her and been accepted, we will announce the betrothal. You will marry by the end of the season. That should provide the dowager with enough time to polish Miss Hindolveston off, so to speak."

Growing increasingly agitated, Percy seemed bereft of speech, although he managed a few squeaks as his immediate future was mapped out so comprehensively.

"Do attend, Percy." Irritated by the unnecessary shuffling of his cousin's unsatisfactory boots, Cosmo went on mercilessly, "I will call upon the dowager in the morning and I expect you to accompany me. You must become better acquainted with your bride's god-mama before you marry, for I expect she will loom large in your future."

Without waiting for his cousin respond, the duke bid him good morning, his parting shot calculated to further disquiet the reluctant bridegroom's heart. "Until tomorrow- and try to look as if this was a joyful occasion Percy, you are to be betrothed, not go to madam guillotine, it is I understand supposed to be a happy occasion."

As the duke went on his way, Percy felt that of the two options, the guillotine was the more preferable.

***

"Harrington, you might have warned me my cousin had taken a foppish turn, I had no notion of it until I beheld him this morning."

While the duke sounded aggrieved, his twinkling eyes held the truth and his secretary held out his hands in appeal. "Your Grace, how does one tactfully inform his employer of such a difficulty?"

"Difficulty? No, no my dear Harrington, it is far worse than that, and let us be clear upon the terminology; my cousin has begun to dress like the son of a merchant with an overly generous allowance and little regard for good taste. It is more than a difficulty, it is a catastrophe. One wonders if I can disinherit him for such a crime. I must investigate the rules of succession more closely."

Wisely, Harrington remained silent, believing such matters should not be taken lightly.

"While I sympathise with your sensibilities, I cannot believe you would wish the title to pass to such a man. Indeed, I nearly wept when I saw his neck cloth."

Harrington winced empathetically. "A bad Mathematical?"

"Worse, much worse," was his employers doom laden

rejoinder.

Torn between horror and fascination, his secretary enquired eagerly, "Worse than a bad Mathematical, your Grace?"

"The most diabolical attempt at a Mail Coach, I have ever had the misfortune to witness. One can only wonder if my cousin's valet has lately given notice, for it would seem the only plausible explanation."

Harrington grinned in appreciation.

"I believe it would be best not to mention it to Watton, he is already but a hair's breadth from quitting me over the boots, and my demanding he catch Miss Hindolveston, and then there was the carriage ride in the dark ..." Cosmo pondered. "Now that I think on it, Watton has every right to give notice. Should he do so, be sure he knows there is a vacancy within my cousin's household. It would, I think, serve them both justly." Having resolved the complicated employment arrangements so soundly, the duke put all thoughts of valets out of his head.

"May I ask how you found the household at Berkeley square?" Enquired his secretary tactfully.

The sharp frown answered Harrington's question long before Bradenham replied. "Out, Harrington, they were out, after I expressly informed Miss Hindolveston that I would call upon her."

Attempting to pour oil upon what were clearly troubled waters, Harrington supplied, "No doubt her Grace has much to do, she is after all behind-hand with the season and will expect Miss Hindolveston to accompany her."

"Undoubtedly, but why do I have the feeling I am being avoided?" He looked at the pile of correspondence and gilt edged invitations awaiting his perusal with something akin to horror. "Harrington, is it possible I am acquainted with all these people?"

"I believe so your Grace, and I have already taken the liberty of discarding the requests I knew your Grace would not wish to attend."

Bradenham looked pained. "Are there really so many dull-witted, charmless, schoolroom hatchlings making their come-outs this season?"

"It would seem so, your Grace."

"And these are the ones upon which I must dance attendance?"

There was no reply, Harrington knew better than to bait his employer on such matters.

Snatching up the pile of cards requesting the pleasure of his company at this soiree, that ball, and the other rout, Bradenham's method of sorting the invitations was simple; if he liked the parents of the girl making her come-out he said yes; if - more commonly - he disliked them, the card was thrown across the desk with a resounding "No!" Accompanied by groans at the prospect of yet another unprepossessing female being unleashed upon the ton.

At one point in the proceedings he paused to consider the engraving upon the card, names he did not immediately recognise.

"Your Grace, I understand Lady Rushford, is a particular friend of the Dowager Duchess of Alconbury," offered Harrington helpfully.

"Now I begin to comprehend, and as ever I am in awe of your scheming Harrington. If you were a woman you would without doubt be in league with Caroline Alconbury, although I am heartily relieved that in his wisdom the Almighty, placed you within male ranks, for we are sorely outgunned, or do I mean out-manned?" As he spoke, Cosmo recalled the dowager duchess saying something similar, and the image of Maia Hindolveston, surrounded by the dark leaves and blossom of the orangery, sprang to mind. It was a bewitching memory. His secretary's voice brought Bradenham back to the present with a start.

"I am informed by a reliable source that the dowager duchess and Lady Rushford, have elder daughters who are of an age."

"So this," Cosmo waved the invitation in his hand, "must be for another daughter making her come-out. One would expect Caroline Alconbury to attend such an occasion, and where the she goes by necessity so does Miss Hindolveston."

Harrington nodded imperceptibly.

"You are of course right, I must attend this most dire of occasions, but it seems remarkably hard having done my utmost to avoid as many of these tedious come-outs as I could decently manage over the years, to be forced to attend the come-outs of second-daughters of people I have not even met. However, as I do not intend to allow any damage to occur to Miss Hindolveston, I am very much afraid I must make a cake of myself keeping her out of harm's way."

"Do you really consider Miss Hindolveston's safety remains in jeopardy? Surely no harm can come to her now she is under the protection of the dowager duchess."

The duke looked grim. "I am beginning to believe Maia Hindolveston could come to mischief in Thomas & Co.'s locked vault, at a ton gathering she should find it easy to fall into a scrape. Harrington, I put it to you, the damnable girl was abducted from a church!"

The secretary was unsure whether to smile, or to match his employers apparent gravity.

"However, perhaps Percy should be made to suffer; after all he is the cause of all of this." Bradenham seemed to be far away, as he murmured, "At least, I think he is."

The moment passed and Cosmo returned to the task of weeding out the social wheat from the obsequious chaff. Shortly thereafter, the desk was littered with cards, while at his right hand there remained a small, neat pile. Harrington knew better than to question his Grace's decisions, and collecting the discarded cards, removed them.

Seated at his own desk overlooking the street below, Harrington opened the silver capped inkwell, and with great enjoyment wrote a carefully worded missive to his Grace's cousin, advising the gentleman that he would be attending the come-out ball for Miss Mary Rushford. Grinning, the secretary could almost see the disgust on Mr Siddenham's face.

Chapter Thirty-Two

There could be no other reason for the squeals of exclamation resonating from Maia's chamber; the first of the gowns had arrived from Madam Aiguille. The squealing had been done by Lovelace Loveday in heartfelt admiration of the workmanship of the gowns, while Maia had observed the arrival of the carefully packaged gowns in silent, horrified wonder.

Now, as she helped the lady's maid-in-training unpack the carriage dresses, day dresses, afternoon dresses, walking dresses, spencers, pelisses and evening gowns, her wonder turned to delight, although she was still reluctant to accept such a magnanimous and expensive gift.

"I cannot possibly need all these, anyone would imagine I have been going about unsuitably attired."

Looking up from the mesmerising drape of the royal blue carriage dress Love had just shaken-out, her god-mother smiled, "If you mean that one would think that you have been wandering around London naked, then by all means say so."

She laughed at Maia's shocked face. "Try not to be prudish dear, one would think you had never seen a naked figure. I am sure you would look perfectly beautiful naked, but since I do not wish his grace to suffer a spasm, or fall over in an apoplectic fit, it behoves me to ensure you are suitably and beautifully attired."

Maia gazed doubtfully at the gowns. "It looks very much as if I will be somewhat overdressed, I had no idea you had instructed Madam Aiguille to make me so many things, or so quickly."

Observing the lady's maid gently shaking out the folds of whisper thin, gauzy, white muslin of a particularly enchanting gown, with white roses embroidered in upon its hem, Caroline spoke hastily, "While it would be too diverting to remain at home and watch you try these on, I am afraid we must hurry. I must have new gloves for mine are past bearing and there is not a moment to delay- tie your bonnet on your way, my love."

Without waiting for Maia to reply, the dowager bundled her out of her bedchamber, leaving Love to unpack the remainder of the gowns. Following in her god-daughter's wake down the stairs, Caroline was well-pleased she had successfully prevented Maia from trying on the magnificent ballgown, having no desire to risk Maia sending it back to the modiste; wickedly hoping the neckline would go unobserved until it was too late.

Chapter Thirty-Three

It was by no means certain whom was more vexed when the Duke of Bradenham, accompanied by his cousin, finally crossed the threshold of the Dowager Duchess of Alconbury's pink salon, having been announced in sonorous tones by Heydon. The duke was certainly grim. While pausing in her perusal of a diverting communication from a particular friend, Caroline tutted her annoyance under her breath, before schooling her features into a practised smile, for despite wishing Bradenham - and more especially Mr Siddenham - to the devil, the dowager knew better than to allow the duke to know it.

Deftly tucking the letter into the cushions behind her, Caro arose with a flurry of skirts, and receiving Mr Siddenham's flourishing bow and the formal incline of the duke's dark head, with an easy curtsy, indicated that the gentlemen should sit. Grateful that Heydon had possessed the foresight to show her unwelcome callers into the pink salon; with its watered silk walls and overtly feminine furnishings, the pink salon always proved so delightfully uncomfortable that unwanted male guests rarely stayed long.

"To what do I owe the pleasure of your company this glorious day?" the dowager beamed. "It is the perfect morning to take a turn in the park. The weather is agreeable is it not Mr Siddenham?"

With this Caroline turned her gimlet gaze upon Percy, although it was debatable whether he was the greater or lesser of the twin causes of her irritation.

Percy had been attempting to seat himself with some semblance of dignity upon the too small, horribly slippery, very pink, silken seat of the gilded chair, he looked up warily; the dowager's reputation doing nothing to ease his discomfiture.

Eyeing the dowager duchess with suspicion, Cosmo commented dryly, "We expected to be able to address Miss Hindolveston."

It was too bad, Caro considered, that as ever, the damnable man had got to the point, She had hoped to fob the pair off without either of them broaching the subject of matrimony. But rather than show her displeasure, she beamed at the gentlemen again.

"Indeed, both of you? How unusual, things have certainly

changed since my day. Does my god-daughter expect you? If she does then she is exceedingly naughty, for she neglected to mention it, and has promised to accompany me upon a walk."

Caroline carefully modulated her voice, taking on a petulant air, which greatly adding to Mr Siddenham's misery and, as he shuffled uneasily upon the too small chair, she quietly gloated.

Bradenham seemed oddly at ease in the ridiculously minute chair. For if Percy was too large for the finely worked seat, the duke positively dwarfed it, yet he did not appear to be unduly concerned by the diminutive furniture.

"Whether Miss Hindolveston, expects us or not, is entirely unimportant, particularly when one considers that I have left my card more once, yet she has not seen fit to receive me," retorted the duke with some asperity, unaccustomed to such cavalier treatment.

"Indeed? Then you may be sure it is I who am at fault." Caroline waved her hand airily. "You know how it is, one finds oneself in London and must by necessity see one's mantua maker and milliner, to say nothing of the considerations of new shoes and gloves. It has been a positive whirl since our arrival, but what else is one to do? It would not do to be poorly dressed."

She cast a disparaging glance at the overly tight knee breeches of the thoroughly miserable Mr Siddenham; his jacket was obviously the recipient of an excess of buckram padding, for one shoulder had slipped, giving him an oddly lopsided appearance. However, he was unaware of the dowager's silent censure of his attire and nodded solemnly in agreement.

It was at this juncture that the lady at the heart of the visit entered the pink salon, and both men rose to their feet to make the somewhat awkward and, in Percy's case, wretched formalities. With the pleasantries over, Maia seated herself at her god-mother's side, and was fascinated to observe Mr Siddenham slide awkwardly upon the pink silk of the small chair, as he attempted to reseat himself.

"My love, his Grace had informed me that he had expected to pay us a visit before this morning, I was not aware such an arrangement had been made."

Caroline's wicked green eyes twinkled at Maia who, trying not to notice Mr Siddenham's floundering, opened her violet eyes wide in guileless articulation; knowing precisely what the dowager was up to.

"I do not believe the details of his Grace's proposed visit had been decided upon, god-mama."

"That explains it," Caro crowed delightedly. "I knew the duke must be mistaken, for I was convinced you would have informed me of such an arrangement."

"Naturally, god-mama."

"A simple misunderstanding," the dowager beamed at this apparent epiphany.

However, Cosmo's displeasure, which had grown with each ridiculous syllable of the exchange, was abundantly clear. He addressed Caroline tersely, "With your leave, I wish to have a moment privately with Miss Hindolveston and my cousin."

Maia felt her temper rising, not only had the wretched man issued decrees regarding his expectations, and then had the audacity to complain when she had not complied with his demands, but he had obviously dragged the unfortunate Mr Siddenham with him to Berkeley square. The wretched man was obviously there under sufferance; certainly his attire indicated his anticipation of something other than being forced to endure a dull social call.

However, Maia's sympathy was only of fleeting duration as she reminded herself that this ridiculous man was to be her husband, and the memory of the duke calling her attire into question, rankled anew in light of Mr Siddenham's resemblance to an overdressed buffoon. The knowledge that she was beautifully gowned was pleasing, and Maia was grateful to her god-mama for the walking-dress in which she was dressed had been well-chosen; its deep violet hue matching her eyes perfectly. Surely Mr Siddenham had to be aware that he was a laughing stock in his padded jacket and tightly fitting breeches? Really, it was difficult to avert one's gaze.

Finding her voice, Maia spoke briskly. "It was gracious of you to call upon us today your Grace, however, you find us about to quit the house for a turn about the square. Our arrangement is of long-standing, for we have talked of little else since yesterday."

As if to emphasise the immediacy of their departure, Maia stood. While relieved that the awkward and exceedingly uncomfortable interview was drawing to a close without any mention of marriage being made, Mr Siddenham leapt to his feet, leaving Bradenham no choice to stand also; his fury evident.

The dowager gave a theatrical sigh. "London is always such a rush, with barely time to enjoy the delights to be found in the square, but one must dash and walk, be seen and see whom else is being seen." Another sigh followed hard on the heels of the first. "My god-daughter is correct, we must take a turn about the square, for I am determined to examine the trees more closely. I was not convinced plane trees would do well in London, and said so when they were planted, but as far as one can tell from the door-step they seem to be thriving. Alconbury would have been delighted to see them flourish; he predicted they would. Will it rain do you think? I do hope not. I will bid good-day to you both; Bradenham, Mr Siddenham."

With that Caroline rose, and first the duke, and then his cousin bent over her hand in parting. She released them by pushing each firmly away as he held her hand, causing both men to take a step back; leaving them in no doubt that they had been summarily dismissed.

Adjusting his gloves as he marched crossly down the steps of the Berkeley square house, Cosmo wondered how it was when it came to Maia Hindolveston, that all his plans seemed to be thwarted - although perhaps only temporarily.

"Percy, you will be attending the Rushford ball this evening." It was command not a question, his cousin noted wrathfully.

"So your blasted Harrrington has informed me, though I cannot think why. The family are hardly well-connected; the daughter is by all accounts not well-favoured and …"

The duke interrupted before Percy could add to his litany of peevish complaints. "The girl's mother is a friend of Caroline Alconbury's, and you will attend because your bride-to-be will be there."

Percy looked even more aggrieved. "Cosmo, surely you must see this whole thing is nonsense; Maia Hindolveston and I are like chalk and cheese, we cannot be expected to spend the rest of our lives together. Good lord, she is an antidote."

Regarding his cousin with disgust, Bradenham enquired coldly, "What the devil are you talking about?"

"Her unladylike behaviour and unbecoming dress to begin with ..."

Percy preened and made an adjustment his badly tied version of what Cosmo assumed was the Mail Coach, or perhaps Harrington was right and it was a poor attempt at the Mathematical, it was difficult to tell.

"And then cousin, did you hear the way she spoke to you? You must be sensible that this is a shocking misalliance, but we can avoid it, we must avoid it."

Turning upon Percy, the duke fixed him with a penetrating gaze, "Had you wished to avoid marriage to such a lady, it would have behoved you to avoid assignations in the long gallery. Let us be clear upon one thing; it is too late dear cousin, far too late to make such statements, for I will not allow you to further drag either Miss Hindolveston's name, or mine, through the mire."

Remaining mulishly mute, Percy knew further argument at

this juncture would be foolish.

"Caroline Alconbury, wants Maia to make her come-out, a singularly foolish notion, but I grow weary of this farce; tonight you will propose marriage to Miss Hindolveston, within my hearing. She will accept you - she has agreed that much - and I trust that when the lines are drawn she will keep her end of the bargain. The announcement of your betrothal will be made, and that will be an end to it."

"An end?" Queried Percy, hopefully.

"Until you are wed, properly, with as much pomp and nonsense as can be managed between now and the end of the season, by which time the girl will have made her come-out to satisfy the dowager, and tongues will cease to wag once the betrothal has been announced. Your wedding, with all the attendant fussing, should delight even my sisters, not that I would have the world deceived for one moment that I wish to please them, but then it is not I who am to be married."

Looking thoroughly disgusted by this turn of events, Mr Siddenham sighed in submission to the combined dictates of society and his cousin. "Oh, very well, but damn it all, it is a high price to pay for a liaison in a long gallery."

"One can only hope you have learned your lesson," was the duke's unsympathetic reply.

"Indeed, you may be sure from now on my dalliances will be carried out with due care and attention, have no fear on that score, cousin."

Registering with distaste the implications of this statement upon the connubial happiness of Maia Hindolveston, Bradenham felt the urge to knock his cousin's teeth down his throat - until they reached the location of the Mail Coach neck-cloth, or what passed within Percy's immediate circle as the Mail Coach. No, Harrington was right, it was the Mathematical.

Chapter Thirty-Four

With her fan held discreetly to her lips, Lady Ormesby turned to her companion and indiscreetly whispered behind it.

The lady at her side, delightfully scandalised and thoroughly entertained, responded, "Why else would the girl simply vanish at the start of the season? You may be assured, Miss Hindolveston is increasing and has been sent away to hide the fact." Lady Bellmont's tone was tinged with disgust. "She has undoubtedly been removed from good society, although one would expect her father to insist she wed Siddenham. I grant you, he is not what one might wish in a son-in-law, but he is Bradenham's heir." Here the lady sniffed disdainfully. "And as the duke himself is no hurry to wed, perhaps Percy Siddenham may inherit after all."

Lady Ormesby paused in her coquettish fanning as a thought occurred to her. "Could it be Maia Hindolveston has stolen a march on the other girls who had set their cap at a title this season? How vulgar."

Looking particularly nasty, Lady Bellmont's reply was vicious, "Not as vulgar as she will be when she produces and remains unwed."

The ladies' salacious conversation was interrupted when the Dowager Duchess of Alconbury swept past, their eyes greedily devoured Caroline from top-to-silk-clad toe. They took in her fine gown, as well as her sparkling earbobs, bracelets and fine diamond necklace; for the late ninth duke had delighted in extravagantly adorning his wife, claiming it gave him joy to see her twinkling - and what was more; as a boon he was always assured of finding her in the dark.

Lady Ormesby whispered, "Utterly tawdry," with considerable venom into Lady Bellmont's ear. However, both were silenced by the slender figure of Maia Hindolveston following in the dowager's wake. Unable to utter a word, the gossiping ladies stood agog as Miss Hindolveston was introduced to Lady Rushton and her daughter.

Belatedly remembering to close her mouth, which had been hanging agape, Lady Ormesby, turned to her companion, "Well! Did you ever see the like?"

Lady Bellmont, who had closed her eyes as if about to swoon, responded wanly, "Shocking, quite shocking. I must find a quiet place where I might recover myself. Come Cornelia, let us remove ourselves from this unrefined melee and sit where we may attempt to still our nerves, perhaps with a small glass of ratafia?"

With that the pair made their way to where they could best enjoy the spectacle of the infamous Maia Hindolveston attending a ton ball.

***

The infamous girl curtsied to her hostess gracefully, grateful to have been invited and welcomed at such an event, having underestimated the considerable influence of her god-mama.

Raising Miss Hindolveston by the chin, Lady Rushford, looked fondly into her eyes. "You are much like your papa, yet I see something of your mother in you. How does she fare?"

"My mother is fragile, but is still in good spirits, thank you."

Briefly lost in the memories of youth, Lady Rushford, was returned to the task of launching her second daughter into the ton, by a gentle cough from the shy, rather gawky girl standing to her left.

"Miss Hindolveston, may I present my daughter Mary. Mary dear, this is the daughter of an old friend of mine, perhaps the two of you will become as fast friends now, as we were then."

The girl bobbed a wobbly curtsy, overwhelmed at being the centre of attention, as well as the burden of expectation which had been placed upon her.

Taking pity on the girl Maia took her by the arm, saying encouragingly, "I am sure we will be friends."

Mary Rushford gave her new companion a shy smile, then ventured to whisper in barely disguised awe. "How can you be so brave and so daring?" Her wide eyes rested upon the revealing neckline of Maia's ball gown of diaphanous white muslin, with its delicate white embroidery and snug, elegant sleeves, which as the dowager and modiste, had intended, emphasised her slender figure.

Maia grimaced inelegantly. "Do not look, it is far too revealing, I made my wishes clear to the modiste, but it seems she did as she pleased. Now there is nothing I can do but reveal half of myself, to half of the ton."

Mary giggled in appreciation. "But you are beautiful, just how I imagine an angel to look."

Grinning at Mary, who was slowly beginning to unfurl like a

flower in the sunshine, Maia lowered her voice. "There is little angelic about me, at least that is what I understand the gossips are saying." She looked at her god-mother and Lady Rushford, who were happily exchanging news. "And yet your mama welcomed me so kindly, although I am convinced I cannot be considered as an asset to any come-out ball."

Mary grew serious, "I have heard a little of what has been said, although mama tried to shoo me away; but Miss Hindolveston, what they are saying cannot be true, I mean ..." The girl blushed rosily, unsure of how to voice the ugly rumours she had overheard.

"If we are to be friends there can be no need to stand upon ceremony, you must call me Maia. The tale you are alluding to is too long, and too dull to tell; it is enough to say that I am accused of much, but am innocent of most of the tittle-tattle."

Relieved, Mary exclaimed, "I knew it must be false, how could such things be true? You are too beautiful to behave with impropriety."

Maia responded with a laugh. "I am not sure the exterior has any bearing upon the soul, but I gratefully accept your compliment. You remind me of one of my sisters."

"Do you have many sisters? I have but one, she was married two seasons ago and was recently confined- oh!" The young lady brought a gloved hand to her mouth in horror at the subject she had introduced into polite conversation. "I ought not to mention such things. Please forgive me."

"Do not worry about such matters on my account, believe me I will not faint dead away at the mention of childbirth!"

Mary sighed with relief. "Thank goodness, it is so very worrying to have to remember what one may, or may not, talk about. I never was so glad as to have influenza last Easter and be laid too low to make my come out last season. It would have been awful to have been compared to my sister, for she is a great beauty and I, as you can see, am not."

Maia looked at the blushing girl beside her. "No, you are not what the ton would call a diamond of the first water, but neither am I, so, we shall not worry about what the ton think." Lowering her voice to a conspiratorial whisper Maia added, "Although I do not think much of the gentlemen of the ton, too top lofty by far. Most of them look like trussed turkeys, or lost calves- look at that one ..." She noded in the direction of a gentleman who had obviously been squeezed with some degree of force into his jacket, which bulged inelegantly, causing the gentleman to move rigidly.

"A trussed turkey if ever I saw one."

Mary's shoulders shook in an effort not to laugh, and she whispered back, "Please be quiet I beg you, for I do believe Sir Thomas Wilbraham is almost upon us!"

"The turkey?"

Unable to speak for fear of giggling, Mary nodded, while at her side Maia barely suppressed a theatrical sigh for Miss Rushford's benefit, as the trussed turkey strutted stiffly past.

***

Not far from the burgeoning friendship between Maia and Mary, the older friends watched with interest. Lady Rushford was delighted to observe her painfully shy, too thin, too tall daughter, smiling and laughing with the equally statuesque, but entirely captivating Maia Hindolveston.

"Caroline, you are a marvel. I confess, I did not believe it when you said your god-daughter would be able to put my poor Mary at her ease. When I think of how I have dreaded this occasion."

The dowager duchess patted her friend's arm fondly. "We shall call the balance even, for you have allowed me to reintroduce Maia, to the ton in a thoroughly proper manner."

"Then your object is achieved?"

Caroline looked purposefully over the assembled throng. "Not yet I think, what is done cannot be undone quite so easily I fear, but I do not intend to fail, after all what is the point of a god-mama if not for a divinely appointed purpose?"

Ann Rushford laughed, "I have never known an occasion when you did not achieve your object, and Maia is a delight. I agree that the ton is a tricky place, but do not doubt you for one moment."

***

Miss Mary's first dance partner was her cousin Mr Scole, a ponderous young gentleman who, despite being up from Cambridge for the occasion, gave the distinct impression that he was in his middle years with a wealth of experience. Maia could not help feeling sorry for the girl as Mr Scole took her hand to lead her out. Really it was too bad; Mary should have had a dashing gentleman for her first dance partner, not be forced to dance with her cousin, who was clearly counting his steps. When compared to her own partner Mr St. Clement, it seemed even more unjust; for Mr St. Clement was very handsome and rather dashing.

He smiled at her kindly as they passed in the set, and whispered, "You dance beautifully, quite like dancing with a feather." Which made Maia blush and lower her eyes, for Mr St. Clement's compliment as well as being unexpected, was quite unlooked for.

However, her partner's evident pleasure made Maia feel wretched, for she was not enjoying herself in the least; feeling as if the entire assembly were looking at her with censure. They were doubtless wondering if she were casting lures in Mr St. Clement's direction, for not only was he handsome, but also highly eligible, and Maia had noticed several mamas watching them with mounting resentment, and not a little apprehension.

Seeing Maia's look of concern, Mr St. Clement squeezed her fingertips reassuringly. "Do not worry, just enjoy the dance and try not let the cats get their claws into you."

As they passed, their shoulders almost touching, he gave her the barest wink of encouragement, and squaring her jaw and straightening her back, Maia continued to dance, pretending not to see the looks aimed her in her direction.

"Well done, show them you will not be cowed." The whisper from Mr St. Clement made her smile, he really was a very kind gentleman and to her surprise Maia began to relax and enjoy the dance after all.

***

"Dashed if I can see her in this blasted crush, are you sure she is here?" Complained Percy in a whining voice.

Bradenham ignored him.

"How can you expect me to propose marriage to the damned girl in this racket? She will not be able to understand one word in ten."

"Percy, if you need ten words, or more, to communicate your desire to marry the lady, then you are sadly lacking. I suggest you take Miss Hindolveston on to the terrace, where I will await your proposal and act as your witness, I trust you will make your offer brief."

Siddenham cleared his throat nervously. "Not going to let me off the hook are you? You should be sitting by the guillotine, knitting, as you wait for the first head to reach the basket."

Eyeing his cousin in the candlelight shed by the tiered chandeliers, Cosmo wondered if Percy was completely sober, certainly he looked flushed and his eyes darted erratically as he searched the ballroom for his bride-to-be. Yet it was the duke who first saw Maia, although he did not inform his cousin of her whereabouts, but stood glowering in her direction. Miss Hindolveston was dancing with a handsome gentleman, and whomever he was, he was making her smile. Suppressing the urge to throttle the stranger, Cosmo watched the pair, experiencing a disproportionate sense of loathing for the man who held Miss Hindolveston so elegantly by the hand. Whatever he was saying to Maia, was making her blush. Uncharacteristically the duke's hands itched to hit something.

To his relief, the set was not a long one and shortly thereafter the gentleman led Maia from the dance floor, their heads almost touching as they spoke, causing Cosmo more anguish than he would have cared to admit.

Percy was still looking vaguely around the crowded ballroom when Cosmo saw Maia returned to her godmother's side, and turning to speak to a plain young lady, must have said something amusing, for both girls laughed. The duke found it odd, that while simpering and artful giggling were considered de rigueur upon such occasions, it was rare to see girls making their come-outs enjoying themselves, particularly when surrounded by the matrimonial prizes of the season; gentlemen who were equally intent upon making a good bargain upon the marriage mart. Unless, like Bradenham, they were avoiding the snare altogether.

He knew when Miss Hindolveston espied him, for the smile died upon her lips, causing Cosmo a sense of disappointment, but banishing such foolish sentiments he nudged Percy, nodding in Maia's direction.

Percy groaned. "I see the antidotes have taken to travelling in pairs."

Wondering to whom his cousin was alluding, the duke was horrified to discover that Percy was referring to Maia and her companion. What was he seeing that Percy was not? For the girl looked like a vision of Aphrodite. Her hair was held back from her face, admirably confined for once, so that her long neck was attractively displayed. While her gown was simple and delicately adorned, Maia was elegant and shown to her best advantage, although Cosmo considered the dress insubstantial and revealing. Indeed, from the admiring glances drawn from the gentlemen in Maia's vicinity, others were in agreement with him.

Belatedly realising he had not noticed what any other girl was wearing, Bradenham glanced at the some of the young ladies, all seemed to be smiling in a forced, brittle manner; several with their heads held artfully to one side, coyly bestowing admiring glances upon eligible gentlemen as they passed by. One girl actually fluttered her eyelashes coquettishly at him, leaving Cosmo to wonder who was the hunter and whom the hunted.

He forged ahead, with Percy reluctantly following in his wake, pushing his way to Maia's side, only to discover, much to his chagrin, the presence of the dowager, who was apparently taking her responsibilities as Maia's chaperone, seriously.

As the introductions and greetings were made, Caroline observed Mr Siddenham coldly evaluating Maia, evidently unmoved by her beautiful gown; while his noble cousin the duke could scarcely take his eyes from her. Maia however, was more concerned for her new friend, and paid no attention to the newcomers; for although the ball was in Mary's honour, the girl was not inundated with eligible, or even personable partners - an inexcusable oversight. It was true that Miss Rushford was taller than many of the gentlemen in attendance, but that was hardly an excuse, for Maia herself was tall.

Poor Mary had paled when introduced to the imperious duke and his disdainful cousin, which had infuriated Maia, the girl was terrified by what should have been the crowing joy of her girlhood, yet she was being intimidated by a fop who was as empty headed as he was vain. Glaring at Bradenham Maia caught his eye and, responding to his raised, questioning eyebrow, she glanced quickly over at the nervous girl and back at the duke once again. Comprehending immediately what Maia was requesting, Cosmo leaned towards Mary, speaking gently, "I would be greatly in your debt Miss Rushford, if you would honour me with the next dance, if your mama will permit."

Of course Lady Rushford permitted, she was not foolish enough to believe the lofty duke had a penchant for her ungainly daughter, but recognising a gift-horse when she saw one, was only to pleased to consent to Bradenham's request.

Mary was both shocked and gratified, and blushing to the roots of her hair, smiled shyly, before remembering her manners and saying in rote-like fashion, "It is I who am honoured, your Grace."

Cosmo smiled warmly at the girl. "I am not known for my dancing skills, but I will endeavour not to tread upon your toes more than once or twice."

"My cousin is no lightly tripping nymph herself," complained Mr Scole ungallantly.

Instantly crushed, poor Mary looked terrified, lest his Grace regret his offer. She need not have worried, for the duke turned a cold eye upon the callow young man. He stated in undisguised disgust. "In my considerable experience young ladies are rarely the ones at fault upon the dance floor, it must be gruelling to be forced to manage a cumbersome oaf, who does not know one foot from the other. Whilst he blunders his way through a dance, the lady must appear to enjoy the occasion and when called upon, make conversation." Cosmo turned back to Mary, "It must be very trying and yet you managed it admirably, you are to be commended Miss Rushford."

The duke offered Mary his arm in order to escort her to the dance floor, and Mr Scole blushed deeply, his clumsy attempt to curry favour with a person of Bradenham's standing at the expense of the shy girl, having rebounded spectacularly.

Mr Siddenham was uneasy; he was an excellent dancer but preferred to dance with women rather smaller than himself, finding in all things smaller women easier to manage. But Miss Hindolveston stood almost eye to eye with him, intimidating him by her mere presence. However, Percy could not allow the gallantry of his cousin to put him to shame, and bowing curtly, stiffly enquired whether Maia would care to dance.

There were already speculative looks in their direction, as other guests observed with interest the objects of the latest scandal, and Maia was aware should she refuse to dance with Mr Siddenham, it would only lead to further gossip. Reluctantly taking his proffered hand, she allowed Mr Siddenham to lead her onto the dance floor, making sure she stepped heavily upon Mr Scole's foot as she did so, She was rewarded by seeing Mr Scole wince; sometimes, Maia reflected as she moved through the assembly, satisfaction came in the most unexpected moments.

Although it was Miss Rushford's come-out, it had not been left up to that nervous lady and her dance partner to lead the second set, the responsibility had fallen to the girl's older brother and his charming wife, who eagerly set the pace of the country dance, while the family's dancing master enthusiastically called out the steps. Enjoying himself greatly, the Honourable Mr Rushford encouraged his young wife to lead a fast-paced dance, leaving many of the young ladies who were unused to such exertion, rather breathless.

The Duke of Bradenham was better than his word, managing to avoid stepping on his partner's toes, and Miss Rushford began to enjoy herself, her eyes sparkled and a gentle glow replaced her former pallor.

Glancing at Mr Siddenham's stony countenance, Maia wondered what he was thinking; her hand felt clumsy against his slim fingers, and he was clearly doing his utmost to avoid brushing against her as they passed in the set. Her heart sank, this was the man she had agreed to accept as her husband.

As her new friend danced the length of the set with the duke, Miss Rushford's hand held firmly within her partner's, Maia felt quite unwell. Perhaps it was the heat, for the ballroom was crowded and the crush of bodies and chatter felt overwhelming. But as the pair passed out of sight Maia recovered her senses and feeling foolish, took her place awkwardly next to Mr Siddenham. Their fingertips barely touched as they danced side-by-side down the line in their turn.

When she returned to the group which included the dowager duchess and her mama, Miss Rushford's face was aglow with happiness, for despite the terror of being asked to dance by someone as grand as the Duke of Bradenham, she had acquitted herself well, remembering to smile, and on several occasions she had responded to the duke's polite enquiries with words of more than one syllable. By comparison, although Maia did her best to smile, she felt chilled and longed to be anywhere other than the Rushford's ballroom. Mr Siddenham had barely uttered one word throughout the entire set. Indeed, his dislike of her was so evident she wondered that the assembly did not see it. Yet, she had given her word that she would marry the duke's wretched cousin, and knew with a sinking heart that she had no choice; she could not live in the knowledge that if she failed to marry Percy, the same fate might befall her sisters as had almost befallen her in Newmarket.

The duke's notice of Miss Rushford had done much to increase the young lady's marketability, and within moments of being returned to her mama's side, Mary's hand was sought once again, this time by an elegant young gentleman with a quiet demeanour. With her confidence soaring, Miss Rushford was borne off by the gentleman to take her place for a reel, and Maia was gratified to observe the gentleman looked delighted with his choice of partner.

***

Heaving a shared sigh of relief, the dowager duchess and Lady Rushford seated themselves upon one of the plentiful sofas her ladyship had so thoughtfully provided for her guests, that they might keep a watchful eye upon the proceedings whilst enjoying a few moments of quiet conversation. Belatedly the dowager realised that the sofa upon which they had so comfortably settled, was separated from that of the ladies Bellmont and Ormesby, by a heavy brocade curtain. It was impossible to remain ignorant of their presence, for Lady Bellmont's carrying voice could be heard above the clamour of the guests and melodious accompaniment of the musicians. Ann Rushford froze in horror at the malice pouring forth in strident tones from the other side of the brocade.

"I cannot imagine what that woman is thinking in bringing the Hindolveston girl here."

Another voice replied, eager to relate, "I was never so shocked in my life and to think, the girl did not even have the decency to wed Mr Siddenham."

The first voice, that of Lady Bellmont, warmed self-righteously to her theme. "What can one expect from such a family? The girl's mother, Margaret Wreningham would marry Hindolveston, despite having no prior knowledge that he would inherit from his cousin, it was a laughing stock of a match."

Lady Ormesby tittered, "As you say, what can one expect? It was Margaret's elder sister Maria who killed herself, was it not? So shocking, one supposes that is why Margaret made such a poor match. I heard tell that her father took to his bed after the trouble with Maria, doubtless he was glad to be rid of the younger girl. It was before I made my come-out of course, but one heard-tell and even in the schoolroom there were whispers of the scandal."

Eagerly, Lady Bellmont took up the account. "The foolish girl cast herself from the stairs the morning following her wedding. The reason was never spoken about publicly, but one assumes his lordship discovered he was not the first and was to put her aside. I was out in the same year as Maria Wreningham, although naturally I was dreadfully young, just out of the schoolroom, and her disgrace was the on-dit of the season."

"Scandalous, tell me my dear, did you know the girl well?" Enquired Lady Ormesby, hanging on every syllable her friend uttered.

"Not well, the Wreninghams' were never considered good ton and one did not care to form a close association with her, although naturally one saw her; she was a mousey little thing as I recall. They claimed she was rather fetching, but I could never see it myself. The Hindolveston girl must take after her sire, assuming that he is her sire - one can never tell with that family, not with the dead aunt all but confirming suspicions, and you know what they say?"

"My dear I am agog, I cannot imagine."

"Blood will out," pronounced Lady Bellmont darkly. "Doubtless the Hindolveston girl will end up like her aunt, you mark my words Cornelia, there is a weakness in that family."

"I am sure you are right, one only has to look at the girl's mother producing all those daughters, even before there was a pressing need for an heir. How vulgar."

Upon the far side of the brocade curtain Lady Rushford watching her friend's face darken with fury, placed a staying hand upon Caroline's arm, for Caro's temper when roused could have far reaching consequences. The dowager patted her friend's hand tenderly, her smile of reassurance doing nothing to reassure.

"What will you do?" Lady Rushford's voice was almost a whisper.

Caro looked thoughtful, her voice unnaturally calm. "Why nothing, I am wounded you would even consider that I might stoop to take revenge."

Lady Rushford was not for one moment deceived and waited patiently for the dowager's pronouncement.

"There is no need for me to act, for these two will shortly discover that gossiping is a most unattractive and unproductive pastime, particularly when done within my hearing and upon subjects upon which they are exceedingly ill-informed."

Rising and abruptly twitching the concealing curtain aside, the Dowager Duchess of Alconbury faced the flushed, shocked faces of the ladies Ormesby and Bellmont.

"Good evening, I trust I find you both in good health?"

Gathering their scattered wits, the ladies inclined their heads in frigid deference, and Lady Ormesby simpered, just a touch.

Caroline smiled at them, reminding Ann Rushford of a lion she had seen in the Tower of London menagerie about to devour it's prey; it had been dreadfully shocking and rather thrilling to watch the spectacle then, just as it was now.

Turning her beaming smile upon Lady Bellmont, Caroline asked lightly, "How is your dear Sarah?"

Stiffening, Lady Bellmont replied, "My daughter is well, your Grace. Thank you for enquiring, she expects to be confined shortly."

The dowager duchess looked gratified. "My felicitations, you must be anxious to be by dear Sarah's side."

"Not yet your Grace, for she does not expect to be confined for another month, I shall of course be with her for the event."

Laughing indulgently, Caroline began to count upon her fingers with casual puzzlement. "My addition was never faulty before, but perhaps I mistake the date of her marriage, remind me was it October or November?"

Looking furious, the mama of the lady in question muttered, "November."

"As I thought, how delightful," came the smug response from the dowager, who turning her attention to Lady Ormesby, assumed an expression of concern and lowering her voice, asked condescendingly, "and how is poor, dear Walter?"

Lady Ormesby smiled a little too brightly before speaking. "Walter does well indeed, how kind of your Grace to enquire." Although her expression betrayed that Cornelia Ormesby considered the question anything but a kindness.

Caro waved her hand expansively across the ballroom, her rings twinkling in the candlelight. "Is the dear boy not here this evening seeking a wife? We shall have to take him in-hand, I shall make a list of eligible debutants for Walter to peruse, surely there must be one to suit his particular tastes."

Lady Ormesby tittered nervously, her fingers anxiously twisting the tassel on the end of her fan. "Walter is kept too busy with his estates to fritter away his time attending balls and routs."

"Indeed? How it must soothe an anxious mother's heart to know her son prefers the company of his estate workers and violent, physical exertion, to wasting his time upon frivolous young ladies. A man's man, is that not how one would describe him? Or perhaps I am mistaken, for I am a shocking shatter-brain." Caroline fanned herself absent-mindedly and looked idly about the room. "I shall leave you to your on-dits, for I have espied dear Heach, and I am longing to speak with him, I have much to tell him and it has been an age since I have had such a delightful opportunity."

Regally inclining her head by way of farewell, the dowager duchess moved away to speak to her particular friend, Sir Louis Heachem.

Sir Louis, Heach to his closest of friends, had a soft spot for Caroline Alconbury whom he had known since childhood. Their lives had remained interwoven through the years, with shared friends, sorrows and the odd intrigue. While not as well-born as many within the ton, Sir Louis had risen within its ranks and was considered a fearsome advisory. His chief skill and danger lay in the devastating combination of rapier wit and a delightfully amoral outlook.

It was widely held that if he so chose, Heach could do more damage to a reputation; assassinate a character; or with a look, sneer or cutting word, repudiate common knowledge faster than any member of the ton. What was less understood was that Sir Louis Heachem used his talents wisely and sparingly; for Heach was not all he appeared to be - he was far more.

Gathering Lady Rushford as she went, Caroline whispered, "What do you think?"

"You are shameless, even more dreadful now than you were

before, but I cannot be cross with you, for they deserve far worse. Are you really going to tell all to Sir Louis?"

Caroline fanned herself languidly with her silk fan. "I do not expect I shall need to; the fact that I am conversing with him be enough to send them both into a decline. Just watch."

Upon reaching Sir Louis Heachem's elite group, the dowager duchess was greeted with much joy by her old friend, while Lady Rushford, anxious not to neglect her duties as hostess, continued on her way, observing with satisfaction the apprehensive glances of the two ladies seated by the brocade curtain.

The dowager duchess having been duly admired by Heach and his followers and having wisely admired back, enquired how long it had been since they had last met, and Heach's followers turned away to allow the old friends to converse alone. As Caroline had known he would, Heach began to count back the months upon his elegant fingers, stopping at November when they had both been present at a ball in honour of Guy Fawkes and his Gunpowder Treason Day; the fireworks had as always been spectacular.

"My love, it has been a perfect age, look at the months upon my hand ..." Sir Louis waggled his gloved fingers under her nose in horror at the time that had elapsed since they had last shared gossip and memories. "Most certainly it was the night of the Gunpowder Plot."

"You are quite right Heach, I recall you wore the most beautiful diamond pin, I quite long for it, but that is the tragedy of being a woman; one must forgo such subtle delights for the vulgar and tawdry." Here Caroline waved a hand at her own glittering finery.

Sir Louis's eyes open wide in delighted shock. "Vulgar? Tawdry? My dear, who would dare call you vulgar? And those are certainly not tawdry, especially when one notes you are apparently wearing the entire contents of a maharaja's strong-room. My lamb, tell me did Alconbury buy you these?"

Caroline nodded, for the Alconbury to whom Heach referred was the dowager duchess's late husband; Sir Louis refused to acknowledge the current Lord Alconbury, or to even refer to him, if he could avoid it.

"The dear man how I miss him, one cannot but be glad that you landed him, for such generosity would be wasted upon a less well-favoured woman. Now tell me my love, for I hear such stories about your god-child."

Heach pouted as he adjusted one of Caroline's earbobs. "Did you tell me you were her god-mama? No, I think perhaps not. Too naughty of you my lamb not to tell your Heach, but we both know I will forgive you for you are too divine to be cross with for long, and far too rich."

The dowager duchess gazed seriously at her friend. "If you have heard rumours I pray you will do all in your power to quash them. Maia is my god-daughter, she is also Margaret's daughter and would have been Maria's niece."

The outrageous Heach grew thoughtful, his thin nose flaring at the memory of the beautiful girl who had been found dead so long ago; the morning after her wedding. His sharp eyes filled with tears, and the brittle veneer of urbanity slipped away, revealing the man hidden beneath the surface.

"My poor little Maria. They should never have married her to that man, it was barbaric. She loathed the very sight of him. Caro, when I think of how she wept … but Wreningham would not listen to reason." He sighed deeply. "Things could have been so very different for both of us. The pity of it was that I was too young to know what to do, and Alice was afraid of her papa, she would not go against him, no matter what I said. Let us not speak of it or I shall be overset and that would never do." His lips trembled as he fumbled for a large, scented handkerchief, holding it to his nose in an extravagant gesture, which belied its true purpose, for Sir Louis was an accomplished performer, only those nearest and dearest to him comprehended the true nature which lay concealed beneath layers of carefully cultivated disdain and artifice.

Regaining his composure, he gave Caroline his full attention once again, "So, your Miss Hindolveston is one of Margaret's girls. I recollect she had several, although I did not realise they were of an age, I must be getting old Caro."

"What nonsense Heach, you have not altered one jot in all the years I have known you. Margaret has seven daughters and a son, Maia is the eldest."

"And you are afraid Maia will go the way of my beloved Maria?"

The dowager shook her head. "No, her papa is not at all like Maria's, although you know, Wreningham never forgave himself for Maria."

"Good, for neither did I." Came the harsh rejoinder. Collecting himself, Heach smiled, "We were speaking of Miss Hindolveston, I am yours to command my lovely Caro."

"I would have you dismiss any rumours that may fall into your elegant ears, my dear."

Eyeing her thoughtfully Heach nodded, a wicked gleam in his

eyes, "You are scheming Caroline, I can see it. What are you up to?"

Caroline fanned herself, batting her eyes at her friend with mock coyness. "Why Sir Louis, what a thing to say to a respectable dowager."

He snorted, "Respectable indeed! Very well, keep your nefarious intrigues to yourself, that I may deny all knowledge of them when pressed, it is so much better to be able to lie with a clear conscience." He paused thoughtfully, then enquired, "Who started these rumours, for it was not I. Not my style at all my dear."

"It was a particularly messy misunderstanding. Sadly, the ladies who misunderstood have shared widely all they believed they saw."

"Indeed, then you need not bother to utter their names, for I already know the source." He turned his head to stare hard in the direction the brocade curtain. The expressions of horror upon the ladies' faces confirmed his suspicions. Adept at his craft as well as his understanding of Caroline Alconbury, Heach merely inclined his head in the ladies direction.

"Interesting, Lady Ormesby, mama to the ghastly Walter, dreadful fellow, crass, one can almost smell the farm about him and perhaps not in a wholesome way." Heach shuddered and raised his scented handkerchief to his nostrils with a flourish, only this time the act was wholly feigned.

He gave a chuckle. "My dear, how simply wicked, how delicious. Do you suppose they know one may only spread rumours if one is able to take the moral high ground? Anything less and one is bound to get mired down, which is always such a tragedy."

Taking his hand and squeezing it fondly, the dowager whispered, "Thank you Heach, I am indebted to you."

Sir Louis's eyes moistened once again as he brought the dowager's fingers to his lips, "No, my lovely Caro, this is not your debt, this is the least I can do for my Maria's niece. Tell me, would Maria have liked the girl?"

Caroline smiled warmly, "I think I may safely say that Maria would have adored her."

Overcome by emotion Heach was unable to speak and he swallowed several times with difficulty, before waving his omnipresent silken handkerchief and saying in a loud and languid voice, "Your Grace, I fear I have been dazzled beyond compare, but whether by your beauty or by your diamonds I am unable to tell. Necton my good fellow, I beg of you, come advise me, which is it that dazzles me so, her Grace's beauty or her diamonds?"

***

The duties of chaperone to her daughter, and hostess to her numerous guests, were not so onerous that Ann Rushford had neglected to keep an eye on the ladies by the brocade curtains, as well as Caroline Alconbury and Sir Louis. The latter were lost from view as Sir Louis Heachem's court eagerly reassembled, anxious to examine the Alconbury diamonds.

Lady Rushford had known of the heartache and heartbreak which had followed young Maria Wreningham's forced engagement and subsequent marriage to a man she disliked. Rather than live a life without Louis Heachem, Maria had found death a preferable alternative. What had made it all the more senseless, as if mocking Maria's self-destruction, was that her husband had out-lived her by but a few months.

Ann had not needed to hear the pronouncements of the ladies Bellmont and Ormesby to be reminded of the tragedy, but having heard their sordid account of the events, she hoped the dowager's verbal equivalent of putting the proverbial cat among the terrified pigeons, would cause the ladies to suffer the most fearful, self-inflicted torments, knowing that the ton would believe, as it always did upon such occasions, the worst. Which in this case, happened to be true.

***

"Cosmo, it is you, and Percy, my dear how unexpected."

A laughing voice caused Maia to turn, she found herself looking into the upturned face of a woman who resembled a Cornish Porcelain doll. The lady greeted the duke and Percy with a kiss on the cheek in a most casual manner. The family resemblance was striking; for the lady possessed the same shaped face, even features and like Percy, she too had golden hair.

The duke spoke first, "Allow me to present my cousin, Mrs. Lyth-Hudson, Connie this is Miss Hindolveston."

Percy's sister smiled and curtsied elegantly, before looking round the crowded room in mock frustration. "I seem to have mislaid Rowland, drat the man, where is he?" Beaming at Maia she explained, "My husband. Percy, be a sweet love and see if you can prise him from the card room, for I am convinced he is there." Needing no further encouragement, Percy quickly disappeared into the assembly.

"My dear, remind again, for as Cosmo will tell you I am

fearfully jingle-brained ... you are?"

Maia found it impossible to dislike this beautiful, charming version of a Siddenham, for now that she looked closely she could see the same dark eyes and wide smile she had observed in the duke.

"Miss Hindolveston," supplied Cosmo, somewhere between amusement and frustration that his carefully laid plans were already going awry.

Mrs Lyth-Hudson's eyes opened wide with comprehension and delight.

"In that case I am overjoyed to make your acquaintance, but we must rid ourselves of Cosmo, must we not? Men do get in the way so." The lady turned upon her cousin, "I am utterly parched and I dare say Miss Hindolveston is in need of refreshment, take yourself off and find me something wicked to drink." With this splendid dismissal, she pushed the duke away. "Such a nuisance, men are never there when one wants them, but when one does not you may wager your best fan they are breathing down one's neck in a most unattractive fashion. Do you not agree?"

Too stunned at the prospect of the duke breathing down her neck, Maia was unable to supply a rejoinder, but far from appearing to be affronted by his cousin, Bradenham grinned at her, revealing what Maia considered to be the characteristic Siddenham smile.

"Miss Hindolveston, perhaps you would care for some lemonade? I recall that you like lemonade, unless I am mistaken."

Greatly surprised, Maia was not entirely sure which was more shocking; that the duke had made a joke at her expense, or his allusion to her abduction.

He did not wait for her to respond. "If memory serves, you do not care for lemonade to be bitter. I will take care to make enquiries before I procure a glass; it is always better to be safe than sorry is it not? Connie, I dread to think what you are asking for, but until Rowland is by your side to keep you in order, I think you had better stick to lemonade as well."

Constance Lyth-Hudson made a face at him. "Oh, very well, perhaps Percy will not be long in finding him, although it is possible Rowland has already wagered away his inheritance."

"Possible? I would say there is every likelihood," retorted the duke dryly, as he went on is way to procure the requested refreshments.

He had no sooner disappeared from view when Mrs Lyth-Hudson took Maia's arm, "So you are Miss Hindolveston, you have no idea how I have longed to make your acquaintance."

"You have?"

"How could I not? All the talk of goings-on in the long gallery have had me agog, but now I have met you I can see why Percy should fall so, for you are a delight. Oh dear, I see I should not have mentioned it, forgive me. I am Percy's elder and very much wiser sister, so naturally I have desired to know the lady who has captured his attentions."

Maia looked so horrified that Constance began to laugh, "Oh! I am the curse of my family, always saying the wrong thing and usually at the wrong time, but I mean no malice. I am just as cross as crabs at hearing the gossip and knowing nothing of the facts. It is too galling to have a member of the family other than myself involved in what could be the scandal of the season, and having nothing of note to be able to offer the scandal mongers. All I could do is stare down my nose at them, when I have been longing to hear every last detail."

Shocked but nonetheless curious, Maia asked, "Are you usually the cause of scandal?"

"Frequently, but allow me to tell you a closely guarded secret; it is just gossip, sadly none of it is true. I love my husband dearly, despite his affair with that most pernicious of mistresses, the gaming table."

Mrs Lyth-Hudson paused to smile coquettishly at a gentleman who had been gazing at her admiringly since the duke had stepped away. The neckline of her gown made Maia's look almost prudish by comparison, in addition Mrs Lyth-Hudson filled the décolleté to the point of abundance, and even Maia could not hide her fascination with a dainty beauty spot, almost hidden by the edge of the gown which seemed to draw the eye.

Noticing Maia's glance, Mrs Lyth-Hudson laughed delightedly, "It is hard not to look is it not? Please do not blush on my account, for I am used to it and my husband finds it greatly diverting." While the lady's candour was refreshing, it was just a little startling.

Constance Lyth-Hudson gave a shuddering sigh, causing the beauty spot to heave. "It is common knowledge that I have indulged in affairs with the most notorious rakes. Dozens of them, but sadly it is not true, there have been no affairs, not even one. Shh, let us not whisper too loudly for the ton like to indulge me as they would a wayward child, and it would be cruel to spoil their fun." She dropped her voice to whisper. "I am informed that I have shockingly wanting morals, but they kindly overlook the unfortunate deficit."

Beginning to comprehend that the lady was not as empty headed as the ton would have liked to believe, nevertheless Maia was taken aback. "What does your cousin have to say upon the matter?"

"Cosmo? Why nothing, of course," Mrs Lyth-Hudson continued, "my cousin is odiously omnipotent and I shudder to think what he would say were the rumours and on-dits true, but sadly, there is no deceiving him, so there is nothing to be said."

So different was this perception of the duke to her own experience of the wretched man, that Maia was rendered speechless. It was incomprehensible having hounded her to marry Mr Siddenham as a matter of urgency, that he allowed his cousin to be seen as a shocking flirt, or worse, a woman who conducted numerous liaisons, yet did nothing to reveal the truth or to put a stop to Mrs Lyth-Hudson's undeniable enjoyment of the misapprehension. Maia had not yet recovered her equilibrium when the object of her confusion returned with two delicate glasses of what appeared to be lemonade.

Eyeing the drink with distaste, the duke's cousin pronounced, "How I wish Percy would hurry and dislodge Rowland from the tables, for I fear this stuff will poison me."

Cosmo raised an eyebrow at Maia and muttered "Many a young lady has fallen victim to such a poison, with fearful results."

At this Maia found herself unutterably furious, the despicable man had hounded her, goaded her and persuaded her to marry his vile cousin, while turning a blind-eye to the gossip about Percy's sister; he now had the audacity to mock her and her hand shook as she took the proffered glass, spilling just a little upon the duke's perfectly polished dancing shoes. He looked at her dolefully, but too cross to find it amusing, Maia had the urge the fling the contents of the glass in to his face and tell him exactly what she thought of him.

"Is there something the matter?" His voice was low and Mrs Lyth-Hudson's attention was temporarily engaged elsewhere.

Maia smiled tightly, through gritted teeth. "No your Grace, why ever would you think that?"

Before Cosmo could offer his thoughts upon the subject, Percy returned to their midst, bringing with him a genial gentleman to whom Mrs Lyth-Husdson instantly appealed.

"Rowland my love, Cosmo has been trying to make me drink lemonade, the very thought of it is enough to send one into an instant decline. Be the sweetest man and fetch me something which is unlikely to make me feel ill."

Rowland Lyth-Hudson laughed. "It will do you no harm to drink the stuff, but I cannot believe you had Percy drag me from the tables to tell me that."

His wife looked interested. "Were you winning?"

He pondered the question before answering. "The strategy of

win or lose is not decided upon one throw of the dice, or one hand, it must be established over several hours of careful play."

Laughing delightedly, Constance explained to Maia, "What he means is that he has neither had a chance to win, or lose enough to signify."

Then recollecting Rowland had not met Miss Hindolveston, Mrs Lyth-Hudson made a point of introducing her brother's amour. Rowland Lyth-Hudson was as fascinated as his wife had been, although to Maia's relief he was not as outspoken, or as overtly curious.

However, naggingly aware that something had occurred in his brief absence and seeking a chance to speak to her privately, Bradenham requested the honour of being allowed to partner Maia in the next set. He was not pleased when Maia declined claiming "A slight headache your Grace, you must hold me excused." While Cosmo was unconvinced by this implausible excuse, surrounded as they were by so many people, there was little he could do or say.

Intervention came from Mrs Lyth-Hudon, who spoke up kindly. "It is overly warm in here, perhaps a turn on the terrace would do you some good. Percy, you must accompany Miss Hindolveston outside for a few moments." Patting her kindly on the cheek, Percy's sister took the lemonade glass from Maia's hand and placed it with her own untouched glass upon a small rosewood table. "I feel sure a breath of fresh air will put the roses back in your beautiful cheeks my dear. Come Rowland, you may dance with me." With that she took her smiling husband by the elbow and pushed him, unresisting, towards the dance floor.

Maia began to quietly panic, the look of dismayed determination upon Percy's face leaving her in no doubt the direction this turn of events was taking, and feeling like a fly in a spider's web, she began to look about her for a means of escape. There was none.

"Connie is quite right, Miss Hindolveston requires a little air, Percy we shall accompany her." Bradenham's voice sounded the death knell.

Hearing himself speaking, it seemed to Cosmo the words must surely have been spoken by another. He was actually going to see this through, he was going to hand Maia over to his cousin, bound and ready to be sacrificed. Hell, he himself held the knife.

Percy offered Maia a cold, formal arm and led her towards the terrace, the duke following but a step behind.

Standing side-by-side as they awaited the start of the next dance, Constance Lyth-Hudson and her husband watched the threesome make their way through the double-fronted doors onto the terrace.

Connie frowned, "You know my love, if I did not know better I would say there is something horribly amiss."

Rowland looked down at her fondly. "Put it out of your mind and dance with me, Bradenham will sort the matter out, he always does. Meanwhile, there are at least five of your lovers here this evening, and I plan to make each and every one of them livid with envy."

Constance beamed at her husband. "I knew there was a reason I married you, and I am just reminded of it."

"Do you care to share this knowledge, or am I doomed spend the rest of the evening guessing at it?"

"If you cannot guess then you deserve to lose your entire fortune at cards, although I implore you not to. I rather fear I must love you, goose."

Well-satisfied with his wife's declaration, Rowland held her hand a fraction longer than necessary and gently kissed the top of her golden head, as the collective hearts of those watching the well-liked, delightfully scandalous couple, melted just a little.

***

The terrace was not deserted as Bradenham had hoped; there was at least one other couple - possibly more - decorously arranged although half-hidden by the trailing trellises, in well-concealed recesses. The terrace was not for the faint of heart, for it was still only early spring and while the evening was dry, it was undeniably cool after the warmth of the crowded ballroom.

Shivering, Maia was aware the step she was about to take was irrevocable and the enormity of it froze her to the core.

While Percy walked Maia to the end of the balustrade, Bradenham lingered by the stone steps, within hearing of the conversation which was about to take place. He was determined to act as witness to Maia's verbal consent to become Mrs Siddenham. Once her acceptance was given there would be no turning back. Waiting, he stared down at the cracks between the stone flags, his hands clasped tightly behind his back. Had anyone scrutinized the duke closely, they might have observed that his knuckles were white, the fingers clasping his hands like iron manacles.

After what felt like an age, he allowed himself to glance in the direction of the couple and noticed that Percy was at least holding Maia's hand. Immediately he wished he had not looked, for it would have been easier to bear this moment had he not seen her face; her eyes huge in the moonlight, her face serious and so very apprehensive. What he had done to her? Where was the Maia Hindolveston he had first met, pointing an accusing finger at him, her dress mud splattered, her hair awry? Was the towering virago so vanquished?

Shifting restlessly from the steps to a stone parapet which served as a makeshift seat, the duke sat, but finding it cold as well as uncomfortable, returned to the teps, glancing again towards the pair, surely his cousin had done the thing by now?

But Mr Siddenham was still stammering helplessly over his proposal speech; if Cosmo wanted him to make an offer marriage to this blasted girl, then it would be done in a way that would win him admiration upon the retelling of the tale. Percy was determined this moment should not be wasted merely on Maia Hindolveston; there was a prime article in one of the establishments he frequented who would fall into a swoon at his feet when he related his tale of romance and passion to her later that evening. With this in mind it was important to get the speech right. Feeling every inch the hero of his tale, Percy was not about to be rushed into the shackles of matrimony, not when he could make a meal of it.

Mr Siddenham was a pompous ass, Maia considered as she struggled to prevent her teeth from chattering - but from cold or nerves she could hardly tell.

At the moment Percy finally reached his objective, an entwined couple hidden in the recessed shrubbery - finding the pacing figure of the duke did little to add to the ambiance of the evening - disentangled themselves, planning to return to the house. The lady, her face half-hidden behind her fan, carefully smoothed her crushed and tumbled skirts. She had almost passed the practically betrothed couple when she paused and, with a sharp intake of breath, dropped her fan. This as it turned out, was her undoing.

Relieved to find something to divert her attention from the catastrophe unfolding before her, Maia looked distractedly at the woman adjusting her gown, straight into the face of her cousin.

"Emme!"

Maia was shocked, almost as shocked as Emmeline and her gentleman friend. The auburn-haired gentleman, wisely deciding that discretion was the better part of valour, continued on his way to the ballroom without so much as a backward glance; anxious to distance himself from whatever was about to unfold.

Comprehending the calamity of the situation, Miss Wreningham pulled her cousin away from Percy, who still clutched coldy at Maia's hand.

She hissed, "Not one word, please Maia think of what is at stake."

Unable to think, Maia did not know what to do, or to say to her cousin. She been aware there were lovers of some description in the alcove, but had not stopped to question the nature of the tryst, or the identity of the lovers. Seizing Maia's free hand, Emmeline tried to wring some sort of reassurance from her cousin, while Percy stood immobile; his declaration dead upon his lips.

It was the duke who restored some sort of order to the situation by calmly suggesting that he escort both ladies to the ballroom, and clutching gratefully at his arm and this straw of salvation, Emme consented. Maia however, remained rooted to the spot, until Bradenham removing her cold hand from Percy's, placed it upon his own arm and together the unexpected threesome returned to the gathering.

The golden Lyth-Hudsons, stepping from the ballroom floor, watched in fascination as Cosmo, flanked by Maia and Miss Wreningham, entered through the French windows.

Gazing at his wife with renewed respect, Rowland murmured, "As ever your instincts are correct my love, there is something very wrong here."

Constance, who had noted Maia's pale face, as well as Cosmo's grim expression, put her head thoughtfully on one side. "Indeed, but what exactly? It all seems rather a mystery."

Rowland whispered, "Time will no doubt tell." Adding brightly for the benefit of those around them, lest the good ladies of the ton become too interested in the sweet-nothings he was most unfashionably telling his wife. "How I wish I could persuade you to bring your instincts to the card table, for I feel sure you would prove an invaluable asset."

Laughing, Constance shooed him away. "Go, for my instincts and I mean to dance and it is unseemly to dance more than once with one's husband, but I warn you, do not lose above a king's ransom or I shall cry myself to sleep, which always upsets you."

With this threat ringing in his ears, Rowland Lyth-Hudson returned to the card tables, leaving his wife to ponder what her instincts were missing, while choosing with whom she would next dance, causing scandal anew, to the delight of the assembled ton.

***

Emmeline led the way back to her party. Maia, the duke and Percy

Siddenham following in her wake. She arrived not a moment too soon, for her anxious mama was surreptitiously perusing the surrounding guests in an attempt to locate her daughter. At Mrs Wreningham's side stood a well-preserved gentleman in an un-modish, well-powdered wig, of the sort fashionable in his youth. The venerable gentleman had happily relinquished the care of his bride-to-be to a young friend of her brother, for Lord Stibbard no longer found dancing as diverting as he had upon his first betrothal. Nevertheless, his third bride was a taking little thing, and would - his lordship hoped - present him with a son and heir within a year of their marriage. Although he had once nurtured a vague partiality for each of his previous wives, their inability to breed had been bitterly disappointing, and he was well rid of them.

Stibbard would be glad when the exhausting London season was over and he could retire to the seclusion of his estates. Still, he considered, it had been a worthwhile investment of his time, although he had no intention of spending another season standing about in ballrooms, wearing uncomfortable dancing shoes, when he could be dozing in his chair, with a glass of port beside him.

Relieved to have avoided arousing any suspicious, Emmeline was delighted the potentially difficult moment had passed without comment. Indeed her be-wigged fiancé seemed not to have noticed her disappearance from the ballroom with her paramour.

"Mama, look whom I have found. My lord, you must, I am convinced, recall my dear cousin Miss Hindolveston? She is lately returned from Norfolk."

The venerable gentleman bowed in a stately manner over Maia's hand, shaking a quantity of powder over her, along with his delight at the opportunity of becoming reacquainted with any relation of dear little Emmeline. Her aunt looked unhappily at Maia, whom she had neither expected, nor rejoiced to see. Emme had done well to ensnare a baron, but Mrs Wreningham knew that until the knot was firmly tied it would be preferable to avoid questions being raised regarding their connection with Maia, and her antics in the long gallery. It had been trying in the extreme to keep the suicide of her late husband's sister from Lord Stibbard's recollection; Mrs Wreningham had no wish to add another unsuitable female to the list of family skeletons.

The duke and Lord Stibbard, already known to each other, required no introduction, yet the group struggled to make polite conversation of even the most prosaic variety.

At length, finding neither the company, nor their unease palatable, Bradenham took his leave of the group. "Pray excuse us, I must return Miss Hindolveston to her god-mama, the dowager duchess will be wondering where she is."

Greatly relieved to be rid of Maia, her aunt immediately acquiesced, effusively repeating meaningless adieus. It was only as they approached the French windows that Maia realised the duke was not taking her back to her god-mama, of whom she had lost sight, he was returning her to the terrace. She about to voice her disapproval, when Bradenham's hand closed about hers on his arm.

"I think you need a few moments to collect your thoughts, you look pale."

Maia had the wit to realise the wisdom of this statement, and permitted him to lead her out into the moonlight, where she fully expected to see Mr Siddenham waiting by the balustrade. She was surprised therefore, to discover that he had disappeared; the terrace was deserted, all the erstwhile lovers,- like Emme and her paramour - had returned to propriety.

Resting her hands upon the balustrade overlooking the dark gardens, overwhelmed with a heady relief that she was not to be proposed to, Maia tried to understand all that had transpired. While standing behind her, Cosmo shielded her from any prying eyes which might be peeping from the ballroom, and waited patiently for her to speak.

When she did, her question took him by surprise. "Why are you not married, your Grace?"

Unable to utter a witty reply to lift her spirits, Bradenham had to settle for the truth, admitting to himself as much as to Maia. "I have never found a woman with whom I have wished to spend my life."

The duke winced at his lack of originality, however Maia appeared to comprehend what lay at the heart of his sentiment, and in the cold moonlight he could see the tendrils of her hair, which having managed to free themselves, gently brushed the nape of her neck as she nodded in empathy.

"I thought as much. It is a tricky business is it not?"

Not sure where the question was leading, and afraid to further voice his thoughts, Cosmo stepped forward, as Maia turned to face him. Finding herself looking into the duke's shadow-wreathed face, Maia tried to distance herself from him, but with her back against the balustrade, she was unable to move, and wobbled unsteadily.

Without a moment's hesitation Cosmo's arms were about her, his lips against hers, clasping her tightly to him. As unforeseen as this moment was, he was not going to allow her to flee this time; but this time Maia did not attempt to flee, this time she returned his kiss.

Her response was startling, but by no means unwelcome, and with the nagging doubts banished - at least for the time being - feeling her trembling in his arms, there was no question; this was exactly what he wanted to do.

How much time passed before placing her hands upon his chest, Maia pushed him away, neither of them knew.

"This is not a good idea."

Cosmo could taste her breath, and her lips just beyond his, he could have touched her lower lip with his tongue. Of course she was right, it was a terrible idea for so many reasons; he would remember what they were later, however at this moment Maia was in his arms and he was damned if he was going let her go.

"A terrible idea," he agreed, and kissed her again.

It was the Dowager Duchess of Alconbury who espied the duke's broad back and the flutter of a white dress. Slipping out onto the terrace she stood for a moment taking in the unfolding scene, before coughing, clearly and with great deliberation.

As the couple stiffened and pulled apart, Caroline bit her lip to suppress a smile. Ignoring their discomfiture, as well as the nature of their very private interaction, she spoke brightly. "There you are Maia, I was wondering where you had got to. Bradenham, perhaps you would be so good as to escort us in, I fear it is a little chilly out here."

***

Rising from a sweeping curtsy made to her gallant dancing partner, Constance was intrigued; for although Maia and the duke had made their way to the terrace unobserved, the same could not be said of their return. They might be in the company of the Dowager Duchess of Alconbury, but there was no doubt in Connie's mind, Miss Hindolveston looked as if she had been thoroughly kissed. What was made things all the more fascinating was that Percy was nowhere to be seen. Instincts aside, Constance had a good idea of what had been going on out on the terrace.

***

While the ball was delightful, and the evening relatively young by society's standards, after witnessing the scene upon the terrace Caro believed it was high-time Maia returned to Berkeley square; she had no desire to risk further scandal at the hands of the haute ton, or worse still, rash decisions on the part of her god-daughter.

The dowager had been horrified when she thought Maia had been proposed to by Percy Siddenham, and had almost fainted with relief when she beheld Maia in quite another gentleman's arms. However, Maia was a strongly principled girl and there was no knowing what she would do if left to her own devices; better by far to ensure the girl was safely tucked up in bed at Berkeley square, where no harm could befall her. Caroline looked at the Duke of Bradenham thoughtfully, no harm at all; for the duke was not the climbing sort, which was a pity.

Chapter Thirty-Five

The carriage ride back to Berkeley square was anything but joyful. Wisely, the dowager duchess kept her god-daughter fully occupied in conversation; refusing to allow Maia to fall into a fit of silent despondency, but it had taken all of the dowager's ingenuity to not ask the obvious question of what was Maia doing in the duke's arms when against all reason the girl stubbornly claimed she must wed Percy Siddenham?

The answer to this was as much a mystery to Maia as it was to her god-mother. It taunted her throughout the night as she tossed and turned in her bed, running her hands wildly through her hair in abject misery until her curls were in coiling disarray and her nightgown wrapped tightly about her legs.

Maia was no fool; she had know as Bradenham's arms encircled her that this was a dangerous encounter; far more than just an accidental caress, to be regretted a moment later when passions cooled. Such an embrace should not have been exchanged. His touch had been spellbinding; holding the unspoken promise of more than mere desire; a promise which, despite her better judgement, she had responded to.

Blushing to think of it, Maia desperately turned her pillow that she might find a cool spot in which to rest her flushed cheek. But having blushed, she thought about it again, until her heart pounded and her blood raced. In the end she had been forced to rise from the tumbled bed and finding her fan upon the dressing table, had spent some time fanning her face and the open neck of her nightgown; for the night seemed unaccountably warm. Yet even after this futile exercise, sleep had been impossible; for while the heated memory of the duke left Maia exhilarated, the recollection of her cousin inelegantly entangled with the gentleman upon the terrace was numbing. Despite trying to focus upon Mr Siddenham and the ghastly declaration he had been on the brink of uttering, the furtive movements from the alcove had not gone unnoticed. Despondently Maia sat heavily upon the ottoman at the foot of the bed, and held her head in her hands.

Her disturbing thoughts were interrupted by a gentle tapping upon the bedchamber door, and before Maia could respond, the dowager opened the door and peered into the chamber.

"I suspected you would still be awake my love, and while I have no wish to press you, I am here should you need a listening ear."

Maia's gratitude was tinged with amusement; she had known since the moment upon the terrace that her god-mother had been longing to quiz her. Indeed, it had taken Caro's curiosity far longer than Maia had anticipated, to get the better of her.

Wary of entering uninvited and trespassing upon any goodwill, or hindering confidences, Caroline waited in the doorway with rather more restraint that she felt.

"May I come in, or shall I leave you to your thoughts?" She was relieved when Maia acquiesced; the prospect of sharing the confusing burden outweighing any reticence Maia may have felt.

The dowager paused to stir the coals in the grate back to life once again, then seated herself in the gilded chair beside the hearth, giving Maia an uninterrupted view of the flames. As she settled comfortably, Caro reflected that it was helpful to have something beautiful to gaze upon while barring one's soul. Indeed, it was easier to be honest with oneself when staring into the burning coals; a fact the Spanish Inquisition had no doubt been aware of.

Even with the encouragement of the glowing coals, Maia was silent for so long that the dowager duchess began to wonder if a little subtle prompting might be in order. However, her fortitude was rewarded when Maia sighed deeply, evidently ready to unburden herself at last.

"Did you never wonder why I was with Mr Siddenham in the long gallery?"

While this was not the start Caro had expected, she smiled knowingly. "Why should I do such a thing my love? I am sure you had a sound reason, besides, I trust you."

"That's more than Bradenham does," was the rueful rejoinder.

The dowager frowned at god-daughter. "Nonsense Maia, he does not trust himself, which is not the same thing at all. Really my love, you must start looking at what you are seeing, not what you think you are seeing, for the two are entirely different."

Momentarily baffled, Maia returned to the point. "I saw something tonight which disturbs me greatly."

Sensibly Caro remained silent.

"It concerns my cousin Emmeline Wreningham, she is betrothed to Lord Stibbard."

Her god-mother was clearly irked by these tidings. "They say there is no fool like an old fool, but I daresay each of them will get what they deserve."

Taken aback by the vehemence in her tone, nevertheless, Maia continued with her tale, "I wish I could have spoken privately to Emme this evening, to discover what is in her heart. You see, tonight -" Maia faltered, however, taking a deep breath she blurted out, "- tonight I saw Emmeline in another man's arms, yet she was attending the ball with Lord Stibbard. Is is possible she loves another? I thought she loved his lordship, that she was happy to marry him." Maia stopped, feeling even more confused now her thoughts had been spoken aloud.

"My love, why does it matter what is in Emmeline's heart?"

"Why? It just does."

"Maia, that is not good enough. I repeat, why does it matter to you what is in Emmeline's heart? Your cousin strikes me as a particularly knowing sort of girl, she would not be easily coerced into such a marriage."

Maia bit her lip, hesitant to put the nature of the scene into words, "She was not just in the man's arms ..."

The dowager was far from naïve and comprehended at once what Maia had unwittingly stumbled upon. "I take it this was no platonic admirer?"

A shake of Maia's dark curls confirmed the speculation.

"Nor was it the first time I witnessed her," her hands waving wildly, Maia gesticulated what she could not bring herself to articulate.

Understanding began to dawn upon Caroline, and she spoke with no small degree of relief. "So that was why to threw yourself at Percy, you were trying to shield your cousin."

"She and Percy were- that is- they were in the long gallery, when I came upon them."

Caroline snorted unattractively and with great scorn. "How utterly unimaginative, the long gallery indeed. I take it your aunt did not feel inclined to rid herself of that dreadful statue of Leda after your uncle's death, heaven knows it is a remarkably unattractive depiction."

"Leda remains in the collection, for that is where I came upon them."

The dowager choked upon a gurgle of laughter. "What a place to conduct a tryst, and damnably uncomfortable I should imagine." However, Emmeline's comforts or lack thereof were the least of Caro's concerns. She enquired gently, "So you thought to be heroic my love, am I correct?"

Her suspicions were confirmed when Maia nodded shamefacedly.

"I could not leave them to be discovered by Lady Ormesby

and Lady Bellmont, for Emme was practically betrothed to Lord Stibbard, so I threw myself at them. In the confusion Emme fell from her perch upon Leda, and was hidden from view by the swan and my skirts, and I kissed Percy because there was no time to think of anything else to do and … he needed to be covered …"

Clapping her hands to her mouth, Caro rocked back and forth as tears of mirth streamed down her face, until at last regaining control of herself, she wiped her eyes upon her handkerchief and she shook her head in wonderment.

"You are the most noble creature I have ever had the pleasure to meet, yet you have been pilloried, denounced, abducted, drugged and now persuaded to marry Percy Siddenham, all for trying to shield your cousin. How odious, and how utterly unfair."

"Tonight as Mr Siddenham was about to make me an offer of marriage, Emme tried to slip away from the terrace and, as I said, she had not been alone."

"Great heavens has the girl no decorum? First the long gallery and now the terrace, really, someone should speak to her, although I am heartily glad you noticed her in flagrante delicto before you agreed to marry Mr Siddenham." Looking hastily at Maia her godmother clarified. "You did not agree did you, not formally?"

The shake of the dark head vastly relieved the dowager duchess's mind, although the knowledge that she had not yet bound herself to the gentleman, offered Maia little solace.

"Do you not see? It makes no difference whether Emme has had liaisons with a dozen or more gentlemen, I am the one who was seen with Percy Siddenham; I was the one who was kidnapped and I am the one who must by necessity wed the very man with whom I saw my cousin in … intimate congress. I am so confused, you see I thought …" Perplexed, Maia held her head in her hands again.

"You thought by agreeing to marry Mr Siddenham, you were protecting Emmeline, ensuring that her marriage to Stibbard would be safe? Maia, I fail to see why you would do such a thing."

"I did not want her to suffer the same fate as mama's sister." Maia sounded even more unhappy than she had before.

"My love, your aunt Maria was cruelly forced to marry against her wishes, when her heart was irrevocably fixed elsewhere. She was bullied unmercifully; her life made a misery until she acquiesced, and was then quickly married before she could change her mind. She only understood what she had done when it was too late, and rather endure such torment she chose …" Caro swallowed hard, for she had known Maria Wreningham since childhood. "But I do not understand what bearing this has on Emmeline, you are making no sense."

Desperately Maia tried to explain her muddled reasoning. "Emme wanted to marry Lord Stibbard, it had been her sole object since she first met him, so when I saw her arranged with Percy Siddenham, I did not stop to consider whether she loved Mr Siddenham or not, I only sought to prevent a scandal."

"By creating one of your own?"

"I thought if she were found with Mr Siddenham, she would be forced to marry him, and it would be poor aunt Maria all over again. But now I wonder, was I wrong? Was she so miserable once she had agreed to marry Lord Stibbard, that she fell into a liaison with Percy Siddenham? Or did I confuse the two; was it Percy whom she really cared for? But if that were the case, then what of the gentleman on the terrace? Why was she with Mr Siddenham if she loves Stibbard?" Raking her hands through her tousled curls, Maia drooped in despair, her chin resting upon the heel of her hand.

Incredulous over the depth of the entanglement, the dowager enquired, "Did you not talk to Emmeline about the incident, the one in the long gallery, I mean?"

"No, the gossips descended upon my aunt Wreningham's house so quickly the next day there was barely time to think, let alone speak."

"And now you wonder if your sacrifice is worth the cost?" Caro mused. "Well, I can tell you, it is not. Percy Siddenham will make your life a misery, that much is clear."

"After Newmarket it seems I have no choice," Maia's wretchedness was palpable. "If I don't marry him what of my sisters, will they too end up at the mercy of some unknown gentleman, stolen away, drugged and debauched?"

The dowager looked at her god-daughter shrewdly. "I think it highly unlikely, and other than Bradenham and myself, whom else knows of the jaunt to Newmarket, for I have heard nothing of it, not even a whisper? I think we may discount Newmarket as a reason to waste your life upon Mr Siddenham. As for the rest, it is no more than fustian nonsense. Any attempt to debauch Eley would be far more entertaining than any mill, and the gentleman would certainly come off worst in the encounter."

While the summary of her sister's character was not lacking in accuracy, it did little to assuage Maia's concern. "But there are the others," she argued.

"Indeed, but consider for a moment as the rational woman I know you to be; your sisters are my god-daughters and thus I am uniquely placed to offer them protection, should such a thing be necessary. All we must do is to promote the understanding that they are under my protection, ensuring it is common knowledge. I am at a loss to comprehend why you believe the only path to salvation is the one leading to Mr Siddenham's door. Allow me to inform you that there are other options, all of which are infinitely more preferable."

Scratching her head, Maia wondered how and when she had started to believe this.

"The duke said ..."

The dowager duchess interrupted crossly. "Bradenham's actions upon the terrace this evening were not those of a man offering a welcome to the newest member of his family, Maia, are you so blind?"

It seemed that she was, as reeling, Maia could only gape at her god-mother who smiled smugly. "Bradenham is head-over-ears in love with you, and no more wishes you to marry Percy Siddenham than he wishes to marry me. Do show a some sense dear."

Shocked, and just a little thrilled by the revelation, Maia began to rally. "He is the one who has pushed and goaded me to marry Mr Siddenham, he cannot possibly have feelings for me."

Caro gazed at the confounded girl in amusement. "The man followed you like a foxhound on the scent all the way to Norfolk, chased you to Newmarket, and even dropped you from a window to keep you from harm. He has been more than attentive; and let us not forget his actions upon the terrace."

Attempting to dismiss the notion which, against her will, was taking root, Maia shook her head. "No, you misunderstand it all."

"How so? Pray enlighten me, my love."

"The duke followed me to ensure I would marry his cousin, to keep Mr Siddenham from scandal."

"Indeed? Yet had he left you to your abductor's tender mercies, you would have been rendered publicly and completely un-marriageable and the point would have been null and void."

Having not considered matters from this point-of-view, Maia was unable to utter a word, but merely stared at her god-mother, her mouth open in bewilderment.

"Bradenham has never cultivated a reputation for the indulgent treatment of gently bred young ladies, Maia. I do wish you would open your eyes and see what is plainly before them." Yawning expansively, Caroline rose to her feet and daintily stretched before the fire/ "Give me your word that you will make no rash promises to Mr Siddenham, before we have unravelled this coil."

"I have already told his Grace, I will wed his cousin."

Leaning to bestow a kiss upon Maia's flushed cheek, her godmother smiled. "I do not believe such a statement is binding, nor do I think his Grace will hold you to it. Now, let me have your assurance, that I may sleep well."

Her violet eyes were shining as Maia observed both truthfully and with delight, "You are a wicked woman."

"Perhaps, although you do not know above half of the tale, but as I have vowed your mama to behave with the gravitas befitting my station, I shall refrain from enlightening you. Promise me Maia."

With a soaring heart Maia promised.

Chapter Thirty-Six

Preening as she inspected her reflection in the glass, Emmeline congratulated herself upon her adroit management the previous evening, despite the momentary panic she had experienced upon catching sight of Maia. It was a nuisance to have been discovered, but with Maia being persona non grata; she was no longer a welcome visitor to Wreningham House, so would not be able to ask any awkward questions.

She gave her gold curls a shake and frowned. Although she was not looking forward to marriage to the dreary Lord Stibbard, she must contrive to bring the ceremony forward. Her betrothed might wish to combine their honeymoon with his annual shooting party, but she was going to have to manage him rather better than that. Emme smiled as she smoothed out the front of her gown, she would start with her mother.

The unsuspecting Mrs Wreningham was seated in the morning room reading a letter when her daughter interrupted her.

"Mama, I am convinced it will not do to have the wedding at the end of the season, to be seen as a last consideration when the people who matter will have already quit London for their own estates. I will not have my wedding viewed as an afterthought, or be poorly attended. We must make a good showing at all costs."

Adding a practised pout for good measure, Emme waited for the effect of her words upon her mother, who was invariably ready to clutch at whatever straw was proffered when it came to the social climbing aspirations of her daughter. The conniving Emmeline was therefore delighted when her fond mama was thrown into a fluster by the pronouncement.

Mrs Wreningham was accustomed to Emmeline's demands, which usually heralded family discord until the girl got her way. Dropping the letter in anxiety, she devoted her attention to her peevish offspring. "My love consider, 'tis all arranged and his lordship himself determined the date."

But Emme had won enough battles to know she must stand her ground. Should that fail she was adept in the use of manipulative tears.

"Mama, I do not wish for my wedding to be the last of the season, I want to be among the first."

The girl's petulant face grew even crosser, and her mama could see that a fully fledged tantrum was in the offing. Wishing to prevent such a calamity, Mrs Wreningham fidgeted in agitation, considering what her daughter had said. "Tis true, it would be better to be amongst the first of the brides this season and to be seen to have been snapped up quickly, but how do we broach the subject with his lordship without seeming - for want of delicacy - too eager?"

Emmeline pouted; for she has not considered this aspect of the coil. Never before has she faced such a dilemma; she was used to making demands and having them met. Eyeing her elder brother as he strutted self-importantly into the morning room, Miss Wreningham was struck by an idea.

"John shall speak to him."

Her brother instantly suspicious, enquired warily, "Speak to whom?"

"John dear, Emme is desirous of bringing her wedding forward. It would be more stylish for her to wed sooner rather than as an addendum at the end of the season."

Mr Wreningham's eyes narrowed as he looked at his sister, whom he suspected was up to something.

"Dear brother, do speak to his lordship and make him bring the wedding forward, if you do I will be eternally grateful."

But well-used to his sister's sweeping declarations, John was not swayed. "I have no intention of asking your fiancé to do any such thing, I am looking forward to a good shoot in August. Dash it all Emme, that is the best thing about you marrying the old coot, a deuced good estate in Scotland at my disposal while you are playing lady of the manor. Blow'd if I'll fool enough to miss the start of the grouse season just so you may be wed a month or two earlier. I am convinced after a month you will be bored rigid and demand to return to London, putting an end to my chances of shooting this year."

Furiously, Emmeline stamped her small silk shod foot. "I want to be wed sooner, I want it John."

Her brother remained unmoved. "Then you will have soften the old man yourself. I have already spent more than enough time in your betrothed's company, listening to him prose on about taxes, war and heaven knows what else. I warn you, Stibbard is an out-and-out bore, when one ventures to offer an opinion he merely says it is a young man's argument and my views will change when I reach my prime. Prime indeed. I tell you Emme, the old fool passed his prime before you were born, but you never did listen to reason. You may have your old lord and I wish you joy, but you may not have him until August, a decent shoot is the least I am owed."

As the exchange showed signs of growing less genteel, the mama of the quarrelsome pair collected that she must speak to the housekeeper. It had been Mrs Wreningham's policy to avoid such confrontations between her children, and closing the salon doors behind her she was not privy to the rest of the conversation, as Emmeline's pout faded, leaving in its place a look of desperation, which even the self-obsessed John could not fail to notice.

"What's to do? Do you want to wed the old man before you lose your nerve?" He enquired, not unkindly.

Weighing up her fast diminishing options, Emmeline settled for the cold, hard truth. "I am with child John, the wedding must be brought forward or there will be a scandal."

Mr Wreningham stared at his sister with distaste and horror. "Why the old lecher, how dare he?"

Emme retorted scathingly. "Do not be foolish, is it likely I would risk my marriage to a lord by allowing him such indulgences before the ring was on my finger?"

John opened his mouth to speak, but his sister had not finished. "Of course it is not his, do not be beef witted." Emme rose and standing that she might view herself in the mantle-glass, considered her abdomen critically.

Grasping at the gravity of the situation, John did not waste his time or breath upon the lost cause of moralising. "Stibbard will need a damned good reason for being rushed up the aisle. May one enquire how long we have to bring this about before the date of your confinement is called into question?"

Dissatisfied by the drape of her gown, Emmeline moved away from the glass. "I think under the circumstances a special license is going to answer."

"Meaning we do not have time to publish the banns?"

She shook her head.

"Emme, are you sure?"

"That I am with child? Of course I am sure, do you think I am play acting?"

The thought had crossed her brother's mind, wisely he did not voice it.

"What of the child's father?"

Emmeline raised her chin defiantly, "What of him?"

"Does he not wish to speak up for your hand?"

With a snort of derision, Emme laughed at her brother's naivety. "Do not be missish John. He does not know I am with child, it was a dalliance, nothing more."

Mr Wreningham was scandalised. "A dalliance?"

"Do not come it so strong brother, I am not so green that I don't know what gentlemen get up to away from the drawing rooms. Why should I be any different? Did you expect me to go to my marriage bed with that old fool, uninitiated? Not that Percy was the first," she giggled. "You cannot imagine the fun of it, pretending to be a shy innocent with his lordship and all the while I was taking a tumble with Percy!" She laughed delightedly as John gaped at her in horror.

While he had heard ladies of the demi-rep speaking in such a way, and even found it rather thrilling while indulging in their company, being a man of limited imagination John had only ever viewed his sister as spoilt miss to be married off to most eligible man she could manage to ensnare, as was right and proper. Now she stood before him utterly ruined. And to make matters worse, his own steep climb up the social ladder was hanging in the balance. He could have slapped her.

However, there was no question about it, together they must contrive to bring this about, although first John wanted some clarity.

"Percy? I take it that you are referring to Percy Siddenham?"

Nodding, Emmeline giggled. "How many other Percys do you know? It was you who introduced us, if you recall."

John did recall, only too well, for in turn was Percy Siddenham who had introduced John to the charms of a certain house in Half Moon street.

"May I inquire how you expect me to persuade Stibbard to wed you within the next few weeks?"

His sister shrugged prettily. "The sooner the better, after all an eight month, or even seven month babe is entirely unexceptionable and will not cause the barest whisper. Just think how delighted his lordship will be to have an heir at last, I will be the toast of the town."

Emme twirled around happily, well pleased with herself. With the problem neatly consigned into John's care, she could concentrate on managing her early-morning queasiness and growing appetites.

It was a pity the liaison the previous evening had been forced to conclude so abruptly. Maia was a nuisance. Still, there would be other parties, with more hidden alcoves, and once she was Lady Stibbard and had presented her ageing husband with a mewling brat, Emme would have a free rein to indulge herself, and had every intention of doing so.

Chapter Thirty-Seven

There came a time in every employer's life when he entered what Watton considered to be a prickly stage; inconvenient at best and invariably difficult for a valet to negotiate. All a man could do was to weather the storm as best he could, and hope it was not an indication of things to come. And there was no doubt about it, his Grace had entered such a stage.

It was true the duke had said nothing to convey such a sentiment to his valet, but Watton had been in service for long enough to know the signs and symptoms of a man in love. Which, as far as Watton was concerned, meant a prickly temper until such time as the knot was tied, or some alternative, less formal arrangement could be reached. Not that it was a valet's place to speculate upon the nature of the alternative solution. And staring out of the window at nothing, was in Watton's opinion, a sign of a man in love. It was not like the duke to behave like a lovelorn calf, but as the valet did not anticipate his Grace getting leg-shackled anytime soon, he could only conclude that it was going to be a trying season.

Sighing, he picked up the duke's dulled dancing shoes. He might have known it, someone had spilled something on them, something sticky.

Upon hearing his valet's long-suffering exclamation, the duke turned from his bedchamber window and seeing the ruined shoes in the man's hands, supplied, "Lemonade, Watton."

The valet made no reply, for there was really nothing to be said in the face of such wanton carelessness.

"In case you were wondering about the perpetrator, it was Miss Hindolveston."

Watton had not been wondering, he had already guessed. Doubtless the lady was also the cause of the duke's current fascination for windows. In the valet's opinion, his Grace had been spending far too much time staring out of windows of late, when he was not riding across the breadth of Norfolk and dropping the young lady in question from a great height upon his poor, hapless valet. It was no way for a duke to carry on, and Watton had given notice to previous employers for less, yet he found himself possessed of a curiosity to see this particular venture to its ultimate end - whatever that end might be. It was of course to be hoped that his Grace would see sense, for Miss Hindolveston was not only a spiller, she was also a defiler of boots.

Shaking his head sadly, the valet bowed deferentially in the direction of the ducal back, which now was turned to him. His employer resumed his monotonous staring out of the window.

Cosmo had not slept well; every time he closed his eyes he saw Maia's violet gaze before him, discovering that remarkable as Miss Hindolveston's eyes were, when viewed in the form of a waking dream they were not conducive to a restful night.

The dawn chorus brought little solace, as he brooded over the debacle at the Rushford ball. Maia had been shaken to discover her cousin in the intimate company of an obvious son of Venus, while the man had scurried off like a rat. And where the devil had Percy hidden himself? The last the duke had seen of his cousin was on the terrace, yet upon returning from depositing Miss Wreningham into the tenuous care of her mama, there was no sign of him.

Agonisingly, before the interruption by Maia's cousin and her amour, it had seemed that Percy was indeed going to offer marriage to Maia. Cosmo had barely been able to breathe. What the devil was he to do? Having spent the greater part of the last weeks convincing Maia that the only solution to the problem in which they were embroiled was for her to marry Percy, to the duke's remorse he had persuaded Percy with equal success. Never had victory been so hollow.

What of his own behaviour? It was one thing to kiss Maia briefly in a spring-garden, where it could almost be forgotten, dismissed as a fleeting whim, but to kiss her again and for her to not only return the affection, but reciprocate with a warmth that he was unlikely to forget, even if he should want to.

What a hypocrite he was. He had hounded Maia to marry Percy for being seen in his cousin's arms, yet what were his own intentions towards her last night? What would have transpired had not the dowager duchess so opportunely chosen to take some air? Cosmo hardly knew, but understood with terrifying clarity that the rest of his life was destined to be a living purgatory, where Maia would be always beyond his reach.

Groaning he pressed his head against the window. "Damn Percy."

But at that moment the damned man was not aware he had been thus cursed by his cousin.

Chapter Thirty-Eight

As was fast becoming his custom, Mr Siddenham had made his way home in the dull grey light, after an enjoyable evening spent in Half Moon street. His fair face and more importantly heavy purse, meant he was assured a warm welcome within the perfumed portals, sharing the genial society of ladies who expected payment in-full. Not that the arrangement was inconvenient, for when he tired of the charms of one, he could easily chose another. It was Percy considered, an excellent bargain.

The considerably embellished tale of his offer of marriage, thwarted at the eleventh hour, had earned him both sympathy and succour amongst the congenial ladies who were always so attentive. It was to them he had betaken himself following his flight from the Rushford terrace.

His house was in darkness, for the candle left by his footman had long since burned down to a pool of wax, but the fan window above the door allowed sufficient light for Percy to be able stumble his way towards his bedchamber. Treading heavily on the stairs he wondered if it would be useful to have a wife to warm his bed, for it would mean upon colder nights he could take his pleasure at home, it was certainly a consideration.

Having rid himself of his evening clothes, Percy had partaken of the cold meat and generous brandy left at his bedside by his valet, and falling into his bed he slept the slumber of the self-righteous.

He was awoken far too early, by the sound of loud and persistent knocking upon his bedchamber door.

"Go to the devil, whomever you may be."

The knocking continued, forcing Percy to sit up. "Come in if you must, but stop that infernal racket."

Hesitantly the door opened, revealing the fearful face of the Percy's valet, who knew better than most; while Mr Siddenham might look like an angel, appearances could be deceptive. Mr Siddenham was a man of uncertain temper, especially in his own home, where the urbane veneer wore thin, particularly if roused before noon after an evening of business.

Glaring at his valet, Percy did not at first see the gentleman whose fist had so unceremoniously hammered on the bedchamber door.

"The house had better be aflame, or at the very least Bradenham dead and I the new duke." Percy's voice was but a pale imitation of his cousin's, but his valet was impressed by it.

The newcomer viciously elbowed the anxious valet out of his way, "Sit up and pay attention Siddenham, for this concerns you."

Upon seeing whom had entered his chamber Percy sat up, prudishly clasping his bedclothes about him. "Good heavens, what the devil is this about? What are you doing here Knox-Gorely?"

Percy's associate was not a frequent visitor to his residence, although the gentlemen saw each other regularly enough in houses of quite a different nature.

It was clear from Knox-Gorely's demeanour that something was amiss and this was not simply a mistimed social call. "Get up man, 'tis the devil to pay, that's what. Wreningham has been asking for you."

Still not fully cognisant, Percy did not grasp anything of significance from this statement. "He knows where I reside, why would he be asking for me?" Sliding back into the warmth of his rumpled bed he added, "Seems to be a deal of nonsense. Pull the door to on your way out."

Yawning widely, Percy closed his eyes and prepared to resume his slumbers, when he was seized and shaken roughly by Mr Knox-Gorely. Shocked to have hands laid so violently upon his person while he was still a-bed, Percy squealed.

"Listen you damned fool." Knox-Gorely's voice hissed ferociously, "Wreningham is on the hunt for you, to call you out."

"What?"

Percy sat bolt upright, the sheets falling away unheeded, while Knox-Gorely nodded in satisfaction. Having made his way to Mr Siddenham's residence in some haste, he was gratified by the reaction he had been seeking.

Noticing his apprehensive valet hovering about the doorway, Percy waved the man away with an imperious hand. "Dismissed. You may wait outside." However, his bravado was instantly forgotten as he motioned for Knox-Gorely to shut the door behind the retreating servant.

"You must be misled, why in the world would Wreningham call me out? I am his friend." Percy's voice trembled as he spoke.

Knox-Gorely grinned appreciatively. "Friend? By the devil, you had his cousin abducted and thought have her ruined, what sort of friend do you call that?"

Dismissing his associate's remark, Percy argued, "But Wreningham knows nothing of the debacle, that at least is a comfort." Mr Knox-Gorely's irritation did not go unnoticed, causing Percy to hastily reassure him. "Not that you were to blame. Who could have foreseen the dratted hoyden would contrive to escape before you had a chance to see to her? Damned unlucky I call it, but you did your best, and I will always be grateful to you. My blasted cousin has managed to hush the matter up; for I have not heard so much as a whisper of it, although I would pay dearly to discover how it was brought about."

Still irked by the insinuation that he was at fault for the failure of Miss Hindolveston's ruination, Knox-Gorely remarked dryly, "It seems you are about to pay dearly, what other reason can there be for Wreningham to call you out?"

"Perhaps because I have delayed in offering for the blasted girl. If he would take the time to speak to Bradenham, he would learn that I am about become leg-shackled to the shrew."

Knox-Gorely sucked his narrow moustache thoughtfully. "He means to do it Siddenham, he is making no secret of the matter."

Clasping at the tumbled sheets, his knuckles white, Percy gulped visibly. "What's to be done? I can hardly hide."

This was met with a derisive snort, "I should think not, for we are expected at a rout of a singular nature in Old Compton street this evening."

The reminder only added to Mr Siddenham's woes; for although he had not hesitated to employ his associate's expertise when the need arose, Knox-Gorely's proclivities, more extreme than his own, were not entirely tasteful.

"Whatever course of action you pursue it would be advisable dress first. Do get up Siddenham."

Lacking an alternative scheme and recognising the wisdom of his friend's suggestion, Percy rose, only to hear the sound of forceful knocking upon the front door. He stared at Knox-Gorely in horror, for there was no question about it; John Wreningham had arrived.

***

The vengeful Mr Wreningham was kept kicking his heels for quite sometime, while, with the assistance of his valet, Percy managed to dress. Both were suffering from trembling hands which further protracted the process, and despite discarding several hopelessly crumpled neck-cloths, Percy's badly arranged Mathematical looked worse than ever.

When at last Percy stood before his study door with Knox-Gorely squarely at his shoulder, he reminded himself that no matter what; it could not be as bad as facing Bradenham. Once he had explained to Wreningham that he was about to make all right with the Hindolveston girl, the misunderstanding would be resolved with much mirth and a drink or two, thus with an expression of false joviality Percy made his entrance.

It was as well he had taken the precaution of fortifying himself with brandy while he dressed, for John Wreningham's face was frighteningly grim. Attempting to dismiss it as nothing but the over-imagining of a guilty conscience, Percy remarked brightly, "What's to do Wreningham? Quite thought the sky was falling when I heard you knocking."

John Wreningham eyed Knox-Gorely with a steely look, before turning his disdainful attention upon Percy. "You know damn well why I am here, blast your eyes."

With a show of empty bravado, Percy clapped the glowering John upon the back. "Now then, what's come over you old man? Have a drink, sit down."

But Wreningham remained resolutely standing, his hands clasped behind his back as if to prevent himself from taking a swing at Percy there and then.

"I say again, you know why I am here."

"If this is about your cousin you may rest easy, I will shortly be making an offer for her; all will be tied in clean linen and there will be no scandal, I assure you. Good lord, there is even a chance she may be the next Duchess of Bradenham, for Cosmo has been looking peaky of late. So you see, there is no need for any upset."

While he was aiming at confiding reassurance, even Percy could see the approach was not having the desired effect upon Wreningham, who appeared to be growing more wrathful with each moment.

"My cousin be damned. You may do what you will with her for all I care. I am here because of my sister."

"Ah, yes." Somewhat abashed, Percy cleared his throat nervously. While intrigued by the sordid saga which was unfolding delightfully before him, Knox-Gorely smiled attentively; here was a scandal he had not been privy to, until now, and his nostrils flared in ruthless anticipation.

"She is with child," supplied John flatly.

Horrified, Percy squeaked. "The devil take it, you cannot pin it on me, I was not the first not by any means and you cannot prove I was. Hell's teeth, I cannot marry 'em both."

"Emmeline will marry Stibbard, but damn it all, you were my friend, she is my sister."

"If you think I seduced her, you are wrong. She was ... a damned ripe plum, we all thought so." Percy was defiant now, perhaps showing off for the benefit of Mr Knox-Gorely. Yet while John Wreningham was no longer under any illusion with regard to his sister, it would perhaps have been wiser for Mr Siddenham to refrain from pointing out that Miss Wreningham was no better than a common doxy, and the pedigree of her child was apparently unknown, even to her.

"I will meet you tomorrow morning, in Hyde Park."

Percy swallowed hard. "Look here old chap, no need for such a take on, if she is to wed Stibbard there is no harm done. 'Tis not as if she was unwilling, far from it, I had to rein her in myself once or twice."

Had Percy had been paying attention he would have observed the hue of Wreningham's face change from red to white.

"May I enquire upon how many occasions you met with my sister?"

Considering the question, Percy tried to be accurate and spoke with an almost naïve candour, "Not more than two or three ... four or five lias- meetings, at most."

John Wreningham's face contorted with fury. "You met with my sister on at least five occasions, yet you deny siring the bastard she carries and see no reason for my demand to meet you in Hyde Park?"

"There were others, did you ask her about the others?"

In his desperation Percy was about to supply Wreningham with a list of possible candidates, but was prevented from doing so by a restraining hand upon his arm.

Knox-Gorely hissed into his ear. "For pity's sake man, be quiet."

Comprehending that nothing could be done to placate Wreningham, the wisdom of keeping silent began to dawn, somewhat belatedly upon the ashen faced Mr Siddenham.

"My second will call upon yours, to what address will I direct him?" enquired Wreningham stiffly, as if he were arranging a social engagement with an outcome which was not likely to endanger life and limb.

Percy, for whom duelling etiquette was uncharted territory, opened his mouth and then closed it with a snap, whom should he ask? His cousin's name sprang to mind, but if he told Bradenham the whole sorry tale, it was entirely likely Bradenham would shoot Percy himself.

To his surprise Knox-Gorely spoke up cheerfully. "I will be your second."

Before Percy could respond, his associate addressed himself to Wreningham. "Your man may meet me at my lodgings, here is my card."

***

Cramming his hat down forcefully upon his head as he made his way along Warwick street, John Wreningham felt a sense of victory. It would give him great satisfaction to put a bullet into Percy Siddenham, then he would be able to concentrate upon getting Emmeline swiftly wedded and duly bedded by her lord, which would put an end to the matter. John threw his chest out purposefully, with that accomplished he would take himself off on a repairing lease for the reminder of the season. As for Maia, shortly to be bereft of a fiancé, Wreningham did not trouble himself overly much.

***

Behind the closed door of his study, Mr Siddenham was taking brandy, generously administered by Knox-Gorely.

"What am I to do?"

His second seemed befuddled by the question. "Do? There is nothing to be done other than to meet the man in the morning. I can hardly blame him, if a fellow bred as carelessly with my sister I would slit his throat."

Choking upon his brandy, Percy looked decidedly uncomfortable but remained wisely silent on the subject.

"Which would you prefer, pistols or swords? Do you know if Wreningham regularly attends Manton's, or Angelo's, for the choice of weapon is yours?"

To Percy's mind Knox-Gorely was being horribly matter-of-fact about the impending ordeal, but he was unable to supply his friend with any information regarding John Wreningham's sporting tastes, other than his being a client of an establishment on Half Moon street, and another in Tavistock court; for Wreningham's purse was not deep enough to run to the Bond street beauties Percy indulged in. However, this information was hardly likely to improve Percy's chances of being alive at this hour on the morrow.

Indicating to his self-appointed second that he should refill the glass, Percy slumped in his chair and held his head in his hands.

Chapter Thirty-Nine

Rowland Lyth-Hudson was feeling flushed in more ways than one. Over the years Crockford's had seen him lose his first and win a second fortune, now he was well on his way to winning a third. Hazard was not a game Rowland cared to play regularly, for he usually played too deep, but he was the first to admit when the dice went in his favour it was impossible to walk away. This evening walking away had never even crossed his mind; calling as caster for an unrivalled number of throws-ins, with each call and rattle of the dice the Lyth-Husdon fortune had increased significantly; not that Rowland played solely for the money, he played for the enjoyment of winning, no matter how large or small the reward.

He played too for the pleasure of seeing the laughter in his wife's eyes when he placed a bundle promissory notes - or better still bank notes - beside her golden head upon the pillow, and he never tired of hearing her squeals of excitement as he related the play of the night before. It was after all, just a game.

Game or not, Rowland not pleased to see the pale face of his brother-in-law at his elbow; clearly the man wished to speak to him. Nor was Percy's arrival welcomed by the remaining players who, acting as setters, had lost a great deal to Lyth-Hudson and were anxious he should not leave the table before offering them a chance to recoup their losses. In addition, a number of side bets had been placed amongst the avid spectators, for when Lyth-Hudson was on form he was a joy to watch, the man always gambled deep, rarely wisely and frequently won.

"Rowland, I would speak with you."

Percy's nasal whine irritated his brother-in-law even more than usual. "Ye gods man, can you not see that I am winning? Do you wish me to inform Connie that she must live in penury because her brother's timing is as ill mannered as he?"

But Percy was insistent. "Tis important Rowland."

Struck by Percy's unusually urgent tone, Lyth-Hudson eyed him suspiciously. "What's amiss?" Knowing Percy was not a gaming man, he speculated dryly, "Troubles in the petticoat line?"

There were calls of 'play on' and 'poor show Siddenham, leave the man alone' from the gentlemen in the room who objected to this unwarranted interruption, as well as several coarse recommendations of a more forthright nature, which did not improve Percy's frame of mind.

Taking a draught from the port at his elbow, Rowland scrutinized his brother-in-law over the rim of the glass.

Realising this might be the only opportunity afforded him, Percy turned his back towards the room and spoke to Lyth-Hudson in a hushed voice.

"I need to borrow your pistols. I cannot explain now, perhaps you could write a direction I may take to your man instructing him to let me have them." He waited, expecting a torrent of questions from Rowland, but believing play had been held up for long enough, the other players had appealed to Mr William Crockford himself, who stepping forward handed Rowland the dice, play could no longer be delayed and this was certainly no time to write letters.

With his fingers closing about the dice, and his mind upon the play and what the room stood to win or lose upon his next throw, Rowland frowned at the hapless Percy as he rattled the dice in his hand.

"Tell my man I sent you, instruct him to give you the Wogden's from Bradenham."

As an afterthought Rowland called over his shoulder at Percy's departing back. "Tell whomever is using them to 'ware, they have the devil's own trigger, he will need to take time to aim."

And turning his attention to the table, Rowland threw the dice with a flourish, whilst the room held their collective breath.

***

The reluctant combatant had received the heavy box containing Rowland's prized duelling pistols from the sleepy butler, with a slight sniff of disdain, how like Bradenham to present Rowland the pair of pistols as a wedding gift.

Taking his cousin's new husband aside during the nuptial celebrations, the duke had produced the mahogany case, saying, "If you are fool enough to marry Connie you deserve all you get, but I am indebted to you for taking her off my hands, perhaps knowing these are within your possession will deter all but her most ardent suitors!"

Having laughed loudly, Lyth-Hudson proceeded to share the joke with his bride, who was delighted and called Bradenham 'a wretch', before being kissed soundly by her husband. It had been Percy considered, in very poor taste.

Scrutinizing the case lying open before him upon his desk,

Percy was disappointed to discover the weapons were not more interesting, finding upon closer inspection than he had previously been afforded, that not only did they possess little ornamentation, but that their only inscription was that of their makers names, Wogden and Barton, although it was enough to instil fear into the heart of a man. It was held that Robert Wogden was responsible for more deaths amongst the ranks of London gentlemen than the French disease, although Mr Wogden's method was usually quicker. Shivering, Percy closed the lid of the baize lined box.

Chapter Forty

It had been, Rowland considered, a most agreeable evening; for despite the ruinous nature of the game, he had emerged victorious. The gentleman-spectators who had upon this occasion backed the right man, had celebrated his triumph; while others who had tied their purses to those who had lost their shirts or more, had commiserated wholeheartedly with the losers.

With a pocketful of promissory notes, Lyth-Hudson made his way home in the still of the hour before dawn, eagerly anticipating Connie's delight at his success. Thoughts of his wife and her tumbled golden curls reminded him of Percy for, since carelessly agreeing to the loan of his duelling pistols, Rowland had put him completely from his mind, and he wondered idly for whom his brother-in-law had begged the loan of the Wogden's.

It was with a growing sense of unease that he mounted the steps to his door where, unusually for this hour, Rowland was greeted by his butler; the man had awaited his master's return and was obviously in a state of high anxiety.

"Pardon me sir, for intruding on what may be a private matter, however, Mr Siddenham was here some hours ago requesting the use of your pistols. He claimed you had given him your permission, I allowed him to take them, I hope I was correct in so doing."

Whilst being relieved of his redingote, Lyth-Hudson set his man's mind at rest, although his own was far from easy, as he enquired, "What would you say of Mr Siddenham's demeanour?"

The butler hesitated, reluctant to express his less than favourable impression of Mr Siddenham. "I did wonder if all was well sir, for the gentleman seemed nervy."

Rowland took this information in, and adding it to his own thoughts, swiftly reached a conclusion, "I was premature in believing I was about to go to bed, I will require my coat after all. Damn Percy."

Making no comment, the butler adroitly helped Lyth-Hudson back into the heavy overcoat and pulling the fur collar up to his ears and drawing on his gloves, Rowland turned to go out into the murky early morning.

Upon the top step he whispered conspiratorially to the butler, waiting to close the door behind him, "Do not mention a word of this to my wife, I would not want her to be upset."

Horrified by the prospect, the butler nodded in silent agreement; for upon the rare occasions when Mrs Lyth-Hudson chose to indulge her sensitivities, she did so with gleeful abandon and little respect for the sensibilities of those in her immediate vicinity. He watched his employer vault down the steps and hurry purposefully down the street, before closing the door.

***

It was apparent that while he had not been abed when Rowland knocked on the door, nevertheless the duke had not expected to be disturbed; for his unexpected guest was astonished to note Bradenham's startling blue and gold silk banyan dressing-gown as he joined Lyth-Hudson in the study.

"Rowland, I find it hard to believe you have awoken my household in order to inform me that you have lost another fortune at Crockfords," was the duke's wry comment upon discovering the gentleman pacing to and fro the Turkey rug in great agitation.

"I do not recall advising you the last time, and will no doubt first inform my wife upon the next occasion. This is far more worrisome ... I would have come sooner, but the gravity of the situation did not dawn upon me until I reached my own front door."

"Sit down, I am listening."

"It is that damnable fool Percy."

Leaning against the edge of the desk, Cosmo folded his arms across his chest in resignation. "What has he done now?"

"To my knowledge nothing, yet. But he came bothering me at the hazard table this evening, wanting to borrow my pistols. The Wogden beauties you gave me."

The duke was incredulous. "Percy wished to borrow the Wogden's? Whatever for? Do not tell me he had got himself mixed up as a second in a duel. Impossible. Percy?"

Warming his hands by the fire, Rowland shook his head sorrowfully. "I fear it is worse than that; for what man in his senses would ask Percy to be his second?"

Thunderstruck, it dawned up Bradenham to what Lyth-Hudson was alluding. "You cannot mean someone has called Percy out? The man incapable of holding a gun, let alone firing one. You did not lend him your pistols?"

Rowland nodded ruefully. "Alas, before I realised the true

nature of the request. I was at hazard after all. What's to do?"

Having risen from his perch against the desk, Cosmo tugged sharply upon the bell-pull in order to summon his butler. "We must ascertain the facts before it is too late."

Advised of the unexpected arrival of Mr Lyth-Hudson by the footman, the duke's butler had risen and judiciously taken up his post, ready for duke to ring - knowing from experience that he surely would.

"Burnum, I need you to awaken Harrington with my abject apologies, and advise him to prepare immediately for a jaunt to the park. Also, I will need my coach brought round as soon as may be managed. Convey to Yaxley that haste is required, as well as discretion. It would perhaps be as well to take brandy with us, if only for ourselves."

The unruffled butler received this information as calmly as if his Grace had been making enquiries about dinner, then betook himself off to complete the necessary offices.

While this was being accomplished Cosmo went to dress; proving he was not so dependent upon the ministrations of Watton, as the valet might wish to believe.

Upon his return to the study he discovered Harrington had arrived ahead of him and was being apprised of events; he too was incredulous at the preposterous prospect of Percy Siddenham being a participant in a duel, albeit an unwilling one.

"There must be some mistake, this seems too fantastical to understand."

Buttoning his greatcoat, the duke's expression was grim. "I agree Harrington, yet despite all prior evidence to the contrary, we must believe that Percy is on the brink of taking part in his first, and in every likelihood his last, duel."

Rowland pulled at the collar of his own coat anxiously. "If I had thought about it I would never have let him take the Wogden's, they've a deuce of a trigger."

"I recall, which is why we must reach him before he shoots his own foot off, although one has to wonder whom has called-out my cousin and, more to the point, why." This consideration had been uppermost in Cosmo's mind since Percy's probable involvement in a duel came to light.

Moments later the three uneasy gentlemen descended into the damp morning and the awaiting coach.

Rowland commented, "T'would have been quicker to ride."

"You are right," the duke agreed. "However, there is every likelihood we will need to convey Percy back, and I prefer to do so in an enclosed carriage." With this grim pronouncement the three sat in silence as the coach swiftly made its way through the almost deserted thoroughfares to Warwick street and Percy Siddenham's house.

The arrival of the coach in front of the sandstone building threw Mr Siddenham's valet into confusion; fully expecting it to contain the gentleman's mortal remains. Nevertheless, the distraught man tearfully answered the questions put to him by the duke, for in his heart of hearts he did not expect his employer to return intact from the murderous meeting in the park.

The poor man could hardly be blamed for his agitation,; for not only has his employment prospects declined significantly with Mr Siddenham's recent foray into sartorial experimentation, but that fateful morning his employer had, with shaking hands, tied his neck cloth in a shameful mockery of the Osbaldeston, and the valet had known his fate was sealed. Mr Siddenham would die with a shockingly arrayed neck cloth and he would never find employment as a valet again.

It did not take the duke long to learn both the whereabouts of the duel and the identity of the other protagonist, although the information was somewhat baffling and, as the coach lurched on its way to Hyde Park, he conveyed this piece of the puzzle to the other occupants.

Harrington greeted the tidings with surprise. "John Wreningham called out Mr Siddenham? Why would he of all people risk harming your cousin?"

With steepled fingers pressing against narrowed lips, Bradenham acknowledged of the truth of his secretary's words. "Why indeed. It appears we are missing some vital element, but I fear we may be too late."

Meanwhile, Lyth-Hudson was focused upon the pistols, which for him were at the heart of the matter. "Damn me Bradenham, if only I had known or guessed at it, but dash it all, the man asked me in Crockford's and it was hardly the time for a discussion." Staring glumly out of the window as the grimy streets flew past, he continued, "Connie will never forgive me if my blasted pistols do for Percy = for all that he is a fool, he is still her brother."

Harrington tried to reassure him. "Perhaps it will not come to that; this may simply be Wreningham's way of bringing Mr Siddenham to point non plus."

"You mean, that Wreningham plans to let Percy off once he is assured a wedding will take place?" Lyth-Hudson sounded hopeful.

The duke's voice drawled thoughtfully. "A little drastic I feel, and can Wreningham be sure Percy would not prefer to stare down the barrel of a Wodgen, than wed Miss Hindolveston?"

Harrington and Lyth-Hudson stared at Bradenham in amazement as he continued, "Percy has after all, been an unusually reluctant suitor, can Wreningham be assured of the outcome?"

With no satisfactory answers to their speculation, silence fell upon the trio, as the coach clattered on towards Hyde Park.

Chapter Forty-One

The unwilling duellist shivered miserably, but whether his trembling was caused by nerves or the inclemency of the weather, it was impossible to distinguish. The meeting had been arranged - as such meetings usually were - to avoid undue attention, and although the occasional figure of a passer-by could be distinguished through the mist, there were no bystanders other than the seconds to witness the event about the take place.

Within the confines of John Wreningham's hired chaise the morose physician huddled in his decrepit travelling cloak. As protocol dictated, he would remain in the carriage until after the pistols had been discharged and thus not be able to act as an eyewitness to the grisly outcome. He had acknowledged Percy's quaking presence, but gruffly announced that he would stay where it was warmer; feeling no need to exchange further pleasantries with a man who might soon require his ministrations.

Stating bluntly, "No point in my catching my death of cold until such time as I am needed." The pronouncement did nothing to calm Percy's nerves, or the feeling of impending doom.

A short distance away, the seconds paced out the distance across which the protagonists would face each other. But unable to recall what Knox-Gorely had told him about the number of yards they had agreed upon, Percy tugged fretfully at his restrictive neck cloth; supposing morosely, as he loosened the extravagant bow, that the difference would make little difference to the outcome.

Given the delicate nature of the incident which had resulted in demanding satisfaction at the end of a firearm, John Wreningham had dispensed with the tradition of a phalanx of supporters as witnesses to the affair of honour. The fewer of his cronies who knew of Emmeline's unfortunate predicament, the better. This way there could be no risk of gossip reaching Stibbard's ears until after the knot was tied, by which time if Emme managed the old man cleverly, it would no longer be relevant.

Knox-Gorely briskly rubbed his thin hands together as he strode towards Mr Siddenham. "Not long to wait, we will just inspect the pistols." Clapping Percy heartily upon the shoulder in a misplaced show of encouragement, he removed the mahogany case from Percy's care and betook himself to join Wreningham's second; a slight, nervous, auburn haired fellow.

Opening the case with a flourish as if revealing a great treasure, Knox-Gorley and his counterpart leaned forward and with their heads together proceeded to inspect the matched duelling pistols.

Wreningham's second was visibly impressed, murmuring, "What beauties. A fine pair, a pleasure to use 'em no doubt." Then recalling the gravity of the event, he cleared his throat anxiously, dismayed by his callous display of enthusiasm.

However, unencumbered by such niceties, Knox-Gorely took a pistol from the case and stroking the polished walnut stock, gauged its weight experimentally. "Damned nice piece, wonder where Percy found 'em." Anxious to make a good impression, the other gentleman ignored Knox-Gorely, and peered myopically down the muzzle of the remaining pistol, ensuring the barrel was not fouled.

Not far away John Wreningham watched the proceedings with a marked degree of interest, although naturally he was careful to avoid looking directly at his opponent. He had heard of inept seconds neglecting to load the pistols correctly - with disastrous consequences - so was reassured his second appeared to undertaking his rôle with a pleasing degree of solemnity.

Duly loaded and primed, the flintlock pistols were placed on the open lid of the case. Time was now of the essence, for prolonged exposure to the damp, misty air might prevent the powder from igniting and the pistols from firing. Or worse still, prevent one pistol from firing.

Percy felt quite faint as he observed the pantomime of the weapons being readied, scarcely believing the moment was upon him. The oak trees coming into leaf, the grass was muddy beneath his feet and everything seemed to be extraordinarily vivid, as if he were noticing the world for the first time. Even the dismal prospect being married to Maia Hindolveston, held fewer terrors than the step he was about to take, and while Percy was the first to admit that he had thoroughly enjoyed his time with Emmeline Wreningham, the price he might have to pay was too high for such an indulgence. As for the accusation that she carried his bastard, there was no proof it was his and he very much doubted even she could be sure.

Upon hearing Knox-Gorely call his name, Percy walked with a thudding heart to where the seconds stood with Wreningham, the pistols ready before them. The weapons, he considered, looked malevolent. The implacable Wreningham scowled at Percy, who could feel his legs shaking as he waited for Emmeline's brother to select his pistol first. Not that it mattered to Percy which of the guns Wreningham chose, for they looked identical. With an effort Percy tried to keep his hand from shaking as he took the remaining weapon from the lid of the case. It seemed heavier than when he previously handled the guns, but now it was loaded and half-cocked.

Wreningham's second spoke; the air about him filled with the lingering miasma of his breath as he addressed John solemnly, "Will honour be satisfied with an apology? Or must we proceed with pistols?"

For a brief moment Percy's heart rose, clutching at the hope that the duel may yet be avoided; that they would shake hands and all would be resolved.

"It will not be satisfied." John Wreningham's voice was harsh and sure.

"In that case gentlemen- "

Wreningham's second proceeded to advise the protagonists of the code duello which would be applied to the morning's meeting. "Upon the signal you will take your marks, when I drop my handkerchief you may fire as you will. There will be but one shot each," looking at Wreningham he inquired hastily, "assuming that one shot will satisfy?"

John nodded, sneering nastily at Percy, who was left in no doubt that one shot was all that would be required.

But Knox-Gorely was disappointed. "One shot only? Not to à l'outrance, or even to first blood?"

Yet although Wreningham looked startled by the second's blood lust, he would not be goaded beyond the dictates of honourable conduct, "One shot will suffice."

"Very well gentlemen, if you would take your marks." The auburn haired man's voice shook as he spoke.

The marks had been made upon the muddy ground by the simple process of each second dragging a booted heel through the soft earth; for neither second wished his friend to adopt the alternative, that of standing back to back before pacing off, which would only have served to add a theatrical air to the proceedings.

John walked resolutely, his shoulders squared and with no discernable doubts, confident in his skill, as well as his righteousness. Percy meanwhile, felt as if each step were an eternity; his legs shook and his feet gave the impression they were being dragged down into the mire, while the pistol felt cumbersome and awkward in his sweating hand. Wholly unsure of what to do with his left hand, he began to push nervously at his oiled hair as it flopped lankly across his forehead.

Once he reached his mark Percy was at a loss to know what to do; afraid to raise his arm before the handkerchief had been dropped, lest he appear to be cheating, and terrified that Wreningham would take aim before him.

Facing his adversary, Wreningham saluted him. It was a perfunctory gesture, merely part of the procedure, and belatedly Percy followed suit, feeling like an actor who had neglected to learn his lines.

Both men turned; Wreningham fractionally before his nervous counterpart, standing side-on, exposing as small a target area as possible to his opponent. Finally they stood, weapons raised, their seconds waiting some way off, John's demeanour demonstrating - as if demonstration were needed - his utter disdain for his former friend.

From the corner of his eye, Percy saw the cloth in the hand of Wreningham's second. For the longest moment the white handkerchief seemed to hang motionless then, with sickening finality, it began to fall to the mired ground. There could be no mistaking it. Percy's hand shook as he struggled to manage the weapon, hearing the echo of Rowland's admonition to, 'take time to aim'. But if he had expected Wreningham to prove a good sport by deliberately firing into the air, then he was disappointed.

Chapter Forty-Two

The carriage drew to a halt beyond the line of trees. Despite the mist, its occupants could distinguish the protagonists as they faced each other; Rowland's precious Wogdens raised and as they watched, unable to intercede, the first shot was fired.

The shower of sparks from the muzzle of Wreningham's pistol, together with the simultaneous engulfing cloud of sulphur smoke, left the onlookers in no doubt which gun had been fired first. In response, the blonde haired figure of Percy Siddenham crumpled heavily to the ground, his pistol discharging as he fell.

To the amazement of the assembled gentlemen, the ball met its target, throwing John Wreningham, still shrouded in the sulphurous cloud, onto the muddy ground.

"I warned him about that hair trigger," muttered Rowland, wondering how he was going to tell his wife her brother was dead and that it was he who had provided the weapon.

With long strides the duke swiftly covered the sodden ground between the coach and the prone figure of his cousin. He was the first of his party to reach the fallen man, arriving at his cousin's side moments before Knox-Gorely. Wreningham's shot had found its mark, and if the loss of blood was any indication, the ball lodged in his left thigh had struck deeply.

"You hit him, you hit him." Crowed Knox-Gorely delightedly, clapping his friend upon the shoulder with little regard to Percy's plight, in fact he seemed wholly unaware that Percy was in grave danger of bleeding out before his eyes.

Arriving after his employer, Harrington shouted the news to Lyth-Hudson that Mr Siddenham still lived, greatly relieving Rowland's mind. The secretary then turned his attention towards the inert form of Wreningham, who was solicitously attended by both his second and the physician, having engaged the man for such a purpose, although doubtless John had anticipated it would be Siddenham upon the receiving end of the doctor's ministrations.

While Percy was still conscious, he was fast losing blood and Cosmo did not need a third-rate physician to advise him that his cousin must be removed as quickly as could be achieved. At last taking notice of Knox-Gorely, he was taken aback to recognise Maia's abductor, whose acquaintance he had neglected to make in Newmarket. However, oblivious to the duke's revelation, Knox-Gorely was still congratulating Percy upon a 'Fine show!'

Cosmo was less complimentary as he bent over his cousin. "You are as damned a fool as one could hope to find."

At this pronouncement the ashen faced Percy began moaning.

Reaching his brother-in-law's side in time to witness the duke snatch the mangled neck-cloth from Percy's neck, Rowland was bemused at the relish with which Bradenham twisted the much maligned article, before tying it forcefully around Percy's bleeding leg.

With a momentary flash of a smile, Cosmo offered the explanation, "The wound had to be staunched, it seemed to me to be the obvious solution," adding with the utmost gravity, "a sacrifice I was more than willing to make, given the circumstance."

With the neck cloth serving a far more noble function than merely adorning the throat of Percy Siddenham, Bradenham took hold of his cousin's shoulder and, indicating that Rowland should do likewise, together they half-carried, half-dragged the wretched figure towards the carriage.

Feeling that his position as Percy's second had been usurped by the unknown interlopers, Knox-Gorely began to protest. "What in hell's name do you think you are about? I will see Siddenham home. Who the devil are you?"

His demands received no response, for having noted with foreboding his secretary's grim expression having seen Wreningham, the duke said nothing.

Between them the three men managed to haul the now screaming Mr Siddenham into the waiting coach. Percy's cries grew so violent that Yaxley was forced to hold the horses' heads to prevent them from bolting.

As Percy was stowed away out of sight of any passers-by alerted by the pistol shots and general commotion, Knox-Gorely restrained Bradenham's arm roughly. "Where the devil do you think you are taking him?"

The duke looked down at the man's hand in utter disdain, whereupon it was swiftly removed.

He asked Percy's second, "Tell me sir, do you travel to the continent?"

Knox-Gorely was surprised by the enquiry, made at such a time as this, by a man who was unknown to him.

"Damn it, what are you talking about?"

Cosmo repeated coldly, "I asked you if you travel."

Looking over the stranger's shoulder to where John Wreningham was still being attended by the physician, Knox-Gorely spoke tersely, the gravity of the situation beginning to dawn upon him, although he was unable to fathom to where this conversation was leading.

"Not often but occasionally I find my- er- interests take me to the continent," adding irascibly, "not that it is any damn business of yours, whoever you are."

The duke, satisfied he now knew how the vile substance given to Maia had been obtained and by whom, responded coldly, "You may not know me, however, I am well aware of you. My name is Bradenham and while I will not put a shot between your eyes upon this occasion, do not make the mistake of again straying into my path, or that of Miss Hindolveston. Should you do so I assure you, you will regret it."

The name of Bradenham was not unknown to Knox-Gorely, who horrified that the duke knew of his involvement in the scheme to ruin Maia Hindolveston, could think of no appropriate response.

Cosmo smiled grimly. "I see you comprehend my meaning, now remove yourself from my sight." He turned to go, but recalling the wound to Maia's head and her befuddled state, added, "One more consideration - I intend to ruin you financially; we will consider it fair and just compensation."

Astonished Knox-Gorely demanded, "For what? I did not touch the damned girl."

The duke wheeled to face the man, his eyes ablaze with fury. "You should be grateful you did not get the opportunity, had you done so your end would have been of an exquisitely violent nature."

Turning abruptly on his heel Bradenham strode to the coach where Lyth-Hudson was belatedly clambering up the step, panting heavily, greatly relieved to have retrieved his treasured Wogden's from the mire of the duelling field. He lovingly cradled the mahogany box, as Bradenham took his seat beside the groaning Percy.

Watching the departing carriage with a sinking heart, not for one moment did Knox-Gorely doubt that the duke would be as good as his word, and roundly cursed both his luck and his involvement with Percy Siddenham.

***

Had Mr Siddenham been conscious he might have been surprised to discover that instead of being carried into his cousin's house with loving care and placed in one of the duke's fine bedchambers, he was instead bundled with little ceremony into the library and deposited upon the long table, to await the ministrations of his cousin's physician. However, it so happened that the coach's arrival in St. James's square coincided with one of several occasions since leaving Hyde Park, when Percy had fallen into pain induced swoon.

Upon coming to, Percy was painfully aware that in addition to the burning agony of his left thigh, he was lying upon something hard and unyielding. Sitting by the fire which burned brightly in the hearth, Rowland inspected his Wogden and Barton pistols with a loving eye, murmuring quietly to himself.

Trying unsuccessfully to raise himself upon his elbows, Mr Siddenham was forced to abandon the attempt, and finding the lead ball lodged in his leg a source of excruciating pain, he gazed down at the source of his discomfort, noting with horror that his newly purchased buckskins were awash with blood, and a bloodied cloth was tied tightly about his leg, which unless he was very much mistaken, was his neck cloth.

"Bradenham?" Percy's voice was weak but his wits had not left him.

"I am here," came his cousin's terse reply which, despite his brevity, reassured Siddenham; for if Cosmo were in control all would be well.

"What the hell is going on Percy? What are you about?"

The injured man attempted a feeble laugh as if to dismiss the ordeal. "That damned fool Wreningham called me out."

Wanting his cousin to tell the whole in his own unguarded words, the duke was careful not to allow his anger to colour his speech. "He called you out over Maia? Surely she must have informed him of your intent to marry her?"

Percy laughed bitterly. "Not over Miss Hindolveston, over his damned sister." Wincing with pain, he was forced catch his breath. "The trollop is with child, she claims 'tis mine, and bloody Wreningham would not listen to reason. There was no need for such nonsense, Emmeline is to be wed soon enough, so no-one need be any the wiser." Flinching once again, he paused momentarily, before resuming his tale of woe. "I told him I was not the doxy's first, but the fool would not listen, now look at me, still I dare say I made a good showing - that damned pistol of Rowland's went off before I was ready."

Rowland's voice growled crossly from the hearth, irritated

that Percy should impugn his beloved pistols. "I warned you, they're Wogden's, with the devil's own trigger."

But Percy did not respond, instead he gripped his cousin's arm in pain. "Get me brandy Cosmo, for pity's sake."

However, not disposed to follow Percy's bidding at this juncture, the duke asked, "Did Wreningham know you are to offer for Maia?"

Percy nodded dismissively. "Yes, the fool told me I may do what I will with her - not that I would want to." He laughed bitterly.

"What of your second?"

"Knox-Gorely?"

"Ah, is that the gentleman's name? I do not believe we had been introduced before today, although I had seen him."

Percy missed the menace in his cousin's voice. "Damned good friend, do anything for me."

"Including abduction and ravishment?"

Again, consumed with his own woes Percy missed the danger. "Hardly ravishment, for I dare say he would have persuaded her to comply, one way or another. To tell the truth, I did not ask him how he planned to go about the matter, for it was none of my business how he managed it. I just needed the girl ruined, for not even you would expect me to marry a doxy and disgrace the name of Siddenham." His voice was nasal, shallow with pain and self pity.

"And what of Maia now?"

Percy rolled his eyes in irritation. "I neither know nor care - the damned girl should have minded her own business and not come snooping about the long gallery, spoiling a fellow's sport."

At last Cosmo understood the rôle Maia had played in the farce, "You were with her cousin?"

Grimacing in pain Percy nodded. "Who else but that strumpet would suggest a liaison over Leda, during a rout? Damned good joke it was too."

"And yet Percy, one must note that you are not laughing."

This time there was no mistaking the disgust in his noble cousin's voice, but before the stricken man could wonder at the unwarranted repugnance, Harrington ushered the duke's physician into the library, bringing the discussion to an abrupt halt.

The examination which followed was carried out with zeal, causing more discomfort than the patient felt was strictly necessary. At length the doctor wiped his bloodied hands and addressed his pronouncement to Bradenham, as if Percy were of no consequence. "The shot must be removed immediately, he has lost a lot of blood, but with care he should make a reasonable recovery; although there is always the risk of poisoning of the blood."

Meditatively Cosmo eyed Percy. "Will he be fit to travel today?"

The physician was shocked. "Today, your Grace?"

"You will have surmised that Mr Siddenham did not shoot himself."

The wise doctor said nothing; believing it was better in such cases to know and say as little as possible.

"The other gentleman in this matter has come off rather worse than my cousin, it is unlikely he will survive."

"I see." The physician eyed the wound shrewdly and pronounced, "Very well, let me patch up Mr Siddenham as best I can and send him on his way. I will need brandy for the gentleman, your Grace."

"Thank the devil," came the grateful response from the table. Percy was relieved to discover he would not have to endure the agony of having the lead shot removed from his leg while sober.

"Before you begin I would like a few words more with my cousin, while he is still in a condition to comprehend. Harrington here will see you have all you need."

Tactfully the physician removed himself from the immediate vicinity of the library table, in order to remove his jacket and set out the cruel tools of his trade, while Bradenham loomed over the figure lying sprawled upon table.

"Before you depart I would have you know that you disgust me. From this day onwards I no longer recognise our connection. Know too that I will not delay in marrying and producing an heir, thus removing all possibility of your tainting the title. Your conduct from start to finish has been revolting, and I am ashamed of my association with you."

Percy gaped at his cousin, shocked and bewildered. "What have I done to earn such condemnation?"

"Is it possible you are truly ignorant of the depths of your own depravity? Allow me to enlighten you. You have tried your damnedest to ruin a lady who did nothing to deserve such treatment, and whose feet a snivelling creature like you are unworthy to kiss. Even now as you lie here, a victim of your own dishonourable conduct, you think of no-one but yourself; certainly you spare no thought for the lady who stands to be ruined by your folly."

The duke was interrupted by his cousin, protesting. "How can you accuse me of dishonourable conduct? I met John Wreningham honourably enough."

"Honour?" Bradenham almost spat the word. "Tell me, whose honour was at stake this morning? Yours? Miss Wreningham's? For it seems to me neither of you have honour worth fighting for."

Percy opened his mouth to argue, but was prevented from doing so by Cosmo, who had heard more than enough. "If you do not bleed to death within the next few minutes, you will be conveyed with your valet to Harwich and from thence to Rotterdam, after that you may go to the devil. One thing is certain, Wreningham will die and when that happens, should you be upon English soil, you will hang." The duke whispered softly into his cousin's ear. "And once Wreningham is dead, be assured I will not lift a finger to prevent your scrawny neck from stretching in the noose."

A gentle cough from the waiting doctor advised Bradenham that the time for talk had ended. Percy cried out, although whether from fear or pain it was impossible to know.

"The brandy, your Grace?" The physician reminded Bradenham.

Harrington hastened forward with the decanter, but his employer waved him away. "Thank you Harrington, but it will not be necessary to waste my best brandy on the snivelling wretch."

Percy gasped in horror at both the insult and what it implied. Looming over his cousin, his face unyielding, the duke brought up his right fist sharply under Percy's chin, rendering him senseless.

Flexing his hand and tugging gently at the cuff of his jacket to straighten the sleeve, Bradenham addressed himself to the astounded physician. "Dig away man, my cousin feels no pain, although one can only hope that his jaw may be broken." With that he left the library, smiling in grim satisfaction.

Chapter Forty-Three

While never an early riser, of late Emmeline Wreningham had found mornings increasingly difficult; for while she might sleep soundly enough, she awoke to nausea and violent retching. To make matters worse, the discovery that Mrs Wreningham and Lord Stibbard were awaiting her presence did nothing to relieve her symptoms.

Adding insult to injury, her pallid reflection in the glass revealed not only her wan complexion, but also unattractive dark rings which encircled her eyes. Forced to press her hand to her lips to prevent the nausea from overtaking her, Emme deftly slapped at her face in an attempt to bring some colour to her faded cheeks, although there was little she could do about the rings. Perhaps his lordship's eyesight was sufficiently poor to prevent him from noticing them. Her figure, which had always been voluptuous, was now even more generous, she hoped it would serve to distract Lord Stibbard's attention from her deficiencies.

Emme smiled slyly she recalled how it had distracted Mr Stokesby the previous evening. A flush of excitement at the memory of the illicit meeting in the hidden stairwell, brought a rosy glow to her pale cheeks.

"Here she is, my dear little gel."

Lord Stibbard's greeting made Emme's skin crawl, but hiding her disgust she dimpled and curtsied prettily to her betrothed, who shuffled unsteadily on his feet, beaming indulgently at her.

However, far from greeting or even acknowledging her daughter's, presence, Mrs Wreningham was lying, weeping upon the arm of the chaise longue.

Unable to comprehend what was amiss, Emmeline took her place on the sofa where her fiancé had been seated, wondering fearfully if Stibbard had discovered something amiss; something to cause him to end their betrothal. She cast her eyes down demurely at her hands in her lap, eyeing him surreptitiously from beneath lowered lashes, but there appeared to be nothing awry with the elderly lord as he laboriously took his place beside her, grunting as he sat.

The noise from the chaise longue could be ignored no longer and schooling her face in to an expression of concern, Emmeline spoke with unaccustomed gentleness. "Mama, is something amiss?"

Unable to articulate, Mrs Wreningham began to weep anew, waving a tear-stained letter at her daughter, who bewildered turned to Lord Stibbard for an explanation.

The elderly gentleman shook his head sombrely at her, causing a fine sprinkling of white power to fall from his wig onto his shoulders. "'Tis bad news little Emmeline, but you must be a brave gel and not sully your pretty face with tears."

Emme suppressed an urge to cast up her accounts, instead she looked from Lord Stibbard to her mother in bafflement.

With an innate sense of theatrics, realising that her moment had come, Mrs Wreningham waved the letter in her hand, wailing, "My son! My own boy ... ", but overcome by tears she was unable to continue, much to the obvious disapproval of Lord Stibbard, who found the ill-bred display most distasteful.

"Now, now, you must remain calm Mrs Wreningham." He patted his betrothed's arm, with a hand bearing the marks of liver spots and grubby nails which required paring. "It is your brother my dear little Emmeline, it would seem he has met with a most unfortunate occurrence."

Emme waited for the man to explain himself, but when no further explanation was forthcoming, she looked to her mother for clarification.

Mrs Wreningham, who had no desire to have the thunder of the occasion stolen by her prospective son-in-law, clutched at her breast as if having palpitations. "My boy, has been brutally shot. My own child! How will I go on?" Her cry reached a crescendo, before subsiding into a series of sobs, punctuated by gasps and shuddering.

With her mind a-whirl, Emmeline turned to her turned to Stibbard, "What does my mother mean, my lord?"

"You must prepare yourself for a shock my dear, but you will hear it in the end, so it as well you hear it from me."

She waited, but still Stibbard delayed, shaking his head censoriously, until Emme could have screamed in frustration. Why would he not get to the point?

"The news I share with you is dire indeed." Lord Stibbard eyed his fiancée, ensuring he had her undivided attention, then announced ponderously. "Your brother most unwisely challenged Mr Siddenham to a duel."

Emme's blue eyes opened wide in dismay, for she alone understood the truth of the encounter. However, not privy to such information, Stibbard could only feel satisfaction at Emmeline's appropriate response to such shocking news. She was obviously a delicate girl, not one of these coming young misses who revolted him so.

Well-pleased, he continued, warming to his theme. "Most unwisely. Lest the event not reach a favourable conclusion, your brother wrote a letter to your mama, the letter was delivered to her a short time ago. I was most shocked to hear of it; for I was to meet your brother here this morning to go over the settlements and so was naturally perturbed when he failed to keep our appointment." His lordship appeared to be as much concerned by John's unreliability as by the injurious nature of the duel, although he murmured despondently, "Tis a sad day."

Without thinking Emme clutched at his jacket. "What of John, of Mr Siddenaham?"

As if seeing the girl's pale face and ringed eyes for the first time, Lord Stibbard placed a restraining hand upon her arm. "Emmeline, you must not overset yourself, I forbid it. This is no subject for a lady and is not one I willingly share with you. T'was your mama who insisted you be told." He inclined his head in disapproving acknowledgement of Mrs Wrengingham's prior claim upon Emmeline. "Nonetheless, the details are unfit for a lady and I will not permit you to learn of them."

Stibbard's tone was not one Emme had encountered before, and realising the need to tread carefully, she dabbed at her eyes with her handkerchief, nodding as if in submission to her masterful fiancé.

"It is all to shocking to be borne, I am quite beside myself- pray advise me- what must I do?" That she did not appear to be beside herself, neither her weeping mama, nor her unexpectedly authoritative fiancé seemed to notice, for Emmeline's words were not laced with feeling.

Grasping the side of the sofa for support, the baron rose slowly to his feet. "I will pay your brother a call and see how he fares. He was taken, I believe to his lodgings by his second."

Emme looked up sharply, "Pay him a call? He lives?"

"Yes, yes, he lives, but for how long? That is the question."

Suppressing the urge to scream, Emmeline managed to convey the impression of possessing delicate sensitivities to the delighted Stibbard, who stroked her hand attentively, forcing Emme to tremble in disgust. Then bowing in a stately manner, his powdered wig slipping just a little, the elderly gentleman made his farewell.

The doors had no sooner closed behind his lordship, when abandoning all pretence, Emme rose and roughly snatched the letter from her mother's hand, her fury rising as she read the read the contents of the tear-stained missive. How could John have been so stupid?

Her mother, prostrate with grief would be of no use to her, even if Emme had been able to tell her of the predicament in which she found herself. If her swelling abdomen had seemed a problem before, with John unable to assist her, the situation was dire; while Emmeline believed herself well-able to manage her lord once the ring was upon her finger, getting it there before it was too late would be quite another matter.

Her mother raised a tear-stained face to her daughter's calculating one, and held out her hand, demanding in her own way that Emme pay court to her grief, unaware that any pity Emme might be experiencing was only for herself. "It's all the fault of Maia and that Percy Siddenham," the stricken woman declared. "If she had not been so wanton as to be seen with him the long gallery, none of this would have happened. How like my noble John to take it upon himself to defend the family honour, and now we must lose him, and for what?" Breaking off into a zealous fit of weeping, Mrs Wreningham was rendered speechless once again.

By way of response Emmeline snorted in frustration, yet she was not ignorant of the irony that the blame had fallen upon Maia, ensuring no one would question what lay behind the duel. Once again Maia was shielding her cousin.

Chapter Forty-Four

Of all the chambers in her London residence, the Chinese room was arguably Caroline Alconbury's favourite, although to the uninitiated, stepping over the threshold could prove to be a startling experience, which perhaps explained why so few were ever invited into the chamber, for the dowager duchess did not care to explain either herself or her room.

Maia was therefore justifiably surprised to be informed by Heydon, that the Chinese room was where the dowager had chosen to receive the Duke of Bradenham, and where the pair now awaited her presence. Duly summoned, Maia left the letter she had been writing to Eley, half-written, and within moments the epistle was wholly forgotten. This heavily edited version of recent events would lie upon the morning room escritoire for sometime, until it was discovered and discarded by Caro, who firmly believed that letters should contain fact, not fiction.

The Chinese room boasted sage-green silk walls, complete with exotic, many hued birds, painted in vivid watercolours, and gave the impression one had inadvertently stepped into a lush forest. The ornately inlaid floor was covered with silk rugs, and made Maia yearn to rid herself of shoes and stockings, that she might wriggle her toes in their inviting softness.

As ever, upon gaining entry to the chamber, Maia was dazzled by the beaten brass gong hanging upon a wall; highly polished it caught the sunlight, shimmering like water in a moving pool. Black lacquer screens stood tall in a far corner, their entwined golden painted dragons threatening to crawl from the confines of the framework, so lifelike was their depiction, more dragons were reflected back at the screen from the vast looking-glass upon the opposite wall. The room was a feast for the senses, with rich silks, vivid colours and the illusion of being deep within a forest. However, the tension within the sunlit chamber was unmistakable.

Her god-mother was seated upon a high-sided, concealing sofa, barely visible to the perplexed Maia, while his Grace lingered by the gilded harp which stood by an open window, allowing the breeze to draw gentle notes from its strings as if unseen fingers ran lazily across the taut wires. While he was motionless, his hands clasped behind his back, Bradenham gave the impression of being both distracted and impatient.

Unable to fathom the cause of her apprehension, Maia looked warily from the duke to her god-mother, and wasting no time on pleasantries Cosmo explained the nature of his visit: "Percy was challenged to a duel by your cousin Wreningham, and as incredible as it may seem Percy has had the best of it; at this moment your cousin lies closer to death than life."

Having hitherto believed John to be no more than a committed blusterer, caring only for his own pursuits and pleasures - a man who would do anything for an easy life - Maia was astounded. While wavering in his resolution to impart all he knew, unsure of how to go about the business without inflaming her damnable temper, Bradenham paused.

Noting his hesitation Caro spoke up. "It was not your honour John was defending, but Emmeline's." She could not resist adding wryly, "sadly it was far too late." Not that Maia needed the details to be spelled out to her, having witnessed much that night in the long gallery.

Cosmo cleared his throat awkwardly, but seeing that the dowager was not mincing words, he continued as if addressing Rowland, or Harrington, while unable to contain his restlessness he began pacing about the chamber as he spoke.

"From what I understand, your Miss Wreningham confided in her brother that she is with child, naming my cousin as the sire. Wreningham, acting upon impulse - one assumes - called Percy out with disastrous consequences. For the time being your cousin lives, but for how long he will survive is uncertain. At my instigation Percy has fled to Holland, with a wound to his leg which one can only hope will prove fatal, although I expect it will not."

Maia was taken aback at the vehemence of his sentiments, yet as Bradenham abruptly ceased pacing and faced her, his eyes seeking hers, it was apparent there was more still to be told.

"It was Percy who arranged your abduction; his accomplice was to present you to the world on the morning of the Second Spring Race Meeting as a ruined woman."

Upon observing the duke's ire, Caroline could not help mentioning with relish, "A thoroughly ruined woman." Cosmo flashed her a furious glance.

"Poor Emme, what will she do? She must be heartbroken that Percy has fled." Maia wondered, half to herself.

Her god-mother snorted indignantly. "Do not waste your pity my love, for I do not believe the wretched girl is heartbroken, and unless I am mistaken, Emme has no intention of calling off her betrothal to Stibbard, but intends to pass off Percy's by-blow as his lordship's legitimate child."

The duke nodded in agreement. "I believe you are right, although Percy was far from convinced the child is his."

Deeply shocked. Maia exclaimed, "Poor Lord Stibbard. How could Emme do such a thing?"

There was another snort from the sofa. "She can because she must, your cousin has left herself no other option, and while I confess to finding it abhorrent in the extreme, there is perhaps some justice in this."

At this both Maia and Cosmo looked askance at the dowager, waiting for her to enlighten them.

"Stibbard has buried two wives, neither of whom managed to produce an heir. It seems to me poor luck to choose wives who were both barren, yet for years I have heard whispers that in his youth Stibbard was wont to … well, let us just say he enjoyed exercising what he considered to be his droit du seignior, yet there is no mention of a trail of bastards left in his wake. One has to wonder why."

Frowning deeply, the duke looked uncomfortable in the extreme at the repugnant nature of the dowager's contemplation.

Maia began to assimilate this unforeseen turn of events and, as she spoke to Bradenham, she watched his expression, "Mr Siddenham has fled; while despite being with child, Emme is to marry her ignorant lord, and it seems I am saved from a distasteful marriage. Yet, I am convinced I am missing something important, for other than informing us that John is about to meet his maker - for which you could have sent a message - I can see no reason why you would trouble yourself to call at this hour of the morning."

Cosmo's face grew grim, for this was the heart of the matter. "The letter your cousin left for his mother did not state that his reason for calling Percy out was to defend Miss Wreningham's long-lost honour, therefore the natural conclusion will be that he was defending yours."

"So, in the eyes of the world I remain the guilty party, a ruined woman and John's death will confirm this."

Her god-mother spoke with enthusiasm. "Yes dear, John has generously confirmed that you are indeed a wicked woman."

The duke groaned.

Eyeing him with irritation, waspishly Maia demanded, "What

would you have me do? Cover my head and hide in a convent? Exile myself to Norfolk once again?"

Unexpectedly he grinned at her. "You have already done that with I might point out, disastrous results." There was another undignified snort from the dowager, but she allowed Cosmo to continue. "Her grace and I have contrived a plan, but it will be entirely dependant upon your agreement."

"And upon your avoiding long galleries at all costs," chimed in Caro unnecessarily, who was thoroughly enjoying herself.

Finding the reminder of Maia in Percy's arms to be galling, no matter how innocent, the duke glared at the dowager. However, Maia was not ready to listen to the plans of others - to be decorously arranged like a child's plaything. Bristling with indignation, she rounded on the duke - not entirely reasonably.

"All this nonsense is entirely your fault, had you not hounded me or brow-beaten Percy, any interest in this matter would have long ceased. There would have been no need for my abduction were it not for your intervention, and Percy would not have been forced to hie off to France ..."

"Holland," interjected the duke.

Maia waved her hand dismissively. "Holland, France, it is all of a piece. John would not be about to breathe his last and Emme ... "

"No! You will not place your cousin's predicament at my door, nor am I responsible for throwing myself upon a couple engaged in an indiscreet and reckless liaison. That I will not take responsibility for."

Neither of the pair noticed the dowager duchess slipping silently from the room; experience told her there were times when young lovers needed to be alone, if only for a few moments.

With eyes ablaze, Cosmo advanced upon the equally infuriated Maia, who sensibly and somewhat tactically retreated behind a chaise-longue; her heart racing and her dark hair tumbling about her shoulders, as she tossed her head in indignation.

"I dare you to deny that you have hounded me. Do you know for a while I believed it was you who had arranged for my abduction, to force me to marry Percy?"

Bradenham took a measured pace towards the chaise longue, so that the elegantly furnished piece the only thing standing between them.

"What made you think otherwise?" His voice had a dangerous edge to it, as he considered the almost disastrous consequence of the abduction.

Maia should have known better, she should have kept her wits and her tongue about her. Should have, but did not. With her chin in the air and her violet eyes blazing, every inch a woman possessed, she retorted, "I reflected that had you wanted to kidnap me you would not have hired an underling to do the job, you would have done it yourself."

"Do not tempt me," ground the reply from the simmering duke. "I still might."

Pushed to the bounds of her limited patience, Maia flashed back at him. "You would not dare."

"Is that a challenge?"

Before she could reply, Cosmo vaulted elegantly over the back of the chaise-longue, landing with Maia in his arms and holding her tightly he groaned as he kissed her.

"You are going to have to marry me, although I must be mad to wish be wedded to such a fury."

There was no reply from Maia, who did not feel it was appropriate to argue while she was being kissed. And there was no doubt about it, she was being thoroughly kissed. But then again, so was the duke.

While the duchess was happy to turn a blind eye to much that went on between Cosmo Bradenham and her god-daughter, she felt she ought to draw the line at what might be construed as seduction, although, it did not appear that Maia would put up much of a fight should the event arise. Not that it would, for the duke was utterly honourable, she reflected sadly. Still, it made her rôle as chaperone easier.

While the pair did not exactly spring apart, they moved a few steps away from each other and, as an incurable romantic, the dowager was delighted to note that they were a little out of breath, Maia's cheeks were rosy, and her hair was about her shoulders - it all looked most promising.

"I hate to interrupt your tête-à-tête, but feel I must remind you that Maia is still under my protection, and while I whole heartedly approve of you as a suitor for my god-daughter, according to the dictates of my rôle, I am duty-bound to disapprove of such behaviour, delightful though it may be. Besides, amorous displays in the morning always prove so unsettling to the servants, and one must act with an eye to propriety, no matter how belatedly."

Still beautifully flushed, Maia was shocked by her god-mother's suggestion, "Suitor?"

Cosmo raised an eyebrow at her, "I am well-aware of your

history in long galleries, but my love, I really must protest, you cannot make a habit of kissing gentlemen and expect to get away with it. I fear you must make an honest man of me. I could never again hold my head up in the ton were known I was just another of your conquests. This time my girl, you have met your match, and before you open your delectable mouth to argue, allow me to advise you that if you refuse to marry me, I will abduct you."

Finding the notion of abduction far more appealing when he was cast in the rôle of abductor, the duke believed his newly hatched scheme to be entirely flawless. This sentiment was not shared by Miss Hindolveston, who turned on him irritably, not appreciating his humorous turn.

"And no doubt take me to Newmarket, to ravish me?"

He leaned menacingly towards her, whispering wickedly, "Oh no my love, I will ravish you long before we reach Newmarket."

Maia's violet eyes opened wide in what could only be described as horrified delight.

She asked her god-mother, "Was that the plan?"

With a howl of amusement, Cosmo interrupted. "For me to ravish you? I am convinced not even your god-mama would be a willing party to that! But do bear in mind that ravishment is an alternative, should all else fail."

Feeling the subject had reached a natural conclusion and that she should attempt to restore some decorum to the proceedings, the dowager spoke up. "Ravishment aside, the scheme was that you should continue to make your come out under my aegis, with Bradenham offering ..." here she choked "... moral support. However, it would appear he has pre-empted things somewhat."

Maia's expression took on a mulish air, but Cosmo was having none of it. "For once you must see sense Maia, if you think I am going to leave my wife to the mercy of the ton, when I can protect her, then you have more hair than wit!"

"But I have not agreed to marry you and you have not asked."

The duke looked abashed. "You are right, would you like me to throw myself upon my knees and vow my fidelity for evermore?"

Appearing to give the notion her full-consideration, Maia wrinkled her nose superciliously. "I think not, I just did not want you to assume I was going to marry you."

"Are."

"I beg your pardon?"

"Are. You *are* going to marry me, you *are* going to be my

wife." Sealing his avowal in the time honoured manner, Cosmo raised Maia's hand to his lips and kissed her soft palm tenderly, delighted to observe the return of the tell-tale blush, and the sparkle in the violet eyes which steadfastly returned his gaze.

"We will see," she mused withdrawing her hand. "It does not do to be too sure of one's self you know."

With that gently barbed set-down, Maia removed herself from the duke's immediate vicinity to sit in relative safety at her godmother's side, leaving the vanquished Bradenham behind the chaise-longue, his fingers beating a frustrated tattoo upon the red damask. Caro looked from one to the other; under normal circumstances such a well-matched couple would be a bore, but these two never failed to amuse, although they would have to settle things eventually and by the look of things, Bradenham would not be kept waiting for long.

Setting aside her romantic schemes, Caroline addressed her god-daughter. "The matter as it stands is not so very different while Mr Wreningham lives, for the duel will be hushed-up as well as your aunt is able to contrive, however, once he is dead the tongues will wag and you will again become the on-dit."

"Can you be so sure he will succumb?" Maia questioned, incredulous that John had been so reckless as to risk harm to something he prized so highly, namely himself.

Cosmo nodded gravely. "No doubt whatsoever."

"I am surprised to learn that Mr Siddenham is an excellent shot, perhaps I should have given his suit serious consideration." Maia's wistful sigh was undetermined by the wicked glint in her eye. "Alas it is too late to think of it now."

"Indeed, it is a good deal too late," confirmed Cosmo with feeling. "Percy has always been a shockingly poor marksman, but upon this occasion had the luck of the very devil. The pistols he borrowed from Lyth-Hudson have a hair trigger, the slightest movement upon the trigger would be enough to discharge the barrel, although your cousin fired first - there can be no doubt of it for I saw Percy go down myself. As Percy was struck the force must have caused his pistol to go off, for I cannot believe he was able hit Wreningham through skill, when he possesses none."

Maia's response was thoughtful. "So John's death will be no more than a lucky accident for Mr Siddenham?" With the duke's nod of confirmation, her voice grew more strident. "How like John to neglect to use his brains, avenging Emme's honour indeed. What of Emme's honour now? If she is with child she will need to hasten the wedding if she is to pass the child off as Stibbard's, for they are not due to be wed until August, and that still some months away. How will she hurry his lordship up the aisle without John's help?"

The silence which followed was broken by the dowager's measured voice, "How indeed?"

Dismissive of Miss Wreningham, whom he had disliked on sight and cared for even less now he had been afforded a glimpse into her nature, Cosmo retorted with asperity. "I am more concerned with how to keep you and your less than spotless reputation safe, while the ton are obsessed with the intimate details of this scandal. Yet as you have not shown the least inclination to return to your home, although I doubt you would be safe even there, and you seem reluctant to wed anyone, including myself, the only course of action is for you to continue to make your come out. After all you have already made your curtsy before Queen Charlotte, have you not?"

Maia nodded.

"You will continue to make your come-out while we," he glanced at Caroline, "will do what we can to keep the gossip-mongers at bay, although it would be a damn sight easier if you would marry me."

A martial light shone in Maia's eyes and neither the duke nor her god-mother were deceived, but then they had not expected her to acquiesce without a fight.

"How is this different to what was being endeavoured before Mr Siddenham and John attempted to murder each other?" she demanded stubbornly.

Feeling that the duke had omitted the more pertinent facts of the matter, the dowager spoke up. "My dear, the difference is that now you have no smoke screen in the form of Mr Siddenham who, unattractive as he undoubtedly is, would have provided you with a useful betrothal had things become difficult. Although, I confess to never being comfortable with the notion of you as his wife, but there is no use crying over spilt milk, particularly when it was already sour. So my dear, what the duke is trying to say," she looked at Cosmo severely, "is that, there may be more difficulties ahead than we had first anticipated, especially once it is known that John died to defend your apparently lost honour."

Maia's shoulders slumped in resignation. "And what is my rôle to be in this nonsensical drama?"

"Why, you are the heroine." Bradenham spoke without any trace of irony.

Maia responded with an un-lady-like noise of derision.

"In order to minimise the difficulties I must insist that you do not stray in long galleries; you would do well to stay away from empty churches and inns too!"

The heroine glared at the duke wrathfully. While wearing an expression of smug satisfaction, the dowager happily smoothed out the skirts of her morning gown, noting with interest that Bradenham had not mentioned Chinese rooms in his list of prohibited venues.

Chapter Forty-Five

As a social climber with an eye to self-promotion, John Wreningham would undoubtedly have found it galling to know that as he lay at death's door, or more accurately halfway across the threshold, that only those closest to him were aware of this fact. For despite his very public demands for Percy Siddenham's head on a proverbial platter, the threats had not been taken seriously by those acquainted with the pair. Consequently, there were no enquiries into his welfare, no weeping ladies languishing upon their chaise-longues in various stages of decline, and until such time as a death notice was placed in the newspapers, the world was none the wiser.

Indifference was not wholly to blame, for John was also indebted to his sister's creaking lord, who had done his best to hush-up the affair by brushing aside such rare enquires as were made into the health of the Wreninghams, and when the need arose by the employment of outright lies. Stibbard was anxious to avoid being associated with the shocking episode, or have his betrothed besmirched or tainted in any way. Having managed to secure a bride, he had no desire to begin the exhausting process all over again. However, never one to miss the opportunity of sharing the wisdom of his considerable years, his lordship was as good as his word and had betaken himself to visit Emmeline's foolish brother.

The dingy rooms in Davis street were hushed; the shutters closed against the joyful spring light, giving the bedchamber a pre-emptive funereal aura, where all hope flown. The fire was banked to keep the patient warm, but the fetid smell which assailed Stibbard's nostrils as he was shown in to the chamber by a surly, ill-kempt manservant, was unmistakable.

Wreningham lay sprawled untidily upon the rumpled bed, covered by a grubby sheet, the occasional muscular spasms causing his hands to jerk sharply were the only signs of life detectable within the stifling, gloomy room. The chamber was littered with the accoutrements of a young man of society burdened with a smaller purse than he might wish. All was as John had left it when he had departed to keep his appointment with Mr Siddenham. Had he known his return would be far from triumphant, it is possible Wreningham might have instructed his man to tidy the chamber, or at least have arranged for the removal of the less savoury items he had collected during his dubious progress. The stained, cheap garter thrown carelessly upon the tallboy spoke volumes - would be the cause of much weeping and hand-wringing when his mother visited to shed tears over and upon her son. As for the hastily scrawled letter to the most recent object of his ardour which - in his haste to set out for the duelling field - John had neglected to direct, Mrs Wreningham spitefully tore the declaration of passion to shreds, for she would never consider its intended recipient a lady.

Peering in the squalid melancholy, Lord Stibbard sighed long and hard over the folly of youth. He had been prepared to deliver a homily upon the pride of the foolish man, and believing Miss Hindolveston to be the cause of the duel, upon misplaced family loyalty, but even he could see that John was beyond such redemptive speeches. Instead his lordship embarked upon a solemn farewell to the man, but was interrupted by John's manservant abruptly opening the door to admit the person of an overly cheery and rotund physician. Unable to spare her own doctor, Mrs Wreningham had insisted that his colleague be dispatched to minister to her beloved son in his darkest hour.

The good doctor bowed with much creaking of his whalebone corset and bobbing of his spherical head; delighted to have an audience to witness his remarkable skills.

"Good day to you sir, I hope I do not intrude. I must do what I can for my patient, much good may it do him. Such a waste, such a pity. Are you aware of the facts of the matter?"

Remote with formal dignity, Stibbard affirmed that he had been informed of the tragic event by none other than the hand of the patient himself. While pulling aside the bed sheet and layers of linen which lay across John's chest, the physician looked closely at what their removal revealed. The stench nearly knocked Stibbard from his feet, forcing the coughing, gagging man to make his way to the chamber door, that the relatively fresh air from the upper hallway might revive him.

Made of sterner stuff and accustomed to such irritations, the physician shook his head sorrowfully. "Tis a bad business, but there is not much that I can do for the boy, I have dosed him with as much laudanum as I dare, any more and I shall be delivering him to the archangel myself." Opening the small bag he carried with him, the doctor enquired conversationally, "Will his family visit?"

Still holding the encroaching man at a social arm's length, his lordship pondered the question. "This is no place for a lady, and I have recommended that the boy's mother stay away. As for my betrothed, under no circumstances will I allow Miss Wreningham to be associated with such an episode. Quite beyond decency."

Despite feeling heartily sorry for the young lady, the physician nodded in judicious agreement. "And yet, the patient's mother must wish to bid her son farewell." He lowered his voice, conspiratorially. "You might consider it, lest she take ill and become wearisome. I have seen it many times; they fall into decline borne of remorse at being denied the opportunity to say adieu, and linger, sometime for years. Often a great trial and always a great expense. You mark me, the boy's mother will prove a burden in the end." As the horror of his words sank in, he added practically, "I will remove the maggots, for it would not do for the lady to see her child being eaten alive, although I do not expect him to linger for long." The sound of straining whalebone could again be heard as the physician bent over John Wreningham, muttering, "I had hoped their application would keep the rot at bay, but there is no hope."

Hastening to remove himself from the bedchamber before this gruesome procedure could commence, Lord Stibbard nodded a terse farewell to the doctor. Betaking himself to his club for a restorative brandy before paying a call upon the household of Mrs Wreningham, his lordship resolved to take a firm line with Emmeline. It was entirely unseemly for an unmarried young lady of good breeding to pay calls upon gentlemen; even if that gentleman was her brother and he had the misfortune to be dying. There was a price to be paid for being a member of the ton, even one who resided on its fringes. Not that the baron was overly concerned, his little Emmeline was a lady through and through; he had chosen well and was content she would give him no trouble. He was quite looking forward to having a young gel in the house once again, doubtless she would restore the vigour of his youth.

With this reassuring thought, the exhausted lord sank back in the wing-chair before the fire, his wig slipping to one side, as through a slackly open mouth he began to snore, dribbling as he did so. It was perhaps as well Miss Wreningham could not see her fiancé at that moment.

Chapter Forty-Six

The obvious solution to the difficulty of brazening out the insidious rumours and speculation, Caroline Alconbury considered, was not to hide away in a timid manner, but to hold a ball - although Maia had taken an inordinate amount of tedious convincing upon the matter. She would have preferred to stay quietly away from public view, attending only a few small, select, wisely chosen social engagements, but the dowager was adamant that the bull of the ton must be firmly grasped by its gilded horns. So with Maia's unenthusiastic consent, and the duke's outright horror, a ball was arranged.

If Caro had any concerns that her last minute gathering might be poorly attended, she kept her thoughts to herself. It is unlikely such a consideration even crossed her mind, for a ball at her Berkeley square house was a rare occurrence, and promised to rank high among the season's events - such was the lure of Caroline's hospitality and the unashamed magnificence of her residence.

Much of the splendour of the dowager duchess's London house was inadvertently due to the tenth and current Duke of Alconbury, whilst he was still Mr Thurlton. When advised by his cousin, the ninth duke, that Caroline was unable to bear more children and that it was likely Mr Thurlton would in due course find himself assuming the ermine mantle of Alconbury, Mr Thurlton was delighted. Unable to contain his eager and unattractively grasping anticipation, the foolish man made the mistake of telling the lady he planned to make his duchess. Metaphorically rubbing his hands with glee, regretfully Mr Thurlton voiced aloud that Alconbury House, together with Alconbury Hall, would be his - just as soon as the ninth duke was cooling his heels in the mausoleum, and Caroline could be prised from the property before being dispatched with a meagre allowance. This, as it turned out, was neither diplomatic or prudent, for he was overheard by the duke.

If Mr Thurlton believed that blood and title were all that mattered to the ninth Duke of Alconbury, then he was guilty of a grave miscalculation, for the furious duke acted swiftly and mercilessly to protect those dearest to him.

The entailed Alconbury House, a delightful but modest London residence, was brutally abandoned by his Grace, who stripped it of everything not in the entail, and abandoned it to the mice, leaving the fascinated members of society under no misapprehension of where his true passions lay.

Within three months of that fateful conversation, the duke had purchased the Berkeley square residence for his beloved Caroline, and under his watchful eye and deep purse, the house had every care and attention lavished upon it. No detail was overlooked and to the chagrin of Mr. Thurlton, no expense spared.

The ballroom was unashamedly rococo with its inlaid parquet floor set out to form flowers - the ornate painted ceiling depicted upon closer inspection insubstantially clad nymphs, who appeared to be frolicking with equally unsheathed, mythical heroes. It was rumoured that if one had the opportunity to see the ballroom by daylight it was possible to see the resemblance of both the duke and duchess among the ranks of heroes and nymphs, as well as one or two of their particular friends. While young ladies were advised to avert their eyes from such scenes, young men were at liberty to look and speculate, craning their neck to peer past the numerous chandeliers at the ceiling beyond.

A riot of gilt and white moulding, the room had two tiers of windows, with gilt looking-glasses between each, reflecting the dancers as they were lit by the glittering chandeliers, whilst looking-glasses at either end of the ballroom reflected the dazzling grandeur ad infinitum.

The opulent room had been described by more than one envious matron as 'the height of bad taste', nevertheless, even she had to confess that it made a startling impression and quite took the breath away.

***

With her eyes wide in astonishment, Emmeline took in the lavish surroundings, for the dowager duchess's ballroom was every bit as fine as she had been led to believe. Normally immune to girlish jitters, Emme could not help being more than a little swept away by heady anticipation, for tonight she was attending a ball without either her mother, or dreary fiancé in attendance.

The distraught Mrs Wreningham had insisted upon remaining with her son, although little would be achieved by her bedside vigil. Torn between accompanying his betrothed to the Alconbury ball, and overseeing the demise of her brother, Lord Stibbard had allowed his aching feet, as well as his sense of obligation, to win the day. Having taken the physician's observations to heart, with ponderous solemnity

Stibbard had accompanied Mrs. Wreningham to sit beside her son's bedside and weep over his pale hand, although his lordship had taken with him a well-worn hip-flask and a kerchief, liberally sprinkled with sweet woodruff to mask the gangrenous odour of both John Wreningham and his chamber.

In the ladies-withdrawing room, Emme glanced at her reflection in one of the looking-glasses so thoughtfully provided by the dowager, and was delighted to note how well she looked, despite her unfortunate condition. Her eyes were bright, her cheeks delicately flushed and her bosom abundant. Best of all the dark rings which had encircled her eyes had at last receded. Ensuring that she was alone in the room, Emme strategically removed the fichu of lace from the neckline of her ball gown and carefully shifted her breasts against the straining fabric of her bodice, to display them to their best advantage. She was going to enjoy this evening.

The twittering confidante of Mrs Wreningham, Mrs Whitwell, who was fulfilling the rôle of duenna for the duration of the ball, was no match for Emmeline's well-practiced cunning. Completely taken in by the wide eyes and golden curls of this diminutive angel, counted herself a fortunate woman that her charge was such a well brought up young lady, secure in the knowledge that the evening would be pleasantly spent in the company of other like-minded matrons, with only half an eye upon dear Emmeline.

Taking the delicate fichu, Emme ruthlessly tore it in two. Rendered useless, the lace was stowed carefully in the reticule hanging from her wrist. Then tossing her golden curls and viciously biting her lips to induce a deeper hue, Emmeline preened, before setting her shoulders and smiling delightedly at her reflection.

***

The vicar of St. Mary's, in Stow-cum-Quy was mildly disapproving as he watched the worldly display of dancing from the safety of the outskirts of the great ballroom, his wife nervously clinging to his arm. He would have preferred to be safely ensconced behind his desk with his beloved texts, but Mrs Chedgrave, although unable to bring herself to join the ranks of the whirling dancers, was mesmerised by the glittering beauty on display before her.

Mr Chedgrave's cousin, the genial Lord Babingly, was engaged in conversation with their hostess. "Delighted to have received your Grace's request. You could have knocked me down with a feather when Chedgrave said we were to be invited, deuced good of you."

"My dear Lord Babingly, it is I who am indebted to you, for ensuring Mr Chedgrave accompanied you this evening. He works far too hard and I am convinced that to be among mere mortals as he will find within these walls will prove good for his soul, if not his sermons."

Babingly laughed appreciatively, for Mr Chedgrave's fascination for church doctrine to the exclusion of all else, was no secret.

Feeling he should say something in order to acquit himself well, and in an attempt to relieve the levity of the conversation, Mr Chedgrave spoke up. "How delightful to see your god-daughter with you last week your Grace, such a charming young-lady." Mr Chedgrave explained for the benefit of his cousin, "Her Grace returned to us at Stow-cum-Quy, with dear Miss Hindolveston. I collect you had both been visiting your dear daughter upon a very happy occurrence."

Caroline nodded. "Indeed, Charlotte has made me a grand-mama, and while I dote upon little Ingham, I cannot help but feel Charlotte has served me an ill turn, to be known henceforth as a grandmother is almost too much to bear!"

There were renewed felicitations on the part of the Chedgraves and jocular congratulations from Lord Babingly, who gallantly reassured the dowager that no-one would believe she had enough years behind her to mistake her for anyone's grand-mama.

The dowager may have reached the elevated ranks of grandparenthood, but the new grand-mama's eyesight was not impaired, and it had not escaped Caroline's notice that Lady Ormesby was standing close to the Babingly party, mesmerised by Mr Chedgrave's words, which would have made his clerical heart swell had he been delivering a sermon, for the woman was actually straining, the better to hear the speaker.

Fixing the eavesdropper with a hard stare, followed by a condescending smile, Caro turned her attention back to the Chedgraves. While she enjoyed entertaining, being entertained was equally rewarding.

***

Secure in the knowledge that she looked well, Emmeline demurely threaded her way through the other guests to Mrs Whitwell's side. The chattering woman's notice was immediately drawn to the striking change in Emmeline's hitherto chaste appearance, but adept at such easy manipulation as this, Emme was prepared and lowering her eyes, allowed her lip to tremble as she clutched her chaperone's hand.

The concerned lady was immediately alarmed and anxious for her charge. "Why my dear child, whatever is the matter?"

"Mrs Whitwell it is too dreadful, look at my gown." Casting her sorrowful eyes down at the expanse of flesh, once so admirably concealed by the now rent lace, Emme continued, "My fichu must have become entangled when my evening cloak was taken from me, for when I looked there was a shocking tear in it and I did not know what to do. I could not possibly make an appearance looking so dreadfully frowzy with rent lace, but I am convinced I must seem shockingly fast." A large tear trickled down Emmeline's flushed cheek, causing her chaperone much anguish.

"My dear child, do not distress yourself so, where is the article in question? Can it not be repaired? I feel sure we can contrive."

Looking earnestly into Mrs Whitwell's concerned face, Emme whispered breathlessly, "I do hope so, for I have it here in my reticule, shall we hasten to the ladies-withdrawing room?"

Mrs Whitwell patted Emme's cheek fondly. "My dear, I think it would be best if I take your reticule and see what may be done, we do not wish to draw attention to ourselves by bobbing in-and-out in an unseemly manner. You may remain here and I ... I am convinced, will be able to mend such little thing as a tear."

In a convincing display of gratitude, Emme breathed, "You are so kind, I should have trusted you would know what to do. Here is my reticule." She bundled the drawstring bag into the matron's hands and watched calculatingly as Mrs Whitwell wound her way through the milling crowd, towards the withdrawing room. Carefully holding the delicate ivory sticks of her silk fan, Emmeline fanned her face as she thoughtfully noted the groups of gentlemen thronging about the ballroom.

***

Naturally, Bradenham had himself informed Constance Lyth-Hudson of the recent events in Hyde Park, the extent of her brother's injury, and the precise nature of the occasion upon which it had been acquired. While Connie was inclined to be tearful upon receiving regrettable tidings, she had been both horrified and furious with Percy; for never one to mince words, Cosmo had apprised her of the greater part of the whole sordid affair. She had wept quietly alone, but the enormity of the horror her brother had attempted to perpetrate upon Maia Hindolveston had not been lost upon her.

That Constance loved her brother was not in question, but

love aside, his behaviour disgusted her and it was with relief that she acknowledged Cosmo's wisdom in arranging for Percy's removal to the continent in the care of his valet. On the other hand, she could quite cheerfully have wrung Miss Wreningham's neck if she thought it would make a jot of difference, for Connie could see the yawning abyss which now stood just beyond Miss Hindolveston's feet, should she set a dainty dancing shoe out of place.

However, her own emotions notwithstanding, Mrs Lyth-Hudson had noted with interest the set of the duke's jaw and rising tide of his fury, as he related the events leading up to the ill conceived duel and protracted, yet apparently imminent demise of the equally foolish Mr Wreningham.

In the marvel of the rococo splendour of the dowager's ballroom, Constance wondered even more, for Cosmo had barely left Miss Hindolveston's side all evening. He had danced with the girl but once, yet when she danced with other eager gentlemen, Cosmo had not taken his eyes from her; his brooding gaze following Maia's progress around the glittering chamber. Miss Hindolveston, Constance considered, looked undeniably beautiful - her dark curls held high above her head, displaying her neatly arched neck in a gown scooped unexpectedly low at the back.

Leaning towards her attentive husband, Constance whispered admiringly, "I must ask Miss Hindolveston whom her modiste is, she looks utterly breathtaking."

Rowland chuckled in her ear. "It would seem Bradenham agrees with you my love, he has not looked at anyone else since we arrived. If he were not such a confirmed eschewer of the parson's mousetrap, one would begin to suspect him."

His wife looked up at him through lowered eyelids. "Even the most confirmed of bachelors has a weak spot, as I recall."

Rowland's hand squeezed hers. "Indeed my love, however, I was never as confirmed as Bradenham, and I would certainly never to refer to you as my weak spot." Seeing her eyes widen in enquiry, he grinned at her. "You dearest, are my tower of strength."

As he kissed her hand gallantly, Constance dimpled in delight, causing anguish in the hearts of several gentlemen, who misguidedly believed themselves to be favoured by her smiles. The show of affection also delighted the matrons of the ton, who despite scheming in the matrimonial stakes, ruthlessly jostling their daughters into the path of eligible partis, liked nothing more than a love match, especially when the players were beautiful and rich. And there was no denying it, the Lyth-Hudsons were both.

***

The tenth Duke of Alconbury gritted his teeth as he and his wife made their way into the dazzling ballroom. Invitations to Berkeley square were rare, and although they never brought the duke unmitigated joy, no matter how much he protested his loathing of the dowager duchess, he did not dare to snub her. It was galling to witness the excesses of Caroline's Berkeley square house, while the tenth duke was left to scape by with only the entailments to provide for his myriad needs. Overawed by the splendour, his duchess said nothing, but wide-eyed and with her mouth open in concentration, she squinted upwards, trying to distinguish the figures upon the ceiling, illuminated in the candlelight from the sparkling chandeliers.

Following his wife's gaze the tenth duke tutted judgementally, "Avert your eyes my dear, do not give her the satisfaction of your interest. 'Tis too bad, to think of what we could have done with such a fortune."

His wife was thinking, but to her credit did not believe the fortune could have been better spent, unless one considered the nagging problem of damp at Alconbury House.

***

Cosmo felt an unpleasant stab of jealousy as he watched Maia being borne off to the dance floor by Mr St. Clement; discovering that the desire to render that gentleman as unconscious as he had rendered the hapless Percy, did little to improve his temperament. Nor did the dowager duchess's remark of, 'what a nice pairing they make, do you not agree Bradenham?' help matters.

He glared at the dowager and resolved when it came to choosing god-parents for their offspring, he would demand a say in the selection of god-mothers for their daughters. The thought of children made him smile, which unnerved Miss Wreningham as she passed by upon the arm of a young gentleman. Not liking the duke's expression she hurried away and therefore did not see his eyes narrow as he gazed thoughtfully at her choice of partner. For Bradenham recognised the auburn haired young man who surreptitiously edged his way to the side of the ballroom towards the open doors leading to the garden terrace, Miss Wreningham clinging to his arm like a vine. The couple waited, half hidden by a tall pedestal crowned with cascading white roses and ivy tendrils, then darting through the doorway they disappeared into the relative anonymity of the terrace, lit only by flaming torches.

Cosmo's could not conceal his disgust; it was a clandestine act such as this that had caused so much pain and suffering; Maia's near ruination; the certain death of John Wreningham; and Percy's bastard about to be placed like a cuckoo into Stibbard's unsuspecting nest. While Percy was already paying and would continue to pay for his crimes - with his life if he chose to return to England's shores - it was high time Miss Wreningham was brought to heel.

He was still considering this point when Mr St. Clement returned Maia to her god-mother's care, and glared with as much disdain as was possible to muster in the direction of the gentleman who was obviously a suitor for Maia's hand, before the thoroughly unnerved Mr St. Clement beat a hasty retreat.

Maia turned upon the duke wrathfully. "What is the matter? You positively terrified poor Mr St. Clement, anyone would think you were about to bite the man."

Bradenham raised a lofty eyebrow at her. "Another trophy to add to your considerable collection? Really my love, I am wounded you would abandon me so heartlessly to dance. When we are married, I will have to learn to be more interesting, perhaps then you will not wish to dance with such gentlemen." He sighed as if deeply distressed.

"I am not going to marry you and I will dance with whom I please, when I please. I like dancing with Mr St. Clement, he is charming." Her emphasis was unmistakable.

Undeterred, Cosmo looked smug. "We shall see, but I would have you know that I too have a fine pair of Wogden's, and am assured that Yaxley is familiar with the road to Newmarket."

With her cheeks flushed, Maia hissed, "If you ever abduct me I shall poison you."

The duke grinned appreciatively, then his face grew sombre. "Do you care to spoil your cousin's evening?" Maia eyed him questioningly as he continued, "Miss Wreningham and the gentleman I believe was John Wreningham's second, have just availed themselves of the terrace. Miss Hindolveston, I am finding it rather warm; shall we collect Constance and Rowland and take a turn in the evening air?"

With the barest of nods, Maia chatted conversationally, "I understand my god-mother's tea-roses are considered to be particularly beautiful, is that not so god-mama?"

The dowager, who despite appearing to give her full attention to the distinguished member of the wilder side of the Russian aristocracy at her elbow, responded immediately, "Indeed my dear, they are a delight." Excusing herself from the wild Russian, Caroline joined Bradenham and Maia, and the trio they made their way through the crowded ballroom in search of the Lyth-Hudsons.

Constance's eyes gleamed when informed of the object of the exercise, and taking her husband's arm in her own, gracefully led the way through the doorway onto the terrace.

***

Eyeing the ballroom ceiling with evident disgust, Lady Bellmont whispered to her companion, "To my mind it does not improve with renewed viewing, but remains now as it ever was, utterly vulgar."

At her side, Lady Ormesby squinted at a particularly well-muscled depiction of a hero with his helmet strategically, if disappointingly placed, and tittered, "Is that? No, surely it cannot be ..."

Her companion looked about her, misunderstanding, she hoped to see she knew not who.

"No dear, above us." Lady Ormseby indicated with her fan towards the ceiling, "I am sure the warrior must be Alconbury."

Lady Bellmont spoke reprovingly. "I will not lower myself by looking," adding a moment later, "which one? The one with the shield or the hemlet?"

"The helmet, but by this light it is so difficult to tell."

The ladies, their eyes heavenward, did not notice Sir Louis Heachem approaching.

"I see you are admiring dear Alconbury. He was a fine figure of a man, was he not?" His drawling accents had a clipped, cutting edge.

Turning sharply towards the exquisite speaker, Lady Bellmont was horrified to have fallen into such a snare, particularly when she done her best to avoid the man all evening. Lady Ormesby, too overcome to gather her scattered wits, hid her confusion behind the overused gesture of ferocious fanning.

"Sir Louis, how pleasant," was the best Lady Bellmont could muster.

Heach, however, was not ready to abandon the scandalous subject so soon. "Alconbury posed for the likeness himself, for I remarked upon it at the time. You have perhaps already seen the depiction of her Grace? Quite superb." He waved his ever-present scented handkerchief with a flourish, indicating the diaphanously clad depiction of a nymph who could only be Caroline Alconbury, beckoning in the direction of the helmeted hero, with an expansive amount of leg on display and a 'come hither' look in her eye. Sir Louis murmured appreciatively, "They posed together. Simply breathtaking."

Gulping, Lady Bellmont could not find the words to express herself, which in itself was significant. Capitalising upon this Heach pressed his advantage. "How is your daughter? Remind me, whom did she marry, in the end?"

This was dangerous ground and Lady Bellmont knew it, for the end to which Sir Louis referred was the culmination her mendacious pursuit of several eligible gentlemen on behalf of her daughter. With an eye to title, prestige and wealth, Bradenham was not the only aristocratic member of the ton who had made a narrow escape, although another titled gentleman had not been so fortunate.

She smiled nervously. "Sarah married Lord Foulden."

Sir Louis Heachem sighed in mock sympathy. "Good heavens! Now I recall. Most unfortunate, although one supposes someone had to. Perhaps it was all for the best. Still, Foulden has several estates, so Lady Foulden may avoid him without undue effort."

Unwisely Lady Bellmont bristled, "It was an excellent match and my dear Sarah is perfectly content, and although one should not whisper it, she is in a rather delicate condition."

Heach wrinkled his nose distastefully. "You mean she is increasing. So soon? How very interesting." The silken handkerchief flicked from side-to-side, not unlike the tail of a cat as it prepared to pounce.

Wishing she has not risen to the bait in a futile attempt to establish the fiction of her daughter's domestic felicity, Sarah's mama subsided into a nervous silence.

Lady Ormesby's fanning took on a desperate air, as the Machiavellian Heach turned his amoral gaze upon her. "Is dear Walter not with you? I am sorely disappointed, my dear you must prise him from his animal husbandry and drag him to town."

With her knuckles turning white in an effort to not drop the sticks of her overworked fan, Lady Ormesby twittered, "Walter is busy overseeing the harvesting upon his estates, my son is always occupied you know."

With evident delight Sir Louis crowed, "Harvesting? Surely you mean ploughing? Quite different my dear, quite different!" His inference was unmistakeable, as was the hoot of laughter that accompanied it.

Pausing to wipe away a tear of merriment from his eye, he surveyed the ballroom. "Where is the beautiful Miss Hindolveston? How kind of Caroline to take the dear child under her wing, but then she is the girl's god-mama, so one would expect nothing less." Noting the ladies dismay with satisfaction, he smiled, "You were not aware of the connection? How strange, I felt sure it was widely known."

The handkerchief flicked mischievously. "I must be getting old, for I confess to feeling an avuncular sentiment towards the girl." Heach lowered his voice as if to take them into his confidence and, unable to prevent themselves, the ladies leaned forward, anxious to be party to whatever the unscrupulous gentleman was about to utter.

"I must arm myself that I might protect the dear child from the wicked tongues of the gossips, for I understand she has been shockingly maligned."

"Arm yourself? Do you mean weapons, Sir Louis? Lady Ormesby's eyes were wide in consternation.

"Nothing so vulgar, my dear, nor so unsubtle."

Beginning to understand the direction in which the conversation was leading, Lady Bellmont gasped. "Surely not revenge?"

"An eye for eye, tooth for tooth?" Sir Louis murmured sotto voce. "I think not, for revenge is nothing without justice and I am nothing if not just." His tone took on an affectation of solemnity. "One must do what one can, with the gifts bestowed upon one."

The omnipresent handkerchief waved expressively. "I have often pondered the irony of how quickly gossip becomes common knowledge, and from there it is but a brief step before it is accepted as fact. Yet irony was ever a false jade, and I confess to finding her delicious." He dabbed his lips with the silk handkerchief as if it were a napkin and he had consumed a rare delicacy.

"One has to wonder at the talent necessary to turn mere speculation into damning fact; such a venomous tongue is required it is remarkable that the whisperers do not upon occasion, find themselves poisoned."

There was a horrified silence as Heach gave his handkerchief a wicked shake, reminiscent of a coiling serpent. "Even if the whisperers escape their own forked tongues, I fancy they will not evade the justice so beloved by those with a literary bent." Observing their mystified expressions he hissed, "Poetic justice, always so enjoyable. Ah, there is my dear friend Necton. Ladies I bid you adieu, for now." As he quit their company, Sir Louis Heacham conveyed the depth of his contempt with a singularly adept bow.

***

Unhampered by the awkward fact that the beauty and variety of the climbing roses were barely visible in the torch-lit night, with great admiration for the trellises, the small party strolled about the terrace. There were joyful exclamations from Mrs Lyth-Hudson upon the fineness of the buds, while the Duke of Bradenham admired greatly the fountain in the gardens beyond, despite the impossibility of distinguishing it the darkness, beyond the remote sound of splashing.

Finding herself unequal to the occasion, Maia was reduced to making small murmurs to indicate her fascination, as her god-mama proceeded to point out the rare roses bought by the late duke which, had to everyone's incredulity, flourished in the grimy London air. Yet for all their joviality, the the group were straining to hear any sounds from the terrace's hidden seats and niches.

Emmeline held her breath as she shrank back against the prickly foliage lining the recess; not only were she and Mr Stokesby in grave danger of being discovered, but worse than that, they were about to be discovered by her meddlesome cousin and the odious Duke of Bradenham, again. Putting her gloved hand over Stokesby's mouth to ensure his silence, she waited, willing the party who seemed intent upon admiring every shrub to be found within the vicinity of terrace, to the very devil.

With the sound of their footsteps drawing ever closer, she brusquely pushed Stokesby away, making rapid adjustments and smoothing her crushed silk gown. She dared wait no longer, Emme knew she must return to the ballroom before she could be seen. Peering round the leafy alcove she recognised none other than the Dowager Duchess of Alconbury, and cursing her ill-fortune together with Mr Stokesby's poor choice of venue, she ducked back behind the concealing greenery once again. This was fast becoming the stuff of nightmares. Holding her breath Emmeline resolved not to conduct any more al fresco liaisons, at least not until she was safely married to Lord Stibbard, and was in possession what she hoped would prove to be extensive terraces and gardens of her own.

While the party were wholly fascinated by an unutterably dull flower growing on the far side of the terrace, Emme seized the moment, and elbowing Mr Stokesby in the direction of the open ballroom doors, made her way silently across the flagstones.

A clear, authoritative voice arrested her progress, "Do you care for roses, Miss Wreningham?"

Until she heard her name Emme did not think she had been seen, but there was no other course of action open to her but to turn and make the best of things.

"R-roses?" She stuttered, glad the flush of her beet-red cheeks would barely noticeable in the flickering torch-light, but was unaware that her crumpled skirts had already betrayed her.

The dowager smiled in a feigned act of benign interest. "Yes my dear, these were a gift from my husband. Sadly I do not think they would grow as well in cooler climes, so perhaps would not thrive in the chill winters of Scotland. I collect that is where Lord Stibbard has an estate, is it not?"

Tongue-tied, Emmeline could only nod like a gauche schoolgirl, the disdain upon the duke's face was plain to see, while her cousin and the lady she knew to be Mrs Lyth-Hudson, remained coldly expressionless.

In truth, Maia was somewhere between incredulous fury and heartbreak. She had been willing - albeit reluctantly - to marry Percy Siddenham, to protect Emmeline's reputation, while her cousin cared for nothing and was incapable of seeing beyond her own pleasures. Wondering how she could have been so foolish, and to have misunderstood so much, Maia's hand began to tremble upon the duke's arm.

Hidden by shadow, Bradenham placed his own hand over Maia's, his thumb gently stroking her fingertips. Startled by this intimate act, Maia looked straight into the dark eyes which sought hers. The closeness of his presence was both reassuring and unnerving, and she shivered, although she was not cold.

Cosmo's delight that Maia should react so to his touch knew no bounds. How could he have believed she should marry Percy? How could he have been so deluded? However, feeling it prudent to refrain from further inflaming his passions at this juncture, his hand closed over Maia's.

Having no desire to address Miss Wreningham, Bradenham was satisfied to leave the wretched girl in the dowager's capable hands, and mused that he would not care to face Caroline in cross-examination. His object in leading the party to the terrace had been to prevent any further scandal from attaching itself to Maia, lest another discover her cousin's tryst, the association tainting Maia anew. The opportunity to put a spoke in the wheel of Miss Wreningham's liaison had been an additional boon.

The young woman in question did not need to be informed that she had stepped beyond the bounds of decorum and propriety; the dowager duchess, by her calm, precise demeanour, pointed observations and cold looks, conveyed to Emmeline the depth of her fall. The girl was all but a social pariah, if only in the eyes of the select few upon the terrace.

The sombre figures of Percy's sister and Mr Lyth-Hudson did

nothing to ease Emme's discomfiture, but although she did not dare contradict the dowager duchess, her sentiments were hardly in accord. For Emmeline firmly believed herself to be the injured party; it was her brother who lay at death's door, with her mama and fiancé dancing attendance, while she was forced to make a show of attending the ball with only a twittering chaperone. It was the outside of enough to be treated so disdainfully.

In the flickering light the golden locks of Mrs Lyth-Hudson were illuminated and Emme struck by the lady's resemblance to Percy, wondered if her unborn child would have the Siddenham colouring. She rather hoped so, having a preference for flaxen hair, her own artfully constructed curls had been encouraged for the past weeks to appear to their best and most golden advantage by her hair-dresser, who enjoyed an occasional dabble into alchemy.

Emboldened by the knowledge that for all her disapproval the dowager was unlikely to cause a scene during the middle of social occasion, Emmeline found her voice and entirely unashamed, made her excuses, hastening back to the throng of the ballroom. Believing she had managed the unfortunate situation rather better than might have been expected.

Her unaccompanied return might have given rise to speculation, however Miss Wreningham slipped cleverly behind a group of well-chaperoned young ladies sadly in want of dancing partners, in whose company she would scorn to be seen under normal circumstances. Attaching herself to the insipid coterie, Emme bided her time, calculating the moment she might seek more illustrious companionship now she was back within the relative anonymity of the seething crowd.

Displaying a feigned interest in a flower adorned pedestal, Emme pondered her next move. Yet her arrival from the terrace had not gone entirely unnoticed, for as she reached up to smell a particularly fragrant bloom, an urbane Lothario detached himself from a predatory clique and approached, smiling wolfishly.

Placing himself between the girl and the eyes of the crowd, the gentleman addressed her quietly, "My dear, we are not acquainted, yet."   His eyes lingered upon Emmeline's gown and all that it revealed, "I should very much like to make myself known to you." Licking his thin lips with innuendo and anticipation, he pressed closer. "What do you say? Shall you entertain me, privately?"

His lascivious gaze made Emmeline fearful, not only did the man frighten her, but he was far from discreet, overtly ogling her in such a manner. She attempted to appear a naïve, young debutante by averting her eyes from his and covering her bosom with her fan.

"Sir, you must hold me excused for we have not been introduced."

Not taking kindly at being toyed with by a chit, who by all accounts was no better than a common doxy, the gentleman restrained Emmeline with a cool hand, his chilly gaze malevolently assessing her creased skirts.

"You misunderstand me Miss Wreningham, perhaps I neglected to myself clear. I am not asking my dear, I am informing you. Shall we say, while the others are at supper?" He indicated the doors to a card room leading off from the ballroom. "I shall be waiting." With this the gentleman released Emmeline's arm and sauntering away was soon lost in the crowd.

There was, Emmeline discovered a vast difference between gleefully ignoring the precepts of common decency with a number illicit meetings, stolen from under the noses of her mama and dull fiancé, and being informed she had no choice in the matter. The distinction hinted darkly at the social morass and inevitable fall which must surely follow.

Until now it had been a game, and even finding herself with child had not unduly bothered Emme, who had assumed John would effortlessly bring forward her marriage, until his poorly timed duel put paid to such delusions. Even so, as recently as this very evening she had been able to put from her mind the enormity of the risks and huge stakes for which she was playing. Yet for all her worldliness and proficiency in the sordid, naively Emme had not realised her liaisons had not always been afforded the discretion which was so vital to her scheme. Nor had she known that some gentlemen were wont to gossip, vaunting the details of the hurried coupling to their peers, with little thought to the consequences. Thus the confirmation that her reputation was known in certain circles, was shocking indeed. If such rumours were abroad it could not be long before they reached Lord Stibbard's ears, and Emmeline had no doubt should any suggestion of improper conduct be mooted, that he would not hesitate to discard her.

The fact that she was increasing could not be hidden forever, and once it became public knowledge she would not even receive an offer of carte-blanche; such an offer was something Emme had been counting on if all else failed, when her mother cast her out, as she would surely do.

With her schemes turning to ashes before her eyes, Emmeline turned blindly, going she knew not where, and bumped straight into Maia.

While they had successfully thwarted Miss Wreningham's

plans upon the terrace, there was no sense of victory amongst these she left in her wake, only a stunned silence. And in Maia's case, anguish. However, mindful of her duties, Caroline had led the party's return to the ballroom while the duke and the Lyth-Hudsons had been drawn into conversation by an elderly couple, remaining aloof from their conversation, Maia had witnessed the exchange between her cousin and the unpleasant gentleman. Observing the fear and horror etched across her cousin's face, Maia did not have to guess the gentleman's intentions as he leered rapaciously at the girl.

When Emme knocked against her unheedingly, Maia stayed her with a gentle hand. "You are unwell."

Emmeline stared at Maia with unseeing eyes. "I am in health, but find the room overly warm."

Maia responded adroitly, recognising the standard phrase to excuse almost any ailment, or desire to escape the confines of a formal situation. "Allow me to join you, together we will find somewhere to refresh ourselves." Without waiting for a response, she took her cousin's arm and marched her from the ballroom.

Having made polite conversation for longer than he would have liked, Cosmo turned, expecting to find Maia in the vicinity of the small group, but finding her gone, immediately sought to discover her whereabouts. Thus he was in time to see Maia's slender figure departing from the well-lit ballroom, making her way along a dimly lit corridor which was evidently off-limits to guests, with Miss Wreningham by her side. He spun on his heel intending to speak to the dowager duchess, but discovering her to be gone also, wondered frowningly what further could be amiss? Finding no answer to his question, he had no choice but to reluctantly return his wandering attention to the elderly couple who had again claimed his notice.

Chapter Forty-Seven

As the cousins, all darkness and light, stole into the sanctum of the dowager duchess's Chinese room, Emmeline seemed barely aware of Maia's presence.

Caro did not make a practise of insisting that the doors of her private apartments remain locked during social gatherings, but neither did she make the rooms she preferred to keep private, welcoming. Therefore Maia glanced cautiously around the deeply shadowed room to ensure they were indeed alone before drawing her cousin in and closing the doors behind them.

The fire cast a flickering, mellow light about the hearth, making the painted golden dragons upon the lacquer screens appear to dance, their counterparts following suit in the eager reflections of the looking-glass.

Resting against the arm of the deep sofa Maia patted a silk cushion, encouraging the distracted Emmeline to be seated, but as the girl sat her face remained drawn, her mind elsewhere. Together they sat motionless; the only sounds the occasional crackling of the logs as they burned in the wide grate, and the strains of music from the ballroom, which reached even the furthest recesses of the house. For the first time that evening Maia took in the brittle figure of her golden-haired cousin.

Aware she was being appraised and beginning to revive, Emmeline looked with pride at all the discarded fichu had carefully concealed, and the gaze which met Maia's was not that of a vanquished maiden.

"I suppose you know that whole?" Emme enquired spitefully.

While there was no point in hiding the truth, Maia tried to temper her response with mercy and merely nodded.

Emme sighed self-pityingly. "Even that I am so unlucky as to be breeding?"

Again Maia nodded, wondering how her cousin could speak so carelessly, and yet despite all the evidence to the contrary, willing Emme to vindicate herself. "I know it, but I am not sure I understand."

"What is there to understand?"

"I am confused, you are with child by Mr Siddenham, yet you

are to wed Lord Stibbard. Which of them do you love, for if you love Mr Siddenham, why would you consent to marry Lord Stibbard?"

"Love?" Emmeline laughed, scoffing at her cousin's naivety, "How foolish you are Maia." She gave her cousin a sly glance, "I did not wish to go to my bridal bed inexperienced, I wanted to have some sport first. Do you really believe I could love that man?"

"Mr Siddenham?"

"Do not be simple, I am talking about Stibbard." Emme sneered. "All the old fool wants is an heir and I planned to give him one, but not his, although I had not expected to be got with child so soon." Her voice grew petulant, as if she were a small child preparing to indulge in a tantrum. "I wanted to be Lady Stibbard, but John has ruined everything with his stupidity."

"Why do you not marry Mr Siddenham, he is, after all, heir to a duke?" Maia suggested reasonably.

"Heir to his cousin, for how long? How dull-witted you are, Bradenham will fill his own cradles and I want a title. I will not spend the rest of my life a nobody like my mama."

Thoroughly disgusted by all she had heard, Maia enquired, "The gentleman who spoke to you in the ballroom, who is he?"

"I did not ask his name." Emmeline shrugged in an effort to appear to be nonchalant, but Maia noted the hunted look which crossed her cousin's face.

"Why did he scare you so? I want to help you –"

Her desire to be of assistance to her selfish cousin was made in earnest, and Maia was entirely unprepared for the venom with which Emme spat forth her furious reply. "How can you help me? You are a fool, upon whom a title would be entirely wasted, so it is as well no-one will offer you one. It would have made me laugh to see you wed to Percy, not that he relished the prospect of being leg-shackled to you. How dare you, of all people, speak of helping me."

Although her hands itched to slap some civility into the girl, patiently Maia waited for the torrent of abuse to stop, but Emmeline was in full-flow: "Is it not amusing that I am the one to bear Percy's child and not you? He should be grateful to me for that, indeed, now the duel has been fought, your disgrace will be confirmed and he will no longer be expected to marry you, Percy must be grateful for saving him from the horror of being wedded to you." She sniffed self-pityingly, as if she alone were the victim of the duel and its consequences.

Maia did not think Percy would be grateful to Emmeline for anything just at present, but refusing to be distracted, persisted,

"Emme, that man?"

Brought back to hard, cold reality, Emme looked up at Maia, announcing in a voice devoid of emotion, "I am to -"

Despite being unknown territory to Maia, she could hazard a guess at the nature of the man's request and narrowed her eyes in disgust. "Emme!"

Her cousin glared at her, scornfully. "He intends that I should indulge him here, tonight. Did you learn nothing in Newmarket?"

There was triumphant desperation in Emmeline's words and as the implication of what her cousin had said hit Maia with awful finality, she gasped, "Newmarket? You knew?"

"Of course I knew, Percy and I arranged it together, who else knew where to find you in Norfolk? He had no wish to be saddled with you, so we thought to have his friend Mr Knox-Gorely ruin you. Such a pity he did not manage to see it through, for it would have rid us of that damned duke too, incessantly hounding Percy and poking his nose where it did not belong."

Despite the warmth of the chamber Maia shivered, sickened by such a betrayal at her cousin's merciless hands.

Her own thoughts gathering a-pace, Emmeline giggled - the sound was not wholesome. "To think, had Mr Knox-Gorely succeeded it would be your company gentleman would be seeking, not mine."

In an attempt to banish her revulsion, Maia enquired coldly, "The gentleman wishes for a liaison?"

"Liaison? I do not think he wishes for anything so formal." Emmeline's voice was even more contemptuous.

"You cannot stay, I will fetch your chaperone, you must leave quickly."

Vulnerable in the face of unexpected compassion, Emme hesitated, "I am not sure what to do for the best."

"What else can you do? Surely you can see that to meet his demands must be impossible."

Her cousin shrugged, appearing to consider the choices before her, until Maia wanted to shake her.

"Emme, you have to leave."

At this the vindictive flame flared once again, and Emmeline turned on Maia angrily, "To do what? Wait for my fiancé to inform me of John's death, with the declaration that the facts need not concern me as I am too much a lady to know of such matters? What then Maia? Am I to sit meekly and wait until August, when I can no longer hide the fact that I am increasing, and must suffer the ignominy of being abandoned by my fiancé, before being thrown from the house by my mother, for John was ever her favourite. Are you really so ignorant Maia?"

Never known for her patience, Maia had at last had enough of her unspeakable cousin. "It seems to me you have remarkably few choices left, other than to wed Lord Stibbard before he is sensible that your child is not his, no matter how repellent the idea may seem. To claim you have no choice but to be used by all and sundry is the talk of a mad woman."

Spoilt, indulged Emmeline Wrengingham was no match for Maia when roused, and with her bravado fading, she dissolved into messy tears. Hiccupping, "B-b-but L-l-lord S-s-stibbard will n-n-not con-s-sider b-bringing the w-w-wedding ceremony f-forward, a-all is already l-lost, for the g-g-gentlemen seem to h-have h-heard of my i-i-indiscr-r-retions."

Maia looked askance at her cousin; indiscretions would not be how she would describe Emmeline's scandalous actions. However, in the spirit of not casting the first stone, she remained silent upon both the subject and indiscretions in question; after all, it was she who had been seen in Mr Siddenham's arms in the long gallery. As far as the haute ton knew Emmeline was as pure as the driven snow, and as Maia was now bitterly aware, equally cold-hearted.

She rose from the arm of sofa. "I will tell your chaperone you are unwell and must be escorted home at once. As for bringing Lord Stibbard to the point and to the altar, that we will undertake tomorrow, for I am convinced it can be achieved. Dry your eyes and tell me who is your chaperone and where I might look for her."

Sniffing richly, Emmeline wiped her eyes upon the sleeve of her long mousquetaire gloves.

"Mrs Whitwell will be with the rest of the old biddies, wearing a frightful lace cap; she looks not unlike a half-plucked chicken." She hiccupped and sniffed again. "Perhaps it would be better to meet with the gentleman, after all one never knows -" Her voice trailed off hopefully, as she weighed up the myriad possibilities.

While speaking, Emmeline had risen until she was half-standing, in a display of irritation Maia pushed her cousin back to sit upon the sofa.

"No, it would not be better -. You are already in too deep, any deeper and you will surely drown. Sit here and do not move."

Without waiting for a response from Emmeline, beyond the girl's squeak of surprise at finding herself pushed unceremoniously against the cushions, Maia departed from the Chinese room, the harp thrumming softly in her wake, wondering at her misplaced loyalty to such a creature as her cousin.

***

Masking his tedium with practise borne from too many evenings spent in dull ballrooms, Cosmo barely listened to the conversation of the elderly couple, whom although he knew them, inexplicably could not recall their names.

Noting his dark eyes darting about the ballroom searching for Maia, Constance interrupted the conversation to ask winsomely, "Cosmo, I beg of you; procure a glass of lemonade for me, before I expire with thirst."

Her cousin was taken aback; for Connie to request a drink of lemonade was shocking, but one look at her twinkling eyes was enough for the duke to grasp both her intention and the salvation she offered him. He nodded dutifully to the couple and eagerly made his way towards the passage down which he had last seen Maia disappearing with her cousin in tow. That she was in Miss Wreningham's company did little to reassure him, for despite being well-aware that Maia could take care of herself, he did not trust her cousin as far as he could throw her.

The corridor echoed his firm footsteps as he ventured into the semi-darkness of Caroline's private chambers. Some of the rooms he was acquainted with, indeed the pink salon and library were both known to him, but a glance inside each revealed no-one. He hesitated at a bisecting corridor, trying to get his bearings in the unfamiliar surroundings, yet despite opening several doors, he was unable to find Maia and Miss Wreningham and was forced to retrace his steps to began his search anew along a smaller corridor. A flickering light emanating from the crack in the double doors caught his eye, if he were not mistaken beyond them lay the beguiling Chinese room, and one door was ajar.

***

Mrs Whitwell was not difficult to distinguish, she sat amidst other likeminded matrons, supremely confident in her misplaced trust in her charge. The view from their seats provided a fine line of vision, so that a weather eye may be kept upon the young ladies as they danced and promenaded. That she had not set eyes upon dear Emmeline for some time did not disquiet the good lady's heart for one moment; after all, Emmeline was happily betrothed to Lord Stibbard. It was a fine match for the girl, and Mrs Whitwell was secure in the knowledge that Miss Wreningham was not the sort of girl to give rise to the least hint of anxiety.

The chaperone, Maia mused, did indeed look strikingly like a half-plucked chicken; her many tiered lace bonnet resembling the indignant feathers of a ruffled hen, while Mrs Whitwell's frequent head nodding was distractingly reminiscent of a fowl hunting for insects.

However, Maia's progress in approaching the formidable row of matrons came to an abrupt halt as Lady Bellmont hove into view, and reaching the fleet conclusion that she would prefer not to undergo public scrutiny, Maia withdrew into the relative anonymity of the darkened hallway.

"Miss Hindolveston, may I be of assistance?"

While she started violently at the sound of the unexpected voice, Maia refrained from making an undignified shriek of alarm. "Heydon, how glad I am to see you."

In the semi-darkness it was entirely possible that the dowager duchess's butler smiled indulgently, having known the Hindolveston girls since they were in leading strings.

"I was looking for Mrs Whitwell," Maia explained, "and I - er - found her."

Heydon followed her line of vision to the clucking duennas, until his eyes alighted upon the sloping shoulders of Lady Bellmont, leaning over the mesmerised form of Emmeline's chaperone, as if she were about to devour her.

The impassive butler's demeanour took on a monolithic air. "May I impart a message to Mrs Whitwell on your behalf?"

With grateful relief Maia relinquished the task into Heydon's capable hands and waited in the safety of the shadows, aware of the moment the chaperone was informed that her presence was requested as, rising with an air of self-importance, Mrs Whitwell haughtily waved her hand at Heydon, indicating he should lead the way.

Although previously unacquainted with Mrs Whitwell, upon making herself know to the lady in the seclusion of the hallway, Maia was greeted with a supercilious stare and evident disdain. She was forced to rein-in her rapidly ebbing temper in order to explain to the disapproving matron that Emmeline was unwell and wished to return home immediately. Whereupon Mrs Whitwell seemed to temporarily overcome her prejudice towards Emmeline's less than proper cousin.

Clutching at Maia's gloved arm with a claw-like hand, the chaperone wailed, "The poor child was overwrought over the dreadful ruination of her fichu. I told her that her appearance was perfectly proper, but the dear girl was dreadfully upset at what others might think."

Recovering herself, Mrs Whitwell sniffed self-righteously. "As behoves a well brought-up young lady, with a care for the proprieties."

That Maia did not inform Emmeline's chaperone just how deeply she had failed in her duty of care, or how Emmeline had long since ceased to care about the proprieties, was admirable. Her only concern was to get Emme away as soon as might be accomplished, for she was very much afraid that having already fallen so far, Emmeline would consider the final descent into utter depravity but a short step. Indeed, she would be right, but that was no reason to take it.

"My cousin is resting in my god-mother's private chambers, I will return her to the ladies-withdrawing room immediately, but did not wish to leave her in a pubic place in a state of ill-health."

Mrs Whitwell inclined her head to indicate that despite Maia's obvious failings with regard to morals, she had on this occasion behaved in a fitting and proper manner.

Although she would very much have liked to visit the dowager's private apartments, the chaperone had no desire to be seen in Miss Hindolveston's company, and released Maia's arm as if it were something unclean. Replying frostily, "I will await her in ladies-withdrawing room."

***

Pushing wider the partially open door, the duke called anxiously: "Maia, are you here?"

Catching sight of a pale gown peeping around the side of the deep sofa, which almost completely concealed the figure of a woman, he pushed the door to, relieved to have found Maia and grateful to have a rare moment alone with her. Too late he realised it was not Maia who reclined upon the sofa but her cousin, and recoiling in horror at his mistake, Cosmo took a step back.

With a feline smile, Emmeline gazed coyly at him, her hands running sinuously along her skirts. "Well, well your Grace, how delightful to see you. Pray tell what brings you here? Can it be you are seeking the company of my dear cousin? How very amusing." Lowering her eyes in an act of feigned innocence, she rose to stand before the fire, the embers casting an orange glow about her. "And yet you find me entirely alone."

The dripping menace of her honeyed tone was not lost upon

Bradenham, who took a step back, anxious to put as much distance as possible between himself and Maia's cousin.

He attempted to speak as if he were addressing any other member of the ton, not this grotesque parody of virtue. "You must excuse my unwarranted interruption Miss Wreningham, I was looking for Miss Hindolveston, but as she is not here I will leave you to your meditations."

He took a further step back as Emmeline pursed her lips, almost mocking him, a calculating look in her eyes.

"Unwarranted perhaps, but it does not mean your interruption is unwelcome." There was a hint of malice lurking beneath the silky smoothness of her words. She giggled, "I wonder what the ladies of the ton will say when they discover that you and I have been together, un-chaperoned?"

Cold and businesslike Cosmo eyed the girl distastefully. "It would be better for all concerned if I bid you good evening Miss Wreningham." Without waiting for a reply he turned on his heel.

Emmeline giggled again, an unattractive exaltation. "Oh no, I do not think so. You cannot debauch a lady and expect to get away with it. Your Grace, even you must pay for such an insult."

She lifted a hand to the low décolletage of her gown and grasping it firmly, rent the delicate cloth. Already stretched beyond its limit, the silk gave way easily, exposing her swollen breasts, and digging her fingers deep into her hair, she raked them violently through the carefully arranged curls, which glinted in the orange light as they tumbled about her shoulders and exposed torso.

There could be no mistaking it, as she stood upon the hearth rug Emmeline Wreningham was the picture of a ravished woman.

She hissed at the duke's back. "No one will ever believe that you did not force yourself upon me. It will be your word against mine, and when I am found to be with child, you will have to marry me."

Cosmo turned; the full horror of the trap into which he had fallen, dawning upon him.

Chapter Forty-Eight

Relieved that Emmeline would soon be on her way home, safe from both herself and the rapacious gentlemen who prowled even the best ballrooms throughout the season, Maia was about to return to the Chinese room in order to fulfil her self imposed obligation to see Emme into her chaperone's hands before further incident could befall her wretched cousin, when she heard her name spoken. She did not recognise the voice and was forced to move closer to the light emanating from the ballroom in order to see whom had called to her, but not wishing to be seen un-chaperoned she lingered hesitantly beside a small table.

"Miss Hindolveston, is it not?"

With dismay Maia realised too late, the voice was that of Emmeline's intimidating gentleman. He looked at Maia appraisingly, as if he were viewing an inanimate object, trying to ascertain its worth.

Making no reply, Maia waited warily.

"We are not acquainted, yet," he continued with vile inference, "although I hope to rectify the oversight this evening."

Again, Maia did not respond, maintaining an icy silence.

"I have heard of you my dear; you seem to have caused quite a stir in your first season. I understand you have a certain weakness for the classical." His perusal took on an air of calculated consideration, and he ran his tongue across his narrow lips, as if he were savouring all that was hidden beneath Maia's gown. The insinuation of his words was explicit.

The gentleman's mistake lay in that he was entirely unprepared for his first meeting with one of the Hindolveston girls, particularly one who had been hounded, abducted, drugged, almost engaged against her will, and betrayed by one of her own family; for Maia had finally had enough.

Her violet eyes flashing with fury, she drew herself up and standing almost as tall as the gentleman, raised her lip in an unladylike sneer. "A reputation is a strange thing, is it not? I too have heard of you, although I scarce believed that even men who prey upon foolish girls would consider this house an appropriate setting for such debasement. However, while I stand corrected, you sir are about to depart from my god-mother's house."

The gentleman's eyes widened in consternation; he had overlooked that Maia was the dowager duchess's god-daughter - another mistake. Had he been aware of this fact he might have trodden with more care, more likely he would have avoided the path altogether.

Fearlessly Maia continued, "As you mentioned, it is my first season and we green girls are apt to make a shocking mull of etiquette during our rudimentary forays into the ton, although -" to the gentleman's rapt delight she leaned forward and said conspiratorially, "- etiquette aside, as you so thoughtfully pointed out I am not known for my decorum." With that she swept up a half-drunk glass of what appeared to be ratafia, from the small table and unhesitatingly dashed the concoction down the gentleman's silk twill breeches.

While he stared at the sticky liquid, rapidly soaking across the front of his tight britches, Maia gasped in feigned horror. "Oh, forgive me, I am most dreadfully clumsy. Heydon, this gentleman appears to have had an accident, perhaps you would be so good as to assist him?"

Waiting in the shadows in case his presence might be required, the butler who had overheard enough of the gentleman's proposition to Miss Hindolveston, to be aware of the man's intent, stepped forward. Although his carefully schooled features did not betray it, Heydon felt more than a touch of pride in the dowager duchess's protégé; for while the girl's god-mother might have managed the situation differently, she could not have done so with more aplomb.

With her head down to hide a wicked grin, Maia retraced her footsteps to the Chinese room, while following in Heydon's glacial wake the gentleman did his best to leave the ballroom unnoticed, attempting ineffectually to hide the spreading stain.

***

The golden dragons reflected in the great looking-glass appeared to pause in their dancing, perhaps the nightmarish scene unfolding before their gleaming eyes was as distasteful to them, as it was to the duke himself.

However, oblivious to all else but the man staring at her in abject horror, Emmeline announced happily. "I wish to be a duchess and it will be a fitting career for Percy's child, to inherit where his father cannot."

"You are deluded if you believe I will be forced into marriage with you." Barely able to contain his loathing, Cosmo spat the words at Miss Wreningham, who pouted childishly.

"Once the shocking depths of your turpitude are known, you will have no other option, and I will see to it that your debauching of my cousin in Newmarket becomes common knowledge - while my own screams will shortly be heard alerting the ton of your wicked ravishment of me. Maia will be ruined, and you will be glad to wed me; if only to put an end to the scandal."

"I would rather shoot myself," ground out the duke with cold finality.

"I would rather shoot Emmeline." Maia's crisp voice was heard from the doorway, where hidden from view by Bradenham's broad shoulders, she had remained in the shadows as she slipped silently into the room.

Unsure of how much Maia had heard, Emme held out her arms in a display of helplessness. "Maia, look at what the duke has done to me, I could not withstand him!"

However, Maia was not the sympathetic audience Emmeline had hoped for - or perhaps expected - as with her disgust evident, Maia marched past Cosmo and stood before the dishevelled figure of her cousin.

"Cover yourself Emme, you look like a harlot."

Not one to give up easily, Emme appealed to Maia's finer sensibilities. "Have you no pity to speak so? It is too shocking to be borne."

What Miss Wreningham discovered to be shocking was the resounding sting as her cousin's hand struck her cheek, as with her eyes ablaze, Maia's contempt could leave no-one disabused as to her true feelings.

"You are the most disgusting creature I have had the misfortune to know, using people cruelly for your own ends and with no thought for anyone but yourself. Because of your selfishness your own brother is dying in unimaginable agony, while you care for little but for your own amusement. Your lover has been shot, not that it matters to you, for already there is another to take his place. You had no qualms about arranging my ruin at the hands of a terrible man; you planned to plant your bastard in an innocent man's cradle and, failing that, sought to ruin a man's reputation in the most damning way possible. The only thing worse is that you planned to make him suffer by foisting yourself upon him as his wife. Have I neglected any aspect of your nature, cousin?"

Although Emmeline appeared to be unaffected by this litany of her crimes, she had the sense to shield her body with the ravaged silk.

"Have you nothing to say Emme?"

Miss Wreningham's chin tilted defiantly. "It will be his word against mine, and I have the proof in the child."

Cosmo remained silent, his future, indeed his life hung in the balance, for marriage to such a creature was unthinkable.

Maia's eyes sparkled in merriment as she looked at the duke. "Not if I say that he was engaged elsewhere - with me."

There was an audible gasp from both Cosmo and Miss Wreningham, but while Emme's expression was one of stunned surprise, the duke gazed at Maia as if she were indeed the celestial body for which she was named.

Hardly daring to believe this sacrifice he demanded, "What did you say?"

"I shall swear I was with you, after all, my penchant for intimate liaisons with gentlemen during parties is a well-known fact, and my god-mother has some fine statuary in the conservatory."

Turning her attention back to her cousin, Maia continued: "If you persist with your tale of fictitious ravishment at the duke's hands, I will be forced to confess that he was privately engaged with me," adding for good measure, "for some considerable time. The true identity of your seducer will naturally be of great interest to all, especially I imagine to Lord Stibbard, and will keep the ton occupied for some time to come, although alas, doubtless your wedding ceremony will be cancelled. Stibbard will after all expect his bride to be innocent." Maia snorted in derision as she uttered the last word.

Desperately clinging to such threads of truth as would support her claim, Emme countered, "You were seen in the ballroom when you spoke to Mrs Whitworth, you cannot have been in two places at once."

However, any hope she might have in this knowledge was ruthlessly dispelled. "No-one of consequence was aware of my presence, Heydon brought Mrs Whitworth to speak with me and the lady will require no convincing of my guilt, indeed she will be expecting such an event."

Behind her Cosmo held his breath.

With the shifting sands of her lies sinking beneath her, Emmeline appealed to her relative. "You would not pay me back so, how could you? We are cousins."

Maia snorted. "I am unlikely to forget that I was to be raped at the instigation of my own cousin, nor would I lower myself in order to pay you back. However, I would do much to prevent an innocent man from suffering at your hands, even more someone who despite himself, has proven himself so much your superior. Go, marry poor, deluded Stibbard, put your child in his cradle. I am sure it will not trouble you to deceive the wretched man, nor will you lose even a moments sleep over the matter. May your schemes bring you joy Emme, for I will always be disgusted by you."

Completely deflated, Emmeline wailed, "How can I marry Lord Stibbard? He is in no mood to hurry the wedding, if I must wait until August before I am wed he will know the child cannot be his."

Eyeing the snivelling girl distastefully, Cosmo spoke up, slipping his hand into Maia's as she stood before him, shielding him from Emmeline, "I might be able to assist, but must have your word that there will be no more schemes and machinations; this must be the end of it. I will speak to Stibbard, you will be wed before the end of the week, but Miss Wreningham, be sure this is indeed what you wish, for I will not again lift a finger to assist you. I have no stomach for your method of doing business."

Even Emmeline could see the straw of salvation he had offered would be the last if its kind, and that without it she would surely drown. She nodded, unable to voice her acquiescence.

The duke, suddenly terrible in his repugnance, waved her away, "Leave, I will bring matters about, on that I give you my word."

Not knowing how to return to the ballroom with her gown rent and her hair in disarray, Emmeline stood looking from one implacable face to the other.

From the shadows beyond the dragon screen came a voice, "Miss Wreningham allow me to loan you my shawl, it grows chilly does it not?"

In dismay, Emmeline turned to face the gimlet, green eyes of the Dowager Duchess of Alconbury, as she stepped from a doorway, well-concealed behind the ornate screen.

Draping the large fringed shawl about Emmeline's shoulders so that it hid the front of her ruined dress, Caroline announced blithely: "The worsted will kept you warm." Her firm fingers pressed against the girl's shoulder, pushing her towards the sofa. "Allow me assist with your hair, it seems to be in a state of disorder and it would not do to be seen so, people might talk."

With deft movements, and not a little tugging, the dowager formed Emmeline's tousled curls into some sort of symmetry. While the coiffure would not pass muster should it be viewed by a hair-dresser, it would do to get Emmeline out of the house un-remarked.

Her aims achieved, Caro took the girl by the arm, almost lifting her to her feet. "It will be my pleasure to ensure you are reunited with your chaperone, she must be anxious. Did you say that her name was Mrs Whitwell?"

Emmeline nodded miserably.

"Very well, I will see you into her safe hands and make sure your carriage is brought to the door immediately; it would not do to be kept waiting when you are so dreadfully unwell." With that the dowager duchess swept Emmeline out of the room without so much as a backward glance at either Maia or Bradenham.

As the doors closed in her god-mother's wake, Maia felt Cosmo's grasp tighten upon her hand.

"I can never repay you for what you just did."

She smiled, perhaps a little smugly, but said nothing.

"You risked your reputation for me."

At this Maia laughed. "It might be argued that my reputation is already in tatters, all I did was to offer to confirm what the ton accepted as fact, some weeks ago."

But he was not listening, instead Cosmo was thinking over all that had transpired in the last few minutes, incredulous that Maia had so swiftly dealt the death blow to her cousin's vile schemes. Upon finding himself being led to the concealing sofa, recently vacated by Miss Wreningham, he sank into it gratefully. He was likely to require some time to come to terms with the world shifting so irrevocably upon its axis, and so he sat, the only sounds the logs burning in the hearth and the distant strains of music from the ballroom.

At last, lifting his dark eyes to Maia's violet ones, Cosmo announced, "To think, I believed I was the one to save you."

Smiling indulgently at the bewildered man, Maia replied, "And so you did, rather nicely as I recall, although I confess to being somewhat muddled at the time."

The duke shook his head dismissively. "That was nothing - What you did tonight, you risked all for me – if ... if Miss Wreningham had called your bluff - " His voice trailed off as he contemplated the uproar which would have ensued.

Entirely unconcerned for either the scandal, or her reputation, considering both to be inconsequential, Maia snorted matter-of-factly, "If Emmeline had been so foolish as to believe she could win this hand, I would have provided you with a thoroughly scandalous alibi."

Discovering her words to be a remarkable panacea, Cosmo reached for Maia and drew her down upon his knee. "How scandalous?" His words were warm in her ear and she shivered at the depth of his velvety voice.

"Thoroughly, your Grace."

Holding her at arm's length, Bradenham appraised her reprovingly, "While there is a time and place for formality, I cannot say that I approve of it in an intimate setting, perhaps you could call me by my Christian name?"

"This is not an intimate setting," argued Maia. "But we shall let that pass, Cosmo."

The duke kissed her lightly on the nose. "As you are finally about to accept my proposal, this qualifies as an intimate setting."

"You seem very sure of yourself," Maia laughed, the reverberations of joy echoing through her slender frame, as a wisp of corkscrew curl detached itself from her coiffure and snagged softly against his cheek. "Although I do not recall that you have ever actually asked me to marry you, informed me, yes, but never asked me."

A familiar, crisp voice could be heard from beyond the screen. "If Maia cavils Bradenham, I shall insist you borrow my coach and take her immediately to Newmarket, after all a god-mother can only endure so much."

But before either of them could respond, the hidden doors were closed and locked.

Satisfied they were alone in the flickering firelight, Cosmo's arms clasped Maia tightly.

"Marry me, I beg you. If you wish, I will profess my undying love and devotion, but what I will really mean is that I do not want to live without you, and while I might delight bundling you into a carriage and abducting you, I would rather you marry me because you wish to."

Taking his face between her sender hands, Maia perused him as if he were a painting, smoothing the frown lines with her thumbs and brushing the dark hair from his forehead, she smiled. By way of response Cosmo nestled his head into her hand, but dissatisfied with the glove that lay between, them, he removed the offending article, peeling it deftly from her arm and over her fingers, before discarding it behind the sofa. He pressed Maia's hand to his lips and kissed her bare palm, his dark eyes holding her violet gaze.

"You may spend the rest of your life telling me how odious I am, just promise to kiss me and only me in long galleries from this moment on."

His lips brushed hotly against her wrist, causing Maia to gasp.

"I promise," she whispered, adding firmly in an attempt to regain control of her dangerously spiralling emotions. "However, we must add a caveat to our vows - for if you believe I will tolerate your attempted seduction by ladies in Chinese rooms, you are sorely mistaken."

Cosmo shuddered at the mention of his narrow escape. "I promise most willingly my love, never to be seduced in a Chinese room again."

He whispered in her ear, "The duchess's drawing room at Swanton Chatteris is not Chinese, but has a Mogul theme, and I make no promises against allowing you to seduce me there, so do not ask it of me."

Maia frowned severely. "I would not dream of asking such a thing." She sighed wistfully, "Is too much to hope there is statuary at Swanton Chatteris?"

The duke's arms tightened around her and his voice grew seductively husky. "Before you become my duchess there will be, and all with a classical theme."

***

In the anteroom beyond the dragon screens and hidden doors, long after the last guests had departed, Caroline lay back upon the silk cushions of the window-seat with a satisfied sigh. Despite frequent appearances to the contrary, the dowager duchess took her responsibilities to her numerous god-daughters seriously, and was therefore delighted to be able to hand Maia's welfare into the very capable hands of the Duke of Bradenham, once-and-for-all.

A kiss upon the back of her neck brought Caro back to matters of a more personal aspect, as the gentleman whispered things of a most delightful nature to her in flowing Russian. For the language of love is very much the same, no matter in what tongue it is spoken, and her Grace was nothing if not fluent.

Chapter Forty-Nine

In later years Bradenham would view the morning's work in a more forgiving light, but as gazed upon the corpulent form of Lord Stibbard, he could not help reflecting that there were several places he would rather be at that moment, and innumerable things he could be doing, none of which were as distasteful as the task ahead; for the knowledge that he was complicit in assisting Miss Wreningham achieve her vile ambition did not sit well with the duke.

Ensconced in a comfortable chair at his club, Lord Stibbard listened to the Duke of Bradenham with a growing sense of disquiet. Thus far the sordid facts of the duel had been kept quiet, although naturally as the cousin of one of the protagonists, it was only to be expected that the duke should be well-versed in the details of the unhappy affair. Stibbard was therefore grateful that Bradenham spoke in a low tone, for the fewer who knew of the debacle, the better.

The real reason for the duel could never be known to the baron, a fact which Cosmo sought to remind himself, galling though it was to hear Maia being repeatedly slandered and maligned by the ageing gentleman, who did not think to question the conclusion to which he had jumped upon first hearing the shocking news.

"Not that I altogether blame young Wreningham," Stibbard's head bobbed sagely. "For he was doing no more than one would expect in defence of Miss Hindolveston's reputation," adding judgementally, "one wonders if she was worth the price to be paid."

His lordship took a sip of port from the brimming glass he had been nursing, and intoned lecherously, "Nor can one entirely blame Mr Siddenham, for the gel is not of the usual stable is she? Not that she is to my taste, not now at least, for a man does not care to come late to such a feast, 'tis better to sup first, while the dish is untouched, is it not?"

Suppressing an urge to ram the ageing baron's yellowing teeth down his wattled throat, Cosmo reminded himself that his purpose was to encourage the damned man to wed Miss Wreningham, not to make matters worse - tempting though it may be.

Stibbard however, blundered on, blithely ignorant of the danger he was in. "'Tis a bad do, Wreningham will not last the week I fear, I wonder if the dratted gel knows what she has done." This time the be-wigged head shook in such enthusiastic dismay that a liberal dusting of powder fell lightly upon the gentleman's shoulders.

Seizing the moment, Bradenham responded coolly. "It is to be hoped Wreningham will not expire quite so soon, should he do so it would throw your plans into disarray, would it not?"

Greatly puzzled, Lord Stibbard's glass was suspended in its progress to his bulbous, saliva encrusted lips, "How so?"

With the air of a man greatly shocked, the duke looked askance at his companion. "My dear Stibbard, once Wreningham makes his departure, naturally his sister will be expected to observe at least six months of mourning, anything less would be unthinkable. More likely a year, when one considers the nature of the man's demise. Will this not delay your intention to beget an heir? One assumes that is your aim in taking another wife. Heaven's man, under such circumstances you cannot expect to wed Miss Wreningham before the girl is out of weeds."

Utterly taken aback Lord Stibbard gaped, having not previously considered this aspect of John Wreningham's death.

The duke took a measured sip of port, scrutinizing the older gentleman through narrowed eyes and observed dismissively, "Still, you have waited this long, another year will be of no moment."

With a shaking hand the baron brought his glass to his lips and drank deeply. "Good lord, I had not thought, that is to say - I did not consider. What's to be done?"

Shrugging his shoulders as if it were an unimportant detail in the grand scheme of things, Cosmo suggested, "One supposes you could marry the girl before her brother dies, or alternatively wait another season."

"Another season?" Horrified by such unfeeling counsel, Stibbard did not need to reflect upon what another season would entail before rejecting it out of hand. However, the practical nature of the alternative suggested by the duke, struck him as an eminently sensible resolution to the thorny problem, and rising he grasped Cosmo warmly by the hand.

"You have my sincere gratitude, had you not been so forward thinking I would have tarried, and there is no time to be lost in the getting of an heir. It might be considered unseemly for a man in his prime to be rushing to wed, but that cannot be helped; for the heir is what matters." Stibbard pumped the duke's hand jovially. "I must inform my bride she is to be married immediately, no time must be lost."

Shaking his be-wigged head at his own lack of foresight, he shuddered, "When I consider, I have even looked in upon the unfortunate Wreningham, willing him to hurry up and get on with the business of dying- it is to be hoped he tarries but one day more, until the ring is upon little Emmeline's finger. My word! Indeed -."

Stibbard rubbed his hands together gleefully, and Bradenham almost felt pity for Miss Wreningham, but recalling how he had very nearly become entrapped in her snares, his pity receded sharply, concluding that Emmline Wreningham and her lord deserved each other and were perhaps, after all, well-matched.

"I wish you joy and a happy conclusion to your bridal, Stibbard."

With that the interview was over, and Lord Stibbard hurried away to make such arrangements as he deemed necessary for a hasty wedding, leaving Bradenham shaking his head, revolted by the pretty pair.

***

In an uncharacteristically unselfish final act, John Wreningham lingered until Emmeline and Lord Stibbard were safely married by special licence, before breathing his last and paying the price for his sister's folly.

However, having greater woes to contend with, Lady Stibbard was only mildly troubled by the event; for not only had she been informed by her husband that not a single tear was to be shed over her brother's violent propensities, more distressingly he demanded that she devote herself solely to the task for which she had been wed.

Delighted with his young bride, Lord Stibbard congratulated himself for taking to the Duke of Bradenham's advice. Providentially, he ensured his domestic felicity by installing his wife in his decaying, ancestral home in the Scottish highlands, well-removed from the distractions of the ton, for his lordship had decreed that his bride's dancing days were now behind her.

Even the precipitate birth of his daughters only temporarily dampened Stibbard's spirits; believing that next time Emmeline would doubtless bear him a son - meanwhile, he was enchanted by the auburn-haired girls who lay squalling in his nursery. Proud of how large they were - despite being twins and barely of eight months duration - Lord Stibbard did not doubt that at last he had married the right woman.

Epilogue

"Are you sure you are not disappointed?" The Duchess of Bradenham's adoring gaze turned from the dark eyes of her husband, to those of her daughter, held safe within her papa's cradling arms.

Bending to place a kiss upon his wife's tumbling curls, the duke asked, "How could I be disappointed, my love?" Tendrils of the silken spirals attached themselves to his stubbled cheek, for it had been a long night for both of the newly arrived lady's parents.

"Aurelia was convinced she would be a boy."

Cosmo snorted disparagingly, "Aurelia is a fool!"

However, before he could expound upon his theme, cataloguing the gravest of his sister's follies, the sound of smashing china resonated from the dressing chamber beyond. Perplexed, the duke went to investigate, while sleeping peacefully in his arms his daughter was blissfully unaware of the disruption.

Warily opening the door, Bradenham was perhaps not altogether surprised to be greeted by the sight of his valet, dripping from head to toe, surrounded by the remnants of what had possibly been an arrangement of wild flowers. Three curly, dark heads emerged from behind the sodden man, but far from sheepish, their dark eyes were alight with mischief.

Yet for all the mayhem there was something missing from the tableaux, an excited bark of delight was followed by the exuberant Monk, who with a drooping elderflower caught upon one ear and his tail thrashing excitedly, bounded forward to greet his master.

Content that everyone was present and accounted for, Cosmo ordered, "Down sirrah."

From her vantage point upon the bed, Maia ineffectually attempted to stifle a laugh, as her husband intoned sonorously, "One wonders why Aurelia would wish more sons upon me."

However, as so often happened these days, his meditations were interrupted, upon this occasion by his second son: "'Scuse me papa, but is it a brother or a sister? Aunt 'Ralia said it would be a boy."

The duke regarded his son attentively. "This time your aunt is wrong, this is your sister. Although I fail to see why you feel the need to mark her birth by half-drowning poor Watton - dragging that hound upstairs and breaking what appears to be your great-grandmother's Chinese bowl, doubtless all will become clear. Would you boys care to see the baby?"

The three curly heads nodded in unison, even the drenched Watton, who as a rule preferred to keep well away from his employer's offspring until they were able to communicate with some degree of accuracy their immediate requirements, was enraptured by the bundle in the duke's arms, although it was to be hoped that the little girl would not prove to be a spiller like her mama.

The only member of the party unmoved by the new arrival was Monk, who commenced scratching his ear, concerned only by the cause of the irritation and the relief provided by his vigorous efforts.

Maia patted her bedside invitingly. "Come, sit beside me and papa will let you hold her."

Needing no second invitation, the boys dashed into the chamber; the elder two scrambling adroitly upon the bed, while the youngest slithered and slid, his legs kicking valiantly as he struggled to obtain purchase upon the silk bed-cover. Seeing his son's predicament, Cosmo placed a booted foot beneath the boy's flailing ones, creating an impromptu stepping-stone, which allowed the child to join his siblings next to their mother. To his credit, Watton observed the newly added scuff marks upon the duke's highly polished boots, without flinching.

Placing his daughter with great solemnity into her elder brother's outstretched arms, Cosmo stepped back to better view the scene, while the two younger boys leaned their dark, curly heads over this oddity that was their sister.

"Hmm ..." intoned the Marquis of Chatteris, as he considered the newest addition to the family with some suspicion. "She looks like us, but she has no ribbons or frills or whatnot" his dark brows were drawn into a frown. "Are you sure it's a girl?"

Patting her eldest son's arm lovingly, his doting mama smiled, "I expect the fills will arrive before too long, indeed, I believe there will be no avoiding them, for she is most definitely a girl."

This was met with a collective "Humph " from the brothers of the lady in question.

Wriggling anxiously for his turn to hold this strange creature who would one day require ribbons and frills, Philip's eyes were huge with excitement, although he hoped 'whatnots' might prove to be weaponry of some description. While Constantine, not fully cognisant that his position as the baby of the family had been usurped, contented himself by bouncing up and down, unable to contain his glee.

Meanwhile, Watton remained dripping reverentially upon the

threshold, ignoring the errant Monk, who free from the burden of floral embellishment, yawned widely, having long since outgrown the need to investigate smashed china.

The water dripping from Watton, onto the Turkey rug, did not go unnoticed by the duchess, nor did the fact that her husband's valet had received a second baptism, this time at the hands of her own, unholy offspring.

"Watton, do not tell me it was simply an accident this time, for I shall not believe it, what happened?"

Drawing himself up with great dignity the valet replied, "Your Grace, it was a misunderstanding, nothing more."

The young marquis opened his mouth to refute the man's version of events, but upon catching his father's eye closed it once again with a snap.

"Chatteris, if Watton says it was a misunderstanding, then that is what it was. It is a wise man who accepts an olive branch when it is placed so generously before him. You will doubtless find a way to express your gratitude to Watton, perhaps by not attempting to drown him in future?"

Three pairs of dark eyes looked at Watton gratefully, while the sodden valet tried unsuccessfully to hide his pleasure and pride in his occasional charges.

"Watton, we seem to have added another Siddenham to the household."

The valet beamed at his employer. "Indeed your Grace, and if I may be so bold as to offer my felicitations and enquire if the lady has a name?"

The lady's brothers immediately took up the question, with a chorus of: "What's her name?" Followed by various unsuitable suggestions from the elder boys, the youngest being engrossed in exploring his sister's diminutive nose with a stocky finger.

Upon voicing her disapproval at such an unwarranted imposition, the baby was removed from her brother's grasp by her papa and placed in the safety of her mama's protection, before he responded to their question.

"I rather like Leda."

There was a gurgle of mirth from the duchess.

"However, your mama informs me that your sister is called Thalia, according to your grandfather she was one of the graces." Frowning at his wife in mock severity the duke mused mournfully, "Although I did like Leda -"

As the boys struggled to say their sister's name with varying degrees of success, Cosmo observed, "Watton, you are in danger of taking a chill. If you would be so good as to deposit these dreadful children into the tender mercies of their aunts and remove that hellhound to the stables on your way to dry off, I would be most grateful."

Shepherding the protesting boys from the bedchamber, with Monk trailing behind, the dripping valet encouraged the trinity in their departure by the expedient proposition that once dry, he would be making a batch of his secret black potion to put upon his Grace's boots, adding with a touch of genius, that only those lords who did as they were requested, would be permitted to assist and only if they did not attempt to drop their younger bother into the foul brew this time.

As the door closed behind the vociferous male scions of the house, the duke mused, "I suppose it will have to be Thalia, that is if you are quite sure about Leda?"

Maia was firm. "I am convinced my love, after all, you do not want our sons in years to come, following their sister around every ballroom, terrified lest she go statue hunting for her namesake, do you?"

Shuddering at the prospect, Cosmo drew his wife's hand to his lips and tenderly kissed her palm. "As ever you are right my love, one young lady in the long gallery is more than enough for any family."

"Quite so," agreed the duchess, smiling as her husband kissed her wrist, but refusing to be distracted, said brightly, "Now, about Thalia's god-mama -"

The Duke of Bradenham groaned.

END

Printed in Great Britain
by Amazon